ANNIE LYONS

A GIRLS' GUIDE TO WINNING the WAR

REVIEW

First published in 2024 by Headline Review
An imprint of HEADLINE PUBLISHING GROUP

1

Cataloguing in Publication Data is available from the British Library

Hardback ISBN 978 1 0354 0107 9
Trade paperback ISBN 978 1 0354 0108 6

Typeset in Bembo by CC Book Production

Printed and bound in Great Britain by Clays Ltd, Elcograf S.p.A.

MIX
Paper | Supporting
responsible forestry
FSC
www.fsc.org FSC® C104740

Headline's policy is to use papers that are natural, renewable and
recyclable products and made from wood grown in well-managed forests
and other controlled sources. The logging and manufacturing processes
are expected to conform to the environmental regulations
of the country of origin.

HEADLINE PUBLISHING GROUP
An Hachette UK Company
Carmelite House
50 Victoria Embankment
London EC4Y 0DZ

www.headline.co.uk
www.hachette.co.uk

*For the women who quietly weaved their magic
during the Second World War in Britain.*

'*I know nothing in the world that has as much power as a word. Sometimes I write one, and I look at it, until it begins to shine.*'

Emily Dickinson

Prologue

London, 1917

'Got yer nose in another book, 'ave yer?'

Peggy Sparks snapped her gaze up from the storybook dragon and his plume of impressive silver smoke to the bulldog-faced expression of Sid Kemp, the meanest boy on the street. Panicked, she cast her eyes left and right, searching desperately for Joe. 'I-I . . .'

'I-I-I . . .' mocked Sid in a sing-song voice, snatching the book from her hands. He peered at the pages with narrow-eyed suspicion. 'My dad said only sissies read books.'

'Please don't,' begged Peggy as he carelessly held the volume by one page so that a minuscule tear began to snake from its edge like ice cracking across a frozen pond.

'Don't what?' said the boy, giving the page a shake as the tear became a rip. He eyed her with triumphant glee, holding the torn page in his hand as the book fell to the floor. 'Oops,' he said. 'I broke it.'

Peggy tried her hardest not to cry, but it was impossible today of all days. Her father's funeral. Her mother had stroked her cheek that morning and told her to be brave. She had managed it, too, as her father's coffin was carried to the front of the church. She noticed her gran squeeze her mother's hand tightly and tried to mimic her expression, face fixed forwards, jaw set in fierce defiance whilst others around them sniffled and sobbed. Peggy had held everything inside throughout the service, like a jack-in-the-box, but now she could bear it no longer. Her eyes brimmed with hot tears as she pleaded with Sid. 'Please. Give me back my book.'

Sid considered the question like a cat casually observing a skittering mouse whose tail was trapped beneath its cruel paw. He sighed. 'I don't think so. I think I might rip another page,' he said, picking up the book. 'In fact, I might rip them all out, and you know the best part?' Peggy shook her head forlornly. Sid grinned with malevolence. 'You won't stop me. And no one else will neither.'

'I will,' said a voice.

They both turned to see Peggy's twin brother, Joe, standing in the doorway, with her best friend, Florence, beside him. Sid adopted a bored expression. 'Oh, here we go. Peggy the bookworm's stupid brother and stupid friend come to rescue her.'

'Give her back the book, Sid,' said Joe.

'Yeah, Sid,' said Flo. 'Give it back.'

'Meh meh. Meh meh meh,' mimicked Sid, pulling a face at Flo.

'Don't do that,' said Joe, taking a step forwards.

Sid sighed and raised himself to his full, not-inconsiderable height. 'Or what?'

'Or I'll knock your block off.'

Sid squared up to Joe now. He was five years older and

a good foot taller than him, with fists the size of meat pies. 'I'd like to see you try,' he said, shoving his challenger hard in the chest. Joe reeled backwards. Sid pulled a face. 'You couldn't knock down a daisy in the wind. You Sparks lot are all weak. Your sister's a cry baby and your dad got his head blown off in France—'

It took Peggy a second to realise that the sharp crack was the sound of Sid's nose breaking as Joe delivered a deft blow squarely to the centre of the bully's face. Flo screamed, but more from delight, which in turn brought Peggy and Joe's grandmother, Emily, charging through the door. 'What the blue blazes is going on?' she demanded.

'Sid was picking on Peggy and said horrible things about Mr Sparks, God rest his soul,' said Flo, crossing herself.

'Is that right?' said Emily, narrowing her eyes. Sid clutched a bloodied handkerchief to his wounded nose and stared up at her in terror. He may not have feared many people, but everyone was scared of Emily Marsh. She reached forwards and grabbed him by the ear. 'Let's see what your mother has to say, shall we, Sidney Kemp?' she said, ignoring his piglet-squeal protests. 'Your father was a wrong 'un and it would seem that you are too.' She glanced back at Joe. 'Look after your sister, there's a good lad.'

After she'd gone, Joe and Flo knelt either side of a sobbing Peggy. 'It's all right, Peg,' said Joe, handing her back the book. 'We can fix it.'

Peggy dabbed her eyes with the freshly pressed hand-kerchief her mother had given her that morning. 'I'm not really crying about that. I'm thinking about Dad.'

Joe put an arm around her shoulder. 'I miss him too, but you know what?'

'What?'

'You don't need to worry because I'll always be here to look after you.'

She gazed up at him, eyes saucer-wide. 'Always?'

'Of course. I'm not going anywhere.'

Peggy linked her arms first with Joe and then with Flo. 'We'll always be together. Us three,' she said. 'And you two can get married and I'll be auntie to all the children.'

Florence and Joe grinned at one another. 'Now, come on, Peg,' said Joe, pulling the book on to her lap. 'Read this story to us. You know how the words go all blurry for me, but you always make them come alive.'

'Yeah, go on, Peg,' said Flo, snuggling beside her. 'Is this the one about the dragon who doesn't want to fight?'

Peggy nodded. 'He loves making up poetry and is a very kind and gentle dragon.'

'Read that bit where the boy takes St George to meet the dragon again, Peg,' said Joe. 'It's so funny. I love the way the dragon talks.'

Peggy smiled as she leafed through the pages, smoothing the book open so they could see the pictures. As she began to read, she thought of her father, of how he used to read to her and Joe, and how much she missed him, but she also knew that as long as she had her books and her brother, everything would be all right.

Chapter 1

London, 1940

'Got yer nose in another book, 'ave yer?'

Peggy Sparks looked up from the page in front of her into the disapproving face of Elsie Cooper, who had just boarded the busy morning train and was making a beeline for her. Peggy had known Mrs Cooper all her life and couldn't remember ever seeing her smile or laugh, or do anything except look perpetually disappointed with the world.

'As nosey as a crow, that one,' her grandmother would remark whenever she noticed Mrs Cooper's net curtains twitch, 'and as sour as a bag of sherbet lemons.'

'Oh, come now, Mum,' Peggy's mother would say with gentle admonishment. 'She lost both her sons in the Great War. You know how that knocks a person.'

Emily folded her arms. 'You lost your husband in the Great War, Alice. I don't see you walking about the place with a face like a wet weekend in Clacton. I've known Elsie Cooper since she was a nipper. She's always been a sourpuss.'

'Perhaps, but it's important to love your neighbour,' said Alice. 'She and Mr Cooper must be very lonely in that house without the boys.'

'I don't think Ted Cooper's lonely. He's always in the pub.'

'Mum!'

Emily shrugged. 'It's true. It may be important to love your neighbour, but it's also important to tell the truth,' she said, winking at her granddaughter.

Peggy closed her book. 'Good morning, Mrs Cooper.'

'Not sure you can call it good,' she said, sitting down beside Peggy and looking out towards the bedsheet-festooned washing lines in the back gardens of the neat, terraced houses they were passing. 'This weather's playing havoc with my rheumatism. Where are you off to then?'

Peggy cast her gaze around at their fellow passengers. The carriage was packed with stern-faced older men in hats and unsmiling younger women mostly of around Peggy's age, all busy minding their own business. 'I start my new job today. At the Ministry.'

'Ooh, yes,' said Mrs Cooper, eyes sparkling. 'I heard about that.' Peggy's grandmother's voice rang loud and clear in her head. *Listening in on the party line, no doubt.* 'Your mother's very proud of you and your dear brother Joe, away with his tank regiment. And now you'll be working for the government. You'll be having tea with Churchill soon, no doubt.'

Peggy smiled. 'I just hope I'll be good enough for them.'

Mrs Cooper patted her hand. 'They wouldn't have asked you to do the job if they didn't think you were capable, dear.'

Peggy hoped she was right, remembering the day she'd found out about the position. She hadn't been home long after her shift at the local library when the front door opened and there was a familiar skittering of paws as Badger, the family's teddy-bear-faced terrier, shot down the hall.

'Get that kettle on, will yer, Peg?' called her grandmother from the doorway. 'Two hours in the ration queue gives you a thirst.'

'Right-o,' replied Peg, seizing the kettle from the range.

'Hello, dear,' said her mother, appearing in the kitchen with Emily close on her heels, each carrying a large wicker basket.

'How did you get on?' asked Peggy, leaning over to kiss her mother.

'All the usuals, but your mother came up trumps,' said Emily.

'Three herrings for ninepence,' confirmed Alice proudly.

'Well done, Mum,' said Peggy, smiling at them both. She dearly missed her father and longed for her brother's return, but in their absence, Peggy basked in the presence of these two women.

Emily Marsh had been as constant as the night sky in Peggy's life. She had been too young to recall the tiny cottage where her grandmother had lived with her grandfather, Charlie, and a blind, three-legged dog called Silver, but she could picture it from her mother's description: 'Spick and span, warm as toast and full of the smell of baking.' The day after Charlie died, Emily had packed up her things and arrived on their doorstep with Silver in tow. To his credit, Peggy's father had welcomed them both with open arms. Emily had always been able to make him laugh, and they had a common bond in that they both adored Alice. Emily was stubborn, opinionated and made the best Victoria sponge Peggy had ever tasted. Alice Sparks, on the other hand, was a gentle soul. Peggy always suspected that Emily offered enough opinions for both of them, but this didn't mean her mother lacked grit. She had received a widow's pension but it was barely enough to make ends meet. She worked by day at the greengrocer's in town and by evening at the local White Bear pub, whilst Emily cared for Peggy and her brother. Certain people muttered about the propriety of a lone woman working in a pub full of men, but if they ever uttered it in Emily's earshot, they never dared again. The family had little to show for their efforts, but Peggy couldn't imagine a happier childhood.

'Mr Harris reckons they'll be rationing tea next. And then we'll definitely lose the bloomin' war,' declared Emily as they unpacked their baskets.

'Don't say that, Mum,' scolded Alice.

'Sorry, dear,' said Emily, looking mildly chastened. 'The poor man had to count over seven thousand coupons last week. Said his fingers were red raw by the end of it.'

'Where are Flo and Nancy?' asked Peggy. 'I thought they'd be home by now.'

'Gone to the park after school. Trying to wear the littlun out. She's got more energy than a box of frogs,' said Emily.

'Flo does look tired,' said Peggy.

'She's about to drop at any second,' said Emily. 'I give it a week before that baby makes an appearance. Unless it's a boy. Then he'll be late. Boys are lazy.'

'At least yesterday's letter from Joe put a bit of colour in her cheeks,' said Alice.

'I'm not surprised she's tired,' said Emily. 'That nipper doesn't stop talking. Question after question. It's never-ending. All those ideas and opinions.'

'I wonder where she gets it from,' said Alice, firing a knowing look at Peggy. Emily huffed but without much vigour.

Peggy smiled. 'Shall I pour the tea?'

'Please, and let's have three of those raspberry buns I made,' said Emily, plonking herself in her sage-green armchair and putting her feet up on the rose-coloured footstool.

Her tea-making was interrupted by a rapid succession of barks as Badger leapt up and scampered out into the hall at the sound of three purposeful raps on the door knocker.

'Saints preserve us!' cried Emily, as the dog's persistent barks gave way to growls. 'You'd think Hitler himself was at the door. See who it is, would you, please, Peggy dear?'

'On my way.'

Peggy dragged the reluctant dog back to the kitchen before opening the door to be greeted by a tall, debonair man sporting a neatly trimmed moustache and a Savile Row suit. 'Sir James. This is a surprise,' she said, glimpsing the sleek black chauffeur-driven car behind him.

He lifted his homburg hat in greeting. 'Good afternoon, Peggy.'

Peggy had been seven years old when she first met James Miles. He was the officer in charge of her father's regiment and had been deeply affected by the fact that many of his men didn't return from the Great War whilst he survived. He had assumed something of a guardian angel role within these families. Peggy could remember trips to the zoo and holidays in Clacton all paid for by this benevolent man. Now in his sixties, he had lost nothing of his charm or influence. He held a senior position in government but never divulged exactly what he did. Peggy relished this air of mystery. He was like a character from a John Buchan novel.

'Well, if it isn't the Lord of the Manor himself,' declared Emily, appearing behind Peggy, closely followed by Alice with Badger on her heels.

'Always a pleasure to see you, Mrs Marsh, Mrs Sparks,' he said, his moustache twitching with amusement. The dog stopped in its tracks as the man held out his hand in greeting. 'Hello Badger, old boy,' he said and was promptly rewarded with feverish licks and tail wags. He straightened up, smoothed his emerald silk tie and smiled at them all, resting his gaze on Alice. 'Pardon the intrusion, but I wondered if I might have a word with Peggy?'

'Of course,' said Alice. 'Come through. Peggy was just making tea. You'll have a cup?'

'That would be most agreeable. Thank you.' He followed them through to the kitchen. 'How are you, Mrs Marsh?' he asked, as Emily settled back in her armchair, regarding him with a critical eye.

'When's this war going to be over then, young man?' she demanded.

'Mrs Marsh, you know I always enjoy my visits. You make me feel twenty years younger than I am.'

'You didn't answer my question.'

'Mum,' warned Alice. 'Sir James is our guest. Could we at least have our tea before you start your interrogation?'

'He enjoys it. Don't you, dear?'

'I do. When you spend your day dealing with the double-talk of politics, it's extremely refreshing.'

'You be sure to let Churchill know I'm waiting for his call,' said Emily.

Peggy held out a cup and saucer to Sir James. 'Milk, one sugar.'

'I'm touched that you remember. Thank you.'

'Raspberry bun?'

He glanced at Emily. 'Made by your fair hand?'

'Of course.'

'Then I accept with gratitude. My wife has me on some terrible eating scheme at the moment. She has seized upon rationing as a way of weaning me off all sweet treats.'

Emily snorted. 'Ridiculous.'

Sir James accepted the plate, holding the cake under his nose and inhaling its sugary scent. 'I couldn't agree more, dear lady. Now. To business. If it's not too indelicate of me, Peggy, may I ask how old you are?'

'Twenty-nine.'

'And still working at the library?'

'Yes, sir.'

Sir James gave a nod of approval. 'Our esteemed leader

11

always asserts that books have the means to carry civilisation triumphantly forwards, and I'm inclined to agree with him.'

'Are you going to start dropping copies of the King James Bible on Hitler's noggin, then?' snorted Emily.

'Mum. Please,' said Alice, taking a sip of tea. 'Sorry, Sir James. You were saying?'

He turned to Peggy. 'And you're still writing your Mass Observation diaries?'

'Yes, she bloomin' well is,' said Emily. 'Makes me nervous every time I see her writing in that notebook. I don't want every Tom, Dick and Harry knowing my business.'

Alice turned to her. 'Mum, we've talked about this. Peg, explain it to your gran again.'

Peggy smiled. 'They're accounts of what ordinary people like us think and feel, Gran. It was started as an experiment by three Cambridge students and means that our voices are heard.'

'Hmm, well. Maybe it's not so bad when you put it like that,' said Emily.

Peggy turned to Sir James. 'But how did you know about my writing, sir?' she asked.

'Your diaries have come to the attention of the powers that be at the Ministry of Information. They think you might be a welcome addition to the staff.'

Peggy and Alice stared at him in astonishment. 'Our Peggy working for the Ministry of Busybodies?' said Emily, folding her arms.

'I can assure you, dear lady, that the Ministry has been established with the most laudable of aims.'

'Like telling us working people what to do all the time.'

Sir James looked amused. 'I'm sure the authorities would never presume to tell Mrs Emily Marsh what to do.'

'It'd be a brave man who tried,' muttered Alice into her teacup.

'Cheek,' said Emily.

'So, Peggy, what do you think? You don't have to decide now.'

Peggy glanced at her mother who raised her eyebrows in encouragement. 'Well, I'm not sure. I enjoy working at the library. I don't know if I'd fit in a place like that. I don't know anything about the government.'

'It acts separately from the government and really deals with the flow of information to the public. Your job would be working in the Publications department where all the books and pamphlets are produced. It's not been established for long, but I have high hopes for the impact it could have on the war effort.'

'Really?' said Peggy, her mind diverting immediately to thoughts of Joe and anything that could be done to bring him home sooner.

Sir James nodded. 'Never underestimate the power of words, Peggy. Although I know I don't need to tell you that, given the power of the words you produce. Why don't you give it some thought, talk it over with your mother and grandmother and let me know.'

'All right. Thank you, sir.'

'Jolly good,' said Sir James, taking a bite of his bun. He closed his eyes for a moment before exclaiming, 'It's as if a thousand angels are dancing a sweet jig on my tongue. Exquisite, Mrs Marsh.'

Emily fixed him with a look. 'And now, tell me when this war's going to be over so that my grandson can come home. There's a baby about to be born who needs a father.'

It had taken the birth of the baby, Charles Reginald Sparks, or Charlie as he would forever be known, to confirm to Peggy that she had to accept Sir James's offer. He arrived the day before his father came home on leave, entering the world without a wail or a whimper. In fact, the midwife was so concerned by his casual indifference to being born that she gave him a firm pat on the back, resulting in a plaintive wailing, which was only calmed when he was reunited with his mother. As soon as Joe arrived home, he rushed upstairs to find Florence sitting up in bed with Charlie in her arms and Nancy by her side. Peggy, Alice and Emily followed behind.

'Daddy!' cried Nancy, leaping into his arms.

'Hello, sweet pea,' he said, kissing the top of her head before leaning over to embrace his wife and stroke his son's downy hair. 'Well done, my love,' he whispered.

'Would you like to hold him?' she asked.

'More than anything.' Flo passed the bundle to Joe with tender care and he perched on the bed. Nancy put an arm around her father's shoulder and planted a kiss on his cheek. 'What do you think of your new brother then, Nance?' he asked.

'I like the way he smells.' She threw a wide-eyed look towards Florence. 'Most of the time.' Everyone laughed.

14

Peggy stood arm in arm with her mother and grand-mother, watching the new family with a mixture of soaring joy and plunging sorrow. She saw the way Joe looked at his son, how he encouraged Nancy to trace a gentle finger along his soft cheek, how he curled his arm around Flo, blanketing them all with love.

She had telephoned Sir James that very afternoon. 'I've made up my mind, sir. About the job. If you'll still have me. I'd like to accept your offer, please.'

She could hear the delight in his voice. 'I'm very glad you've decided to accept, Peggy. I think you'll be splendid.'

I'm going to be more than that, thought Peggy, her body pulsing with secret determination. *I'm going to help bring an end to this war. There'll be no children left without fathers in my family this time round.*

'Peggy. Peggy.' Peggy blinked back to the present and the frowning face of Mrs Cooper. 'Dearie me, you were in a proper brown study there. We're here.'

'Oh. Sorry, Mrs Cooper,' she said, rising to her feet and following her and the rest of the crowd as they dispersed across the concourse, its ceiling hung with Union Jack flags, its walls with posters insisting that 'Careless Talk Costs Lives'.

'Well, goodbye and good luck, dear,' said Mrs Cooper, waving over her shoulder before disappearing into the crowd.

'Bye,' said Peggy. After the quiet routine of Edenham library, London seemed so vibrant and alive that she had no choice but to keep walking.

Sir James had assured Peggy that she wouldn't be able to miss Senate House where the Ministry was housed. 'It's a huge, ugly brute of a building,' he'd said. As it appeared before her half an hour later, a towering incongruity beside the Bloomsbury grandeur, she realised he was right. The forbidding stone and brick structure was certainly awe-inspiring. It loomed above Peggy as she approached, reaching hundreds of feet into the sky. The small grey windows which studded the outside did little to soften its appearance.

A serious-looking man with bushy eyebrows emerged from the front gate whistling to himself. He touched his hat when he saw Peggy. 'Like an art deco prison, isn't it?' he said, glancing up towards the Union Jack flag fluttering half-heartedly on top of the building. 'The architect, Holden his name was, wanted to blend the modern with the classical.' The man shook his head. 'It's like asking Glenn Miller to play Mozart.' Peggy wasn't sure how to answer. The man didn't seem to require her input as he sighed. 'Dreadful waste of Portland stone.'

'Excuse me, but do you work here?'

The man looked at her. 'I did, but I have recently been relieved of my duties.'

'Oh. I'm sorry.'

'Don't be,' he said, studying her face. 'First day, is it?'

Peggy felt her cheeks burn. 'Yes. Do you know where I should go?'

'If I were you I'd turn round and go back to where you came from.' He gave a barking laugh before glancing towards a sentry box by the front door. 'Jarvis, could you show this young woman where she should go? The poor thing has a job here.'

A uniformed man with greying hair and kindly eyes emerged from the box. 'Certainly, Mr Greene. It's this way, miss.'

'Oh, thank you,' said Peggy.

'Good luck,' called the man over his shoulder.

Peggy glanced back at him before following Jarvis. 'Excuse me,' she asked, 'but that man. Was it . . .?'

'Graham Greene,' said Jarvis. 'The very same. Terrific writer.'

'Goodness,' said Peggy, her heart thumping in her ears. She knew the Ministry of Information was the workplace of several famous writers but hadn't reckoned on one of the authors of the books she stacked on the library's shelves greeting her on her first day.

Peggy followed Jarvis into the entrance hall, which reminded her of a Roman temple leading to a gladiatorial arena where no doubt the lions would be released at any moment to devour her. 'It's just through there, miss.'

'Thank you,' said Peggy, feeling in her coat pocket for the letter her gran had given her the night before, willing it to give her the courage she needed to walk through the doors.

February 1940

Dear Peg,

I asked Gran to give this to you for your first day as I can't be there in person to wish you luck. Hopefully they'll put us on a slow boat to China after our training, drifting away from the fighting. You know me. I'll do my duty but I'm a bit like the reluctant dragon from that book you used to read to Flo and me. I'd rather not fight. Not that I can say that aloud these days. England expects and all that. Saying goodbye to you all was the hardest thing I've ever done. I still picture Nancy's sad face every night when I close my eyes and I've got the picture she drew of us all in my jacket pocket. I'll take it out from time to time for courage. I don't know what lies ahead and maybe it's better not to think about it. Maybe it's better to just get on with it like Gran would. I'm scared though, Peg. I know I can admit this to you. I want to make you all proud and I want you to know how proud I am of you. You're clever, Peg. Cleverer than all of us put together. Like I told you when we went for that walk with Badger and Nance before I left, you're wasted working at the library. You've got to grab your chance. I know you'll show those blokes at the Ministry a thing or two. I was tickled pink when you said you're going to make it your job to get me home again. The thought of that will keep me going. Knowing that my sister is fighting for me while I'm fighting for her. Write and tell me about it soon. I promise to write as often as I can and be as honest as I can in my letters like you told me to. I'll always sign off with we'll meet again because then I know we will.

Love, Joe

18

Chapter 2

As Peggy stepped into the echoing marble hall, she did her best to display more confidence than she felt, breathing deeply in an attempt to slow her thumping heart. Luckily, the buzzing throng of suited men and smart young women paid her no notice. They were too intent on hurrying towards the grand stone staircase or disappearing into lifts. Peggy couldn't imagine ever walking these corridors with such purpose. She approached the wide marble reception desk where a woman, who was at least five years younger than Peggy, regarded her with an icy expression.

'Yes?'

Peggy heard her grandmother's voice very loud and very clear in her head. *She's no better than she ought to be.* Peggy swallowed her nerves and spoke with similar clarity and volume, her words resounding around the hollow chamber. 'My name is Peggy Sparks and it's my first day working in the Publications department.'

'All right, there's no need to shout,' said the receptionist, throwing a glance towards another woman beside her, who snorted with laughter.

It's like being back at school, thought Peggy. *It's Sid Kemp and his like all over again, except there's no Joe to fight my battles any more.* 'Sorry,' she said more quietly, hoping that her cheeks weren't as flushed as they felt. 'Here's my letter of introduction.'

The woman snatched the document from Peggy, lifting her eyebrows slightly when she spotted Sir James Miles as the signatory. She plucked her telephone from its cradle and dialled. 'Yes, hello. This is reception. I have a Peggy Sparks here for you. Very well. Thank you.' She slid the letter back towards Peggy. 'Take a seat. Someone will be down to collect you shortly.'

'Thank you,' said Peggy. She walked towards the low leather seats which lined the reception area, trying to ignore the other woman's whispered comment to her snickering friend.

'Honestly, Mary, I swear the secretaries get plainer every day.'

Peggy remembered her mother's advice to ignore anyone who had nothing nice to say and focused on her surroundings instead. The place was bustling with industry, its stone walls echoing with clipped accents very unlike her own. It had a cold, closed-in atmosphere that somehow made Peggy want to run and shout. She was used to the hushed atmosphere of the library, but this had an air of secrets and intrigue. She watched as a young man wearing thick-lensed glasses and bicycle clips entered the building. The two women on reception nudged one another as soon as they saw him. He ignored them, approaching the lifts and pressing the 'call' button. The man glanced in her direction, offering a timid smile which she returned, grateful for this small but encouraging human interaction. As the lift doors opened, an irate-looking man of about the same age shot through them, almost knocking him over in the process. He offered no apology. The first man shook his head and disappeared into the lift.

Please don't be coming to collect me, thought Peggy as the angry man cast his gaze around.

'Miss Sparks?' he barked.

Peggy and her dread rose. 'That's me.'

The man registered her with barely a blink. 'Well, come along then,' he said, frantically pressing for another lift. He glared up at the lights.

Peggy came to stand beside him. Despite her shyness, she always did her best to be polite. She held out her hand. 'Peggy Sparks,' she said. 'And you are?'

The man sighed, shaking her hand with begrudging impatience. 'I'm Cyril Sheldrake and I'm incredibly busy. Fetching secretaries really is below my remit, you know.'

The lift doors slid open and he shooed her inside. Peggy scurried forwards, her cheeks hot with shame. As the doors closed she glanced at the two women on reception watching her with nudging amusement. They rode in silence until the doors pinged open and Sheldrake hurried out. 'This way,' he said, setting off at such a pace that Peggy had to jog to keep up. He veered left and right along corridor after corridor so that by the time they entered a large, stuffy office containing half a dozen desks, Peggy was beginning to feel dizzy. She had no idea how she would ever find her way around this bewildering maze. 'Home sweet home,' said Sheldrake. Peggy peeled off her coat, wrinkling her nose against the musky stench of a room which was no doubt invariably filled with men. Sheldrake was already gathering armfuls of paper and folders and making for the door. 'I've got a meeting.'

'But what should I do?' she asked.

He shrugged, gesturing towards a desk situated in a cramped corner next to the window. 'You can set yourself up over there, I suppose, and . . .' He glanced back at his overflowing desk before plucking a document from a teetering pile. 'Read this and mark any errors in spelling, punctuation and so on.' He handed her a thick sheaf of papers with the heading, *High Quality Silage by the Ministry of Information and Ministry of Agriculture.*

Peggy stared down at the document. 'But I don't know anything about –' she said to Sheldrake's retreating back, '– silage.' She sighed, making her way over to the desk, shuffling past two others on her way before plonking her bag on the chair. 'Sorry, Joe,' she murmured. 'Doesn't look as if I'll be bringing an end to the war today, not unless I can rewrite this so that they tip their high-quality silage over the enemy.' She took in her surroundings properly now. The whole office looked as if it had been put together in a hurry with its mishmash of office fur-niture and stark white walls. The desk to the left of hers was a chaotic mess with an overflowing in-tray, dusty typewriter and piles of what looked to her like fashion magazines.

Peggy took a deep breath before walking across the room to unfasten the window, which took a certain amount of effort as it had clearly never been opened before.

'There,' she said, returning to her desk, retrieving a pencil and setting to work.

Despite the fact that the contents of the pamphlet could have been prescribed as an effective cure for insomnia, Peggy soon fell into a rhythm of reading and correcting which she found satisfying. She may have been persuaded to accept this job out of a longing to help her brother, but she was pragmatic enough to know that this would take a while.

By the time Sheldrake returned from his meeting, she had finished the task. He entered the room wearing the strange smile of a man who didn't use this set of muscles very often. Peggy soon realised this wasn't meant for her but the man beside him, who she guessed to be around the same age as her father would have been. He was tall and thickset with a careworn face that bore glimpses of a handsome youth. Sheldrake was several inches shorter than him and looked up at the man in a way that made Peggy realise he was his superior. She rose to her feet and sidestepped the desks to greet them.

'I thought you were very assertive in that meeting, Mr Beecher. It's important that we don't let the other departments walk all over us,' Sheldrake was saying.

'Thank you, Mr Sheldrake. It's good to know you're on my side.' He turned his attention to Peggy. 'Good morning. Miss Sparks, is it?'

She took a small step forwards. 'Peggy Sparks.'

'Clarence Beecher,' he said. 'I head up this department, for my sins. You come highly recommended, Miss Sparks.'

'Thank you, sir.'

'Right. Well, if you'll excuse me. One of the many perks of my job is the endless string of meetings I am expected to attend. Mr Sheldrake will show you the ropes.'

'It would be my pleasure,' said Sheldrake with an obsequious bow.

'Jolly good.' Mr Beecher disappeared through the door leading to his office before emerging moments later with a fresh sheaf of papers. 'Onwards.'

'Onwards, Mr Beecher,' said Sheldrake, maintaining an alarmingly toothy grin which reminded Peggy of the gurning clowns who had terrified her during a childhood trip to the circus with her gran. He dropped the smile as soon as Mr Beecher left before turning to Peggy. 'Have you finished correcting the pamphlet?'

'Yes,' said Peggy, retrieving the document and handing it over.

'Really? All of it?'

'Yes,' she repeated.

She held her breath as Sheldrake frowned his way through the pages. 'You missed one typographic error here,' he said, pulling a pencil from his top pocket and marking it. 'And another grammatical error here.'

'Right,' said Peggy. 'Sorry.'

'And next time, use a blue pencil.'

'Right,' repeated Peggy. 'Understood.' Sheldrake grunted before taking his seat at a large desk to the left of the door to Beecher's office and picking up a document to read. 'What should I do now?' she asked.

Sheldrake sighed. 'Well, really you're supposed to be working under Lady Marigold Cecily, but unfortunately she's rather fonder of dancing the war away at the Café de Paris than turning up for work on time.'

Peggy was surprised by his honesty and, given his description, not in a great hurry to meet her new superior. 'I could make some tea perhaps while I'm waiting for her to arrive? I don't suppose you've had time for one this morning.'

Sheldrake seemed momentarily caught off guard. *Kill them with kindness, Peg*, as her gran would say. 'Yes, actually. That would be rather . . . Thank you.'

Peggy nodded. 'I think I noticed the kitchen on our way here. Back in a tick.' As she retraced her steps along the narrow corridor, Peggy had to pause several times to allow other employees past and was irritated that not one of them either acknowledged or thanked her. *Bloomin' toffs*, as her grandmother would say. Eventually, she spied the kitchen. As she walked towards it, a man approached and immediately stood to one side to let her past.

'Dear lady. Please,' he said with a courtly bow.

'Thank you,' said Peggy, relieved to finally meet someone with manners.

The man lingered in the doorway as Peggy set about placing cups on a tray and searched fruitlessly through the empty drawers for a teaspoon. 'You won't find one for love nor money,' he told her, reaching into his top pocket and retrieving a shiny silver spoon. 'But you can borrow mine if you tell me your name.'

Peggy coloured a little under his scrutiny. He was what her grandmother would have called a dandy with his neatly pressed suit, pristinely styled hair and pewter-blue eyes, which were watching her intently. She cleared her throat. 'Peggy Sparks. It's my first day working in the Publications department,' she said, fixing her gaze on the spoon.

The man held it out to her as a knight might offer his sword with head bowed. 'My lady. It is my deep honour to meet you and offer you full use of my teaspoon. Wallace Dalton. At your service.'

Peggy couldn't help but laugh. 'Thank you, Mr Dalton.'

He grinned. 'It is my pleasure, Peggy Sparks. I have a feeling we're going to be great friends. Have you met old Beecher yet? He's a good bloke. Bit put upon but decent.'

'He seems nice. And I've met Mr Sheldrake.'

Dalton raised one eyebrow. 'He's as snappy as a turtle and as officious as they come. Don't mind him. No one else does. Shall I carry that for you?' he offered, gesturing towards the loaded tea tray.

Peggy was buoyed by the gesture. 'Thank you.'

They heard the raised voices as soon as they neared the office. Dalton threw her a sideways glance. 'Once more unto the breach,' he said before leading them into the room.

The young woman perched on the edge of one of the desks was a good few years younger than Peggy and looked as if she'd just stepped off the set of a Hollywood movie. She wore a figure-hugging rose-coloured silk dress and a string of pearls which she caressed absent-mindedly as Sheldrake berated her. She seemed unmoved by his words, flashing a stunning smile towards Dalton and Peggy as they entered. 'You made tea. You darlings,' she said, rising to greet them.

'Lady Cecily, I haven't finished,' insisted Sheldrake.

Lady Cecily rolled her eyes at Peggy and Dalton before turning back to Sheldrake with an angelic expression. 'Dear Mr Sheldrake. I've told you before, you must call me Miss Cecily. Just because my father's a lord, there's no need to doff your cap to me. And as for my slight tardiness, I can only apologise and assure you that it won't happen again.'

'You promised that last week. Every day,' said Sheldrake.

'Well, I'll do better this week. My word is my bond,' she said, placing a hand on her heart. Peggy watched as she helped herself to tea without offering it to anyone else. 'Delicious,' she declared, closing her eyes as she took a sip. 'Nothing cures the misdemeanours of the night before more than a cup of tea.' She glanced at Peggy. 'I don't think I know you.' Peggy shifted slightly under her scrutiny, suddenly aware of her plain librarian's tweed skirt and cream blouse.

'This is Miss Sparks. Our new secretary. She'll be working under you, Miss Cecily,' said Sheldrake.

'Oh, what fun,' she cried, reaching out a hand. 'Marigold Cecily, but please call me Marigold.'

'Peggy Sparks,' said Peggy, her skin prickling with dread as they shook hands.

'What a delightful name,' said Marigold. 'So full of vigour.'

'Thank you,' said Peggy, unsure of what else to say.

'Dalton,' said Sheldrake, glancing in the man's direction. 'You appear to be in the wrong department. Shouldn't you be getting back to Campaigns so that you can give us even more to do?'

27

Dalton gave a short barking laugh. 'If you insist, Mr Sheldrake. We've got some marvellous ideas brewing.'

'I'm sure you have,' said Sheldrake.

Dalton clicked his heels together and bowed. 'Goodbye, Miss Sparks, Miss Cecily. It was a great pleasure as always. Sheldrake,' he added in a tone that suggested it was anything but.

Sheldrake muttered something under his breath before returning to the document in front of him.

'Here,' said Peggy, pouring milk and tea into a cup and handing it to him.

Sheldrake glanced at the tea in surprise. 'Oh. Thank you.'

'Be a peach and top me up, would you, Peggy Sparks?' said Marigold. 'Not only do you make the best tea I've ever tasted, but you also have the most delightful name I've ever heard.'

Peggy avoided her gaze as she refilled Marigold's cup before pouring one for herself.

'Chin, chin and welcome to our delightful department,' said Marigold, raising her teacup.

'As Miss Sparks has just arrived, perhaps you could explain what we do here,' said Sheldrake, as if issuing Marigold a dare.

'Please, Mr Sheldrake. Not until I've finished my tea,' she said.

He shook his head and turned to Peggy. 'Officially we're part of the Publications department which is located on the other side of Russell Square, but there's not enough room for everyone, so our department, headed by Mr Beecher, works here. We're one branch of the publishing

28

arm responsible for all books, pamphlets and leaflets which aim to maintain morale at home and exert influence abroad.'

'Gosh,' said Marigold, beaming at Peggy. 'Don't we sound jolly important.'

Sheldrake scowled. 'Lady Cecily, you started here the same day as me. Were you not aware of our fundamental aims?'

Marigold shrugged. 'There just seem to be an awful lot of pamphlets about animal feed and how to put on a gas mask.'

'That's because we are expected to deal with the leaflet requirements of almost every other department and organisation with links to the Ministry,' said Sheldrake with a sigh.

'Oh dear,' said Marigold. 'No wonder your desk is always overflowing.' Sheldrake gave an exasperated shake of his head.

'I've seen some of the books on the W. H. Smith's bookstands,' ventured Peggy. 'And we used to hand out leaflets at the library.'

Sheldrake nodded. 'Some are published for sale via publishers or the Ministry; others are given out for free if they're of import to the public. They tell us we're a vital cog in the machine of war, but most of the time it feels as if we're working ourselves into an early grave.' He glanced over at the pile of magazines on Marigold's desk. 'At least some of us are.' He drained his tea and looked at his watch. 'Right. I've got another meeting,' he said, gathering his papers and hurrying out through the door.

'Always rushing about,' said Marigold, shaking her

head. 'What a funny little man.' She sat herself down at the desk beside Peggy's, retrieved a copy of *Tatler* from the top of the pile and began leafing through it, pausing to take another sip of tea.

'So, what should I do now?' asked Peggy.

Marigold glanced up at her as if she'd requested two tickets to the moon. 'Are you asking me?'

Peggy breathed away a flicker of irritation. 'Mr Sheldrake did say I was working under you.'

Marigold screwed up her pretty face and guffawed. 'That's too funny. Wait until I tell Cordy that someone is working for me.' She looked down at the magazine she was reading. 'Right. First of all, I'd like to know if you think I could carry off this look?' She pointed to a stylish photograph of Katharine Hepburn wearing a white silk shirt tucked into wide-legged trousers.

'I'm not quite sure what that's got to do with this job.'

'Oh, it's got nothing to do with the job. It's just for fun.'

Peggy longed to tell her that she wasn't here for fun. She was here to help with the war effort, to bring her brother home, to end this nightmare. They were interrupted by the telephone on Sheldrake's desk ringing. 'Should we answer that?' asked Peggy.

Marigold shrugged. Exasperated, Peggy approached and lifted the receiver, wincing as she spoke. 'Publications?'

'Where's Sheldrake?' barked the voice.

'Erm, he's in a meeting. Can I take a message?' she asked, casting around for a notepad.

'Message for Beecher. Tell him Longforth called. Wilfred Buchan has said yes.'

'Wilfred Buchan? The writer?'

'Is there another Wilfred Buchan?'

'No, I don't believe there is.'

'Very well. Tell him to call me to discuss.'

Peggy was about to ask if he had his number, but the man had hung up. She stared at the receiver for a moment before replacing it in its cradle. Marigold glanced up and noticed her worried expression. 'Whatever's the matter? Was someone beastly to you? Do tell and I'll have them court-martialled.'

'It was a man called Longforth.'

'Henry Longforth?'

'I think so.'

'If he's phoning about an author it'll be Henry. He heads up things on the other side of the square. He's a horror. Likes to terrify all the juniors. My pa and he are members of the same club.'

This didn't surprise Peggy. She was about to return to her desk when she spotted a folder on Sheldrake's labelled 'For Proof-reading'. 'Do you think Mr Sheldrake would want me to check through some of these?' she asked.

Marigold gave another shrug. 'Probably. He's always asking me to go through them but it's deathly boring. He's been trying to get me to read some ghastly pamphlet about silage for weeks.' She yawned, stretching her elegant arms above her head. 'I usually liaise with the divine bunch in the Photographs department on suitable images for our publications. I simply adore photographs, don't you?'

'Yoohoo!' called a voice from the doorway.

Peggy glanced round to see a tall, grinning young

31

woman with hair the colour of cinnamon, wearing elegant, wide-legged trousers and a fitted teal-coloured blouse. 'Cordy, darling, you're doing the Hepburn and you look magnificent!' cried Marigold, leaping from her chair in delight. The woman struck a film star pose before giving an airy laugh. 'I was just talking about your divine Photographs department. Come and meet the sublime Peggy Sparks.'

Peggy had never been described as sublime in her life and could feel the colour rise to her cheeks as Marigold's friend approached with a perfectly manicured outstretched hand. 'Ecstatic to meet you, Peggy. I'm Cordelia Fitzwilliam but all my friends call me Cordy.'

'Nice to meet you,' said Peggy.

'Oh, but your accent is darling. Where are you from?'

Peggy shifted uncomfortably. 'Edenham. It's south of the river.'

Cordelia turned to Marigold. 'Didn't we go to a party south of the river once?'

Marigold nodded. 'Greenwich.'

'Oh yes. At Queen's House. Marvellous ball. Have you ever been, Peggy?'

'I don't believe I have.'

'Ah. Pity. Well,' said Cordelia. 'I was just popping by . . .'

'To invite me for an early lunch to discuss those photographs I need?' asked Marigold, raising her eyebrows mischievously.

Cordelia laughed. 'Precisely. Wonderful to meet you, Peggy. You should come along to one of our soirées, shouldn't she, Marigold?'

'Oh yes. That would be marvellous,' said Marigold, fetching her handbag from under her desk. 'Right. Toodle pip, Peggy Sparks. You'll be all right, won't you?'

'Of course,' said Peggy, welcoming the idea of having the office to herself and being rid of these irritating women with their airs and graces. She'd known that the staff at the Ministry would be different to her but she hadn't reckoned on working alongside someone as downright lazy as Lady Marigold Cecily. Didn't she realise there was a war on? She carried on as if this was all a hobby. Something to pass the time while the servants put in the graft. Clearly Lady Marigold had never done a day's work in her life. Peggy could imagine her gran giving this upper-class sloth a piece of her mind and wished she had the gumption to do the same.

Chapter 3

With the office free of preening aristocrats and ill-tempered colleagues, Peggy was soon happily immersed in an *Air Raid Training Precautions Manual*. She quickly forgot where she was and even found herself temporarily shaking off the concern that she didn't belong here. She grew bolder with every strike of her blue pencil, every dot, dash and correction. It was as if each minute impression she made on the paper was for Joe. She wouldn't say this to anyone else for fear of sounding daft. She was just happy to let the idea rest in her heart like a seed in warm earth.

By lunchtime, Peggy had finished a third of the document as her stomach began to rumble. In the absence of anyone to tell her otherwise, she decided to take the fish paste sandwiches her mother had insisted on making ('In case the Minister doesn't take you out for lunch on your first day,' she'd said with a grin) and stretch her legs. She was worried about straying too far from the office for fear of not being able to find her way back, so retreated to the lift but decided to take the stairs rather than risk its creaking mechanics.

As Peggy entered the stairwell, she heard the cheering,

unexpected sound of birdsong. She looked up at the wide, bright staircase twisting away from her. It was then she glimpsed the words, 'To the Library'. Peggy heard it like a whispered command in her head as she instinctively continued up two more flights before coming to a stop before a glass-fronted door. She peered like Alice through the looking glass to a world lined from floor to ceiling with mahogany bookcases filled with cloth-backed spines in shades of chestnut, damson and jade, their gold lettering a glittering temptation. For the first time that day, Peggy realised she was smiling, her nerves dissolving. Without questioning her actions, she pulled the door open and stepped inside. During her twenty-nine years on earth, Peggy had never found anything to match the hushed calm of a room filled with books. It made her heart soar with hope to be in the presence of so many thoughts and ideas, and she often felt that if she closed her eyes and listened very closely, she would be able to hear their whispered wisdom. She loved the idea of the likes of Charles Dickens, Jane Austen and Agatha Christie all sharing their words, like an orchestra of story-telling sparrows.

Peggy's mind drifted to thoughts of Edenham's Public Library, where she used to work. Its unprepossessing struc-ture looked as if the architect had taken the design from the drawings of a child, producing an entirely symmetrical outline with a hexagonal roof, only adding the windows and doors as an afterthought. 'It looks as if it's smiling,' Nancy had declared. 'The windows are its big eyes and the door is its happy mouth. See, Auntie Peg?'

Though the outside of the building was unremarkable,

it was the inside which always stirred Peggy's heart. Firstly, there was the silence. Having grown up in a family where only the dead were quiet, she relished silence. The children's library could be full of eager young readers, but its hushed peace managed to quieten even the unruliest child. Peggy knew mothers who brought in their youngsters just to calm them down. Secondly, there were the floors with their honey oak herringbone pattern and the balmy whiff of the beeswax and linseed oil Mrs Cope the cleaner applied every week. Thirdly and above all, there were the books. Shelf upon shelf, floor to ceiling, on every subject, telling every type of story you could wish for.

The Sparks family didn't have space at home for books, so the library had always been a haven for Peggy. She could remember her first trip, hand-in-hand with her mother, and the thrill when Miss Bunce, the then librarian, handed over her treasured reader's ticket. For Peggy it had been like someone reaching into the night sky and fetching her the shiniest of stars.

'Would you like me to help you choose a new book?' the freckle-faced librarian had asked.

Alice had given her daughter an encouraging nod. 'Yes, please,' Peggy whispered.

As the young woman led her to the children's library, Peggy caught the scent of her rose perfume, but more intoxicating than that was the smell of the books. It was difficult for Peggy to pinpoint what this smell reminded her of. It was sweet yet musty and laced with hope. Peggy inhaled deeply and decided she'd like to stay in this moment forever.

'Here we are,' said Miss Bunce, plucking three volumes from the shelves. Peggy glanced back towards the other books with a shiver of panic. *What if there was another one she liked more?* It was as if the young woman could read her thoughts. 'Don't worry, you can come back next week and exchange them for more.'

Peggy had felt dizzy, but not in a topsy-turvy way, like when she fell off the merry-go-round in the park. It was a happy dizziness, as if someone had opened up the sky above her head to reveal the secrets of the universe. 'Thank you,' she whispered, accepting the books carefully.

Peggy loved *The Secret Garden*, wasn't keen on *Rebecca of Sunnybrook Farm* and after reading *The Wonderful Wizard of Oz*, immediately asked her mother if she could have a pet lion.

She walked beside the shelves of this far grander library now, allowing a hand to stroke their spines as she passed. She glimpsed books on the Civil War, the French Revolution and the Tsars of Russia. After the dark, closed-in atmosphere of the corridors and offices, this room was open and full of light. Peggy found herself drawn to the window at the far end with a small desk and view of what looked like a castle, its twin jade-green turrets conjuring up stories of dragons, knights and princesses with exceptionally long hair. Peggy glanced back towards the door and decided to try making this her lunch-break haven. She would never usually entertain the thought of eating in a library, of course, but told herself that needs must in times of war, and besides, she would be sure to leave without dropping a single crumb. She retrieved her writing pad and pen from her bag along with her sandwiches. She needed to write down everything that had happened that day in a letter to Joe. She couldn't wait to tell him about Sheldrake and Lady Marigold. She became so lost in her writing that the first she knew of someone standing behind her was from the sound of him clearing his throat. Peggy turned, her cheeks flushing scarlet, overcome with the same feeling as when she and Flo had been caught trying on her mum's hats and shoes when they were six years old.

Peggy recognised the man with his thick-lensed glasses as the one who'd offered her an encouraging smile whilst she waited in reception. He wasn't smiling now, however, and had the appearance of someone who was trying to look cross but who'd had little practice at it. Even though he was frowning, his blue eyes had a softness to them and he kept folding and unfolding his arms as if he'd somehow lost control of them.

'I'm sorry,' said Peggy, rising to her feet, deciding that contrition was her best and only defence. 'I saw the books and couldn't resist. I used to work in a library, you see, and I love places like this.'

The man hesitated as if he didn't want to say what he was about to say. 'Well then, I hate to tell you this, but you really should know better than to eat in a library,' he said, gesturing towards her half-eaten sandwich.

Peggy's cheeks turned from scarlet to crimson as she hurriedly re-wrapped her lunch and tucked it into her bag. 'You're right. I'm sorry. I'll go.'

'No,' said the man. 'It's all right. You can stay. To be

honest, it's nice to have someone visiting the library. We're a little quiet without the students now.'

'Do you work here?'

He nodded. 'I'm Laurie Parker. I'm a librarian, one of the few remaining, actually. All the other chaps have gone off to war but they didn't want me because of my eyesight.'

'Peggy Sparks,' she said. 'It's nice to meet you, Laurie.'

He offered the smile she remembered from earlier. 'You're welcome to eat your sandwiches in the librarians' office if you'd like. I could make us some tea if that's not too forward a suggestion?'

Peggy returned the smile. 'It's the nicest offer I've had all day.'

'How was your first day?' asked Alice as they sat down to dinner that night.

'It was better than I expected,' said Peggy.

'Did you meet Winston Churchill?' asked Nancy.

Peggy and Flo exchanged a look. 'I didn't,' said Peggy. 'I think it might have been his day off.'

Nancy frowned. 'He shouldn't be having days off. There's a war on.'

'Quite right,' said Emily. 'What about the toffs? Did you put them in their place?'

'Not exactly,' said Peggy.

'Give her a chance, Mum. It's only her first day,' said Alice.

'I did find the library though.'

''Course you did,' said Emily teasingly.

'I met this nice man called Laurie. He's the librarian.'

39

'Like Laurie from *Little Women*,' said Nancy. 'Are you going to marry him?'

This was Nancy's usual question whenever Peggy mentioned meeting someone of the opposite sex. Peggy laughed. 'I don't think so. It's nice to have a friend though.'

Alice kissed the top of her head. 'I'm proud of you, Peg. And Joe will be too.'

Chapter 4

The next day, buoyed by her mother's words, Peggy arrived early at the Ministry. She was determined to make a good impression and show willing for any task thrown at her. She stopped in her tracks on reaching the doorway of the office, however. There were piles of boxes all over the desks and floor. In amongst the chaos, Sheldrake was piling items into one of them with his customary pursed-lip impatience.

'Is everything all right, Mr Sheldrake?' asked Peggy.

'If you consider moving our entire office and its contents to a different floor as being all right, then yes, we're tickety boo,' he replied.

'Oh dear,' said Peggy, taking off her coat. She picked up a box. 'Let me help you.'

He grunted his thanks. 'Apparently, it's not enough for the News Division to inhabit the ground floor. They need this floor as well.'

'But where will we go?'

'For some reason known only to the powers that be, we're moving to the library.'

'The library?' Peggy was cheered by the idea of working

near to her new friend, Laurie. 'But what about all the books?'

'We're to work around them. I suppose it makes more sense for a publishing department to be in a library. At least it'll be peaceful,' he added as a roar of laughter went up from further along the corridor. 'You need to box up your things, carry what you can. The porters will bring up the rest later today.'

'What about Marigold?' asked Peggy, glancing over at her chaotic desk.

'Well. If she can't get to work on time, these things are bound to happen. She'll work it out.'

Once packed, they made their way up the stairs and were greeted at the entrance to the library by a wild-eyed, rake-thin elderly man, who waved his arms frantically as they approached. 'Get out! Get out!' he cried. 'I refuse to allow the annexation of this library. It's 1938 all over again!'

'Professor Minton,' called Laurie, hurrying out of the librarians' office. 'It's all right, Professor Minton. I will personally ensure that none of the books are damaged.'

The professor stared up at him with mournful, milky eyes. 'They're my life, you see.'

Peggy caught Laurie's eye and approached the man. 'We won't damage anything, sir. I promise. I worked in a library, you see. I understand how precious books are.'

Professor Minton gave a weary nod of resignation. 'Thank you,' he said before shuffling off.

'Apologies,' said Laurie. 'Some of the older academics have been somewhat resistant to . . .'

'The invasion of the Ministry,' said Beecher, entering behind them. 'Which I completely understand. Professor Minton is one of Europe's most-respected historians. I shall personally ensure that he is reassured. We, as a department, are grateful to you and your colleagues for allowing us to share your space. We shall be respectful at all times.' He held out his hand. 'Clarence Beecher, I'm one of the heads of publishing, and this is Mr Sheldrake and Miss Sparks.'

'Laurie Parker,' he said, accepting it. 'I'm pleased to meet you all, although of course Peggy and I have already met.' She smiled shyly.

'Excellent,' said Beecher. 'And you will no doubt meet Miss Marigold Cecily whenever she deigns to grace us with her presence.'

'Yoo hoo,' called a voice.

'Ah,' said Beecher, glancing at his watch. 'That's a twenty-minute improvement on yesterday.'

'Gosh, sorry I'm late. It took me an age to find you, and annoyingly, my housekeeper has left to join the war effort so I'm all at sea.'

'Dear me,' said Beecher. 'How ever will you manage?'

She rewarded him with an angelic smile. 'Dear Mr Beecher, so sweet of you to concern yourself.' Sheldrake rolled his eyes.

'Well, if you'd care to follow me, I'll show you where you'll be working,' said Laurie. He led them to the room which Peggy had discovered on her first day. As she looked around, taking in the floor-to-ceiling shelves lined with books, with more on the mezzanine level above, she felt

43

her shoulders relax. 'And there are smaller offices along here, sir,' he told Beecher.

'Thank you, Mr Parker. I'm sure we'll be very comfortable here.'

'It reminds me of Pa's library at home,' said Marigold. 'Although when you take a book off the shelf, you usually find a whisky decanter behind it.' She plucked a volume at random and carelessly leafed through it before casting it aside and selecting another. 'What a lot of dusty old tomes.'

'Actually,' said Laurie, picking up the book she had discarded. 'It's probably best if you don't do that. They're all shelved in a specific order, you see.'

Marigold gazed at him with the wonder of a child, before replacing the book she was holding in the first gap she could find. 'Are they? How clever. That must make them easier to find.'

'That's how libraries tend to work,' muttered Sheldrake.

'Fascinating,' said Marigold, oblivious to the fact that Laurie had extracted and re-shelved the book she'd just carelessly plonked on the shelf.

'Right then, everyone,' said Beecher. 'I've been told that our telephones will be connected later today, so let's enjoy the peace while they still don't know where we are. We will treat the library with the respect it deserves. Any questions?' When no one answered, he gave a brief nod. 'Jolly good. Onwards.'

Over the next few months, Peggy made a great effort to throw herself into work at the Ministry without questioning the tedium of the tasks she was given. It seemed to her that the men, namely Beecher and Sheldrake, spent their lives in meetings which made them prickly whilst the women, namely Peggy, as Marigold was invariably absent, were either required to make tea and take minutes or given the tasks resulting from these gatherings which had the capacity to bore them to tears. For days, Peggy did her best to enthuse about pamphlets on *Fire Guard Training Notes* and *How to Preserve Tomatoes*, and then one day, Sheldrake emerged from a meeting seeming even more irritable than usual.

'Bed-wetting,' he said, throwing a document on to her desk without further explanation.

Peggy's mouth went dry as she stared at the pages in question before Emily Marsh's voice chimed in her ears. *Well, Peggy Sparks, are you going to let this man talk to you like that?* Peggy cleared her throat. 'Mr Sheldrake?'

He glared at her. 'Well? What is it?'

Peggy swallowed. *Well, go on, Peggy. Out with it.* 'It's just that your manner . . .'

Sheldrake folded his arms. 'My manner?'

Come on, Peggy, you can't stop now. 'Yes. Your manner is sometimes . . .'

'Rather abrupt?' said a voice. 'Discourteous? Downright rude?'

Peggy and Sheldrake turned to see Beecher standing in the doorway. 'Forgive Mr Sheldrake,' he said. 'He has something of a bellicose nature thanks, no doubt, to his public school background.'

'I went to a grammar school, Mr Beecher.'

'In which case there is no excuse. Miss Sparks, I

apologise that we haven't had the time to formally introduce you to the workings of the Ministry. To be perfectly frank, none of us are quite sure what they are yet.'

'Actually, Mr Sheldrake did explain our role as part of the Publications department situated on the other side of Russell Square and how it's responsible for all books, pamphlets and leaflets published as part of the war effort,' said Peggy, glancing at Sheldrake who merely scowled.

'Well, that's something. As you know, I head up this publishing section and Mr Longforth heads up another. His is staffed by some of England's finest writers. I'm sure you've heard of them.' Peggy nodded. 'Of course, a lot of them find working for a government-headed organisation somewhat out of kilter with their creative sensibilities and don't stay for long, and then there's the issue that they can be a touch, how can I put this . . .' he gazed heavenwards as he searched for the right word, '. . . vainglorious.' Sheldrake huffed his amusement. Beecher raised an eyebrow before continuing. 'This is not a criticism, of course, for one should never criticise great artists, but it is merely the truth of what we have to deal with. Consequently, our department is small but overstretched as we have the dubious pleasure of dealing with any requests which Mr Longforth deems to be beneath him and his great scribes. Does that give you a fuller picture than perhaps you had before?'

'It does,' said Peggy. 'Thank you, sir. And please don't think I'm unwilling to do whatever is required of me.'

'I understand. It's merely the manner in which you are asked.' He fixed Sheldrake with a pointed look. 'Would you be so kind as to brief Miss Sparks with the same courtesy as you would show me or any other member of staff, please, Mr Sheldrake.'

Sheldrake shifted his weight slightly. 'Of course, sir.' He turned to Peggy. 'Miss Sparks, the Women's Voluntary Service has requested a leaflet on bed-wetting to be issued to all families who are hosting evacuees. Would you be so good as to read through their version and make any amendments as you see fit?'

'Please,' murmured Beecher.

'Please,' said Sheldrake with a tight smile.

'Of course,' said Peggy. 'Poor mites. They must be so homesick. Anything to make it easier for them.'

She thought of Nancy and Flo, and of Emily's reaction when they were told that the council was planning to evacuate Nancy's entire school. 'We stay together,' Emily said. 'And look after one another. There's enough splitting up of families with all the fathers and sons going off to war. You're no safer in the country than you are here. Joe built the shelter to keep us safe while he's away. We'll be right as rain.'

Beecher was about to disappear into his office when Marigold waltzed in through the door. 'Good afternoon, Miss Cecily. Did you get lost on your way to our office?'

She flashed him a stunning smile. Peggy could tell this was the kind of smile which got her off the hook on a regular basis. 'My dear Mr Beecher. I may have overslept. My new housekeeper didn't wake me.'

'I hope you sacked her on the spot.'

Marigold laughed. It was a bright, tinkling laugh which

47

conjured up visions of crystal goblets filled with champagne. 'Oh Mr Beecher, you are too funny.'

'I hope you're still of that opinion when we've finished our conversation, Miss Cecily. Would you mind stepping into my office, please?'

Marigold pulled a comical face at Peggy before following him inside. Although the door was shut, it wasn't difficult to hear Beecher's firm assertions and Marigold's plaintive whines. Peggy glanced over at Sheldrake who was staring very hard at the document in front of him but clearly not reading a word. When Marigold emerged, Peggy turned back to her work, focusing on the first page of the document Sheldrake had given her and the words, 'Train the Child'. She didn't look up when Marigold huffed her way back to her desk and threw herself into her chair, sighing and slamming down a folder, reminding Peggy of Nancy when she was having a tantrum. She tutted as she sifted through the documents, sat back, scratched her head and muttered under her breath, 'What a cross little man.' When no one responded, she leaned across to Peggy and whispered, 'What's wrong with old Beecher, eh?'

Peggy shrugged. 'He's just doing his job.' She resisted the urge to say, *You should try it some time.* She couldn't see the point.

'He's a crosspatch,' said Marigold, studying her nails. 'Worse than Father, and that's saying something.' She flashed Peggy a sideways glance. 'I'm bored. What are you doing?'

'Editing a pamphlet on bed-wetting for the WVS. Unless you'd like to?'

Marigold wrinkled her perfect nose. 'No fear.'

'Miss Cecily?' said Sheldrake.

Marigold pulled a face at Peggy before turning. 'Yes, Mr Sheldrake?'

'One of our publishers has requested a selection of photographs of RAF airmen and unfortunately I'm rather busy at the moment . . .'

Marigold's eyes lit up as she jumped to her feet. 'Understood,' she cried with a mock salute. 'Leave it to me.' He handed her a list and within seconds, she was gone.

Peggy shot him a quizzical look. He shrugged. 'At least we can get some work done now.'

Marigold had only been gone a few minutes when there was a light tap at the door. Peggy turned to see a bewildered-looking man with sandy-coloured hair and a copy of *The Author* magazine tucked under his arm. Sheldrake muttered, 'Not another one,' before turning to address him. 'May we help you?'

'Oh,' said the man, glancing over his shoulder as if searching for guidance. 'You see, I've been sent . . .'

'By Henry Longforth's department?'

'How did you know?' asked the man in surprise.

'Lucky guess.'

'They felt that . . .'

'You'd fit in better here?'

The man gazed at him in awe. 'You're like a fortune teller.'

Sheldrake picked up a file and held it out to the man. 'I've been called worse. Here, take these.' He fished a blue pencil from the pot in front of him. 'And this. Sit at that desk and proof-read the contents.'

The man chewed thoughtfully on the pencil. 'It's just that I'm more of a writer. I'm a creative type.'

'Well, feel free to be as creative as you like with those amendments as long as they're correct and you don't change the words.'

'Right,' said the man, glancing at Peggy.

'Hello,' she said, trying to be more welcoming than Sheldrake. 'I'm Peggy Sparks.'

'Gideon Fairchild. Pleased to meet you,' he said, sliding behind the desk, pulling out the first document and frowning at the words as if they had wounded him deeply. By lunchtime, Peggy had finished working on her pamphlet, adding advice such as 'Be kind and patient' and 'Treat these children as if they were your own. They're a long way from home.' She sat back, eyeing it with satisfaction. It might not have a direct effect on the direction of the war, but it might make life a bit more bearable while they waited for it to end.

'I'm finished so I'll be going for lunch now, Mr Sheldrake,' she said.

'Very well. All done, Mr Fairchild?'

Fairchild gazed up at them with wide eyes. 'I'm still on the first page,' he said.

Sheldrake glanced heavenwards as if praying that lightning might strike him down before approaching his desk. Peggy could still hear his voice as she reached the end of the corridor. 'It's an instructional pamphlet about how to keep well during winter, Mr Fairchild. It doesn't need an injection of dramatic tension.'

She chuckled to herself as she made her way through the

library and was pleasantly surprised to find Laurie already waiting for her by the door. 'I thought we could make the most of the spring sunshine,' he said. Peggy glanced over his shoulder towards the books. 'Don't worry, Peggy. They're not going anywhere.' She laughed.

She had to confess that meeting Laurie had been the best thing about working at the Ministry. They were both diffident to begin with, but as soon as they began talking about books and in particular Laurie's passion for poetry, their friendship blossomed. With Joe away, she relished his straightforward company. She hadn't realised quite how much she'd miss her brother, and although Laurie was different to Joe, they both had a kind heart and openness which made Peggy feel she could tell them anything.

'Here we are,' said Laurie, as they left the bustling corridors behind them and walked across the street to Russell Square. It was a small but well-designed space lined with paths and peppered with evergreens, oak, lime and yew trees, all of which were bursting into life in the spring sunshine. 'This garden was designed by a man called Humphrey Repton for the private use of the residents and their guests,' said Laurie, pointing towards the smart townhouses surrounding the square.

'Well, I'm glad they decided to let us riff-raff in,' joked Peggy, sitting on a bench and turning her face towards the sun.

Laurie took a seat beside her and inhaled deeply. 'If you have a garden and a library, you have everything you need.'

'Wise words.'

'Cicero's, not mine, sadly.'

'I'm sure you could come up with something just as good,' said Peggy.

Laurie laughed. 'You have more faith in me than I have in myself.'

'You'll never know if you never try. That's what I always tell myself, anyway.'

'Well, you know your writing is good. It got you your job here.'

'True. Although I don't write for the Mass Observation now. I write it all down in letters to my brother.'

Laurie looked at her. 'You must miss him a great deal.'

'He's the reason I accepted this job.' She stole a glance at him. 'Can I tell you something I haven't told another soul?'

He put a hand on his heart. 'I would be honoured.'

'I'm going to make sure he comes home. Him and all the others. I'm going to do everything in my power to end this war.'

Peggy felt breathless from saying aloud the words she'd been carrying in her heart, but exhilarated too, especially when Laurie replied, 'I can't imagine a better reason for doing anything, Peggy. If only you were running the country.'

They returned to the Ministry just as Beecher was exiting the doors with a man and a woman in tow. 'Ah, Miss Sparks. Mr Parker. Allow me to introduce you to Frank and Rosa Bauman. They run the printers where we produce many of our publications.'

'Pleased to meet you both,' said the woman, holding out her hand first to Peggy and then to Laurie. The directness of this action and the way in which she held their gaze, eyes sparkling with genuine warmth, made Peggy like her immediately.

The man, on the other hand, couldn't have seemed more offhand if he tried. He gave them a curt smile but no more. 'Rosa, dearest. We really should be getting back. Goodbye, Mr Beecher,' he said, offering his hand.

'Goodbye, Frank. Rosa. Safe journey. Apologies that Longforth couldn't make the meeting. I hope it wasn't a wasted trip.'

Frank Bauman didn't reply. 'Of course it wasn't,' said Rosa. 'It's always a pleasure to see you, Clarence. And good to meet you too,' she added to Peggy and Laurie. Peggy watched them go, feeling immediately sorry for this poor woman with her ill-mannered husband.

'I'm home!' called Peggy as she opened the front door later that evening and Badger catapulted down the hall to meet her. She could hear the sound of Flo crying as soon as she entered. Dropping her bag, she hurried to the kitchen. 'What's happened? Is it Joe?'

Nancy was sitting on Emily's lap, their faces mirroring one another with deep frowns while Alice held baby Charlie in her arms and Florence wailed. 'He's not coming home, Peg. They won't give him leave before they send him off to God knows where!'

Peggy wrapped her arms around her friend. 'Oh, darling Flo, I'm so sorry. But I tell you what we'll do, we'll send him a parcel full of his favourite things.' She sat down at the table. 'Nancy can draw him a picture and we'll use our rations and Gran can make him a nice sponge cake. Okay?' Flo nodded and Peggy planted a kiss on the top of her head. 'It'll be all right. I promise.'

Nancy slid off her great-grandmother's knee and came to stand very close to Peggy. 'Auntie Peg?'

'Yes, Nancy?' she said, pulling her on to her lap.

'I miss you working at the library. It's not the same with Miss Thingummy working there instead of you.'

'I thought you liked Miss Bunce.'

Nancy wrinkled her nose. 'I do, but she smells of mothballs whereas you smell . . .' Nancy sniffed her neck, '. . . of home.'

Peggy shared a look with her mother and pulled her niece close. 'Miss Bunce was the librarian when I was a little girl. She's good at picking out books.'

'True,' said Nancy. 'Although she said I'd like *Pollyanna* but I do not, so I told her so.'

'And what did Miss Bunce say?' asked Peggy.

'She smiled and asked me why.'

'And what did you say to that?'

Nancy folded her arms. 'I told her she's too happy all the bloomin' time. No one can be that happy all the bloomin' time. At least, that's what Great-Gran says.'

'I'm glad my pearls of wisdom are going in, Nancy Sparks,' said Emily with satisfaction.

'And what did Miss Bunce say to that?' asked Peggy, exchanging an amused glance with Flo.

'She asked me if I agreed with Great-Gran,' said Nancy.

'And?' asked Peggy, noticing her grandmother put her hands on her hips in anticipation.

'I told her that I do like to be happy but I'm sad when I think about Dad not being here, so I think Great-Gran is right, because actually, how would you know you're happy if you've never been sad?' Peggy and Emily stared at her in astonishment. 'And then Mr Alderman said I was like a miniature Bernard Russell or something and asked if I would like to train to be a librarian.'

'And what did you say?' asked Alice with a chuckle.

'I thanked him very much but pointed out that I am only seven.' Everyone laughed and Peggy kissed the top of her head. 'I think Mr Alderman misses you, Auntie Peg,' added Nancy.

Peggy sighed. She missed his avuncular presence too. Wilberforce Alderman had arrived in Edenham in 1920, taking charge of the recently built library without fanfare or explanation. This had set tongues wagging with a range of far-fetched suggestions from him being a murderer or spy on the run or even an exiled Russian count. These assertions were largely quelled after Mr Alderman furnished these imaginative souls with the best crime and spy thrillers he could offer, and Emily Marsh told any others that, 'If they had nothing nice to say they should keep their bleedin' traps shut.'

For his part, Mr Alderman never discussed his life outside the library with Peggy, but she did know that he lived alone in a small cottage on the outskirts of town because she'd glimpsed him through the window one day during a dog walk with her grandmother. He had been sitting in a comfortable armchair by the window reading by lamplight, its buttery glow reflecting towards the wall of book-lined shelves behind him. 'Doesn't look much like a murderer to me,' said Emily, nudging Peggy as they made their way past.

'You be sure to give him my best wishes when you're next in the library, won't you?' said Peggy.

Nancy gave an emphatic nod before studying her aunt's face for a moment. 'Auntie Peg, have you ever been in love?'

'Nancy!' said Alice. 'Why do you want to know that?'

Nancy pulled an incredulous face. 'I want to know everything.' She turned back to Peggy. 'So. Have you?'

Peggy laughed. 'I don't think so.'

Nancy wrapped her arms around her aunt's neck. 'I think you should find someone to fall in love with so that I can be bridesmaid at your wedding.'

'I see,' said Peggy. 'Well, I'll do my best for you, Nance.' Nancy planted a kiss on Peggy's cheek.

'Right, young lady, that's quite enough nonsense from you,' said Emily. 'Auntie Peggy has been working hard all day and needs her dinner. And so do I.'

Later that evening, when they were sitting down to listen to the news, Emily turned to Peggy. 'Nancy's right, you know. You deserve someone nice to love you and make you feel special. Am I right, Alice?'

Peggy's mother took a sip of her tea and glanced at her daughter. 'It's not really up to me. Whatever makes Peg happy will make me happy.'

Peggy smiled at them as she answered. 'I've got you lot. And that's more than enough for me for now.'

Dear Peg,

Thank you for your letter. Trust you to end up working in the library again! I love hearing the tales of Lady Marigold and that bloke Sheldrake. Don't let them push you around, mind. Beecher sounds like a good man, though, and I know you're doing a terrific job. Keep going and you'll be running the country in no time.

Flo probably told you that I won't get leave before we move out in the next few days. It was a bit of a blow, to be honest. I can't bear the thought of not seeing you all and not getting to hug Flo and the kids. I'm not sure how I feel about what happens next. I wish we could go for a walk up the hill in Edenham Park to talk about it. You always make me feel better about everything. You're wise, Peg. It's probably all those books you read. I suppose I just want to get on with whatever needs to be done and get home as soon as possible. I try not to think about what's to come, but I get the feeling that I won't be home again until this war is over. I have made a good friend though, a bloke called Albert Cobb. He's from Yorkshire and he's a right card. Keeps us smiling. That's all we can do. Keep smiling through, as the song says.

I'll write whenever I can, but you might not hear from me for a month or two after this letter. Please keep sending the letters and parcels. I can't tell you how much they give us all a lift, and they'll reach me wherever I am. God bless the APO! Ask Gran to bake one of her Victoria sponge cakes to send. They always go down a treat. Take care of yourselves. I know it won't be long before Hitler sets his sights on London and I'm glad I built the shelter before I left. If I can't be there to protect you in person, at least you'll be safe. Please make sure Gran uses it. Give her and Mum all my love and have some for yourself. Thank you for keeping an eye on Flo and the kids. They're lucky to have someone like you in their life. We all are. I'm getting mushy now, but if you can't say these things at times like these then they never get said. We'll meet again.

Love, Joe

Chapter 5

'Right, Miss Sparks, due to the unreliable nature of your nominal superior, Miss Cecily, you are now required to attend the joint publishing meeting which starts in five minutes,' said Sheldrake one morning. 'You'll need to take the minutes, which will hopefully be more comprehensive than those of your female colleague. Last month's seemed to mainly consist of a shopping list for Fortnum's.'

During her first weeks at the Ministry, Peggy had been daunted by Sheldrake's peremptory manner. She had confided this to her grandmother. 'What does this lad look like?'

Peggy shrugged. 'Slight, short, glasses, a pencil moustache. Why?'

Emily folded her arms. 'I knew it. Never trust a short man with a moustache. You have to stand up to them. We wouldn't be in all this bother if we'd stood up to that other lunatic.'

'I don't think you can compare Cyril Sheldrake to Adolf Hitler, Gran.'

'I'm not comparing anyone with anyone. I'm just saying you need to be bolder, Peg. You're a bright girl and they're lucky to have you. Don't let anyone tell you otherwise, short man or not.'

Peggy knew her grandmother was right. In the quiet refuge of Edenham library, she hadn't needed a voice, but the Ministry was a very different place. If she were to be any use to Joe, she needed to follow Emily Marsh's advice.

'Of course, Mr Sheldrake,' she said, picking up her notebook and pen, observing with satisfaction his raised-eyebrow look of approval.

'Oh, I think I'm needed for this one too,' said Fairchild vaguely, following after them like an obedient puppy.

'Needed might be stretching it somewhat,' muttered Sheldrake as Peggy hurried to keep step with him along the corridor back to the lift which took them to the ground floor. They paused outside a vast, forbidding oak door. Sheldrake thrust a sheaf of papers into her hands. 'Dish these out, and just to warn you, Beecher is always in a stinking mood at these meetings.'

Oh good, thought Peggy as they entered the dimly lit cavernous room with walls the colour of over-steeped tea. If an alien had arrived from outer space at that moment, it could have been forgiven for assuming that the world was only populated by men. The large, highly polished walnut table was encircled by several men wearing deep frowns, some of them smoking as if their lives depended on it. The air was a pea-souper of tobacco smoke with no one thinking to open a window.

'At last,' said Beecher, looking up sharply at the three of them. 'Although I was expecting Miss Cecily.'

Peggy avoided his gaze, doing her best to be helpful

by handing out Sheldrake's agendas and surreptitiously propping open a window.

'Sorry, sir. She's late again,' said Sheldrake.

Beecher sighed. 'Do you know the thing I hate more than tardiness, young man?'

'Sir?'

'Toadyness, Sheldrake. I can't bear toadies.' He turned to Peggy. 'Miss Sparks, do you know where Miss Cecily is today?'

Peggy knew it was a test and that she mustn't fail. 'I believe she was called away on urgent business, Mr Beecher.'

Beecher turned back to Sheldrake. 'You see? That's how humans are supposed to co-exist, Sheldrake. With diplomacy. It's so important, particularly when we're in the middle of a war which we would dearly like to end sooner rather than later. Do you see my point?'

'Sir,' said Sheldrake with an abrupt nod followed by a glowering side-glance towards Peggy.

'Right, take a seat,' said Beecher, glancing at his watch. 'Mr Lear, do you have any idea how long Mr Longforth will be?' he added with a note of impatience.

A tall, thin man with a sweep of greying hair and a pipe, who was largely to blame for the tobacco-smoke fug, glanced up from his papers with a shrug. 'I know he had a meeting with Lord Candleford, but . . .'

'Beecher, gentlemen, manifold apologies,' boomed a voice from the doorway as Henry Longforth swept in through it. 'My meeting with Winslow overran. We were reminiscing about our Eton and Oxford days and lost track of time. You know how it is, Beecher. Oh, but wait a minute. I forgot. You're not a public school chap, are you?' Beecher stared down at his papers, offering no reply. Peggy felt an immediate stab of dislike for Henry Longforth and his ruddy, self-satisfied face, recalling his barking telephone manner from her first day. He plonked himself at the opposite head of the table to Beecher. 'Do we have an agenda?'

'Here you are, sir,' said Peggy, handing one to him.

He glanced up at her. 'Hmm. And I'll have a cup of tea if you would be so kind.'

Beecher cleared his throat. 'Miss Sparks is not here to make tea. She will be taking the minutes, and as we are already ten minutes late, I suggest we press on.' He neither waited for a response nor acknowledged Longforth's frown of irritation. 'The first item relates to paper stocks. We have reason to believe that some publishers are hoarding quantities of paper which could otherwise be utilised for the greater good.'

'Oh, come now, Beecher,' said Longforth. 'Surely there are more pressing issues. We have more than enough paper to go round. We need to keep publishers onside. I suggest we don't go poking the hornet's nest.'

'I agree that we need to maintain good relations, but we also need to ensure that everything is done fairly,' said Beecher. 'It appears that some publishers are receiving favourable treatment.'

'Which would never do,' interrupted Longforth with a sideways glance towards Lear, who snorted with amusement. Peggy held her breath as she watched this scene unfold with rising indignation on Mr Beecher's behalf. There was something about him that reminded her of Mr Alderman, which in turn provoked an immediate wave of loyalty. Longforth caught Beecher's eye. 'Look, old boy, maybe you don't really understand how these things work, but Lord Candleford would concur that we should let the Paper Control chaps get on with controlling the paper whilst we get on with the business of publishing. Wouldn't you agree?'

This question was issued like a dare. Beecher accepted it without hesitation. 'Very well. Shall we turn then to the second item on the agenda relating to this tome?' He held up an orange booklet with the title, *How Hitler Made the War*. Peggy noticed Lear shift uncomfortably in his seat. 'As the Publication department's first foray into publishing it has been an utter failure.'

Longforth shook his head. 'There were some misunderstandings with booksellers and a few copyright issues, but . . .'

'I hear the Minister is very disappointed,' said Beecher.

Longforth folded his arms. 'Well, Beecher, old boy. Here's a suggestion for you. Why doesn't my publishing department continue building relations with the publishers whilst your publishing department over here has a stab at producing your own books and pamphlets, eh?'

Beecher fixed him with a glinting stare. 'Challenge accepted.'

Longforth returned the stare with one eyebrow raised. 'Very well.'

The meeting only lasted another five minutes before

Longforth rose to his feet followed by Lear and one other man. He paused in the doorway. 'Good luck, Beecher,' Longforth said with a self-satisfied smirk. 'You'll need it.'

'Are those meetings always like that?' asked Peggy as she rode the lift with Sheldrake and Fairchild, Beecher having excused himself to take the stairs.

'Pretty much,' shrugged Sheldrake.

'Henry Longforth has a reputation as one of the most terrifying men in publishing,' said Fairchild with a frightened look in his eye. 'One of my Oxford chums works for him and says it's like constantly teetering on the edge of an active volcano. I avoided him completely when I worked on that side of the square.'

'It's true,' said Sheldrake. 'I know of three people who have resigned after being subjected to his outbursts, and I heard a rumour that he had once challenged a fellow editor to a duel in his younger days working at the *Daily Messenger*.'

'Mr Beecher didn't seem cowed,' said Peggy.

'He's a good man,' said Sheldrake.

'Yes,' she said. 'I'm beginning to realise that.'

'Now then,' said Beecher as they returned to the office. 'We have quite a task ahead of us.' He placed the orange pamphlet on a desk. 'Take a look and tell me what you think. What's missing from it? What do we need to do to produce publications which grab the public's imagination? It must inspire them, inform them and boost their morale, tall order as that may be.'

'Should I make some tea while you discuss this, sir?' asked Peggy.

Beecher frowned. 'Absolutely not. I need your opinion, Miss Sparks. If you would be so kind.' Peggy's hands grew clammy as she approached the desk.

'It's well-written,' admitted Sheldrake, scanning the text. 'You can't fault that.'

'Could it be that people don't want to read books about Hitler?' suggested Fairchild.

'*Mein Kampf* was one of the bestselling books of last year in this country,' said Beecher. Peggy picked up the pamphlet, leafing through the pages. 'Any ideas, Miss Sparks?'

'I think . . .' began Peggy, glancing up at them. Sheldrake's face was set with his customary frown, but Beecher and Fairchild were regarding her with genuine interest. 'It needs illustrations. Otherwise it's just dry facts and blocks of text.' She shrank under their scrutiny. 'That's just my opinion, of course. I could be wrong.'

'No,' said Beecher. 'I think you've hit the nail squarely on the head.'

'Terrific,' agreed Fairchild.

'Expensive,' said Sheldrake, 'and therefore risky.'

'Well,' said Peggy. 'Correct me if I'm wrong but we do have someone in this department with contacts in the Photographs department.'

Lady Marigold Cecily chose that moment to breeze in through the door, wearing dark glasses and a mustard-yellow swing coat. She lifted her sunglasses, regarding them like a film star ready to greet her public. 'Hello all. Dreadfully sorry I'm late, Mr Beecher. I had a pressing appointment. What did I miss?'

★　　★　　★

Beecher tasked them with producing a pamphlet under the title *Our Mighty Navy*. It was to be fully illustrated for distribution to members of the Royal Navy and the general public.

'Something to galvanise and inspire those brave souls fighting on our behalf,' he told them. 'The sooner they get the job done, the sooner we can bring them home.'

'Pardon me if I speak out of turn, Mr Beecher,' said Sheldrake. 'But do you think these publications can make a difference to the war effort?'

Beecher regarded him for a moment before answering. 'Honestly, Mr Sheldrake? I can't say for sure, but I do know that where posters, films and even radio broadcasts have an immediate impact, the printed word has the power to endure. People love to be entertained on a Friday night by Charlie Chaplin, but they return again and again to Dickens, to Austen, to Shakespeare.'

'So true, dear sir,' said Fairchild with a far-off look in his eye.

Beecher continued. 'Who knows how long this war will last, but it won't be over by Christmas and I doubt it will be over by this time next year. Therefore, we must produce works which encourage us all to persevere. Anyone with a relative fighting abroad would surely agree.'

'I agree,' said Peggy, thoughts of Joe giving her the courage to speak. They eyed her with interest. 'My twin brother, Joe,' she explained. 'He's with the tank regiment.'

'Oh, you're a twin,' said Marigold with uncharacteristic curiosity.

'In that case,' said Beecher, 'it would seem we have an even greater reason to make these pamphlets a success.'

Marigold stood up, catching Peggy's eye as she made for the door. 'I'll go down and speak to Cordy right away.'

'Very good, Miss Cecily,' said Beecher.

'Come along then, Miss Sparks,' said Sheldrake. 'Let's get to work on the text.'

'I'll fetch my notebook, Mr Sheldrake,' she said with a grateful smile.

Chapter 6

The war had dragged the country into a new phase and, like everyone else in Britain, Peggy had no choice but to be dragged along with it. The day and night raids which began in September had become mainly nightly ones now, although you never could bet against a sudden surprise from the Luftwaffe.

Peggy had always known that her family were close, but there was something about the thought that you might bid goodnight one evening and not be around to say good morning the next day that had strengthened that bond.

They were all relieved that Joe had built the shelter before he left. It had been something of a bone of contention with Emily, who was adamant that she wouldn't step foot in it.

'You may as well build me a coffin and set it in the garden beside my gooseberry bushes,' she'd declared.

'Gran, I'm not leaving you all without something to protect you. I know you get a bit claustrophobic, but please, I'm begging you, when the siren goes off, get in the shelter. You don't want me worrying about you all the time I'm away, do you?'

Emily had frowned for a moment before answering. 'Joseph Sparks, you always did know how to winkle your way into your gran's heart, didn't you? Used to be exactly the same when we walked by the sweetshop. Could never make it past without you persuading me to buy a quarter of pear drops from Mrs Huggins.'

Joe had bent down and kissed her on the cheek. 'Love you, Gran.'

The old woman sat up straighter in her chair. 'Yes, well. You better get on with building that thing before Hitler's banging on our door.'

Peggy was relieved that her grandmother had now seemed to accept the shelter as a necessity, packing tea and her always-stocked cake tin, challenging them to games of whist or playing Old Maid with Nancy. Despite the cramped conditions, Peggy found nights spent in the shelter with her family oddly comforting. She would often wake in the morning to find Nancy curled up beside her and Badger sleeping on her feet. 'I feel safe next to you, Auntie Peg,' her niece would say, snuggling her small, warm body closer. Peggy also noticed that Alice always waved her off these days, either blowing a kiss from the doorway or occasionally walking her to the station, handing over the sandwich she'd made and pressing a palm to Peggy's cheek before she boarded the train. Whenever Flo began to fret that they should pack up and leave for the country, Emily would put an arm around her shoulder and tell her, 'You're safe here with us. Nothing bad's going to happen while Emily Marsh is around. Hitler wouldn't dare.' Peggy loved her grandmother's spirit, but she knew in her heart of hearts it was all a gamble. You could be unlucky like poor Mrs Henry, two streets over. There was a gap like a knocked-out tooth where her house had once stood and a gap in the world where Mrs Henry had once stood, God rest her soul. Peggy believed they had to stay together and stay hopeful. It was hard, though, having received little news from Joe. Even though he'd warned it could be months between letters, the fact that they were in autumn with hardly a word from him hung heavy on their shoulders.

'So where is Daddy now?' asked Nancy one evening, spinning the globe he'd bought her for her last birthday and planting a finger to make it stop. 'Maybe here?'

Peggy squinted at where she was pointing. 'I doubt he's in Antarctica, Nance.'

'He might be. With all the penguins. There are six types.'

'Is that so?' said Alice, picking up her knitting with a smile.

'It is, Granny. The macaroni penguins are my favourite. They have orange tufty heads.'

'You're like a walking encyclopaedia, Nancy Sparks,' said Emily.

'Thank you.' And then after a pause, 'Will Daddy be all right?'

Peggy exchanged glances with her mother and grand-mother before looking over to Flo, who was sitting by the fire feeding Charlie. 'Of course he will,' said Flo in a reassuring tone that Peggy knew was as much for her own benefit as her daughter's. 'Now, young lady, it's high time you got ready for bed.'

'Can Auntie Peg read me a story, please?'

'Just try and stop me,' said Peggy. 'I'm enjoying our nightly chapters of *The Little House in the Big Woods*. I like the idea of living in a cabin in a place where a bear could wander past the window. Don't get many of those round south-east London.'

'I wish we did,' said Nancy, kissing them one by one. 'We could train them to fight the Germans,' she added before skipping up the stairs.

'Oh, to be seven years old and imagining fighting bears and penguins with tufty heads,' said Peggy.

'I feel as if I'm lying to her. Saying Joe's all right all the time,' said Flo, her brow creasing with anguish.

'Well, as far as we know, he is,' said Emily. 'And until we hear otherwise that boy is as alive and well as any of us. All right?' Flo nodded. 'That's a good girl. Now, give me that baby and put your feet up. You look done in. I'm world class at winding babies.' Flo handed her Charlie, who at nearly nine months was as round as a currant bun. He wriggled with gurgling joy as Emily plonked him on her lap before letting out a resounding belch which made everyone laugh. 'Told you,' said Emily with satisfaction. 'World class.'

Peggy woke early after another disturbed night spent in the shelter. She yawned and stretched her aching limbs before dressing and creeping out of the house.

It was a bright, cold autumn day and Big Ben was striking eight as she arrived in London. The Ministry never closed its doors, thanks largely to the News Division which processed and rolled out the day's events to members of the press who invariably lined the dimly lit corridors. Peggy had to admit that she felt herself stand a little taller as she walked past them on her way to the lifts these days. Even Jarvis, the security guard she'd met on the first day, would tap the brim of his hat in greeting if ever he saw her enter the premises. She didn't have the confidence of the senior members of staff who swept through the corridors with ease but, encouraged by Beecher in particular, she had started to feel that she belonged here.

On the whole, the department had settled in well to life in their library office. Professor Minton seemed reassured that Beecher and his department weren't a 'gang of book-destroying barbarians' and Peggy loved working in a place steeped in knowledge and history. She hurried to the fourth floor, relishing the idea of the empty library with time to work on the pamphlets, which since the success of *Our Mighty Navy* had developed into a series about other sections of the armed forces. With quiet encouragement from Laurie, she had written the text for two more, which had even received praise, albeit grudging, from Sheldrake. Peggy didn't mind. She was writing them for Joe. She kept in mind Beecher's words about the effect that these publications could have on the war and it spurred her on.

As she entered the office, Peggy was astonished to find Marigold already at her desk, sifting through a pile of photographs. 'Good morning,' said Peggy, peeved that she wouldn't have the place to herself.

Marigold spun round in surprise, knocking some of the

pictures to the floor. 'Heavens above, Peggy, you gave me the fright of my life,' she cried, hurrying to retrieve them.

'Sorry,' said Peggy, moving forwards to help her.

'I can get them,' said Marigold but Peggy had already picked up a couple. One was of two smiling girls carrying bales of birch twigs on their backs and the other was of a small boy sitting amongst the rubble of a bombed-out building staring directly at the camera.

'These are terrific,' said Peggy, handing them over. 'Who took them?'

Marigold looked sheepish. 'I did.'

'You?'

She nodded. 'The girls work on a farm near my parents' house and I got that picture of the boy while I was wandering round London with my camera one day.'

Peggy wasn't Marigold's biggest fan but she believed in giving credit where it was due. 'You're very talented.'

Marigold blinked rapidly, unused to receiving compliments about anything that wasn't to do with her appearance. 'Do you really think so?'

'You should show Beecher.'

Marigold laughed. 'Gosh, no. I could never do that. It's just a silly little hobby. Mama says . . .' She was about to go on but clearly thought better of it. 'Never mind what Mama says.' She tidied the photographs into an envelope and tucked them in a drawer. 'Shall I make us some tea? Truth is, I haven't actually been home after last night's adventures. I'm positively gasping.' Peggy shook her head as Marigold disappeared towards the kitchen, returning a while later with the worst tea she had ever tasted.

73

'Ah good,' said Beecher, entering the office. 'Miss Cecily, you're on time. What a pleasant surprise.' Marigold flashed him a delightful smile. He removed his hat and shouldered off his coat. 'Could I ask for the benefit of your combined wisdom?'

'Naturally,' said Marigold whilst Peggy gave a reserved nod.

Beecher opened his briefcase and retrieved a sheaf of papers. 'As you know, Lord Candleford is my esteemed superior.'

'My papa and he were at Eton together,' said Marigold breezily.

'Of course,' said Beecher, catching Peggy's eye for the briefest moment. 'Lord Candleford likes to consult with close members of his family and invariably use their thoughts and ideas as the basis on which the Ministry then directs the public.'

Peggy raised her eyebrows. 'His family?'

'Oh yes. And their housekeeper. And periodically, he presents these to me for comment.' He held up the papers. 'This document contains Lady Candleford's key recommendations on how to avoid panic and hysteria after an air raid. I would be grateful if you could allow me to share these pearls with you and offer your thoughts.' Peggy and Marigold looked at him expectantly. Beecher cleared his throat. 'According to Lady Candleford,' he began, 'all women take unbridled comfort in getting together with other women and drinking tea whilst talking everything over.'

'I have to admit there's definite truth in that,' said Peggy.

'Oh yes. Super idea. Really helps to calm one down,' said Marigold. 'Although of course, a champagne cocktail from the Café de Paris would also do just the trick.' Peggy raised her eyes to the ceiling as Beecher continued. 'Lady Candleford now offers a further ten suggestions for minimising hysteria following an air raid.' He took a deep breath: 'Knitting, crosswords, board games . . .'

'I do love a game of draughts,' interrupted Marigold cheerfully.

Beecher continued. 'Laughter, sitting quietly, singing songs, dancing the Lambeth Walk, playing charades, reading the Bible and praying.' Peggy gave a small cough. Beecher glanced her way. 'Thoughts, Miss Sparks?'

She shifted in her seat. Peggy wasn't used to offering opinions, but there was something about Beecher's reassuring demeanour which gave her courage. 'It's not really for me to contradict Lord Candleford's wife.'

'God forbid you should contradict the assertions of a woman who spends her life tending begonias and telling Cook that there will be one more for lunch.'

Marigold chuckled. 'She sounds like my mother.'

Beecher raised an eyebrow before turning back to Peggy. 'Please, Miss Sparks, I would genuinely like to know what you think.'

Peggy took a breath. 'Well. If Lady Candleford were to come to my corner of south-east London after a raid, she'd find very little hysteria and a lot of people either helping one another or getting on with their lives. People don't need to be told to knit or drink tea or sing. We do that anyway, and as for dancing, there's not enough

75

room to swing a cat in our shelter with my mother, grandmother, sister-in-law, niece, nephew, dog and me. Everyone's a bit scared and worried, but what can you do except get on with it?' Her mouth felt parched by the end of this speech.

Beecher nodded. 'So, may I glean from your honest appraisal that this well-meant set of guidelines could perhaps, and it's only a perhaps, be construed as a little elementary and indeed a touch condescending? It could in truth underestimate the fact that the British public needs no direction when it comes to the making of tea or indeed the passing of time during an air raid. It begs the question as to whether dear Lady Candleford thinks we should perhaps draw up a leaflet for our grandmothers regarding the practice of egg-sucking.'

Peggy let out an involuntary snort of amusement. 'Sorry,' she said, putting a hand to her mouth. 'That's just rather funny. And yes, I think you've hit the nail on the head, sir.'

'Thank you, Miss Sparks, for both your input and your amusement. My wife often teases me for having become the most tedious of men, but I shall let her know that a young person found me amusing today. Thank you both for your opinions. I shall now spend a futile morning drafting a reply for my superior to ignore,' he said, disappearing into his office.

'What a funny little man he is,' said Marigold.

'I like him,' said Peggy.

Marigold turned to her. 'So, Peggy, it sounds as if it's a squash and a squeeze at your place.'

Peggy was surprised by her interest. 'I suppose, but I've never known any different.'

'Doesn't your family drive you potty?'

Peggy laughed. 'Sometimes, but we're very close, even closer since Joe left.' She hesitated, unsure why she was sharing these details, but Marigold's emerald-green eyes were fixed on her, glittering with curiosity. 'We live in a small house but we've got more than some. It's a friendly neighbourhood. We all look out for one another.'

'That must be nice,' said Marigold.

'Don't you live with your parents?'

Marigold shrugged. 'I go home to the family pile sometimes at weekends, but mostly I stay in the London house.'

'You have two houses?'

Marigold wrinkled her nose. 'Well, three actually, if you count the estate in Scotland.'

'Only three. How do you manage?'

Marigold stared at her for a moment before bursting into laughter. 'Oh I see, you're teasing. That's jolly good. Yes, poor old us with our three houses.' Peggy shook her head. Although Marigold was infuriatingly oblivious to the world around her, it was difficult to stay angry with her. She was as naïve as a child.

Sheldrake chose this moment to burst in through the door, stopping in his tracks to stare at them in amazement. 'Miss Cecily, you're already here.'

She threw a sideways glance at Peggy before tapping her watch. 'Yes, Mr Sheldrake, and you are approximately ten minutes late.'

Chapter 7

The morning was an eventful one. Already peeved by his late start, Sheldrake's habitual state of irritation was only intensified by Fairchild, who had been tasked with checking the transcripts of some of Churchill's speeches and had deemed it appropriate to re-word them.

'I just wonder,' said Fairchild, sending his gaze heavenwards as if appealing to some celestial muse, 'if instead of fighting on the beaches, it should be about fighting on the coast and cliff. It has a more poetic, alliterative edge, wouldn't you say?'

Sheldrake inhaled and exhaled heavily like a dragon stoking up a roaring breath of fire. 'Poetic it may be, but these are the words which have already been spoken by our Prime Minister, inspiring an entire nation, and therefore, these are the words which will be printed and distributed to every man, woman and child in the kingdom. Your job, Mr Fairchild, as I have explained innumerable times, is to offer one final proof-reading check for typographical and grammatical errors. Now do you think you can do that for me?'

'I'm not sure,' said Fairchild. 'My brain is primed to create, you see?'

'I'll do it, Mr Sheldrake,' said Peggy, retrieving the document from Fairchild, who placed a hand on his heart and offered her a gracious bow.

'Thank you, Miss Sparks,' said Sheldrake.

'What should I do now?' asked Fairchild.

Sheldrake hesitated, his eye twitching as he fought the urge to tell the man what he should really do. He picked up a folder from his desk. 'Take these to Lear on Russell Square.'

Fairchild's face brightened. 'Right-o. Will do. I'll see if Dickie Blake wants to take an early lunch at the Russell if it's all right with you, Sheldrake old chap?'

Sheldrake wore a tight smile. 'Take all the time you need.'

'Splendid. Toodle pip.' Fairchild was about to exit the room when a woman appeared in the doorway. She was immaculate in a fitted soft grey suit, a choker of pearls at her throat and a brown fur stole around her upright shoulders. Her hair was elegantly coiffured beneath a mulberry-coloured angled hat. Fairchild stood back with a bow. 'After you, m'lady.'

She pursed her lips in the semblance of a smile before entering the office as if she owned it. 'Marigold,' she said by way of greeting, ignoring everyone else in the room.

Marigold sprang to her feet as if her chair had caught fire. 'Mama. What are you doing here?'

'That's a fine way to address your mother, I must say,' she said, gliding across to kiss her daughter on both cheeks.

'Sorry,' said Marigold. Peggy noticed how she seemed to deflate like a punctured tyre under this woman's scrutiny. 'It's just a surprise to see you,' she stammered. 'A lovely surprise.'

'Yes, well. I dined at the Savoy with the Candlefords last night, and Winnie was in the office today so he picked me up from there this morning.'

'You should have called, Mummy. You could have stayed at the house with me.'

Her mother frowned. 'I don't think so, darling. I'm always much more comfortable at the Savoy. Now come along, I'm taking you to lunch.'

Sheldrake cleared his throat. Marigold glanced in his direction. 'Mummy, let me introduce you first to Mr Sheldrake. He's Mr Beecher's second in command. And this is Peggy Sparks, my . . .' she searched for the right word before surprising Peggy when she said, 'work colleague and friend.'

'Lady Lavinia Cecily,' said Marigold's mother as if issuing a challenge. 'Pleased to make your acquaintances,' she added in a tone that suggested she was anything but. 'Well, come along, Marigold. I've got a reservation at the Russell.'

'Is that all right, Mr Sheldrake?'

'Of course,' he replied, offering Marigold's mother an awkward bow which caused her to frown.

'I daresay you'll be glad to have me take her off your hands for an hour or two,' she said. 'I can't imagine that she contributes much to the war effort. Such a lazy, useless girl.' She swept from the room with a dejected Marigold hurrying after her. Peggy watched them go, astonished not only by the rudeness of this disagreeable woman, but by the creeping sympathy she was starting to feel for Lady Marigold Cecily.

Peggy left the office at lunchtime, eager to share that morning's events with Laurie. She was crestfallen to find the librarians' office locked and no sign of her friend. She plodded towards the staircase, lost in thought, when she heard a voice.

'Miss Peggy Sparks, you owe me a teaspoon.'

She turned to see Wallace Dalton grinning up at her from the floor below. 'Oh goodness,' she said. 'I'm so sorry. I completely forgot.'

He laughed. 'I'm teasing. I don't suppose you have plans for lunch?' Peggy held up her sandwiches in reply. He lifted his eyebrows. 'I can do better than that.'

'I'm not sure an employee at a ministry where we encourage people not to waste food should be wasting their fish paste sandwiches,' she said as she followed Dalton across Russell Square towards the elegant green-turreted hotel where he was taking them for lunch.

He plucked the bag from her hands, retrieved a sandwich and took a bite. 'Delicious,' he said as she laughed. 'Luckily for you, I have the constitution of a man who can eat two lunches.'

The dining room of the Russell Hotel was a lavish affair, hung with dripping crystal chandeliers, which cast a decadent glow across the richly veined marble walls and creamy white columns topped with statues of benevolent maidens. It was all Peggy could do not to stare around her, open-mouthed, and imagine what Nancy would make of it all.

'What will you have?' asked Dalton, plonking himself down in the chair the waiter pulled out for him and accepting a proffered napkin with the casual indifference of a man who was used to the finer things in life. 'The chops are jolly good but so is the Irish Stew. My treat, by the way.'

'I thought I owed you after I stole your teaspoon.'

He grinned. 'You are repaying me with your company. I hate to dine alone. Will you have a glass of wine?'

'Just tea for me, please.'

Peggy looked around the room, spotting Marigold sitting with her mother at a table in the far corner. She could see Lady Lavinia berating her daughter as Marigold sat with her eyes cast downwards. On the other side of the room, Gideon Fairchild was dining with a blond man wearing round glasses who Peggy assumed must be his friend, Dickie Blake.

'So, how is work in the Campaigns department?' she asked.

'I don't work there now. I've moved to Home Intelligence.'

'Oh. That must be quite different.'

He shrugged. 'The Ministry's so disorganised, you never know where you might be working from one day to the next.' He studied the menu. 'So, what's it to be? I think I'm going to plump for the Woolton pie.'

'Me too,' said Peggy.

The lunch was delicious and Peggy had to admit that, in the absence of Laurie, Wallace Dalton was good company. He was effortlessly charming and witty, although there was something about him that was a little too assured for Peggy, as if he had an answer for everything.

'I saw you eating your lunch in the square with that librarian chap the other day,' he said, lighting a cigarette.

Peggy wiped her mouth with her napkin, feeling self-conscious. 'Laurie is a very kind man.'

'They often are.'

'Who?'

He leaned in with a wry smile as he whispered the word. 'Homosexuals.'

'I beg your pardon?'

Dalton gazed at her. 'You didn't know?'

Peggy felt colour rise to her cheeks. 'Well, how do you know?' she demanded.

Dalton exhaled a plume of smoke and shrugged. 'The Ministry is stuffed to the gills with them. You recognise them after a while. Sheldrake, for example, and half the writer chaps, a few of the women too.'

'Oh,' said Peggy, feeling as naïve as a newborn.

'Are you shocked and horrified?' he asked with barely concealed glee.

'No,' said Peggy frowning. 'Why would I be?'

'Precisely, Peggy. Each to their own, is my mantra. Every man for himself.'

'And woman,' said Peggy.

'Quite right.' He lifted his glass and tapped it against Peggy's teacup. 'I'll drink to that.'

'Where have you been?' demanded Sheldrake as she returned a while later.

Peggy glanced at her watch. 'I'm sorry. I was late going to lunch. Is there a problem?'

Sheldrake sighed. 'Beecher's been called away on urgent business and asked me to deputise for a meeting with our printer, Frank Bauman. He's spitting chips about how successful our new pamphlets have been.'

'Why?'

Sheldrake shook his head. 'Something to do with Paper Control. Usually Mr Beecher liaises directly with him as they know one another. Apparently, he can be a bit difficult.'

'Perhaps you should try to put him off,' suggested Peggy.

Sheldrake shook his head. 'I can't. Mr Beecher said he'd been let down before and was insistent that I meet with him.' He gave her an uncharacteristically helpless look. 'Would you come along as an extra line of defence?'

Peggy stared at him. 'I'm not sure what help I'll be.'

'Please, Miss Sparks.'

Peggy had never seen Sheldrake like this and found it both disorientating and endearing. After her conversation with Dalton, she felt she was seeing a different side to Cyril Sheldrake. 'All right, but I'm only coming to take notes.'

'Yes. Of course. Thank you,' said Sheldrake, looking genuinely relieved. Marigold appeared at that moment looking downcast. 'Ah, Miss Cecily. Good. You can come too.'

'Come where?'

'To a meeting with our printer. You were involved in choosing the photographs. He might want to tear a strip off you too.'

'Very well,' said Marigold, not registering what he'd said.

'Are you all right?' asked Peggy as they made their way downstairs.

'What? Oh yes, fine.'

'How was your mother?'

Marigold avoided her eye. 'As critical as ever.' It was the first time Peggy had seen her show anything but sparkling positivity for the world around her.

'Mr Bauman,' said Sheldrake, approaching Frank, who stood in the lobby wearing an impatient frown. 'Apologies for the lateness.'

'Where's Beecher?' he barked.

Peggy and Sheldrake exchanged glances. 'He was called away on urgent business. He sends his apologies. He asked us to conduct the meeting on his behalf.'

Frank gave an exasperated sigh. 'Well, that's my afternoon wasted, which is particularly aggravating given how much work your department is currently throwing at us.' He turned, ready to leave.

Sheldrake threw Peggy a panicked look. 'Mr Bauman,' she said, trying to stop her voice from shaking. He turned, dark eyes flashing as he glared down at her. Peggy guessed he was only a year or two older than her and this gave her a certain amount of courage. She might have even thought him handsome with his mop of raven-black hair and eyes the colour of molasses, but his disagreeable demeanour appalled her. She decided that, for Mr Beecher's sake, they should do all they could to appease him. 'We understand your frustration and believe you have some issues with Paper Control, so please, why don't you allow us to conduct the meeting and do our best to help you. I'm Miss Sparks and this is Miss Cecily and Mr Sheldrake, by the way.'

He seemed momentarily astonished, a sentiment which Peggy shared, before throwing up his hands. 'Fine, Miss Sparks,' he said with a hint of mockery. 'I suppose I'm here now, and as Rosa is in a meeting with Mr Longforth's department, I'll only be waiting around. Let's get this over with, shall we?'

Sheldrake ushered him towards one of the meeting rooms with Peggy and Marigold following on behind. 'Gosh, he's a crosspatch, isn't he?' whispered Marigold. 'But devilishly handsome.'

'Marigold,' scolded Peggy.

'Don't pretend you weren't thinking the same thing,' said Marigold with a teasing nudge.

'May I offer you some tea?' asked Peggy as they entered the gloomy room.

'God, no,' said Mr Bauman, plonking himself in the first available seat without taking off his coat. 'I'd rather drink Churchill's bath water.' Marigold gave a snort of amusement which made Peggy frown. 'I really can't fathom why the English love their tea so much. It tastes vile and looks disgusting.'

'I must say, I do prefer a champagne cocktail,' said Marigold with a flirtatious moue.

'Why does that not surprise me?' said Frank, raising one eyebrow.

Sheldrake cleared his throat. 'So, Mr Bauman, I believe you have some issues regarding Paper Control?'

Frank grew serious again. 'Correct. Grateful as we are for the increased business from these pamphlets . . .' he reached into his briefcase and brought out copies of *Our Mighty Navy*, *Our Mighty Air Force* and *Our Mighty Army*, fanning them on to the desk in front of him, '. . . we are under increasing pressure due to their huge popularity, and Paper Control are reluctant to allocate us more paper to meet those demands.'

'Have you explained to them why it's so important?' asked Peggy.

'Oh, I didn't think of that,' said Frank before rolling his eyes. 'Of course I've explained, but the bureaucracy in this country is such that they don't always have sympathies with a German Jew.'

'Oh, I'm sorry, I had no idea,' said Peggy, her face growing hot.

'Sorry that I'm German or sorry that I'm a Jew?' demanded Frank.

Peggy shrank at his sharp words. 'Mr Bauman,' said Sheldrake. 'We are most dreadfully sorry that you've been having problems with the powers that be. Rest assured I will personally address this matter with Mr Beecher and we will endeavour to smooth the waters as soon as possible.'

Frank regarded him for a moment. 'Please make sure

you do. Rosa and I work hard for this country. We want to do all we can to make sure that the Allies win the war.'

'Of course,' said Sheldrake. 'I shall speak to Mr Beecher as soon as he is back and ask him to call you.'

'Very well.' They walked back to the atrium where Rosa Bauman was waiting. 'How did it go?' he asked her.

Rosa shrugged. 'I'm not sure what irritates these men more. The fact that I'm a woman, or German, or Jewish, or immune to their public school charms, or a combination of all these elements.'

'Right,' said Frank, eyes wild with anger. 'That's it. I'm going over to deal with Longforth myself.'

'You will do no such thing,' said Rosa, grabbing his arm. 'I am perfectly capable of fighting my own battles. I don't need a man riding into the fray on my behalf. It's not the Middle Ages.' She turned to Peggy, who was once again reminded of how much she liked this woman. 'It's nice to see you again, Miss Sparks.'

'You too,' said Peggy. 'This is Mr Sheldrake and Miss Cecily.'

Rosa nodded from one to the other. 'Delighted.'

'Charmed,' said Marigold as Sheldrake tilted his head in greeting.

'Well, we must be going,' said Frank. 'Be sure to speak to Beecher, won't you? I'm tired of being fobbed off by Ministry half-wits.'

'Of course,' said Sheldrake.

Frank turned away and Rosa shot them an apologetic smile before following him.

★   ★   ★

Peggy was still seething as she returned to the library. She wasn't sure if it was Frank Bauman's brash rudeness or Marigold's coquettish behaviour which had annoyed her more. Above all she felt sorry for Frank's wife. Poor Rosa Bauman. Fancy being married to such an ill-tempered man. If she were able to remain civil, why couldn't he?

'Gosh, you look cross,' said Laurie. 'Got time for a cup of tea?'

Peggy bristled as she recalled Frank's damning indictment of their national drink. 'Nothing I'd like more,' she said.

Chapter 8

Aside from having him home to celebrate with them in person, the news that Joe was alive and well was the next best Christmas present for Peggy and her family. It was difficult to predict where he might be, but given his reports of sunny weather, they guessed he was probably somewhere in the Mediterranean or Middle East. Nancy sat beside her, scrutinising her globe one evening.

'So if Daddy is here in Africa,' she said, pointing at Morocco, 'all he has to do when he's finished fighting the enemy is jump back across to here, then here and then back to us.' She hopped her finger to Spain, France and then England.

'That's right,' said Peggy, wishing it were really that simple. 'Now, do you want to help me finish making these paper chains?' She held up the strips of wallpaper cut from the old rolls she'd found in the attic.

'All right,' said Nancy. 'Can I do the gluing?'

'Of course.' They worked in companionable silence, Nancy's face screwed up in concentration, Peggy relishing the quiet, the mantel clock's tranquil ticking the only sound she could hear. After days and nights of raids and the frenetic bustle of work at the Ministry, Peggy was grateful for a peaceful Saturday afternoon with her niece. 'Have you written your letter to Father Christmas yet?' she asked after a while.

Nancy shook her head. 'Didn't need to. He came to our school so I told him what I'd like.'

'That's good,' said Peggy.

'Although,' said Nancy, frowning slightly, 'he smelt of tobacco and peppermints and sounded a bit like Mr Cooper from next door.'

'Oh,' said Peggy, folding her lips together to suppress a smile. 'Fancy Father Christmas being like our next-door neighbour.'

'I know. He was very nice, though.'

'So what did you ask him for?'

'Well, first I asked if he could bring Daddy home.'

'And what did he say?'

'He said that he wished he could but unfortunately Father Christmas doesn't have that power, so I asked for the next best thing.'

'Which is?'

Nancy shrugged as if it were obvious. 'A skipping rope. Alfie Riley snapped my last one when we were playing cowboys and Indians.'

'Good choice, Nancy.'

'I know. What do you want for Christmas, Auntie Peg?'

Peggy thought for a moment. Her dearest wish was the same as Nancy's and nearly every other person in the world with a relative fighting in the war, but that was all it was. A heartfelt wish. What with the nightly bombings and Joe's manoeuvres to goodness-knows-where, it didn't feel as if this war was going to end any time soon. 'I want the same thing as you.'

'A skipping rope?'

Peggy laughed. 'No, silly. I want your daddy home, but if that's not possible then probably a writing pad so I can write him lots more letters about everything that's going on.'

Nancy eyed her aunt. 'Do you tell him all the stories about those funny people at your work?'

'Sometimes.'

'Tell me about Lady Marigold Cecily again. Do you think she's as rich as the King?'

'I'm not sure about that, but I know her family has three houses.'

'Three!' Nancy's eyes bulged.

Peggy nodded as she pressed together the paper chain that her niece had just spread with far too much glue. 'One in London, another big one in the country and an even bigger one in Scotland.'

Nancy exhaled in wonder. 'I bet they have a really huge Christmas tree and a big fire with all her family gathered round it,' she said, glancing towards their small, garlanded tree with its tiny glass baubles and a photo of Joe nestled in the branches.

'I like our little tree. Anyway, I don't think she is going to be with her family. Her mother's a bit of a cold fish.'

'Oh. Poor Lady Marigold.'

'Don't worry about her. She'll be happy going to parties in London with her friends.'

Nancy furrowed her brow. 'I think that's a shame. Iris and Alfie are my best friends, but I wouldn't like to have Christmas without my family.' Her face lit up. 'You should invite her to our house.'

Peggy realised she needed to nip Nancy's bright idea in the bud. 'Where would we put her? We've hardly enough room as it is.'

Nancy shuffled closer to Peggy. 'We could all budge up. It'd be cosy.'

'She won't want to come. We're not grand enough for her,' said Peggy.

Nancy narrowed her eyes. 'It sounds as if you don't want her to come.'

Their conversation was interrupted by the sound of the front door opening as Emily, Alice and Flo arrived home from their Women's Voluntary Service shift. The three women had signed up after Emily declared that they needed to do something to help get their boy home as quickly as possible. Alice had immediately been enlisted as a champion knitter, whilst Flo was a very adept seamstress. Emily dished out tea and sympathy to anyone who needed it whilst often locking horns with Mrs Pike, who was nominally in charge and who Peggy's grandmother declared to be 'a bossy beggar with a bad smell under her nose'.

Peggy stood up to fill the kettle, partly to put an end to Nancy's line of interrogation but also because she knew her grandmother didn't like to be home for longer than five minutes without a cup of tea.

'What's all this then?' asked Emily as she entered the kitchen.

'Auntie Peg and I have been making paper chains,' said Nancy, holding them up for all to see. 'And talking about Christmas. I think she should invite Lady Marigold because she won't be with her family this year.'

'Oh, that's a pity,' said Alice, peeling off her coat. 'Well, you know she'd be more than welcome, Peg.'

'I'd like to meet this Lady Marigold,' said Flo. 'She sounds like a character.' Peggy reached out to take Charlie from her, sitting him on her lap and receiving a gummy smile in greeting.

'Let's ask her then,' said Nancy, bobbing up and down in her chair. 'Please, Auntie Peg.'

'It's a kind thought but she won't come,' said Peggy, avoiding her niece's eye. She looked around at their small, snug kitchen. It was clean and welcoming, but she couldn't imagine Marigold fitting in here. There were no waiters running to bring more cocktails, for a start. She pulled a face at her nephew who gurgled in delight before turning to her niece. 'Why don't you go and wash that glue off your hands, Nancy?'

'All right,' she replied, climbing down from the table. 'But I want you to know that I'm disappointed I won't get to meet a real lady this Christmas.'

'Now then, Peggy Sparks,' said Emily. 'I've got something to say about your Ministry's latest film.'

'I don't work in the film department, Gran,' said Peggy.

'I know, but I want you to give them a message from me.'

'All right. What is it this time?' She was getting used to her grandmother's judgements on everything from a poster of a cheerful pig telling her to donate her kitchen waste ('Tell Winston he can come and get it whenever he wants to') to the King and Queen's visit to the East End. ('They should have come to south-east London. I'd have baked a Victoria sponge in tribute to the King's great-grandmother, God rest her soul.')

Emily folded her arms. 'Tell them to stop saying "London can take it."'

Peggy frowned. 'You want them to say that London *can't* take it?'

'No,' cried Emily, scandalised. '"Course not. I want them to say that London can give it.' She punched the air left and right. 'Come 'ere, Hitler. I'll tan your backside.'

Nancy giggled from where Flo was helping her wash her hands. 'You're funny, Great-Gran.'

'I'll be sure to pass on the message, Gran,' said Peggy, sharing an amused look with her mother.

Flo was just filling the teapot with boiling water as the air-raid siren sounded. 'Right, come on, everyone, grab the pot and the cups,' said Alice, opening the back door and ushering them outside. 'We'll have our tea in the shelter.'

'All I want for Christmas is a break from these bleedin' air raids,' shouted Emily, pointing an accusing finger at the sky. 'Do you hear me, Jerry?'

'Come on, Mum,' said Alice, herding them into the shelter. She placed an arm on Peggy's shoulder before they went inside. 'I think you should at least ask Marigold, Peggy. Out of kindness. It is Christmas after all.'

★   ★   ★

In Peggy's world, it was her grandmother who offered an endless assortment of opinions, some of which were to be adhered to, others ignored, but when her mother made a suggestion, always gently and never forced, you would do well to listen. Which is why Peggy found herself in the strange position on Christmas Eve of not wanting to invite Marigold for Christmas but knowing that she really should. At lunchtime, Beecher called them all together for a drink, producing a bottle of port – 'a gift from Lord Candleford's own cellar,' he said with one eyebrow raised.

'Good old Winnie,' cried Marigold.

'Thank you for your efforts this year,' said Beecher. 'You have all worked extremely hard, especially on the series of "Our Mighty" pamphlets.'

'Mighty is right, sir,' said Sheldrake with bright eyes and pink cheeks, thanks to the port. 'We've sold over half a million copies of each in Europe and the Middle East, and according to feedback from Home Intelligence, the public love them and want more.'

'Indeed,' said Beecher. 'It is most gratifying.'

'Apparently Longforth is spitting chips over the whole thing,' said Fairchild. 'Dickie Blake told me he threw a walnut side table out of the window when he heard how successful they've been.'

'As I said,' continued Beecher. 'Most gratifying.' He raised his glass to them all. 'I pray that we have a peaceful Yuletide and that it's the last one of this war. Merry Christmas.'

'Merry Christmas,' they echoed.

'And God bless us everyone,' said Fairchild, placing a hand on his heart.

'So what plans do you have for Christmas, Miss Sparks?' asked Beecher.

'Just at home with my family. And you?'

'Just my wife and me.' A whisper of sadness seemed to flit across his face before he turned to Marigold with a brisk smile. 'And how about you, Miss Cecily? What hedonistic delights do you have in store?'

Marigold sighed. 'None, actually. I was supposed to be celebrating with my friend Cordelia, but she's going back to the family pile in Norfolk. I'll probably just have lunch at the Savoy and see who's around.'

'You're welcome to spend Christmas with my family if you'd like to,' said Peggy quickly before she had time to change her mind.

Marigold stared at her. 'Oh, but I couldn't. Could I?' She looked towards Sheldrake who shrugged before turning back to Peggy.

'Well, the offer is there if you'd like to,' said Peggy, secretly hoping she'd decide she really couldn't.

She nearly jumped out of her skin as Marigold seized her by the shoulders and gazed at her with dazzling green eyes. 'Thank you, Peggy. That really is terrifically kind. I'd love to.'

Peggy briefly caught Sheldrake's raised-eyebrow look before she answered. 'Wonderful,' she said through gritted teeth. 'God bless us everyone.'

'Peggy?' She turned round to see Laurie standing in the doorway. 'Sorry to interrupt, sir,' he said to Beecher.

97

'Not at all, young man. Come in. Have a drink,' said Beecher, handing him a glass of port. 'Happy Christmas, Mr Parker, and heartfelt apologies for the upheaval we've all caused you and your colleagues. Thank you for making us so welcome.'

'Hear, hear,' said Sheldrake, raising his glass towards Laurie in a gesture which struck Peggy as uncharacteristically friendly.

'Well, there really is no need, but thank you.' He turned to Peggy. 'I got you something,' he said, reaching into his pocket and handing her a small rectangular parcel. She opened it to reveal a blue leather-bound notebook. 'For your writing,' he said.

'Oh Laurie, that's wonderful. Thank you,' she said before reaching into her desk drawer and handing him his own parcel. 'Happy Christmas.'

Laurie's face lit up when he unwrapped it. '*Letters From Iceland*,' he read. 'Thank you, Peggy. That's very kind.'

'It's a second-hand edition,' said Peggy, 'but I know how much you like MacNeice and Auden.'

'I'm a great fan of them both too,' said Sheldrake, sauntering over.

'Oh,' said Laurie with a shy smile. 'Well, I'll lend it to you after I've read it if you'd like?'

Sheldrake nodded rapidly. 'Thank you. That would be most . . .' He caught sight of Peggy smiling at him. 'Well, if you'll excuse me. Lots to do before we, er, finish,' he said, gathering up some files and making for the door.

'What a funny little man he is,' said Marigold to his disappearing back.

98

'I'm not interrupting, am I?' said a voice.

Beecher's face dissolved into a smile at the sight of Frank Bauman standing in the doorway. 'Not at all, my dear fellow. Come in, come in. Please join us.'

Marigold sidled up to Peggy. 'What's the handsome crosspatch doing here?'

'I haven't the foggiest.' She noticed the ease of interaction between the pair of them and the almost paternal way that Beecher patted Frank on the shoulder as he handed him a drink.

'Miss Sparks, Miss Cecily, I believe you've already met Mr Bauman?' Sheldrake appeared at Beecher's shoulder and whispered something in his ear. 'Please excuse me for a moment.'

Peggy couldn't be sure but she thought she detected a flicker of guilt in Frank's expression as he turned to face them. 'Hello again. I was in the area and wanted to call in to wish Mr Beecher season's greetings. He's smoothed out all the issues as Mr Sheldrake promised he would.'

'Oh good,' said Marigold.

The silence threatened to become awkward. 'Is Mrs Bauman not with you today?' Peggy blurted out.

A flicker of a frown crossed Frank's expression before it was replaced with glittering amusement. 'I would be very surprised if my mother were here, given that she died five years ago.'

Peggy was crestfallen. 'Oh, I'm so sorry. I meant . . .'

'Rosa,' he said. Peggy blushed. 'Rosa is my sister, and for your information, she was very displeased with me following our previous interaction.'

'Oh,' said Peggy.

'Yes,' said Frank. 'Oh indeed. She said I was unforgivably rude.'

'She sounds like a perceptive woman,' said Marigold.

Frank laughed. 'She is, actually. And I think you are very perceptive to notice this, Miss Cecily.' Peggy watched their interaction unfold with a stab of envy. It was no surprise, given the way she looked and held herself, that Marigold found it easy to talk to people, men included. There was a confidence that came with class that would forever evade Peggy. Her grandmother seemed to have it despite her working-class background, but Peggy felt that Emily was an exception to the rule. She wondered what it was like to be so sure of yourself.

'Miss Sparks?' Peggy blinked up into Frank's eyes and realised she had no idea what he'd just said.

'I beg your pardon?' she asked, flushing slightly.

'I wanted to know if you can find it in your heart to forgive me as Miss Cecily has.'

'Of course,' said Peggy.

'*Wunderbar*. Then perhaps Rosa will too.' He nodded to the pair of them. 'Season's greetings to you both.'

'Season's greetings to you and Rosa. We look forward to working with you next year,' said Marigold. He smiled before turning to bid Beecher farewell.

'Gosh, what a dish he is,' said Marigold, watching him go. 'Don't you think, Peggy?'

She shrugged. 'I can't say I'd noticed.' Handsome or not, Peggy didn't have time for a man with such erratic manners. There was a war on and she had a brother to save. There was nothing more important than that.

Christmas Day brought a temporary break from the bombs and Lady Marigold with a Fortnum's hamper containing a Christmas pudding, Dundee cake, hare pâté, tinned strawberries in syrup and a tin of mint humbugs.

'You're welcome any time, dear,' said Emily, as she eyed the contents with delight and her friend Dulcie, who always spent Christmas with them, popped a humbug into her mouth.

'It's the least I could do after your kindness,' said Marigold. 'Gosh, doesn't it look wonderfully festive in here,' she added, taking in the holly-decked halls and paper-chain-festooned ceiling.

'I made the paper chains with Auntie Peg,' said Nancy proudly. She had been gazing up at Marigold ever since she'd entered the house. 'You have beautiful eyes and hair. You look like a film star,' she told her.

'Nancy, it's very rude to stare at people and to comment on their appearance,' said Flo. 'Sorry, Lady Marigold,' she added, with a curtseying gesture.

'She's not the Queen, Flo,' whispered Peggy with barely masked irritation.

'Sorry,' said Nancy. 'Am I allowed to say that she smells lovely, like a beautiful flower garden in the sunshine?'

Marigold cupped Nancy's face in her hands. 'Oh, but you are such a darling. And now, I have something for you.'

'For me?' Nancy's eyes were saucer-wide as Marigold handed over a large oblong box.

'I hope you like it,' said Marigold. Peggy tried to catch Flo's eye but she was watching Nancy with delight, as was Alice. Even Emily was looking on with a twinkle in her eye as Nancy opened the box and slid out a large doll looking serenely smart in an ATS uniform. Nancy stared at it open-mouthed. 'She's in the army, like your daddy.'

'What do you say, Nancy?' prompted Flo.

Nancy flung her arms around Marigold's middle. 'Oh, thank you, thank you, Lady Marigold.'

'I didn't think you liked dolls,' said Peggy, immediately regretting her petulance.

'But this isn't a doll, Auntie Peg,' said Nancy. 'She's an army lady and I'm going to call her Marigold.'

'Perfect,' muttered Peggy as Marigold clapped her hands together and everyone else laughed. 'Just perfect.' She watched with arms folded as Marigold held her family in thrall, perched on the edge of the pale green sofa in the front room, regaling Flo, Emily, Dulcie and Nancy with tales of the famous people she'd met.

'And what was Greta Garble like?' asked Dulcie.

'She's called Greta Gar-bo,' corrected Nancy.

'That's what I said,' Dulcie insisted.

Marigold's eyes sparkled. 'She was a darling. Not like you'd expect. Really quite friendly. I think she liked me.'

'Seems like everyone does,' muttered Peggy under her breath.

She felt her mother slide an arm through hers. 'Come and help me with the lunch?' Peggy followed her mother out to the kitchen. Alice reached into the range and pulled out a golden brown pie.

'Looks good, Mum.'

'We've done Lord Woolton proud,' said Alice with satisfaction before turning to her daughter. 'You know you don't need to be jealous of Marigold, don't you?'

Peggy picked up a cloth and started to polish the cutlery. 'I know. I just wish I had the money to buy Nancy a doll like that and a fancy hamper for us.'

Alice picked up a pot from the hamper on the side and held it out to her. 'I can assure you, Peggy Sparks, that I don't want you wasting your money on hare pâté. You know I only like plum jam on my toast.' She caught her daughter's eye and they started to laugh.

'You mean you wouldn't want me to take you to the Savoy for champagne and caviar?' Peggy asked.

Alice chuckled before tucking a strand of hair behind Peggy's ear. 'All I want is for my family to be happy and safe.' She glanced at the photograph of Joe, smart in his uniform. 'That's all any mother ever wants.'

Peggy hugged her as a raucous peal of laughter went up from the front room. 'Come on. Let's get the troops fed,' said Alice.

Peggy had to admit that she enjoyed Christmas more than she expected. It was difficult not to be charmed by Marigold Cecily, particularly when she gave them all gifts of Yardley soap and pulled out a bottle of French brandy, 'liberated from my father's drinks cabinet', she said with a wink. 'He'll never know.'

After lunch, they sat around the wireless and listened to the King's speech. Peggy noticed her mother thumb away a tear as he talked about 'the sadness of separation', and of forces 'guarding the dark seas or pursuing the beaten foe in the Libyan Desert', while Flo gazed down at Charlie through misted eyes, Nancy hugged her doll tightly and Emily stared straight ahead, her chin jutted forwards in quiet defiance.

When the speech had finished, Emily fetched six small tumblers and poured them all a nip of brandy. She raised her glass. 'To those who can't be with us. God bless them all.'

'God bless them all,' they murmured in reply.

Peggy took a wincing sip as Marigold rose to her feet. 'I would like to propose a toast to you all. Thank you for welcoming me into your home. It's wonderful to be part of a family Christmas.'

'What's Christmas like in your house?' asked Nancy. 'Do you have a butler to bring you dinner and fancy maids to do your hair?'

'Something like that,' said Marigold with a wistful air. 'But I think your Christmas is much better. It's full of . . .' her voice trailed off as she searched for the right word, '. . . love.'

Peggy felt her mother place a hand on her shoulder whilst Emily eyed their guest for a moment before topping up her glass. 'Get that down you, Lady Marigold. You might not call it love once we've played some parlour games. Dulcie here can be quite the hothead once she gets going with Are You There, Moriarty?'

'Can we play Wink Murder first?' cried Nancy, hopping from foot to foot. 'Please?'

'I was going to ask if I could take some photographs

of you all if you don't mind,' said Marigold. 'I've brought my camera.'

'Oh, please take my photograph,' said Nancy, standing up taller.

'Well, I could take photographs while you play games if that's all right?'

'She's a good photographer,' admitted Peggy. Alice rewarded her with a gentle smile.

'Thank you, Peggy,' said Marigold.

'I'm not sure why you'd want to take our pictures, but if you bring a bottle of brandy to our house, I say you can do what you like,' said Emily, topping up her and Dulcie's glasses.

'I've had a wonderful time, Peggy,' said Marigold later as she helped her wash up. 'Thank you for inviting me.'

Peggy passed her a plate to dry before plunging another into the sudsy water. 'I wouldn't like to think of you on your own at Christmas.'

Marigold was quiet for a moment. 'Look, I know we didn't exactly hit it off when we first met.'

'Well . . .' Peggy began.

'No, it's all right. I know how I come across. I'm frightfully annoying sometimes. Mother's always telling me so. But I'm glad to have met you, Peggy. In truth, I don't have many people who see me for who I am, but I think you do.'

Peggy glanced at her. 'I think I'm beginning to.'

Marigold wiped the plate she was holding and set it on the side. 'Are you close to your brother?'

Peggy nodded as she rinsed a bowl and handed it to her. 'He's always protected me, ever since I was little. We tell each other everything. I miss that in particular.'

Marigold looked up at the photos on the shelf by the window. 'Is that Joe?'

'Yes. And the one next to him is of my father. He died in the Great War.'

'I'm sorry.'

Peggy shrugged. 'Thousands of people lost their fathers, brothers and loved ones in that war. I just hope we can put an end to this one before that happens again.'

Marigold held her gaze. 'I hope so too.'

'Do you have any brothers or sisters?' asked Peggy.

Marigold hesitated before answering. 'No. Just me.'

'So where do your parents spend Christmas?' asked Peggy, wondering why her mother didn't treasure her only child.

'Scotland. My mother likes to go riding or walking with her dogs.' Peggy noted that Marigold made no mention of her father, her effusive, excitable spirit replaced with an air of melancholy. 'I don't mind. Really.'

'Well, I'm glad you're here,' said Peggy, not sure that she believed her. 'Not least because I'm grateful for your help with the washing-up.' Marigold laughed.

Alice appeared in the kitchen doorway. 'Your grandmother and Dulcie are snoring like a couple of elephants, and Flo has taken Charlie and Nancy for a walk, so I'm going to make the most of the peace by putting my feet up with a cup of tea. Who'd like one?'

'You sit down, Mum. I'll bring it to you,' said Peggy.

Alice leaned over to kiss her daughter on the cheek. 'You're an angel, Peg.'

Marigold watched her go before turning back to Peggy. 'You're lucky to have a mother like that.'

Peggy smiled as she handed Marigold the last plate to dry. 'I know,' she said.

January 1941

Dear Peg,

Thank you for your letter. Unfortunately, the parcel got crushed and nearly everything inside was ruined. Gran's socks will dry out, mind. Don't tell Nancy as I don't want her to think I didn't get her Christmas card. I was a bit down about it, but Albert shared the Christmas cake his mum had sent. Wasn't as good as one of Gran's, but I wouldn't tell him that. Sorry to sound like a moaning Minnie, but Christmas is hard when you're away from your family and particularly hard when you love your family as much as I do. I'm glad you had a good Christmas (honest!). Fancy Lady Marigold spending the day with you. She sounds like a good sort bringing all those gifts. I bet Nancy was in seventh heaven to get the doll and Gran similarly tickled pink with the brandy!

This is the first chance I've had to write for a bit. We had a couple of days' leave when we got off the boat and two good nights' sleep in barracks, which was a blessing as we're in the desert now. It's rough going, although I don't mind sleeping under canvas. The sand gets everywhere, especially when there's a sandstorm. Albert keeps joking about our rations being nothing but sand-wiches, which makes us laugh and groan. Tell that one to Nancy. I know she'll chuckle. She's the one I think about when I'm sleeping in my tent as I know she always said she wanted to go camping. I'll take her and Charlie as soon as I get the chance when I'm home, because I'm determined to come home, Peg. It's this thought that keeps me going. I also think of you when I come to places like ███ because I know you'd love to visit and I can't wait to tell you about the sights I've seen, but obviously that'll have to wait until the censor's not watching.

We get the local paper but it doesn't mention the bombings in London, so I hope you're all keeping safe and still managing to drag Gran into the shelter. Give her and Mum a squeeze from me. Flo told me in her last letter that Nancy is getting tall and was pleased with her skipping rope. She also said that Charlie has got his first tooth and is chewing on the bickie pegs like there's no tomorrow. I wish I could see them just for five minutes. It would make life here a lot easier. But I'm all right, Peg. Don't worry. We've got the Italians on the run so there's lots to be cheerful about. Onwards and upwards, eh? We'll meet again.

Love, Joe

Chapter 9

The woman arrived without introduction or announce-ment, taking up occupancy in the office next to Beecher's. Peggy caught sight of her through the half-open door on her arrival one morning. She was slight with dark hair wound in a tight bun and bore the look of a woman with whom one did not trifle. She glanced up from her desk as Peggy passed but neither acknowledged her presence nor offered any greeting. In fact, she rose without making eye contact and quietly shut the door.

'Who is that woman in the office next to Mr Beecher's?' she asked Sheldrake, shrugging off her coat.

He looked up from the document he was frowning at. 'I haven't the foggiest. Some secretary palmed off from another floor, probably. They're always moving people around. And some of them stay for a very long time,' he said with a pointed glance in Fairchild's direction.

'Good morning, Mr Fairchild,' said Peggy.

'Ah, my dear Miss Sparks. How are you today? Any word from our dear boy fighting the good fight?'

'Nothing since he wrote from the desert.' Peggy did her best to live by her gran's assertion that 'no news was good news', but it was difficult to stay positive week after week. Instead, she had resolved to pour every ounce of effort into her work, feeling that this was the only way she could help Joe. Whenever she received a letter from him, it only served to strengthen this resolve.

'It makes me wish I was ten years younger so I could join him,' Fairchild said.

'Be careful what you wish for,' said Sheldrake. 'They'll increase the age group and then you'll be scuppered.'

'I would sacrifice myself for the greater good,' said Fairchild, bowing his head gracefully.

'They'd eat you for breakfast,' muttered Sheldrake. He glanced towards Marigold's unoccupied desk. 'Well, Miss Sparks, it seems as if you'll be required to take minutes for Mr Beecher's department meeting yet again today, although I daresay you're getting used to it.'

Peggy shrugged. 'I don't mind. Mr Fairchild, are you joining us?'

He gave a gracious bow. 'Where you go I shall follow, dear lady.'

'Good morning,' said Beecher, as they gathered in one of the smaller libraries. It was lined with glass cabinets filled with antiquarian tomes in shades of scarlet, russet and jade which always made Peggy's spirit soar. 'Thank you to Miss Sparks for deputising for Miss Cecily once again.' Peggy caught his eye and smiled. 'And so to business. Mr Sheldrake, what news on *The Battle of Britain* pamphlet?'

Sheldrake's eyes lit up as he spoke. 'Three hundred thousand copies sold to date, sir, and hugely positive feedback from the British public and booksellers alike.'

'I spotted it on a W. H. Smith bookstand at the station this morning,' said Peggy proudly. 'I saw two men buying a copy each along with their morning papers.'

'Excellent,' said Beecher. 'Congratulations to you all. But of course, it's vital that we don't rest on our laurels, so let's discuss projects in the offing. Mr Fairchild, what have you got for us?'

Fairchild glanced up at him from the book of Shakespeare sonnets he was perusing with the naïve wonder of a child contemplating the world around it. He closed the volume, placing it on the table with deliberate care and resting his gaze on each person in turn before he spoke. 'The Bard,' he said, placing a hand on his chest and offering a reverential sigh.

Beecher blinked away his impatience and tried to adopt an encouraging expression. 'The Bard.'

Mr Fairchild clasped a hand over his mouth as he tried to suppress his bubbling emotion before continuing. 'He has everything we need to motivate – to inspire – to galvanise the nation.'

'Indeed,' said Beecher. 'The problem is, my dear Fairchild, that you have been promising to write something about the Bard for the past six months.'

Fairchild's benign face creased with a frown. 'I'm afraid I don't thrive creatively under pressure and the war has made me rather peevish.'

Beecher raised his eyebrows. 'I see your problem. However, *my* problem is that I need to produce publications to help with the war effort, and an inability to do that can make me rather peevish.'

111

Mr Fairchild nodded along, hanging on his every word. 'I understand, Mr Beecher, really I do, but creatively my hands are tied.'

Beecher glanced at Peggy. 'Miss Sparks, would you make a note, please, that Mr Fairchild is requesting a secondment to a different department, preferably one where his creativity is not required. I would suggest Religions or Empire.'

'Oh,' said Mr Fairchild, looking forlorn. 'But I like this department.'

'And we like you, Mr Fairchild, but I would be doing you and the Ministry a huge disservice if we kept you prisoner here when clearly you could flourish elsewhere.'

Fairchild bit his lip. 'If you think it's for the best.'

'Mr Fairchild, I do, and may I take this opportunity to thank you for all your efforts.' Beecher stood up and held out his hand so that Fairchild had no choice but to do the same. 'Goodbye, Mr Fairchild.'

Fairchild walked slowly to the door and paused before exiting. 'Well, goodbye then.' Peggy gave him a cheerful wave. She'd grown fond of Fairchild's gentle presence, even though he was as her grandmother might say, 'as useful as a teapot made of cheese'.

'And that's why I dislike writers,' said Beecher after he'd gone. 'And why it's an even greater shame that, A, I used to be one and, B, I still have to deal with them on a daily basis. Right, Sheldrake, what else is on the agenda?'

Sheldrake cleared his throat. 'The WVS would like a pamphlet on knitting with dog hair.'

Beecher gazed heavenwards. 'Lord help us all.'

As the meeting closed, Beecher turned to Peggy. 'Miss Sparks, would you mind staying behind for a few moments, please? I'd like a word.'

'Of course.' She noticed that Sheldrake remained in his seat as everyone else vacated the room.

So did Beecher. 'Run along now, Mr Sheldrake. My discussion with Miss Sparks does not concern you.'

'Oh,' he said, his cheeks reddening. 'I'll get back to the office then.'

'Good idea,' said Beecher. He turned to Peggy after Sheldrake had left. 'Now, Miss Sparks. How long have you been working here?'

'Just over a year, sir.'

'And do you enjoy the work?'

'Yes, very much. I've enjoyed working on the pamphlets. I feel as if they could be making a real difference to the war effort.' It surprised Peggy how easy she found talking to Beecher. She supposed it was his quiet encouragement and the fact that, unlike most of his peers, he listened to what his staff had to say. She admired the way he conducted himself and knew it had altered the way she conducted herself too.

Her gran had been the first one to notice. 'There's a change in you, Peggy Sparks,' she'd said one evening, regarding her granddaughter through narrowed eyes.

'Oh, really?' said Peggy, knowing that her gran didn't always react well to change. It had taken her a good ten years to accept that Queen Victoria had died.

'Yes,' said Emily with a resolute nod. 'A confidence. I like it.'

'Praise indeed, Peg,' said her mother with a wink.

'I'm glad you enjoy the work, Miss Sparks,' said Beecher, 'but I'm going to be frank with you. I feel as if you're under-utilised. I detect you have a keen brain that could be more productively employed.'

'I suppose my heart did sink a little when Mr Sheldrake put me down to write the dog hair pamphlet.'

'I can imagine. Of course, we all have to undertake the menial tasks at times. But these are rather more palatable if mixed with a few more interesting ones. Wouldn't you agree?'

Peggy sat up taller in her chair. 'I would, sir.'

'Good. Well, heaven help me if Sheldrake finds out that I've told you first . . .'

'Your secret is safe with me, Mr Beecher.'

His expression crinkled with amusement. 'I'm glad to hear it. I have it on good authority that there's a new broom about to sweep through the Ministry. I'm sure I don't need to tell you that operations have been somewhat mismanaged since the start of the war. Three ministers in just over a year is two ministers too many, and I didn't enjoy the Press chanting, *Hush, hush, chuckle who dares, another new minister's fallen downstairs* at every briefing for the duration of May last year. Also, far be it from me to criticise our minister, but he has never quite shaken off the hysterical "Cooper's Snoopers" headline which has painted the Ministry in a largely unfavourable light and somewhat hampered our best efforts.'

'My neighbour keeps accusing me of listening in on the party line,' Peggy told him.

'For which I can only apologise. Added to that, our government has become somewhat obsessed with the so-called fifth column and encouraging the country to "be like dad and keep mum", a slogan which enrages Mrs Beecher on an almost nightly basis.'

'My mother said she wished my dad was still around to keep her.'

'Again, I can only apologise. This is why I wanted to speak to you. I feel as if you are more in touch with what people actually think than perhaps my superior, Lord Candleford. I was therefore wondering if you might be able to write a weekly report for me, offering your honest opinions. It would be purely for departmental use, but I feel it might help us to better understand what information we should be offering the public.'

'You mean like my Mass Observation reports?'

'Precisely. I appreciate that you're offering the opinion of one woman, but I've read your Mass Observation reports and get the sense that your thoughts and feelings are similar to those echoed up and down the country. I also realise that a great number of our campaigns are aimed at a largely male audience and we are somewhat neglecting the women of this country who, let's be honest, are working like Trojans for the war effort. What do you think?'

'I'd be delighted to help in any way I can, sir.'

'Splendid,' said Beecher. 'Thank you, Miss Sparks.

115

There will, of course, be an additional remuneration in your pay for this and for the way that you've deputised for Miss Cecily so capably.'

'Thank you, sir.'

They were just about to leave when the door to the library burst open and Longforth appeared with Lear in tow. 'Ah, Beecher, this is where you've been hiding,' he said, ignoring Peggy's presence entirely. He looked around at the shelves. 'You poor lambs, being consigned to this cave of dusty old relics. Although . . .' He threw a sideways glance towards Lear, who sniggered at the veiled insult.

'Longforth,' said Beecher. 'What can I do for you? We're really rather busy publishing bestselling pamphlets and boosting morale with little time for idle chat, unfortunately.' He slid a copy of *The Battle of Britain* pamphlet across the table.

Peggy noticed a scintilla of irritation flicker across Longforth's expression before it was replaced with a smug smirk. 'Well now, that's exactly why I'm here, dear boy. You see, the powers that be are grateful to you and your department for producing these little pamphlets, but it's been decreed by Lord Candleford himself that our department would be better placed to oversee this particular publishing programme from here on in. You can of course carry on producing the other, more rudimentary publications – leaflets for the WVS, advice on avoiding bedbugs in air-raid shelters and so on. All vital work I'm sure,' he said with a sly glance at Lear.

Beecher's frown was thunderous. 'When was this decided?'

Longforth adopted a quizzical look. 'When was it, Lear? Oh yes, it was last night over drinks at our club.' He gave Beecher a sympathetic look. 'It really is a pity you're not a member. So many important decisions are made during these evenings. Anyway, I wanted to come and give you the news man to man. Didn't want you hearing it through the old Ministry grapevine, what?' Beecher regarded him in stony silence. 'Well, chip chip, old boy. As you say, there's no time for idle chit-chat when you have bestsellers to publish and morale to boost. Toodle pip,' he added before sweeping from the room with a snickering Lear in tow.

Peggy longed to offer a word of comfort to Beecher, to tell him that he shouldn't be bothered by these insufferable men with their superior airs and moneyed connections, but she could see that he didn't want to discuss it as he gathered his papers and ushered her to the door. 'Onwards, Miss Sparks,' he said without further comment.

'Onwards, sir,' she said.

As they returned to the department, Peggy noticed that the door to the mysterious woman's office was open. Her desk was immaculately ordered and she was reading a document through a pair of tortoiseshell glasses. She glanced up. 'Mr Beecher,' she called. 'Might I have a word?' Peggy detected the hint of an accent as she spoke.

'Of course, Mrs Pyecroft,' he said, entering her office and closing the door behind him.

Pyecroft. So that was her name. Peggy wracked her brain to work out if she'd heard it before, but her detective work was swiftly interrupted by Marigold appearing before her looking as excited as a child in a sweetshop. 'Peggy, there you are! I've been itching to see you. Look, I've got the photographs from Christmas. Come see.'

Peggy approached her desk and was amazed by what she saw. Marigold had managed to capture each one of her family perfectly. Nancy grinned out at her with bright, shining eyes whilst Emily and Dulcie laughed uproariously and Alice sat in her tatty old armchair with a cup of tea and a look of contentment on her face. 'Marigold, these are wonderful.'

'Not to be immodest, but I know! They've come out even better than I hoped. Here. These are for you.' She handed Peggy a smaller set of black and white pictures. 'I thought you could send some to Joe.'

'Thank you, Marigold. That's very kind of you.'

'Ah, Miss Cecily, nice of you to join us,' said Beecher, returning from his meeting. 'What's the excuse today? Was the waiter at the Savoy unusually slow in bringing you your morning coffee?'

'Sorry, Mr Beecher,' said Marigold. 'It won't happen again.'

'If only that were true,' he said with a weary sigh.

'Mr Beecher?' said Peggy. As he turned, she held out Marigold's photographs. 'I think you should see these. I wondered if perhaps we might be able to make use of Miss Cecily's photographic skills some time.'

He studied the pictures in silence, his brow lifting in surprise. 'Well, it would seem that this department is a veritable treasure trove of talent. Thank you for bringing these to my attention, Miss Sparks. I'll let you know if an opportunity arises.'

Marigold seized Peggy's arm as he disappeared into his office. 'Peggy, you're a marvel. I would never have had the courage to show them to him. Thank you.'

'You're a good photographer,' said Peggy. 'You deserve it.'

'I wouldn't get your hopes up,' said Sheldrake. 'No one's going to steal Cecil Beaton's crown.'

Marigold looked horrified. 'As if I'd dare. Besides, Cessie would probably share it with me if I asked him,' she added, winking at Peggy.

'Cessie,' muttered Sheldrake, shaking his head.

'Cooee!' called a voice from the door. They turned to see Cordelia striding towards them wearing sage-green dungarees and a honey-coloured satin blouse.

'Cordy, darling!' cried Marigold, clapping her hands together in delight. 'You look fabulous.'

Cordelia struck a film-star pose. 'If it's good enough for the Land Girls then it's good enough for me,' she said with a chuckle. She turned to Peggy. 'Did you see M's photographs? Aren't they top hole?'

'They're wonderful,' said Peggy.

'Guess what Peggy did?' said Marigold. 'She showed my photographs to Beecher and he liked them. Said he might even use some of them in our publications.'

Cordelia stared at Peggy for a moment before pulling her into a tight embrace. 'Thank you, dear Peggy. I've been telling M for years how talented she is. She deserves the recognition.'

'I didn't really do anything,' mumbled Peggy.

'We must celebrate,' said Cordelia. 'M and I are going

to the Café de Paris on Saturday with a gang of friends. Do come.'

'What a splendid idea,' said Marigold. 'You can stay with me afterwards if you like. Cordy always does.' Peggy was momentarily struck dumb. She was used to working alongside Marigold now and was even quite fond of her, but she couldn't imagine socialising with this group of born-again bright young things. Marigold's face fell at her hesitation. 'I understand. You don't want to.'

'No,' said Peggy. 'It's not that. It's just that . . .' Her mind raced as she fumbled for the right words. 'I wouldn't have anything to wear.'

'I could lend you something, or Cordy can.'

'Absolutely,' said Cordelia, regarding Peggy for a moment. 'I have an emerald sequinned evening gown which would suit you to a tee.'

Peggy shrank under their scrutiny. She had no desire to go but didn't know how to refuse without seeming impolite. 'Oh, very well,' she said.

'Wonderful,' said Marigold, clapping her hands with glee. 'This is going to be so much fun.'

'Sorry to interrupt your vital social arrangements, Miss Sparks, but is there any chance I can have the minutes from the department meeting by lunchtime?' asked Sheldrake.

'Yes, of course, sorry. I'll do it right away,' said Peggy, flushing with embarrassment whilst Marigold and Cordelia continued to chatter away like excited parrots.

Peggy completed the task in no time at all and had little inclination to start work on the dog hair pamphlet so decided to turn her attention to the report Beecher had requested. She fed a clean sheet of paper through the roller of her typewriter and set the carriage to the left, then stared at the blank sheet in front of her. She steepled her hands together as she considered how to title it. 'South-east London despatches' sounded rather haughty and 'musings of a south-east London girl' too vague. She glanced at Marigold's photos of her family, calling to mind their worries for Joe, how they made their rations stretch, how they survived the raids and the blackouts. All they were trying to do was to live day to day, to get through this war, and they did it all with as much cheer and determination as they could muster. This was the story that Peggy wanted to tell, of the people she loved and the ones she missed. She wanted to tell her version of events and she knew in her heart that it was a version she shared with many other young women. It might be only Mr Beecher who read it but that didn't matter to Peggy. By committing it to paper, she was making it into something, and that was enough. She felt a shiver of excitement as she placed her fingers on the keys and began to type:

One Girl's Guide to Surviving the War, by Peggy Sparks

It was mid-afternoon when Wallace Dalton appeared in their department. 'Peggy Sparks, stealer of teaspoons and hearts. And Miss Cecily, what a sublime joy it is to see you as ever,' he said, bowing to them both. 'Sheldrake,' he added as an afterthought.

'May we help you, Mr Dalton?' said Sheldrake with a strained air.

'Well, my dear man, it's rather more a case of how I

can help you. I've been transferred to your department, you see.'

'Really?' said Sheldrake, making no attempt to hide his irritation.

'Really,' said Dalton, plonking himself down at Mr Fairchild's now vacant desk. 'And I'm very much looking forward to it,' he added, flashing a grin towards Marigold and Peggy. Peggy looked on as he flirted with Marigold, who seemed to hang on his every word. She could see he was charming, but there was something about Wallace Dalton that bothered her. He was a little too sure of himself. 'Cocksure,' her grandmother would have declared, 'and not to be trusted with your money or your heart.'

Peggy stayed late to finish her report. Even Sheldrake went home before her, leaving Peggy to relish the lamplit hush and the occasional indistinct hum of Mr Beecher on the telephone behind the closed door of his office. Her fingers glided across the keys as she became lost in her writing. When she was finished, Peggy laid out the pages, rereading them with quiet satisfaction. She wanted to be honest, to show what life was really like for people like her. She talked about where she lived, about the library, the town and the neighbours who looked out for one another. She told stories of her walks with her grandmother and Badger the dog, of their talks about Joe and how much they missed him. She wrote about Nancy praying every night by the side of her bed for the safe return of her daddy and of Flo looking paler and paler with worry at each passing day. She recounted how her mother queued long hours for meagre rations but always managed to feed them like kings. This wasn't an unusual story. In fact, it was the story of millions of women living through the war along the length and breadth of the country – in London, Manchester, Liverpool, Bristol, Cardiff and goodness knows where else. This was about women fighting and surviving, not on the battlefields but in their own back yards. Peggy piled the papers together, sitting back with a sense of pride.

She was aware of someone entering the room and turned to see Mrs Pyecroft standing in the doorway. 'Is Mr Beecher still here?' she asked.

'Er yes, he is,' said Peggy, rising to her feet. 'I'm Peggy Sparks by the way.'

Mrs Pyecroft looked her up and down as if deciding whether this was worthy of reply. 'Pleased to meet you, Miss Sparks.' She knocked on Beecher's door and disappeared into his office as soon as she heard his grunting reply.

'Pleased to meet you too,' said Peggy as the door closed, curious to know more about this mysterious woman.

Chapter 10

The evening started well. Marigold and Cordelia's excitement as they transformed Peggy, like a life-sized Cinderella doll, was infectious. She rather enjoyed the way the pair picked out the perfect dress, helped her coiffure her hair in an elegant style which, according to Marigold, was 'the very latest thing from Paris' and set about applying a little too much make-up for her liking. Still. It was rare for Peggy to step out for an evening feeling she could turn heads. Her pulse raced when she found herself the recipient of several admiring glances as they entered the Café de Paris. Naturally, Marigold received far more and was greeted by everyone from the doorman to the band to their fellow revellers as if she were a deity walking amongst them. Peggy looked on with a certain amount of awe and a mild dose of jealousy. It wasn't that she wanted to be like Marigold. It was more curiosity as to what it might be like to glide through life like a swan on a lake.

She had heard tell of the Café de Paris, but nothing had prepared her for its opulent splendour. Peggy had visited dance halls over the years, of course, but this was something else. It was a flawless diamond on the crown of an empress with its buttery gilded interior and sweeping double staircase.

'Of course, the marvellous thing about it is that because we're in the basement, we're as safe as houses against the Luftwaffe,' said Cordelia as they made their way downstairs. Peggy followed in Marigold and Cordelia's wake, noticing how people greeted the pair warmly whilst eyeing her with a flicker of suspicion.

'Pay them no heed,' said Cordelia, handing her one of Marigold's beloved champagne cocktails. 'Drink this. For courage. You'll feel better.'

Peggy smiled, surprised and grateful. She took a sip, wincing against its sharp tang but welcoming the warming sensation. It helped. A little. Yet she couldn't quite shake off the nagging sense that she didn't belong here. She still felt like this at the Ministry from time to time – less so now with Beecher's gentle tutelage – but here, amongst the feathers and finery of the well-heeled, Peggy felt as out of place as a pig at a horse race. Marigold was in her element, of course, introducing her to 'the gang', as she called them. Peggy quickly lost track of their names, but as far as she could see, 'the gang' seemed to consist of several beautiful, bewildered young women who mostly seemed to be cousins or distant relatives of either Marigold or Cordelia.

'Oh, but you are too funny,' said an elfin-featured young woman wearing a choker of pearls embellished with what Peggy guessed to be a real diamond, when she told her that she'd never actually dined at the Ritz. 'Marigold, we must take Peggy for supper at the Ritz at once. I think

I'd die if I'd never eaten the filets de poulet au paprika.'
Peggy sat in silence, letting their chatter wash over her,
telling herself to enjoy it as Flo had instructed her to.

'You need to loosen up a bit, Peg. Have fun. You've
as much right to be there as them. And besides, Marigold
did invite you.'

She knew this was true, but looking round now,
Marigold seemed to have disappeared. Peggy scanned the
room and soon spotted her and Cordelia being led around
the dancefloor by a couple of servicemen. She sighed and
focused on enjoying the music. The band members were a
lively bunch. It was hardly surprising that nearly everyone
in the place except Peggy was dancing. She found herself
tapping her foot along to the music and took another sip of
her drink. She noticed several men in uniform, enjoying a
night off from their toil. She thought of Joe and wondered
where he was right at this moment.

'I don't believe I've had the pleasure,' said a voice. Peggy
looked up to find that its owner was nearer her age than
Marigold's. His dark hair was flecked with grey and his
ice-blue eyes bored into Peggy as if he were a collector
considering an artefact. 'Galahad Munro,' he said, taking
a seat beside her without waiting for an invitation.

'Peggy Sparks,' she said with a polite smile.

'Do I detect an accent?'

'I'm from Edenham,' she said with as much boldness
as she could muster.

'Never heard of it. No matter. I like all women from
all backgrounds,' he said, inching closer. Peggy's neck
bloomed scarlet and her mouth felt parched. She reached

for her drink and took a sip. 'I also like a woman who enjoys a drink. It helps to loosen one up, wouldn't you say?' he added, sliding his arm behind her so that she felt his hot breath on her neck. Peggy threw a panicked look towards the dancefloor, praying that Marigold or Cordelia would return to rescue her, but they were lost in the music. *Think, Peggy, think*, she told herself as she felt him press his body against hers. *What would Emily Marsh do?* Before she had a chance to reconsider, she'd swept her hand across the table and, with one deft swipe, tipped the contents of her glass neatly into Galahad Munro's lap.

'What the blazes!' he cried, leaping up as if his trousers were on fire. 'This is a Savile Row suit!'

'I'm most dreadfully sorry,' lied Peggy, hurrying to her feet and gathering her things. 'I hope it's not too costly to clean. Please excuse me, I have a train to catch,' she called over her shoulder.

Without a backward glance towards Marigold or her friends, she dashed towards the exit and out into the open. Her cheeks burned crimson as she cast around, assessing her options. What had she been thinking, agreeing to this ridiculous charade? She was a fool. Plain and simple. She had allowed Marigold to persuade her that their worlds could happily collide, but Peggy knew better. The sky was buzzing with planes and her instinct was to head in the direction of the train station and find a shelter until the raid passed. She turned down a side street and was promptly knocked off her feet by a blast so thunderous and terrifying, her immediate thought was that it had to be the end of the world.

Peggy sat up. She squinted. Smoke swirled like fog. The world was muted. Her ears ringing. She pulled herself to her feet, dusting down her finery. For a split second there was silence. The world took a breath. And then it began. The screams. The shouts. People running from the hotel opposite the Café de Paris. Faces rigid with shock. She ran towards them.

'What was it?'

'Where did it hit?'

'Where are those screams coming from?'

'Down there.'

'The Café.'

'Oh, dear God.'

Peggy realised afterwards how humans are when terror strikes. They all react in exactly the same way. People to whom you wouldn't normally give the time of day are immediately cast as comrades-in-arms. Strangers helping strangers. That was how it was in a war. The manager of the hotel seemed to take charge and everyone was happy to let him.

'We've sent for help, but let's see what we can do for the poor wretches while we're waiting for it to arrive. Take the walking wounded over to the hotel, and anyone with a torch, come with me and see if we can help those trapped below.'

'I've a torch,' said Peggy, stepping forwards.

The man looked at her kindly. 'Please could you lend it to one of my lads? I don't think it's going to be safe or fit for a lady down there.'

'But . . .'

The man stared at her with pleading eyes. 'You look to be the same age as my daughter and I wouldn't want her going down there either. Please, miss.'

'All right,' said Peggy. 'But please look out for my friend. Marigold, her name is. She was down there dancing and I . . .'

The man patted her hand. 'I'll try to find her.'

Survivors were beginning to filter out through the mangled wreckage now, faces creased in bewildered shock. Glittering evening dresses torn, starched white shirts bloodied and filthy. Peggy scanned the crowd for a glimpse of Marigold and spotted the young woman with the pearl choker. She hurried over. 'Hello,' she said, wishing she'd paid more attention to her name. 'Are you all right?'

The woman gazed at Peggy, seeming to look straight through her. 'Shards of glass like daggers,' she murmured.

Peggy noticed her clutching her arm. 'Shall I take a look at that?'

The woman allowed her to prise her arm gently from her grip. Peggy felt bile rise up from her stomach as she saw the vast bloom of blood on her dress and a cut so deep, the milky bone was visible beneath. She took a deep breath and pulled a clean handkerchief from her pocket. 'Right. I need you to press that firmly against the cut and come with me to the hotel to find a nice clean dressing.'

'So kind,' said the woman, leaning against Peggy as she led her across the road.

'Did you see Marigold?' she asked.

The woman shook her head. 'She was dancing with Cordy. The place was full of smoke. I couldn't see anyone.'

129

No news is good news, decided Peggy, helping her into the lobby of the hotel which had quickly been established as a makeshift hospital. There were a handful of women already doing their best to help people by ripping up tablecloths and napkins.

One of them approached Peggy. 'I'm an off-duty nurse. Can I help you?'

'This lady has a bad cut. I've told her to press my handkerchief against it, but it's quite deep.'

The nurse was unfazed. 'Come here, my love. Let's see what we can do for you.'

'So kind,' murmured the young woman again.

'I need to go and look for someone,' said Peggy. 'I'll be back soon.' She returned to the street just as the manager of the hotel was emerging from the wreckage. 'Excuse me,' she said, approaching him. 'Did you see my friend?'

The man looked up at her, eyes blank and distracted. He shook his head. 'How can they?' he whispered. 'How can they do that to innocent people? It's monstrous.'

Peggy felt panic rise up as she scanned the crowds behind him. An entire troop of dancing girls were standing unscathed and smoking on one corner. Two ambulances had arrived and a stretcher crew was beginning to bring the injured and dead up from below.

'Where the bleedin' 'eck are the other ambulances?' shouted one of the crew. 'We're going to need at least half a dozen more to deal with all this.'

'Please,' said Peggy, hurrying over to them. 'Please. I'm looking for my friend.'

'Sorry, love. We haven't got time to identify people. We've just got to bring 'em out. It's carnage down there.'

Peggy watched in stupefied horror as stretcher after stretcher emerged, but Marigold was nowhere to be seen. Some brought survivors and others bodies covered with tablecloths and coats. Then one emerged and she froze. A body lay on the stretcher draped with the mink coat which Marigold had so proudly flaunted earlier that evening. Peggy rushed forwards, eyes brimming with tears. 'Please,' she said to the stretcher bearers as they placed it in a waiting ambulance. 'This is my friend. I lost her when I left the club.' She began to sob.

One of the bearers frowned. 'I don't think so, love. This one here is a bloke.' He lifted the corner of the coat to reveal the trousers of an expensive Savile Row suit.

'Oh,' said Peggy, taking a step back.

'Peggy?' called a voice. She turned to see Marigold peering out at her from a waiting ambulance, holding a balled-up, bloody napkin to her wounded head.

'Marigold,' cried Peggy, rushing to her side. 'Thank goodness. You're all right.'

Marigold seemed to look through Peggy. 'Cordy's dead,' she whispered as the tears began to stream down her face.

'Oh, Marigold. I'm so, so sorry.'

'Right. Mind your backs,' said the driver, moving forwards to close the door of Marigold's ambulance. 'We're ready to go.'

'Can I go with her?' asked Peggy.

The driver shook his head. 'Sorry, love. No room.

We're taking them to St Thomas's, but your friend should go home tomorrow. She just needs patching up.'

Marigold stared out at Peggy. She looked as if she needed a good deal more than to be patched up. She seemed tiny and helpless as she palmed at her tears before closing her eyes and turning her face away. 'Goodbye, Marigold. They'll take good care of you. I'll see you soon,' called Peggy to the closing door, feeling completely useless and utterly wretched.

Chapter 11

Marigold was absent from the office for a month. Despite Beecher's assertion, when she arrived for work on Monday, that Peggy should go home too, she was determined to stay. She had talked it over with her mother the night before.

'Are you absolutely sure you should be going in, Peg? You've had an awful shock.'

Peggy shook her head. 'It's made me even more determined to help bring an end to this awful war and get Joe home, Mum.'

Alice pulled her daughter close and kissed the top of her head. 'I'm proud of you, Peg.'

Beecher gathered them together to give a short speech before work. Peggy noticed Mrs Pyecroft standing by the door, her expression solemn as they listened.

'I'm sure you're all aware of the terrible events on Saturday night at the Café de Paris, although our press division, in its wisdom, seems to be playing it down so as not to alarm the general public. I, however, find the whole thing most dreadfully sad. I know we are all thinking of the dead and their families.' He paused for a moment to collect himself. 'Thankfully our very own Miss Sparks escaped unscathed and Miss Cecily only sustained a minor injury, but sadly, her friend and our colleague from the Photographs department, Lady Cordelia Fitzwilliam, was killed. I have granted Miss Cecily leave of absence for the time being. I wonder if we might arrange for some flowers to be sent.'

'I'll do that, Mr Beecher,' said Peggy. 'I was planning to visit Marigold.' She had a sudden urge to do something, to help in some way. She'd only met Cordelia a handful of times but knew how close she and Marigold had been. It also made her regret her hasty judgement of the pair, dismissing them as foolish. They had been nothing but kind to her. She valued this and admired their friendship. It made her think of Flo, which brought tears to her eyes as she wondered what she would do if she ever lost her.

'Thank you, Miss Sparks. I also hope this monstrous event serves to strengthen our efforts. That is all,' he said, retreating to his office with an air of defeat.

'Well,' said Sheldrake after everyone had dispersed. 'It's a terrible tragedy but I can't say we'll miss Lady Cecily's contribution to our workload.'

Peggy glared at him. 'How can you be so unfeeling?' she demanded.

He stared at her in surprise. 'I beg your pardon. I'm not being disrespectful to the dead. I'm merely stating a fact.'

'This is not the time,' said Peggy, surprised by her own outburst. 'You should be ashamed of yourself.'

'Quite right, Peggy,' said Dalton, looking up from his desk, clearly relishing the moment. 'That's poor form, Sheldrake.'

Sheldrake swallowed. 'I apologise. You're right. I'm sorry, Miss Sparks.'

'I should think so too,' she said, turning back to her desk, shaking with anger.

Later that morning, Peggy was in Beecher's empty office delivering the next of her reports when the phone rang. She picked up the receiver. 'Publishing department?'

'Where's Mr Beecher?'

'He's in a meeting,' said Peggy, irritated by this abrupt greeting. 'May I help you?'

'I doubt it. Who is this?'

Peggy was stoked with indignation. 'Peggy Sparks. And who is this?'

'Frank Bauman.'

Of course. No one apart from Henry Longforth was as rude as this man. Peggy had no time for his games today. 'Shall I ask Mr Beecher to call you?'

'Don't you want to know why I've called?'

Not really, she thought. Peggy cleared her throat. 'Only if you want to entrust me with that information,' she said, losing patience.

'Well. Here's the thing, Peggy Sparks. As your department is no longer publishing the Official War Books, as they're now called, my company has lost that business.'

'I'm sorry to hear that.'

'You're very good at giving out sympathy, aren't you?'

Usually, Peggy wouldn't have reacted, but she felt differently today and not just because of the events of Saturday night. She was tired of the rudeness of others. 'Look, Mr Bauman, I seem to remember you complaining when we gave you too much business and now you're complaining that you don't have enough. I believe we still use your company for the pamphlets we do produce and it really isn't my job to account for the ebb and flow of printing demand. That is your job as a businessman. Now, I'm afraid, I have other business to address and will ask Mr Beecher to call you at his earliest convenience. Good day, Mr Bauman.' She replaced the receiver with shaking hands. 'Oh Peggy. What have you done?' she muttered before turning to see Mrs Pyecroft standing in the doorway, eyeing her with interest.

'Good morning, Miss Sparks.'

'Sorry, Mrs Pyecroft, that phone conversation, I was merely . . .' began Peggy.

Mrs Pyecroft held up a hand to silence her. 'You were merely saying what needed to be said. I understand. And so will Mr Beecher. And Mr Bauman too. Today is a difficult day. However, I would like to discuss certain matters with you at some stage with a view to you perhaps helping me with some of the work I'm undertaking. I'll ask Mr Beecher's permission first, of course.'

Peggy didn't hesitate before replying. 'Yes. Yes, please. I would like that very much.'

Mrs Pyecroft nodded. 'All in good time. Do give Miss Cecily my condolences and best wishes when you see her, won't you?'

Laurie offered to accompany Peggy on her visit to see Marigold. She was grateful to him. It wasn't that she minded going, more that she wasn't sure what she would find when she got there. Marigold's apartment was located in glamorous Fitzrovia, renowned for its drinking clubs and cafés which attracted famous writers and artists from far and wide. As they made their way along the lively street, offering a nod to Paris with its busy bistros, she was sure she spotted George Orwell emerging from a restaurant, having recognised him from the back cover of the books she used to place on Edenham library's shelves. They turned off the main road on to a mews flanked on either side by smart apartments with a surprising lack of bomb damage.

'This is the place,' she said to Laurie, glancing down at the slip of paper where she'd scribbled the address. She reached over to rap the door knocker. There was silence within.

'Perhaps she's gone out,' suggested Laurie.

'I doubt it,' said Peggy. 'The curtains are still drawn.'

Laurie glanced at his watch. 'It's gone five. She's probably preparing for the blackout.'

Knowing Marigold as she did, Peggy very much doubted this. She knocked on the door again. 'Marigold! Are you in there? It's Peggy. And Laurie. We've come to see if you're all right.' She cast around and noticed a curtain twitching in the house opposite. 'Nice to know people are as nosey here as they would be on my street.' She leaned her ear to the door, detecting the sound of someone moving around inside and then the crash of what sounded like a bottle falling on to the floor. Peggy and Laurie glanced at one another. 'Come on, Marigold. We're getting cold out here. Please let us in.'

'Fine,' shouted a voice from within. 'I'm coming. Just stop all the banging, will you? I've got a dreadful headache.'

'Sorry,' said Peggy. 'We just wanted to see if you were all right.'

It was patently clear that Marigold was not all right as she opened the door. Peggy inhaled sharply at her appearance. Marigold looked otherworldly. Her face was almost translucent with streaks of make-up where she'd obviously been crying. Her head was flecked with scratches and one of her hands was bound in a bandage. Marigold opened the door, barely registering their presence before turning and tottering back along the corridor as if in a trance. Peggy and Laurie exchanged a glance before following her inside. The apartment was small but beautifully decorated with oil paintings and expensive-looking ornaments on every surface. Marigold stumbled into the large lounge with its marble fireplace and huge gilt-framed mirror. She plonked herself back on the sofa before lighting a cigarette and taking a sip of her drink which, from the empty bottle on the occasional table in front of her, contained the last of the vodka.

'Cheers,' she slurred, lifting the glass to them both before knocking it back and taking a deep drag on her cigarette.

'We brought you some flowers,' said Peggy, frustrated at how feeble this sounded.

Marigold blinked up at her. 'How lovely,' she said vaguely.

'Why don't I put them in a vase?' suggested Laurie, taking them from Peggy.

'Yes, good idea.' Peggy watched him go before turning back to Marigold. What could she say? Marigold was clearly in a bad way. How could she make this better for her? Peggy looked around and spotted a photograph beside the overflowing ashtray. It was of Marigold and Cordelia. They were laughing, heads inclined towards one another, two friends caught in the moment, a pose similar to the one in the photograph Marigold had taken of Emily and Dulcie. Peggy tried to imagine what she'd say to her grandmother in the same circumstances, how she'd make it better for her. And then she realised that she couldn't. All she could do was be honest. That was all you could ever do.

She sat down next to Marigold and took her uninjured hand. 'I am very sorry about Cordy. I can't imagine how terrible this is for you.'

Marigold gazed at her through rapidly blurring eyes. She blinked as the tears fell but made no attempt to wipe them away. 'I feel as if I've glimpsed the pits of hell, Peggy,' she whispered, shaking her head. 'It was unspeakable.' Peggy squeezed her hand as Laurie returned, quietly setting the flowers on the mantelpiece and coming to sit on the other side of Marigold. She was silent for a moment, her breathing laboured as she relived the horrifying moments in her mind.

'You don't have to tell us if it's too painful,' said Peggy.

'She died in my arms,' said Marigold. Peggy glanced at Laurie, who placed an arm around her other shoulder. 'One minute we were getting ready to dance to the Andrews Sisters and the next moment . . .' She paused before continuing. 'Carnage. Screaming and crying. I tried to help. I tried to save them. To save her. We ripped up tablecloths and even our dresses, but it was pointless. Useless. I held her in my arms and told her I loved her.'

'Oh Marigold,' said Peggy as she and Laurie held her while she wept. Not for the first time, it struck Peggy how quickly life could be reduced to nothing, but equally how at times such as this, when the world was ink-blank, offering not the slightest shred of hope or light, the thing that remained and which in turn recharged that hope, was love.

Peggy refused to take no for an answer as she bundled Marigold back to 26 Evelyn Street. Alice, Emily and Flo were even more adamant that she should stay ('You can't be on your own with grief. It ain't healthy,' declared Emily), whilst Nancy was positively skipping with joy to see her favourite member of the aristocracy again.

'I'm sorry your friend died,' she told her. 'I would be very sad if Iris died.' Tears sprang to Marigold's eyes again, for which she received the fiercest of hugs from Nancy until the small girl was sure that she felt 'all better'.

It was strange for Peggy to be going to work every day with Marigold staying home. Peggy had batted away Marigold's protests and given up her bed, sleeping perfectly well on the fold-out camp bed which their next-door neighbour, Mrs Cooper, who had lost both her sons in the Great War, had lent them. ('It was my Tom's. He'd want you to use it,' she said with a sad sigh.) Nancy was forbidden from sneaking in during the night but often appeared on weekend mornings when Peggy would make them all tea and her niece would bring in her latest library book and insist on reading it to them. Peggy enjoyed these moments with Marigold and Nancy chattering happily.

One morning, Nancy appeared with a copy of *Little House on the Prairie* under her arm. 'Oh goody,' said Marigold, as she climbed into bed beside her. 'I've been enjoying getting to know Laura and her family.'

Nancy gazed up at her. 'Didn't you read these books with your mother when you were little?'

Marigold shifted a little, plumping up the pillows behind them. 'Mummy was always quite busy. I had a nanny, but she didn't really read to me much. She thought books would give me ideas.'

'Perish the thought,' said Peggy with a wry smile.

'You had a nanny? Like in Peter Pan?' asked Nancy. 'Was she a dog?'

Marigold and Peggy laughed. 'No, but that would have been lovely,' said Marigold. 'Now, where did we get to in this story?'

Nancy frowned at the pages. 'It's the part where the family make the journey across the creek. I'm a bit worried about their dog, Jack.' Badger's ears pricked up from his position at the end of Peggy's camp bed.

Marigold patted her hand. 'I'm sure he'll be fine. Dogs are very resourceful.'

Nancy nodded and began to read. By the time she'd reached the end of the chapter, both she and Marigold were in floods of tears as the poor dog was lost, swept away by the turbulent creek's current.

141

Peggy eyed them both with concern, taking the book from Nancy's hands. 'Let me read the next chapter to you,' she said, knowing what lay in store. Nancy and Marigold clung to one another as Peggy relayed the events of that night and the moment when Pa stood ready with his gun, fearing that the green-eyed creature approaching their camp was a coyote. When Peggy revealed his true identity, the pair laughed and wept with relief, and Badger wiggled over to join in the celebration.

'Oh Jack,' cried Marigold, kissing the top of first Nancy's and then Badger's head. 'Thank goodness.'

'Nancy! Time to get dressed,' called Flo from the next room.

Nancy's face fell. 'But I wanted to read more.'

'There's always tomorrow,' said Peggy.

'All right,' said Nancy. She planted a kiss on Marigold's cheek before leaving. 'I'm so glad you're here.'

Marigold shook her head after she'd gone. 'Your niece should be prescribed as a cure for all ills. She's a tonic and an absolute darling.'

'Most of the time,' said Peggy. 'I'm sorry she asked about your mother, and for the tears. You've had more than your fair share of them lately.'

Marigold fixed Peggy with a steady gaze. 'Honestly, Peggy, being here with your family has been one of the best times of my life.'

Under their watchful care, Marigold grew stronger every day. She still looked pale and drawn, but Emily would take her for daily walks with Badger and she would often accompany Flo when she went to collect Nancy

142

from school. Naturally, Nancy was proud to show off her new friend, telling her open-mouthed schoolmates that 'Lady Marigold Cecily is practically related to the King.' Peggy knew that although Marigold looked better, she was struggling inside. She often woke at night to hear her sobbing or found her staring out of the window with tears streaming down her face. She did her best to offer a word of comfort or place a hand on her shoulder but knew in her heart that she had no power to dissolve Marigold's pain. It would always be there, and for a good while, it would be like a bubbling pot, threatening to rise to the surface at any moment.

For her part, Peggy was glad to be able to offer daily updates at work on Marigold's progress. Even Sheldrake asked Peggy to 'give Miss Cecily my regards' after inquiring about her state of health one day, whilst Dalton promised to 'take her to lunch at her favourite restaurant whenever she feels well enough'.

Of course, Beecher was always keen to know how she was. 'Tell her there is no hurry for her to return, but we'll be delighted to see her as and when she feels able.' Peggy was always struck by his kindness. She got the feeling that there weren't many other department heads at the Ministry who were quite so benevolent as Mr Beecher. She was enjoying writing her weekly reports for him, too. He rarely commented on them but always thanked her for her 'invaluable insight'. She knew that he disapproved of Lord Candleford and his like, who seemed determined to preach to the British public, whereas Mr Beecher was of the opinion that the majority of people didn't need anyone to tell them to 'stay cheerful' or 'make do' or 'carry on'. It was second nature and always had been – at least, that was Peggy's experience.

One Saturday afternoon, Marigold suggested a walk to the top of Edenham Hill. 'I've been promising Nancy I'll manage it, and I feel as strong as a carthorse now, thanks to your mother's home cooking and your grandmother's weekly baking.'

'Why don't we all go?' said Alice. 'Charlie loves to look up at the barrage balloons from his pram, and the sun's out today. We should make the most of it.'

The early part of spring had been chilly, but it felt as if the weather was beginning to turn with daffodils starting to nudge their progress up through the slowly warming soil. The sun was doing its best to warm the day through a hazy sky as they made their way to the park. Nancy held Marigold's hand, skipping along by her side, while Emily and Alice walked behind with Badger on the lead. Peggy pushed a gurgling Charlie in his pram with Flo beside her.

'Seems funny to think of Joe in a place where the ink dries up when he's writing to me while we're shivering in the cold, doesn't it?' said Flo, pulling up the collar of her coat.

Peggy nodded. 'I don't think I'd like it with all that sand and millions of flies.'

'He's been bitten to pieces,' said Flo. She was silent for a moment. 'Do you think he's all right, Peg? It's so difficult to tell from his letters.'

Peggy knew what she meant. Thanks to the censors, a

letter could only say so much. *I'm fine. It's hot. I love you.* There was no way of knowing what was really happening, where Joe was or what he'd seen. To be honest, Peggy wasn't sure what good this information would serve, anyway. If they knew he'd been under fire, they would only worry more. It was enough for now to receive his letters and to know he was alive. She knew he was more honest in his letters to her, but she also knew that he wouldn't want Flo to be any more worried than she was already. Peggy had decided that it was now her role to protect the family as Joe had always done, and it was her duty to do all she could to keep their hopes alive. 'I think he's all right, Flo,' she told her. 'I know you can't stop worrying. No one can, but if Joe Sparks tells me we'll meet again then I believe him. He's a man of his word.'

'He's certainly that,' said Flo, seeming reassured.

They'd reached the park now and Charlie was particularly taken with a group of pigeons. 'Dat, dat, dat,' he told Peggy, pointing a chubby finger in their direction.

'Yes,' she agreed. 'Pigeons, Charlie.'

'Horrible filthy things,' said Emily, letting Badger off his lead and watching with satisfaction as he bowled straight towards the birds, who scattered into the sky with a boisterous flapping of wings.

'Ooh,' said Charlie, gazing up at them before his eyes came to rest on a barrage balloon in the distance. 'Dat, dat, dat,' he said.

'Everything's dat, isn't it, Charlie?' said Flo, chucking her son's cheek.

'Dat,' he confirmed with a gummy grin.

All the while, Nancy was filling the air with a flurry of questions. 'Do you think those barrage balloons are bigger than an elephant? How many are there in the whole of London? How do they stop the Jerries from bombing us? Do you think they will bomb us?'

'Yes, two thousand, the Luftwaffe can't get near and no,' said Emily.

Nancy frowned. 'But what about . . .'

'Nancy,' said Marigold. 'You promised to climb up that big hill when I was feeling better, and today, I'm ready.'

Nancy's face lit up as she held out one hand which Marigold duly took before glancing over her shoulder and holding out the other. 'Come on, Auntie Peg.'

'All right,' said Peggy, following after them with Badger in tow whilst Alice, Emily and Flo found a bench at the bottom of the hill where Charlie could get his fill of pigeons and air defences.

Marigold had to stop every now and then to catch her breath, but she refused all offers of help and managed to keep pace with Peggy all the way to the top. They looked out across the bruised and battered city with buildings still standing proud in the spring sunshine and others like skeletons, their bones exposed to the world, roofs open to the sky. Hitler had turned his attention away from London now, but that wasn't to say there weren't raids. They'd just become more used to them. They could never really be off their guard and knew they wouldn't be until the war was over.

'Makes my blood boil to see my city like this,' said Marigold, staring into the distance.

'Me too,' said Peggy, struck by their common ground.

'It's good to see you with some colour in your cheeks, though.'

'I feel like a completely different person,' Marigold said. 'Isn't it strange how life changes in a heartbeat? One event and your life and the lives of hundreds of others are altered forever.' Peggy watched her. She had never heard her talk like this before. 'All I cared about was having a good time, but now . . .' Her voice trailed off before she gave a shrug. 'I don't know. Somehow Cordy's death makes me want to live even more.'

'That's a good thing, surely?'

Marigold nodded, glancing towards where Nancy was playing a game of chase with Badger. 'It's all down to you and your family's kindness. I would have completely fallen apart without you.'

Peggy nudged her arm. 'It's what people do,' she said.

'Some people,' said Marigold.

Peggy could tell she was thinking about her own family as her eyes travelled towards where Emily, Alice and Flo were sitting on the bench with Charlie, chattering and laughing. The thought had occurred to Peggy too on more than one occasion. She could see that Marigold's mother wouldn't be the kind to throw her arms around her daughter, but still, she'd wondered at the apparent complete lack of contact. She didn't have to wonder about it for much longer, as they arrived back home a while later to find a large official-looking car parked outside the house.

'Coo, no one told me Churchill was coming for tea. I'd have saved my rations and baked something special,' said Emily as they rounded the corner.

147

The car was causing quite a stir with groups of small children watching at a distance and Mrs Cooper outside her front door, pretending to sweep her step. 'Mummy!' cried Marigold, rushing forwards as her mother emerged from the car, immaculate as ever in a tight-fitting rose-coloured jacket and skirt, her pearls at her throat.

She looked horrified as Marigold threw her arms around her, shrinking back and whispering with some ferocity, 'Pull yourself together, Marigold. You're making a scene.'

Marigold stepped back as if she'd been stung. 'Sorry,' she muttered. 'I'm just pleased to see you.'

'Yes, well. Winnie insisted I take his car and come to collect you. I had no idea you were staying here,' she said, throwing a distasteful look towards the house. Peggy noticed that her grandmother was eyeing Lady Cecily with a similar aversion. 'Gather your things now. You're coming back to Greymore. I'll wait for you in the car.'

Marigold threw a panicked look towards Peggy, who glanced at Emily. Quick as a flash, her grandmother was standing before Marigold's mother. 'Why don't you come inside for a cup of tea, dear?' she said. 'Or if you like, I could send Mrs Cooper from next door to keep you company while you wait. She loves to chat about her health problems. She's got dozens of them. Her current issue is bunions.'

Lady Cecily glanced in horror towards Mrs Cooper, who was peering with interest at the unfolding scene. 'Very well,' she said.

'That's settled. I'm Emily Marsh, by the way. This is my

daughter Alice, granddaughter Peggy and my grandson's wife, Florence.'

'And I'm Nancy. And that's my brother Charlie,' said the small girl.

'Lady Lavinia Cecily,' said Marigold's mother, ignoring Nancy entirely and holding out her hand to Emily who chose that moment to turn away.

'Follow me, Your Ladyship,' she said.

Lady Lavinia could not have looked more out of place if she'd been taking tea in the Sahara Desert. She sat very upright and very awkwardly at the kitchen table, sipping from the cup, her little finger outstretched. 'What's wrong with your pinkie?' asked Nancy, pointing at it and receiving a shushing from her mother.

'It's been a pleasure to have your daughter to stay,' said Alice, offering her one of Emily's queen cakes, which was rejected with an upturned nose and brief shake of the head. 'It was a terrible thing to be caught up in.'

Lady Lavinia inhaled and exhaled. 'She should never have been there in the first place. I don't know what she was thinking, but then that's Marigold for you. An utterly foolish girl.'

'That's not very kind,' whispered Nancy to Peggy who gave her a squeeze of agreement.

'She was just out having fun with her friends,' said Alice, catching Peggy's eye. 'They're young, after all.'

Lady Lavinia scowled. 'Fun? Fun? War isn't a time for fun.'

Emily had been watching the scene in silence, her eyes as bright as a crow's. 'Why not? You could be blown to bits at any minute. Why not live a little?'

Peggy held her breath as she watched these two women fix their eyes upon one another. It was like observing two cats squaring up for a fight. You couldn't be sure who would pounce first. 'All packed,' said Marigold, breezing into the kitchen, oblivious to what was going on.

Lady Lavinia's eyes didn't leave Emily's face as she rose to her feet. 'Good. Come along now, Marigold. Thank your friends before we go,' she said, gliding from the room without a backward glance. 'I'll wait for you in the car.'

Marigold had tears in her eyes as she hugged everyone in turn. 'I'll miss you all so much,' she said as Nancy clung around her waist. 'I can't thank you enough for your kindness.'

'You're welcome here any time you like,' said Alice, cupping her face in her hands.

'Well,' said Emily after they'd gone. 'Poor Marigold having to put up with a mother like that.'

'Now, Mum, you don't know why she's the way she is. Everyone's different,' said Alice.

Emily shrugged. 'I know what I see, and that woman is a rude, stuck-up cow.'

Nancy giggled. 'Mum!' scolded Alice.

Emily turned to Peggy with eyebrows raised. 'Sorry, Mum,' said Peggy. 'I can't disagree.'

June 1941

Dear Peg,

Thank you for your letter and the photographs. We've been through a bit of a dry patch with mail so it was a godsend to get them, even though they took their time arriving! I can't believe how clear the pictures are. I almost feel as if I can reach out and stroke Nancy's cheek. I'm so pleased to have them. Please thank Marigold for me. I was sorry to hear about her being caught up in the bombing at the Café de Paris and losing her friend. I understand only too well what it is to lose people you care about.

We lost three blokes on one day last month. Good men. One of them was only nineteen. David, his name was. Albert usually gets on with most things, but he went off into the desert on his own for a bit after that. David was from a village near to his home town and Albert knew his mother. He was a nice lad. Had a sweetheart back home. Albert and I sat and raised our tea mugs to them all that night and then agreed not to talk about it again. You can't dwell on all those unlived lives. You also have to stop yourself from thinking about how it might have been you. You can't help it, of course, but you can't let yourself. You'd go mad if you did. I hope Marigold's better now. It's nice that you all looked after her but then I wouldn't expect anything less.

I nearly forgot to tell you the big news. Guess who I met a month or so ago right beside ███ ████? Only Arthur Morris, the kid with the snotty nose who used to follow us around when we were kids. He was sweet on you as I remember. Can you believe I've bumped into someone from home on the other side of the world? But it seems to happen a lot out here. You'll be glad to know that he's lost the snotty nose but now has a sweaty upper lip. Mind you, we all do out here. What I wouldn't give for a drop of English rain, Peg. I promise I'll never moan about the cold or the wet back home again. It's as hot as hell and the flies drive you potty, but we're all getting pretty handy with the swatters now! Anyway, try not to be too broken-hearted, but Arthur has a sweetheart back home. A pretty young lady called Judy. He's quite the smitten kitten. As for me, I feel lucky to be in with a good bunch, especially Albert. For the most part I'm happy, even though I'd rather be at home, of course. It's a bit relentless at the moment, but if we survive another day, it's another day closer to coming home. I've heard that the Luftwaffe are leaving you alone now. I'm glad. I better sign off. I want to write to Mum, Gran and send another card to Flo and Nancy. Can't wait to hear all the news from home. I miss you. Stay safe, Peg. We'll meet again.

Love, Joe

Chapter 12

Marigold was a changed woman. Everyone noticed it. She was still late nearly every morning but there was a shift in her demeanour. She took more interest in their work, and not just that involving the photographs they published. One day she surprised Sheldrake when she asked him to explain what exactly was going on in the Middle East and listened intently as he told her. Another day, she arrived early to a department meeting and insisted on taking notes, delivering the resultant minutes only two days late. Peggy noticed a change in their working relationship, too. Marigold took an active interest in what Peggy was working on and in turn shared her own work. For once, she seemed genuinely invested in what was going on.

'I want to help,' she told Peggy. 'I'm sorry I didn't understand before why you're so determined to work to bring an end to this horrible war, but I do now.'

Peggy was buoyed by her admission but wondered deep down if this sentiment would endure or how Lady Marigold would cope if a crisis arose. Of course, what she didn't realise was that it would be her facing the crisis and that Marigold would be the one to help her navigate her way out of it.

At first, the missing report barely registered with Peggy. She had finished it late one evening while Beecher was still in his office. Peggy remembered Mrs Pyecroft appearing as she was putting on her coat ready to leave, nodding to her and then tapping on Beecher's door before disappearing inside. Not wanting to interrupt their conversation, Peggy had placed the report on her desk ready to give to Beecher in the morning. When she came into work the next day and it was gone, she assumed that he'd taken it from her desk. In fact, she didn't give any real thought to it until a few weeks later when she returned from lunch to be confronted by an animated Marigold, who was waving a printed pamphlet at her.

'You're a dark horse, Peggy Sparks!' she cried. 'Why didn't you tell me?'

Peggy frowned in confusion but was distracted by her telephone ringing. She picked it up, mouthing 'sorry' to Marigold who shook her head with a confidential wink. 'Peggy Sparks, Publications department.'

'Ah, Miss Sparks. Frank Bauman here. I'll cut straight to it. I'm telephoning to apologise.' Peggy couldn't have been more surprised if the King himself had appeared beside her desk. 'I see that I've stunned you into silence,' he continued, his voice laced with wry amusement.

'I confess I'm surprised.'

'My sister would tell you that I'm not known for my heartfelt apologies, but I learned from Mr Beecher recently that I must have caught you on a bad day when we last spoke. You were of course worried about your friend. I'm sorry for my rudeness. How is Miss Cecily?'

Peggy glanced over to where Marigold was reading the pamphlet she'd been waving around when she first came in and smiling to herself. 'She's doing very well, thank you.'

'Jolly good, as you British like to say. And you were happy with the document? I must say, I had no idea what a talented writer you are.'

'I beg your pardon?'

'Your *One Girl's Guide to Surviving the War*. I thought it was exceptional. Honest yet heartfelt. I was impressed, Miss Sparks.'

Peggy's mind started to turn somersaults. How on earth did Frank Bauman know about the report she wrote for Beecher's eyes only? She craned her neck to see what Marigold was reading and it was then that the title skipped into focus. Her title. Her writing. In print. For circulation to goodness knows how many destinations. 'Mr Bauman, may I ask if the leaflet has already been distributed?'

'Well, of course. It was on the order. Ten thousand copies circulated at home and overseas.'

'Overseas?'

'Yes. To America mainly. Is there a problem, Miss Sparks? Should I speak with Mr Beecher?'

'No,' said Peggy quickly. 'That won't be necessary. There's no problem at all. Thank you for your call, Mr Bauman. Now if you'll excuse me.'

'Of course, Miss Sparks. We have a war to win, after all.'

Peggy returned the telephone to its cradle with a

shaking hand. She rose to her feet, trying not to draw attention to herself as she moved forwards. 'Marigold,' she said, standing beside her desk, keeping her voice as hushed and calm as she could.

'Yes, Peggy?' she replied, gazing up at her with an open, friendly expression.

'Marigold, I need your help.'

Marigold stared at her in genuine surprise. '*You* need *my* help?'

Peggy nodded, leaning over her desk to whisper. 'That pamphlet you're holding . . .'

'It's jolly good, Peggy.'

'Thank you, but in actual fact, it's very bad. It was printed by accident.'

'Printed by accident?' cried Marigold.

'What was printed by accident?' said Sheldrake, bustling in from a meeting, his arms full of folders as usual.

'Nothing,' said Peggy, widening her eyes at Marigold who involuntarily put a finger to her lips. 'We were merely discussing what a dreadful disaster it would be if something were printed by accident and, say, distributed to America.'

'I'll say it'd be a disaster,' said Sheldrake, slumping in his chair and sifting through a mountainous pile of documents. 'Probably cause a diplomatic incident. Can you imagine? The PM's office having to iron it all out with the White House. It would almost certainly stop the Yanks joining the war and then who knows what would happen?'

Peggy gripped hold of Marigold's shoulder. 'A diplomatic incident caused by one small error.'

'And it'd be curtains for the poor dolt who wrote the

156

document in the first place. They might even end up in prison.'

'Prison,' repeated Peggy, gripping Marigold's shoulder even tighter.

'Right,' said Marigold, standing up and removing Peggy's iron grip. 'Excuse us, Mr Sheldrake. We have an important meeting to attend.'

'Where are we going?' whispered Peggy, following her from the office.

'Somewhere quiet where we can think.' She spotted the librarians' office and tapped on the door.

'Come in,' called Laurie and then, on seeing Peggy's distressed face. 'Whatever is the matter?'

It took two cups of strong, hot tea and three of Laurie's mother's honey biscuits before Peggy was able to join in their conversation. Marigold had explained the situation to Laurie who listened with patient concern before reading Peggy's words.

'It's hardly treasonous, Peggy. You're just telling people what it's like for you living through the war.'

'I know, but Sheldrake said . . .'

'Don't pay Sheldrake any heed,' said Marigold. 'That man sees the worst in everything.'

'But what am I to do?' she wailed.

Marigold and Laurie exchanged glances. 'You could let sleeping dogs lie and hope that no one finds out,' said Laurie.

Peggy looked doubtful. 'If Marigold has seen it then there must be copies circulating. Wait. Where did you get it from?' she asked.

'It arrived with the weekly finished copies of our printed matter, so there's only one copy in our department.'

'Well, that's something,' said Peggy. 'Who else will see it?'

Marigold shrugged. 'I'm not sure.'

Peggy put her face in her hands. 'I'll have to confess. Fall on my own sword.'

'But it's not your fault,' said Marigold. 'You're not to blame.'

'Maybe you could plead your case to the powers that be?' said Laurie.

'Beecher?' said Peggy.

'I'd go higher,' said Laurie.

Marigold's eyes lit up. 'I know exactly who to speak to.'

'Who?'

Marigold gave her an enigmatic smile. 'Winnie.'

'Winnie?'

She nodded emphatically. 'Lord Winslow Candleford. He's my godfather. Bit fierce, but a sweetie at heart. I'll talk to him.'

Dread pooled in Peggy's stomach. 'I'm not sure, Marigold.'

Marigold waved away her concerns with a casual hand. 'Leave it to me, Peggy. Let me help you.'

Peggy stared from her to Laurie, who gave a friendly shrug. What choice did she have? 'Thank you, Marigold,' she said, hoping she wouldn't live to regret it.

Peggy decided not to breathe a word about the pamphlet to her family. She told herself she didn't want to worry them, but in truth, she felt ashamed. Instead of working to bring her brother home and keep their hopes alive, she had snuffed it all out by carelessly leaving her report lying around where it had no doubt been scooped up with another copy-edited document. She couldn't quite believe the enormity of her crime.

'You looked tired, Peg,' said her mother, tucking a stray strand of hair behind her ear and placing her dinner in front of her.

'It's been a busy day.' Peggy stared at her plate, not feeling the least bit hungry.

'Something's happened,' said Emily, narrowing her gaze. 'Did one of them toffs say something?'

Peggy shook her head, avoiding Emily's eye. 'No, Gran. Everything's fine.'

'You never were a very good liar,' said Emily. 'Out with it.'

Peggy could hear Nancy and Charlie squealing and giggling as Flo read them a story upstairs and wished they were downstairs creating a distraction. 'Mum,' said Alice. 'Can't you let the poor girl have her dinner in peace?' And then, noticing the tears forming in her daughter's eyes, 'Oh Peg, whatever is the matter?'

'I've messed everything up,' cried Peggy. 'I've made a terrible mistake and I don't know what's going to happen.'

Peggy couldn't remember a time when her mother and grandmother hadn't known exactly the right things to say. Alice was always calm and reasonable, of course, whilst Emily faced any threat to her loved ones' happiness with blazing fierceness.

159

'You haven't done anything wrong,' Alice told her. 'Mr Beecher will surely know that.'

'And if he doesn't, he'll have me to deal with,' said Emily. 'And toff or no toff, Marigold is a diamond. She won't let you down.'

Emily was right. Marigold didn't let her down. She had booked an appointment that very next day with Lord Candleford who, as soon as he heard it was his god-daughter who needed to speak to him, insisted on taking her for dinner at the Ritz. Marigold was all reassuring smiles and soothing words when they reconvened in Laurie's office the next day.

'Actually, it was quite funny, because it turns out he didn't have a clue about your pamphlet being printed but he was delighted that I'd brought it to his attention and told me not to worry. Apparently, he's going to sort it all out with Beecher.'

For the first time in nearly a week, Peggy felt her pulse calm. 'And you're sure he wasn't angry?'

Marigold shook her head. 'Well, to be honest, Winnie's always a bit cross, but no, no more than usual. Trust me. All will be well.'

And for a few days, all was well. Peggy no longer panicked every time Beecher asked her a question or jumped a foot in the air when the telephone rang. Then one day, Beecher asked to see her and Marigold in his office. As soon as Peggy saw his sombre expression, she knew all was no longer well.

'I take it you both know what this is?' He held out Peggy's pamphlet. The words swam before her eyes. *One Girl's Guide to Surviving the War.*

'It's my report, sir.'

'Correct. And do you know who gave me this copy?'

'Lord Candleford,' said Marigold. 'And I gave it to him.'

Beecher blinked in surprise. 'And why on earth did you do that, Miss Cecily?'

'Because they had been printed in error and I was concerned that Peggy would get into trouble.'

Beecher steepled his hands together. 'I suppose I should be impressed by your honesty and loyalty.'

Peggy stole a glance at Marigold. She had noticed how fiercely defensive Marigold had become of late. Only last week she had scolded Dalton for trying to badger Peggy into going for a drink after work. 'She's just not interested, Wallace. Accept it or I'll tell all the girls in the secretary pool what a dolt you are.'

Marigold shrugged. 'It's what friends do.' If Peggy's heart hadn't been skipping with nerves, it would have swelled at these words.

'That's as may be, but as your superior, you should have come to me first.'

Marigold looked downcast. 'I'm sorry, sir. I was acting with the best intentions.'

'I don't doubt it, but the truth of the matter is that those documents were not printed in error.' Peggy and Marigold frowned at one another in confusion. 'And Lord Candleford was not privy to that decision. In fact, very few people were privy to that decision.'

'Oh,' said Marigold, blanching.

'Yes,' said Beecher. 'Oh indeed. Consequently, my superior is now demanding a meeting with those responsible which, as far as he is concerned, means you and me, Miss Sparks. And to add insult to injury, the head of paper rationing has got wind of this apparent waste of precious resources and will also be at the meeting.'

Peggy sank into her seat. 'Oh, this is bad. This is very bad.'

Beecher sighed. 'I can't deny that it's serious, and that's why you and I need to attend a meeting downstairs with Lord Candleford and Mr Burbage from Paper Control in ten minutes. Shall we?'

'Should I come with you?' asked Marigold. 'Winnie is my godfather, you know.'

'That won't be necessary, Miss Cecily,' said Beecher in a tone suggesting he felt she'd done enough already.

Marigold caught hold of Peggy's hand and squeezed it before she left. 'I'm so sorry if I've made things worse, Peggy, but don't worry, Winnie's a nice man. I'm sure he'll be kind.'

As it turned out, Winnie wasn't at all nice. In fact, he behaved as men in power often do when cornered. He deflected any blame towards Peggy and Beecher in a gesture which she could see was largely for the benefit of Mr Royston Burbage, who sat through the meeting grim-faced with arms folded. Beecher did his best to argue their case and intervene on Peggy's behalf, but Lord Winslow Candleford was like a scorpion primed and ready to counter any defence with a stinging attack.

Peggy could see that any contribution from her would be unwelcome or simply ignored, so all she could do was sit in frustrated silence.

'Sir, I must assert this had nothing to do with Miss Sparks. She is an upstanding and trustworthy member of our staff,' said Beecher.

'Upstanding, you say?' raged Lord Candleford. 'Have you read this socialist diatribe? It's like something from Communist Russia.'

'Well, technically, Communist Russia is fighting on our side in this war, sir.'

'Yes, and we all know the only reason is because Hitler gave Stalin a bloody nose and the man wants revenge.'

Mr Beecher's brow furrowed. 'I fear we may be getting off the point, sir.'

'Oh, you do, do you? I know how you conspire against me, Beecher. I've heard in dispatches your opinion of the way I manage this division.' Beecher gazed down at Peggy's pamphlet, unable to disagree with his superior's assertions. 'And clearly you have promoted an environment which enables women like Miss Sparks to spread their own propaganda.'

'Women like Miss Sparks?' said Beecher in a quiet voice. Peggy could see his knuckles clenched, bone-white, fingers trembling with anger.

'Yes. They're everywhere. It all started with that dreadful woman Pankhurst and it's given them all carte blanche to rise up from the gutter, to spread their notions of equality. And of course Bevin doesn't help, carping on about the lower classes all the time.'

'Have you actually read Miss Sparks' words?' Beecher asked.

Lord Candleford snorted with derision. 'What? You dare to question me? I've read enough, and besides, I know the mind of the working classes. I consult with my valet every day.'

'Perhaps your valet is too loyal to tell you the truth, sir,' said Beecher, with barely concealed contempt. Lord Candleford glared at him.

'Gentlemen, I think you may be missing the point,' said Mr Burbage in a thin, reedy voice. 'The real issue here is the dreadful waste of pape—'

'Gentlemen, ladies!' cried a voice. Peggy stared in amazement as Sir James Miles burst in through the door, followed by Mrs Pyecroft. 'Manifold apologies for the interruption and indeed the lateness.' He turned to Lord Candleford first, who was as ruddy as a beetroot. 'Winslow, you're looking the very picture of health, dear boy. So good to see you again,' he said, shaking him vigorously by the hand. 'And you, sir, must be Mr Burbage. Delighted to make your acquaintance. I'm James Miles. Mr Bracken himself has sent me to deal with this extremely sensitive matter.' He nodded to Peggy and Beecher.

'Brendan Bracken?' spluttered Lord Candleford. 'Our new Minister?'

'The very same,' said Sir James with a broad grin.

'But why is a man of his rank getting involved in departmental business?'

Sir James took a seat beside Peggy, who noticed that Mrs

Pyecroft remained standing, watching everything unfold with an unreadable expression. 'Well, firstly, Mr Bracken takes the issue of paper rationing very seriously.' Mr Burbage gave a grave nod of approval. 'And secondly, the Minister is also of the mind that as the course of the war ebbs and flows, we must learn to ebb and flow with it. It is highly regrettable that these leaflets have been printed without your knowledge, Candleford. However, we have received reports from our friends and colleagues in Home Intelligence that some early recipients of Miss Sparks' writing, particularly the women, have responded very positively to the way in which it portrays Britain's endurance of the war. Therefore, Mr Bracken is of the opinion that in the interest of our diplomatic relations and war effort, it is for the best if this matter is merely . . .' he paused, fluttering his hands as he searched for the right word, '. . . forgotten.'

'Oh,' said Lord Candleford.

'Oh,' echoed Mr Burbage.

Sir James turned to Peggy and Beecher like a father dismissing his children. 'Thank you both for your time. Please don't let us hold you up any longer.' He extended his hand to Mr Burbage. 'My dear man, we're very grateful for all you do. Candleford, could I have a brief word alone, old chap?'

Peggy noticed that Mrs Pyecroft remained behind in the room with Sir James and Lord Candleford as she and Beecher left.

'Well,' said Beecher. 'That's a blessed shame. I was fully anticipating being out of a job by elevenses, not that Mrs Beecher would appreciate having me under her feet.'

'I'm sorry, sir,' said Peggy.

He turned to her. 'Miss Sparks, you have nothing to be sorry for and I am pleased that your writing is going down well.'

Peggy dared a small smile. 'May I ask you something?'

'You may, but you probably know by now that there's a good chance I won't have the answer.'

'Is Mrs Pyecroft your secretary?'

'She is not.'

'Does she work for Sir James, then?'

He fixed her with a benevolent look. 'As I said, I have long given up trying to decipher the forces at work in this place. May I suggest that you perhaps do the same?'

'I'll try, Mr Beecher.'

'Jolly good. Onwards, Miss Sparks.'

The announcement of Lord Candleford's retirement was delivered by Sir James two days later. 'He has offered a lifetime of great service to both our country and latterly to the ministry. I know he will be sorely missed,' he said as Beecher stood beside him, rocking back and forth on his heels with what Peggy took to be a gesture of covert joy. 'I'm sure you are keen to know who his replacement will be and I am happy to advise that I will be your new Division Head, but please, don't worry. I am fully aware of what a sterling job Mr Beecher does, so I will do my best not to tread on either his or your toes. Thank you all.'

Peggy was returning to her desk when Mrs Pyecroft appeared before her. 'Might I have a word, Miss Sparks?'

'Of course.' Peggy followed her into her office.

166

'Please, take a seat,' she said, closing the door behind them and taking her place behind the desk. 'I greatly admire your writing.'

'Oh,' said Peggy. 'Thank you.'

'You have a rare gift for speaking the truth about real life. Politicians could learn a lot from you.' Peggy wasn't sure what to say so she remained silent. 'I see you understand when to speak and when to stay quiet, too. That is also a gift. Now, you probably have many questions and I will do my best to answer them. It was I who took your report and showed it to my superiors, who felt that its printing would be helpful in our endeavours to encourage the US to join the war effort.'

'My words?'

Mrs Pyecroft nodded. 'Words have power, and yours have more power than most. Therefore, I want to ask if you would be willing to write more of these reports, but perhaps embellish them with certain details which I will supply.'

Peggy eyed her with curiosity. 'Details?'

Mrs Pyecroft held her gaze. 'The reporting of a war is rarely populated with pure, unadulterated fact. As we know from some of the so-called facts emerging from the Axis powers, it is often littered with rumour. Obviously, it would be a wonderful thing if we could tell the truth, the whole truth and nothing but the truth. However, we are often forced to confront rumour with rumour and half-truth with half-truth. I think the phrase *desperate times call for desperate measures* springs to mind.'

'So you want me to plant certain information in my reports?'

'Yes. If this presents you with a moral quandary, I would urge you to see it as a means to an end. Your writing seems to strike a particular chord amongst women. It is our belief that if we win the hearts and minds of American women in this war, we can persuade their nation to join us, and if they do, we'll change its course.'

Peggy's thoughts immediately turned to Joe. She replied without a moment's hesitation. 'I'll do it.'

Chapter 13

Mr Beecher handed the manuscript to Peggy one evening as she was leaving for home. 'Miss Sparks, would you be so kind as to cast your eye over this and let me know your thoughts, please?'

'*Three Cheers for the Fairer Sex,*' she read, glancing at the document.

'Hear, hear!' cried Dalton. 'Where would we be without the ladies?'

Beecher shot him a reproachful look before turning back to Peggy. 'It's been commissioned by the Ministry who feel that perhaps the representation of women within the war effort has been somewhat overlooked. I detect from previous conversations that you would possibly agree with this statement.'

'Possibly,' said Peggy. 'And has this been written by a woman?' she added hopefully.

Beecher sighed. 'No. In their innate wisdom, Longforth's department have managed to persuade the great Wilfred Buchan out of writing retirement.'

'Gosh, he must be about a hundred years old,' said

Marigold, looking over. 'My pa used to read me his *Hubert the Hippopotamus* stories when I was a child.'

Beecher frowned. 'He's younger than me.'

'Oh,' said Marigold.

'So you'd like me to read through his manuscript, sir?' asked Peggy.

'If you would. I have looked over it, but sadly I am not blessed with the sensitivities of what Mr Buchan likes to term *the fairer sex*. We've been asked by Sir James to offer an opinion, much to Longforth's delight, so I'd like to know how you think it will be received. It's a fait accompli that it will be published, but we may be able to soften some of the perhaps more unenlightened passages.'

'I'll take my blue pencil to it this evening,' said Peggy.

'Thank you, Miss Sparks. And Miss Cecily?'

'Mr Beecher?'

'There's a good chance that we may require your photographic skills with this one. We already have most of the pictures we need but could perhaps do with a few more. Here's a list.'

'Thank you, sir,' said Marigold, throwing a joyful glance in Peggy's direction.

'Read that to me again, Peg,' said Emily who sat with folded arms and a face like thunder.

Peggy cleared her throat. '*The invasion of the weaker sex has come at a price to us men, but we must do our best to applaud and celebrate it.*'

'Invasion? Weaker sex? Bring that Buchan bloke here.

I'll give him weaker sex,' declared Emily, balling her hands into fists.

'I'm not sure you should read much more to your gran,' said Alice. 'I don't think her blood pressure can take it.'

'What's all this then?' asked Flo, who had just returned from putting the children to bed.

'It's a book about the role of women in the war effort,' explained Peggy.

'Written by a man who wouldn't know what women do in this war if his life depended on it,' said Emily.

'He does say that the country owes women its gratitude.'

'Yeah, but what about that bit where he talks about their bewitching feminine wiles and sly ways?'

'True.' Peggy frowned as she read on. '*Women still strive to preserve their beauty. Their pretty hands and beautiful hair remain groomed and lovely.*'

'I've met blokes like him,' muttered Emily. 'Always gawping at girls' hands and hair. Ought to be locked up.'

'I like to be pretty,' Flo admitted, patting her perfectly waved hair.

'It's not all bad,' said Peggy, sifting through the pages. 'It's just a bit . . .'

'Patronising? Perverted? Half-witted?' suggested Emily.

'Old-fashioned,' said Peggy. 'But Mr Beecher asked me my opinion, so chances are we can edit it and show what women are really up to.'

Emily shook her head. 'I'd just chuck it on the fire, Peg, and write your own version.'

'Oh, you should, Peggy,' said Flo. 'You'd tell the truth of what life's really like.'

Peggy pulled a face. She was being careful not to let slip to her family about the work she was doing for Mrs Pyecroft. She had intimated that this work should remain secret, and Peggy didn't want to compromise anything that could help bring Joe home to them. 'I'm not so sure. The last time my version of the truth became public, I nearly lost my job.'

'Well, I think it's a crying shame if you don't, and give that Buchan bloke what for while you're at it,' said Emily.

'I'll do my best to improve it,' said Peggy.

Alice reached over and squeezed her hand. 'And we'll be proud when you do, Peg. Won't we, Mum?'

Emily rolled her eyes as if it were the most obvious question in the world. ''Course we will. We're proud of everything our Peg does.'

Peggy arrived at work early the next day to find Marigold already at her desk. These early appearances were happening more and more regularly. It certainly made Marigold a more productive employee, but Peggy also noticed that she'd lost a certain effervescence and her clothes were considerably more pedestrian these days, her silk and satin replaced by tweed and wool. She still looked as if she'd just walked out of the pages of *Harper's Bazaar* but there was a sad, reflective air about her.

'That's what grief does to a person,' said Emily when Peggy told her. 'It makes you turn somersaults inside. You're never quite the same again.'

'Oh girls, could one of you fix me a tea?' said Dalton, loping in through the door and sliding behind his desk. 'I've got the hangover from hell this morning.'

Marigold glared at him. 'Do we look like tea girls? We're busy. Make it yourself, you lazy clot.'

Dalton blinked at her in surprise. The compliant, appeasing Marigold of old was apparently no more. Peggy smiled to herself. Perhaps this new version of Marigold wasn't one to fret over at all.

'Actually, I'd love a tea if you're making one, Dalton,' said Sheldrake, catching Peggy's eye. 'Milk, no sugar. I'm sure Miss Sparks and Miss Cecily would like one too. That's very kind of you.'

Dalton hauled himself to his feet and exited the office muttering 'Bloody suffragettes' under his breath.

Peggy was still chuckling when Mrs Pyecroft appeared beside her desk. 'Miss Sparks, do you have a moment?'

'Of course, Mrs Pyecroft.'

'Follow me, please.' She led Peggy to one of the smaller libraries filled with antiquarian tomes. They often used it for meetings and it had become one of Peggy's favourite rooms. The book-lined shelves always helped her to think. 'I want you to meet Mr Bauman,' she said, ushering her inside.

Peggy couldn't read the expression on Frank Bauman's face as she entered. It was a mixture of amusement and surprise with a dash of all-knowing. 'Oh, but Miss Sparks and I are well acquainted,' he said, standing up to shake her hand.

Mrs Pyecroft eyed him with interest. 'Really? In that

case, I'm sure it will make our working together all the more straightforward. Please take a seat.' Peggy was reminded of her school days as she and Frank listened to Mrs Pyecroft in obedient silence. 'I thought it would be useful to bring the pair of you together, given that you are the ones producing these particular pamphlets. I'm sure I don't need to remind you that discretion is key and that only the three of us should be discussing their content. Is that clear?' Peggy noticed an uncharacteristic compliance to Frank's demeanour as they both nodded. 'Excellent. Perhaps I could leave you alone to discuss layout and so forth in more detail, and please, do not hesitate to ask if you have any concerns.' She issued this final statement as an instruction before rising to her feet and leaving.

Frank turned to Peggy after she'd left. 'Terrifying, isn't she?'

Peggy let out an involuntary chuckle. 'A little.'

'I'm glad she's on our side. I share her determination.'

'So do I.'

Frank pulled a folder from his briefcase. 'So, here is the layout for the next pamphlet,' he said, sliding it over to her. Peggy concentrated on the document, avoiding Frank's intense gaze. 'Can I ask you if it's true what you say about Hitler planning to invade South America?'

Peggy offered a brief sideways look. 'It's one of Mrs Pyecroft's rumours, but who knows how far-fetched it is? Two years ago, war was just a rumour.'

'Not for the Jews,' said Frank, his face clouding. 'We were already at war then, under attack from people we used to think of as friends and countrymen.'

174

Peggy was encouraged by this shared confidence. 'Do you still have family in Germany?'

He nodded. 'Our parents are dead, but we still have aunts, uncles and cousins. We don't know where they are.'

'That must be hard.'

He shrugged. 'I think war is hard on everyone except for those maniacs wielding the power. What about you, Miss Sparks? Do you have a loved one caught up in this horror?'

'My twin brother, Joe. He's somewhere in the Middle East.' He held her gaze for a moment, and for the first time, Peggy noticed his expression soften. She turned back to the document. 'Well, we better get this right so that we can help them all, hadn't we?'

She could tell he was smiling when he answered. 'Never a truer word, Miss Sparks. Never a truer word.'

'Miss Sparks?' said Beecher a few days later, peering around the door of his office. 'We've been summoned to a meeting on the other side of Russell Square by Lear. He wants to discuss Buchan's book. Are you free?'

'Of course, Mr Beecher.'

It was a warm day and Peggy enjoyed the short burst of sunshine as they walked across Russell Square's oasis of green. She spotted Mrs Pyecroft sitting on a bench in one corner with Sir James and noted that she was the one doing the talking while he listened with interest.

'Are you enjoying your work with Mrs Pyecroft?' Beecher asked.

'Yes, sir. It's very interesting,' said Peggy.

He nodded. 'I am not privy to the details, which is as it should be, but I'm glad that your skills are being utilised in this way.'

'So am I, sir.' Peggy had to admit that she was enjoying the work, not just because she sensed it was making a real difference to the war effort, but she was finding Frank a more engaging and agreeable work colleague than she'd imagined. His moods could be erratic, but she got the sense they were reaching an understanding and found herself looking forward to their conversations.

Beecher and Peggy stopped outside a large building which looked like every other Bloomsbury townhouse but which had been converted into makeshift offices by the Ministry. Beecher led them inside and they climbed the stairs to an office which was filled with men and tobacco smoke. 'Mr Lear?' he called into the fug.

Lear looked up from his typewriter. 'Oh. You're here,' he said coldly. He stood up, leaving his still-smoking pipe in the ashtray on his desk, and joined them in the hallway. 'I've booked a meeting room. Follow me.' They did as they were told, entering a room that, like almost every other room in the Ministry, still reeked of tobacco but at least didn't have the smoke to go with it. 'Take a seat. So, apparently you're here to tell me what you think of old Buchan's treatise.'

'Is Longforth not coming?' asked Beecher.

Lear sighed. 'No, he told me to deal with this,' he said, folding his arms. 'Although I'm not sure why it's necessary.'

Beecher fixed him with a look. 'Sir James and indeed the Minister himself are aware of the fact that we are

176

neglecting our female audience when it comes to the flow of information, and that perhaps, although Mr Buchan is an exceptional writer, it might be wise to consult an actual woman before we publish a book aimed at that audience. I therefore gave the manuscript to Miss Sparks to read. She's an excellent writer herself and I knew that her input would be invaluable.'

Peggy felt herself grow a foot taller at these words. 'Very well,' said Mr Lear, looking bored.

Beecher turned to Peggy. 'Please, Miss Sparks. The floor is yours.'

Peggy's throat was sandpaper-dry, but then her grandmother seemed to hop on to her shoulder. *Tell them the truth, Peg, and don't let anyone, man or woman, make you feel small.* 'I think,' she began, 'that although Mr Buchan's words are well-intentioned, it comes across as a little old-fashioned.' Mr Lear shrugged but Beecher gave her an encouraging nod as she continued. 'Women are more than manicured hands, lipstick and pretty shoes. We have brains and we know how to use them.' She caught Beecher's eye and took courage from his steady gaze. 'It would be perhaps more truthful if it represented the view of women rather than the view of a man observing them.'

'Truthful,' said Mr Lear, staring up at the ceiling. 'Such an interesting word, and one which becomes a real head-scratcher for governments in times of war. I believe that the News Division have pledged to tell the truth, nothing but the truth and as near as possible the whole truth.'

'Yes, but surely people want to know what women are really feeling,' said Peggy with a rising frustration.

She remembered Mrs Pyecroft echoing his sentiment and knew that this disagreeable man had a point.

Mr Lear steepled his hands together as he turned to her. 'If we were living in peaceful times, I'd agree, but sadly, people still nurture a romantic view of the world. Although his writing style may be somewhat archaic, Mr Buchan represents that romantic view of the so-called fairer sex keeping the home fires burning until our brave soldiers return. I'm sorry to say it, but truth doesn't win wars, nor does it encourage the population to continue fighting them. I'm sure you understand, Miss Sparks.'

'So you won't accept my suggestions?'

Mr Lear sighed. 'I will glance over them and change anything glaring. That's the best I can do.'

'All right,' said Peggy, disappointed but aware she had no choice. Beecher barely spoke as they returned to the office. She knew he was bristling with anger on her behalf and, although it didn't alter the situation, it made her feel a little better.

A few days later he called her and Marigold into his office. 'I've had a call from Mr Lear. He has integrated some of your suggestions, Miss Sparks, which is remarkable given how reluctant he was to listen to us in the first place. Sir James has also asked if you would be prepared to liaise with Mr Buchan on behalf of the Ministry. He feels that you might be able to mollify some of his views and pave the way for future similar and indeed improved publications. I thought that perhaps you and Miss Cecily could work together on this. We're hoping for at least another two books.'

'Oh,' said Peggy. 'That sounds promising. What do you think, Marigold?'

Marigold clapped her hands together in delight. 'I think it's going to be splendid. I love old people. I'm sure he's an absolute sweetie.'

'Jolly good,' said Beecher, handing over a piece of paper on which was scrawled a South Kensington address. 'He's expecting you at eleven o'clock tomorrow. Good luck.'

Chapter 14

Peggy had become used to the sight of London's bomb-damaged streets. It was now commonplace to wander along roads where some buildings remained proudly upright while another one a few doors down was completely missing. In fact, it was more unusual to come across an area where all the buildings stood untouched, and yet as she and Marigold turned on to the street where Wilfred Buchan lived, she was immediately struck by the lack of damage. Each bright white concrete house stood gleaming in the morning sun. Peggy wasn't sure if this was a good sign, although Flo had read her horoscope the previous evening, asserting that 'Something dramatic is about to happen.'

'Something dramatic is always about to happen. There's a bleedin' war on,' declared Emily.

Marigold was humming to herself as they approached the front door. Peggy had watched her reapplying her lipstick before they left and detected the heady aroma of a perfume far more expensive than the treasured Evening in Paris scent which she and Flo shared. Marigold had noticed her looking over as she snapped her lips together. 'A gal's got to have her Gala lipstick when going into battle,' she said with a wink. Peggy hoped it wouldn't be a battle, that they would be able to win Wilfred Buchan over with a combination of charm and intelligence.

They gave one another a confident nod before Peggy pulled on the front doorbell and waited. The woman who opened the door was definitely younger than Peggy and almost certainly younger than Marigold. She was wrapped in a silk dressing gown, regarding them through sleep-glazed eyes. 'Hello?'

Peggy stood up straighter and cleared her throat. 'Good morning. My name is Peggy Sparks and this is my colleague, Marigold Cecily. We're from the Ministry of Information and we're here to see Mr Buchan.'

The woman stared at her for a moment before calling over her shoulder. 'Wilfie! There's two women here to see you.' There was no immediate reply so the young woman shouted with some irritation, 'WILFIE! You've got visitors!'

'All right, all right,' called a voice from somewhere upstairs. 'No need to go into a song and dance about it. Show them into the drawing room. I'll be down in five minutes unless they want to see me in my dressing gown.'

The woman rolled her eyes and moved aside to let them in. 'Down there on the left,' she said before disappearing back upstairs with a swish of luxurious silk.

Peggy and Marigold looked at one another before making their way into the drawing room. If it weren't for the overflowing ashtrays, discarded champagne and whisky glasses and general state of disarray, Peggy would have loved this room. The walls were lined with shelf after shelf of books, poetry, literature, mythology. She took it all in with relish.

'Gosh,' said Marigold, gazing around the room. 'Do you think that was his daughter?'

Peggy raised her eyebrows. 'If that was his daughter then I'm the queen of Sheba.'

'Ladies,' boomed a voice behind them. They turned to see Wilfred Buchan sweep into the room like an actor ready for applause. He was tall with a chaotic mop of dark grey hair, a face lined with wrinkles and an intense, ocean-deep gaze. Peggy was relieved to note that he had forsaken his dressing gown in exchange for a burgundy velvet smoking jacket, mustard-coloured trousers and green silk cravat. His attire alone suggested great self-confidence, but it was the way he locked eyes with each of them as they shook hands that said, *Yes. It's really me.*

'It's a great honour to meet you, Mr Buchan,' said Peggy.

'Thrilling,' echoed Marigold. 'We're so grateful for your contribution to the war effort.'

'Firstly, you must call me Wilfred. And secondly, if I weren't so old and crusty, I'd be out there fighting myself.'

'Well, if I may be so bold,' said Marigold, 'you don't look a bit old or crusty to me.'

Wilfred raised an eyebrow in her direction. 'I can tell we're going to be the greatest of friends, but please, you must tell me your names.'

'I'm Peggy Sparks and this is Marigold Cecily.'

He stared at Marigold in wonder. 'Of the Cecily family? I think I may have been to one of your father's soirées.'

182

Marigold grinned. 'He used to read me your *Hubert the Hippopotamus* stories.'

Wilfred pulled a face. 'Now I do feel old.'

'Wilfie?' called a voice from the hallway. 'I'm going out to get supplies. Do you want anything?'

'Cigarettes and some of that French cheese if you can persuade the grocer,' he called. He winked at Marigold. 'We need our little treats in times of war, don't we? Athena is so good at convincing people to give her things.' Marigold beamed at him. He gazed at her, apparently transfixed by her beauty. 'I bet you are too.' Marigold gave a tinkling laugh that made Peggy cringe. 'But where are my manners? Can I offer you some tea?' he asked, his eyes not leaving her face.

'That would be lovely,' said Marigold, allowing him to take her by the hand and lead her to the kitchen, leaving Peggy no choice but to follow. She was unsurprised to notice that the kitchen was in a similar state of chaos as the drawing room.

'Let me make the tea,' said Marigold. 'We can't let the great Wilfred Buchan do it.'

'Oh, but you are utterly charming,' he said, kissing her hand as she let go. 'Thank you, my dear.'

Marigold picked up the kettle and managed to fill it with water before turning to Peggy with a bemused look on her face. 'Give it here,' said Peggy, placing it on the range. 'Marigold,' she whispered, glancing over to where Wilfred was half-heartedly making space at the kitchen table before giving up and lighting a cigarette, blowing an extravagant plume of smoke as he stretched his arms behind his head. 'What are you doing? Are you trying to make Wilfred Buchan fall in love with you?'

Marigold shrugged. 'Not particularly, but Beecher said he was difficult, so where's the harm in using a little charm to make our job easier?'

Peggy sighed. There was a certain amount of truth in what she said, but it made Peggy uneasy. There was something unsettling about this man with his French cheese, cravat and young lady friend. 'Do you have any fresh milk?' she asked him, wrinkling her nose against the curdled offering in the milk jug.

'Afraid not. Unless Athena remembers to get some. Although I doubt it. She's not the brightest but she is beautiful. Just like you, Lady Marigold.' He grasped her fingers and kissed them.

She withdrew her hand with a polite smile. 'Please. Call me Marigold.'

He gave a dismissive wave. 'As you wish. And now, what can I do for you both?' he asked as Peggy placed three cups of black tea on the table. 'Lear said the Ministry wants me to write more books.'

'Yes, if you would be agreeable,' said Peggy.

He looked from Marigold to Peggy and then back to Marigold again. 'If I am to work with you, I would find it very agreeable indeed.'

Peggy gave a small cough. 'That's wonderful news. So all we need to do now is to discuss the subject matter.'

Wilfred threw a sideways glance at Marigold. 'Is she always this bossy?'

'Sorry,' said Peggy, her face growing hot. 'It's merely

that Mr Lear has expressly asked us to discuss these future publications with you.'

'Blah, blah, blah. Goodness, don't you go on, Penny,' said Wilfred, rolling his eyes.

'It's Peggy,' she said, feeling her shoulders stiffen. 'Peggy Sparks.'

'Sorry, Peggy Sparks,' he said, taking a swig of his tea and pulling a face before reaching into his jacket for a hip flask and tipping a nip into it. He took another sip and sighed happily. 'That's better. Want some?' he said, turning to Marigold.

She placed a hand over her cup. 'No, thank you.'

He tipped some into Peggy's tea without asking. 'Well, you should definitely have some. Help loosen you up a bit.'

It was suddenly clear to Peggy that she was in the presence of a man with an ego the size of Russia, who was so monstrous and self-regarding that he would never listen to someone like her. She doubted that he ever paid attention to anyone except perhaps his own reflection in the mirror. However, it was also clear to her that the Ministry had sent her to do a job and as the granddaughter of Emily Marsh and daughter of Alice Sparks, she was not going to allow this pig of a human being to stand in her way. She did her best to adopt a steely look. 'Mr Buchan. We have been sent to ask you to write more books about the role of women in the war. Your first book focused on this subject in a more general sense, so we thought that the next one could perhaps deal with specific roles such as the Land Girls or the Wrens?'

Wilfred took another swig of tea and regarded her with

185

flared nostrils. 'And would I get to meet these women at work? I'll need to properly understand what they're doing, you see.'

'I'm sure that will be possible. Marigold here will be taking the photographs to illustrate your words.'

At this Wilfred's face lit up. 'Ah, well then, that's settled. Marigold and I will embark on these field trips together. I assume that the Ministry will meet all expenses.'

'I'll have to ask Mr Lear,' said Peggy.

'You do that. Although Lear will be fine. He dances to Longforth's tune and Henry and I have a long history.' He sat back in his chair with his hands behind his head, looking pleased with himself. 'I must say, this is turning into rather a lovely war.' He smirked as he leaned towards Marigold. 'Plus I know how mischievous these women can be without the men to keep an eye on them. What is it they say? *Up with the lark and to bed with a wren?*'

Peggy felt her hands ball into tight fists at these words and then noticed Marigold's hand on her arm as if to reassure her. 'Well, Peggy and I wouldn't know about that, Mr Buchan, but we'll do our best to make sure that your requests regarding the work side of things are adhered to.'

Buchan gave Marigold a sparkling look, miming the zipping of his lips. 'Say no more, my dear, say no more. I shall leave it all in your more than capable hands.'

'Well, I shall be telling Mr Alderman to take all the copies of *Hubert the Hippopotamus* off the shelves of the library. Wilfred Buchan is a monster,' declared Peggy as they made their way back to the Ministry.

'I've met worse,' said Marigold with a weary sigh.
'Really?'
Marigold shrugged. 'You know how men can be.'

September 1941

Dear Peg,

It feels like ages since my last letter and I'm sorry for that, but we don't get much spare time for writing at the moment. I'm scribbling this like billy-o on my knee by the light of a candle in what feels like a force 10 gale. Things are rough going at the moment ██ ████████████████████████ but we keep going. As long as Albert's here and I know you're all at home praying for me, I'll get through it. I remember you told me to be honest about what's happening and it is hard, but I don't want you to worry. I'm all right.

We found out today that a lot of mail (including parcels) has been lost over the summer which is a bit of a blow. I'm keeping my fingers crossed that this letter reaches you all right. I did get your letter from last month though. That Buchan bloke sounds like a wrong 'un but I can tell you and Marigold are a good team, like Albert and me. He wants me to propose marriage to Marigold on his behalf. Says she sounds like the kind of woman for him. He's a fool, but a good friend to have around here. Don't worry about sending parcels and tell Mum and Flo not to either. We get all the stuff we need out here – soap, cigarettes, chocolate, the lot. And newspapers, even though they're always months out of date. Still, it's nice to see them. Makes us feel like there's still a world back home worth fighting for. Be nice to see one of your books one day. Anyway, I'm doing well. A bit tired but then that's to be expected as there's a lot going on. I'm hoping and praying that the Yanks will join the war effort. That would be a good Christmas present. Can you put in a word with Beecher and see what he can do? Keep writing. Your words make all the difference. We'll meet again.

Love, Joe

Chapter 15

'I must congratulate you both,' said Beecher, holding up a finished copy of *Three Cheers for our Land Girls*, a fresh-faced young woman beaming out at them from the front cover. 'This has turned out far better than I thought. Lear is grudgingly impressed. Your photographs are splendid, Miss Cecily, and I can see your influence on Mr Buchan, Miss Sparks.'

'Oh really?' said Peggy, throwing a wide-eyed glance towards Marigold. 'Not too obvious, I hope?' Peggy was already on tenterhooks following her decision to reframe some of Wilfred Buchan's more unenlightened turns of phrase following a telephone call with Frank the previous week.

'How on earth did you persuade him to let you edit his writing?' he had asked.

'What do you mean?' said Peggy, with a little too much haste.

'Oh, Miss Sparks. Do you mean to tell me that the great Wilfred Buchan isn't aware of what you've done?'

'I'm sorry, Mr Bauman. I don't know what you're

talking about,' said Peggy, her pulse thundering like a thousand racehorse hooves.

'Methinks the lady doth protest too much,' he said, enjoying her discomfort too much for Peggy's liking. 'Don't worry, Miss Sparks. Your secret is safe with me and besides, the writing is much improved.' Peggy had been a nervous wreck ever since.

'Not obvious at all,' said Beecher. 'You've merely tempered his more old-fashioned tendencies into something really quite powerful. Jolly good work. I know Mr Buchan is not the easiest of men, so thank you both.'

This was something of an understatement. Peggy and Marigold had spent three trying days in the countryside with Buchan whilst he attempted to woo any poor Land Girl who agreed to be interviewed by him. Happily for everyone except Buchan, the farm they were working on was run by a no-nonsense, ruddy-faced woman called Mrs Winthrop who was immune to the charms of this 'preening rascal', as she described him to Peggy. She demanded to be present at every interview and made sure Buchan left for the country inn where he was staying at the end of every day. Peggy and Marigold were then forced to spend the evenings dining with him and watching while he drank himself into a stupor, at which point they would hurry to bed, locking their doors behind them. Peggy had the misfortune one evening to happen upon Buchan leading a giggling barmaid to his room.

'Don't mind us, Penny,' he called over his shoulder. 'Just doing our bit for the war effort.'

She shivered at the memory. 'Yes, well, it's all part of the war effort, Mr Beecher.'

'Quite so. And *Flying High with the Wrens* is agreed as the next title?'

Peggy nodded. 'We're waiting for Mr Buchan to confirm dates for the interviews and photographs. He's keen to make it into an overnight trip but we think we could manage it in a day.'

'Would you like me to speak to Longforth about that?' asked Beecher.

Marigold and Peggy exchanged a look. 'No, sir. We can handle it,' said Marigold.

'I'm sure you can. Onwards,' he said with a smile before disappearing into his office.

Peggy exhaled as she turned to Marigold. 'The sooner we get these books finished, the better.'

'Agreed,' said Marigold. 'In the meantime, we need to celebrate our hard work and kick back our heels after putting up with old Wilfie these past months. Where are you going to be this Saturday evening?'

'At the pictures with Flo?'

Marigold's eyes sparkled. 'Wrong! You're coming to the country pile with Flo for a Christmas party!'

Peggy hesitated before answering. 'It's a kind invitation, Marigold, but I'm not sure.' The thought of spending the weekend in the company of the terrifying Lady Lavinia was not one Peggy relished.

'Why ever not?'

Peggy glanced at her friend's eager face and realised she

would need to tread carefully so as not to offend. 'Well, for a start we have nothing to wear.'

'You can both borrow one of my dresses. I've got dozens.'

'I don't know if Flo will want to leave Nancy and Charlie.'

'Ask her. I bet she'd love a break, and knowing your mother, she'd be only too happy to look after them.'

'I'm not sure . . .'

Marigold held up a hand to hush her. 'Now then, I won't hear another word. I really want you to come. Please. It'll be a little thank you after all your kindness to me this year.'

There was something about Marigold's pleading tone that made her reply, 'All right. I'll ask Flo.'

'I think it's lovely that Marigold's invited you. You and Flo should definitely go,' said Alice when Peggy told her that evening.

'Go where?' asked Flo, appearing in the doorway with Charlie in her arms and Nancy by her side.

'Marigold has invited us to a party at her house in the country.'

'Can I go?' asked Nancy, pirouetting into the room. 'Please?'

'Why don't you stay home with Great-Gran and me?' said Alice. 'Help us look after your brother.'

Nancy folded her arms and huffed. 'That doesn't sound like fun at all. I'm just like Cinderella when she's not allowed to go to the ball.'

192

'How about you do some baking with your fairy god-mother?' suggested Emily.

Nancy reconsidered. 'Can I lick out the bowl?'

'Of course. That's the best bit.'

'I'm not sure, Peg,' said Flo. 'What on earth would we wear?'

'Marigold said she'd lend us dresses.'

'But what about the other guests? Won't we be a bit out of place?'

Peggy shrugged. 'You're right. It's a daft idea. I just thought it'd be nice to get out of London and have some fun, but perhaps we shouldn't given that poor old Joe and his mates are up against it.'

Emily waggled a finger. 'Poor old Joe, as you call him, would want you to enjoy your life whenever you get the chance. Now, the pair of you need to go to this party and have a bit of fun for all of us. You don't win a war by being a martyr to it.'

Peggy raised her eyebrows at Flo. 'Shall we, m'lady?'

Flo laughed. 'Oh, why not? I've always fancied trying my hand at being a lady of the manor.'

The bowler-hatted man who collected them from the station only spoke to confirm their names. He drove at a funereal pace which gave Flo and Peggy ample time to admire the striking Hampshire countryside, populated by skeletal trees casting long shadows in the winter sun. As they turned on to the winding drive leading through the front gates of Greymore, the driver growled. 'That yew tree is over a thousand years old.'

'Fancy,' said Peggy, clueless as to which of the hundreds of trees could be the famous yew. She widened her eyes at Flo who put a hand to her mouth to suppress a giggle.

'And the house dates back to the sixteenth century.'

'I wonder if he was working here then?' whispered Flo to Peggy. It was Peggy's turn to stifle a laugh. She was happy they'd decided to come. It had been a long time since she and Flo had been able to enjoy themselves without life getting in the way. Emily was right. They were both still young. They needed to have a little fun whenever they got the chance. She glanced at her friend. Her face was as familiar to her as her own. They'd been friends since the first day at school when Flo had turned up in a tatty pinafore with unkempt hair and a couple of girls had sniggered at her appearance. When Peggy saw how Flo kept her head down as if she wanted to disappear into the ground, it stoked an unexpected furnace of anger inside her. She shouldered the unkind girls out of the way, put an arm through Flo's and became her ally and protector from that day onwards. It wasn't long before Emily sniffed out the fact that Flo's mother had died two years earlier and her father was either out at work or in the pub, leaving Flo to fend for herself. Encouraged by Alice and Peggy, Flo spent more and more time at their house until she eventually became one of the family, which was made permanent when she and Joe had the good sense to fall in love. Peggy linked her arm through Flo's now, giving her a gentle squeeze as they pulled up at the front of the house.

As soon as they came to a halt, Marigold burst through the huge oak front door and down the steps to greet them. 'Oh, I'm so glad you're here,' she cried, hugging them both. 'Pincher, will you bring in my friends' bags, please?'

The driver's face immediately softened at her words. 'Of course, Lady Marigold.'

'Thank you. Follow me, girls. This is going to be so much fun!'

Peggy tried not to stare as they entered the hall and took in their surroundings. She could picture the lords and ladies through the centuries arriving in their carriages, decked in finery, entering through this door to be greeted by the crackling open fire and a cacophony of excitable, barking dogs. The dark oak floors gleamed with polish whilst the panelled walls were hung with oil paintings of Marigold's ancestors who cast their watchful eyes towards the visitors and the huge, sparkling Christmas tree at the centre of it all. The wide carpeted staircase swept away to the left, lifting Peggy's gaze towards the gilded plaster ceiling and sparkling chandeliers. She caught Flo's eye and knew they were thinking the same thing. It was as if they'd wandered into the pages of a fairy tale.

Marigold had already started to climb the stairs. 'Come on. I'll show you where you're sleeping.'

Peggy's room was the size of the entire downstairs of 26 Evelyn Street and Flo's was even bigger. 'Coo, don't let me get used to this,' said Flo, perching on the edge of her bed and giving a little bounce. 'I'll never want to go home again.'

Peggy smiled. It was good to see her friend at ease for

once. Life was a constant toil of worry about Joe and care for the children. Marigold had excused herself, saying that she would meet them in an hour so she could give them the guided tour. 'Could you imagine living in a place like this?' said Peggy, gazing through the mullioned windows across the vast gardens and verdant landscape stretching as far as the eye could see.

''Course not,' said Flo. 'But it's fun to pretend for a day. And Marigold is very welcoming. I'm going to forget all my cares this weekend and enjoy myself. I can't wait to write and tell Joe all about it.'

'Very well, Lady Florence. I'm going to go and read in my room and I suggest you have a well-earned nap before we go and pretend to be ladies of the manor.'

Peggy felt as if she were strolling through history as Marigold took them on a tour a while later through the Marble Hall and the Long Gallery, before finally coming to rest in the Library. 'I guessed you might feel at home in here, Peggy,' said Marigold.

'I certainly do,' said Peggy, admiring the rows of books which were shelved on two floors with an iron balustraded walkway around the top level.

'I thought we could have tea in here,' said Marigold, ringing a little bell, at which Flo pulled a wide-eyed expression at Peggy.

Moments later, a young girl appeared. 'Tea for three please, Daisy,' said Marigold.

'Yes, Lady Marigold,' said Daisy before disappearing back through the door. They took their places on the crimson leather sofas, set before a fire burning briskly beneath an ornate marble fireplace.

'It's so grand here,' said Flo to Marigold. 'What was it like growing up?'

Marigold shrugged. 'I suppose it was much like any other childhood.'

Peggy snorted with amusement. 'You are joking, aren't you? Look at this place. It's huge. Our back garden is the size of a postage stamp compared with this. We played out in the street most of the time, didn't we, Flo?'

'Hopscotch on the pavement was my favourite,' said Flo.

'I've never played hopscotch,' said Marigold.

Flo's eyes grew wide. 'Wait till Nancy hears that. She'll be digging out her chalks for you.'

Their conversation was interrupted by Daisy returning with the tea. 'Will there be anything else, Lady Marigold?' she asked after she'd set down the tray.

'No. That will be all. Thank you, Daisy.'

'And we don't have people bringing us tea all the time,' said Peggy after she'd gone.

Marigold looked embarrassed. 'Gosh, you must think I'm so spoilt. I suppose I am, but I don't know any different. In truth, it was rather lonely growing up here.' She gazed at them both. 'I know I'm lucky to be surrounded by this wealth, but I'd give it all up in a flash to have Cordy back again.' Flo reached over and squeezed her hand.

'May I?' said Peggy, gesturing at the teapot.

They were on their second cup of tea and finishing the last of the dainty sandwiches when the door opened and Lady Lavinia swept into the room. She regarded the three of them with a coldness that made Peggy wonder if this woman ever found joy in anything. She couldn't imagine her own mother giving her children the same frosty look Lady Lavinia was casting towards Marigold now. 'Oh Mother, you remember Peggy and Flo from when you collected me from their house.'

'Thank you for inviting us,' offered Peggy.

'It's nice to see you again,' added Flo.

Lady Lavinia gave a curt nod. 'Marigold, have you seen your father? Cook has told me that the fishmonger has let her down so we'll have no cod tonight. I just hope that Mr Lansdown still delivers the pheasants.'

'I'm sure it'll be fine, Mama.'

Lady Lavinia narrowed her eyes. 'Of course you're sure, Marigold. It's not you having to deal with the consequences, is it? Honestly, I said to your father that we should abandon the party this year — it's not seemly to be celebrating during a war — but he wouldn't hear of it. Well, I hope they drink his cellar dry. And as for what we'll do when the army move in . . .' She gave a laboured sigh. 'Heaven help us all. Excuse me. I need to get on.' She swept from the room without a backward glance.

Marigold gave them a breezy smile, doing her best to mask her dejection. 'Mother's just peeved because she's found out that the army will be requisitioning the house next year.'

'Oh,' said Peggy, nudging her. 'Shame that you've only got two other houses to fall back on.'

Marigold laughed. 'Oh Peggy, I do enjoy your teasing.'

'Good,' said Peggy with a grin. 'And now, Lady

Marigold. Didn't you say you had some dresses we could borrow?'

Marigold's eyes lit up. 'Would you like to try them on?'

Flo grinned. 'Lead on, Your Ladyship.'

It was a splendid party, like something Peggy had only ever read about in books. It would have been easy to forget there was a war on if it weren't for the blackout panels at the windows. The inside of the house was bathed in a warm glow from the candles flickering on every surface and the crackling fires in every room. Despite Lady Lavinia's vexation regarding the catering, there seemed to be an abundance of food and drink to feed the huge number of guests who began to appear from seven o'clock. There was a sense of joyful hope about the gathering. America had entered the war and the world was feeling more optimistic about what lay ahead. Peggy had taken great delight in the news, not least because she knew how much hope it would bring Joe.

She and Flo eyed the arrivals nervously as they followed Marigold down the grand staircase into the cheerful throng. 'Do I look all right?' whispered Flo, gazing down at her beaded damask rose gown.

Peggy placed her hands on her shoulders. 'Flo, you look beautiful. I can't wait to see the photographs Marigold took. Can you imagine what Joe will say when he sees them? His mate Albert's eyes will be out on stalks.'

Flo laughed. 'I feel done up like a kipper, but in the nicest possible way.'

'You're the loveliest kipper I've ever seen,' said Marigold.

'Now. Let's get a drink and I can introduce you to some people.'

By the time the evening was in full swing, Peggy felt as if her head was spinning and it wasn't because of the champagne from Lord Cecily's cellar. They rubbed shoulders with dukes, actresses, artists, baronesses, politicians and, of course, writers. She was told by one famous actress that she should consider a career on the screen due to her strong jawline, whilst another man who turned out to be the owner of Arnold's Booksellers was delighted to hear that she and Flo lived in south-east London.

'My niece Gertie has a splendid bookshop very close to you. You should visit it some time.'

Flo was led around the dancefloor by a sprightly ageing artist with the most extravagant moustache Peggy had ever seen, whilst Marigold was invariably surrounded by men desperate to either light her cigarette or persuade her to dance. Peggy drank it all in, absorbing as many details as possible, ready to pour them into her next letter to Joe.

She noticed Lady Lavinia standing alone in one corner, nursing a glass of champagne, occasionally throwing a thin smile towards whichever guest greeted her. There was something about her demeanour that stirred a note of sympathy in Peggy.

'It's a wonderful party, Lady Lavinia,' she said, approaching.

'Is it?' she asked. 'I find the whole thing grotesque in times of war, but then Edwin vehemently disagrees with me and so here we are.'

'I haven't met your husband,' said Peggy. 'I'd like to.'

Lady Lavinia looked her up and down. 'Don't bother. He won't be interested in meeting you unless you're skilled at blackjack.'

'Oh,' said Peggy. 'I see.'

Lady Lavinia sighed. 'I very much doubt you do. Now, if you'll excuse me, I need to consult with Cook.'

'Of course,' said Peggy, watching her go. There was something about her upright, curt manner which Peggy sensed was just a mask.

'Peggy,' said Flo, arriving at her side, a little out of breath. 'I don't know about you, but I could do with a break. That artist has worn me out. Shall we escape upstairs for a bit?'

'Good idea,' said Peggy. They made their way up the staircase and along the corridor towards their rooms.

'Do you remember that big old empty house at the far end of the park where we used to play when we were kids? This place reminds me of that with all these secret corridors.'

'We used to think that place was haunted.'

'Do you remember that time we hid in one room and jumped out at Joe after he came looking for us?' said Flo with a grin.

Peggy laughed. 'He leapt about six foot in the air. I thought he'd never stop screaming.'

Flo chuckled and threw a glance down one of the corridors. 'Come on, let's go and have a look down here.'

'Now I understand why your daughter's so nosey. I thought you wanted a rest.'

Flo flashed her an innocent look. 'You're always saying

it's good to be curious, and besides, when will we ever get a chance to have a proper look round a place like this? Come on.'

'All right,' said Peggy, grabbing her arm and following behind. 'But don't touch anything.'

The corridor was flanked by closed doors along both sides of its entire length except at the far end where one stood open. Flo led them to it. 'Oh look. A rocking horse,' she said. The curtains were open and the pale moonlight cast a milky glow into the room.

'I'm not sure we should be here, Flo,' warned Peggy.

'Why? We're only looking,' said Flo, stepping over the threshold. 'What I would have given to buy a rocking horse for Nancy and Charlie.'

'This must have been Marigold's nursery,' said Peggy, looking around at the shelves lined with books, teddy bears and toys.

'Strange that it's been left like this,' said Flo.

'Mmm,' said Peggy, approaching the desk by the window and gazing out towards the silvery moonlit view. She glanced down and spotted a photograph of two young girls of no more than five or six. Struck by a certain familiarity, Peggy reached down to pick it up.

'What on earth do you think you're doing?' Peggy and Flo grabbed one another in shock before turning to see Lady Lavinia standing in the doorway, her face blazing with incandescent fury. 'Well? I asked you a question. What are you doing snooping around up here?' Peggy and Flo looked at one another helplessly. There was no excuse for their actions and Lady Lavinia knew it.

'I daresay they got lost, Mother,' said Marigold in a slurring tone, appearing behind her.

'Lost,' said Lady Lavinia, turning towards her daughter with one eyebrow raised.

'Yes. Not everyone lives in a huge mansion with hundreds of corridors. They were no doubt trying to find their way back to their rooms.'

'Yes,' said Flo breathlessly. 'That's exactly what happened. We were lost.'

Lady Lavinia narrowed her eyes at Peggy and Flo before turning her imperious gaze back towards her daughter. 'This is why I don't like strangers coming here, Marigold. Now, please take your friends downstairs and remind them that they are guests in this house and would do well to treat our home with a little more respect.'

Marigold gave a snort of disdain. 'Respect. You're a fine one to lecture about respect.'

Peggy noticed a flicker of panic flit across Lady Lavinia's face. 'I would thank you not to be rude, particularly in front of strangers.'

'They're not strangers, Mother. They're my friends, and actually, they deserve some respect too.'

Peggy placed a hand on her shoulder. 'It's all right, Marigold. Come on. Let's go downstairs. We're very sorry, Lady Lavinia.'

'So sorry,' echoed Flo. 'It was kind of you to invite us in the first place.'

'Oh yes,' said Marigold in a bitter tone. 'Isn't my mother kind?'

Lady Lavinia regarded her daughter with pursed lips

before approaching the window of the nursery. 'Perhaps you could escort my daughter downstairs. I think she would benefit from some fresh air.'

'Come on, Marigold,' said Flo, putting an arm around her shoulder and leading her away. Peggy glanced back into the room and noticed Lady Lavinia tracing a finger over the photograph she had spotted earlier.

The party was still in full swing as they re-joined the guests. Marigold broke free from Flo, grabbed an open bottle of champagne from one of the servants and wrenched open the front door before disappearing outside.

'She'll catch her death out there,' said Flo.

'Come on,' said Peggy. 'Let's go and bring her back inside.' Marigold was stalking across the lawn, swigging from the bottle. 'Marigold!' cried Peggy, hurrying after her. 'Wait!'

'Go away,' shouted Marigold, turning on them, her face stained with tears. 'Just leave me alone.'

'You've clearly never dealt with the Sparks girls before,' said Peggy, grabbing her by the arm. 'We don't leave our friends alone when they're upset.'

Marigold's eyes flashed. 'Am I your friend, Peggy, or do you just feel sorry for me?'

'Why would I feel sorry for you?'

'Because my mother hates me, my father doesn't even know I exist and my dearest friend is dead. I've got no one.'

'You've got us,' said Flo.

'Have I?' asked Marigold. She turned to Peggy. 'Do you like me? I know you'll be honest about it, so tell me. Do you?'

'All right,' said Peggy. 'I'll admit, you weren't my cup of tea when we first met, but now? Of course I like you. We tamed the monster who is Wilfred Buchan together. That sealed our friendship there and then.'

'And your mother doesn't hate you,' said Flo.

'Doesn't she? Do you see any warmth or love from her towards me?'

'But she's your mother, Marigold. Why on earth would your mother hate you?'

Marigold was silent for a moment before gazing at them both with tears in her eyes. 'Because my twin sister died when we were six years old.'

Flo threw a sorrowful look at Peggy before putting an arm around Marigold's shoulder. 'But why would your mother hate you for that?'

Marigold gazed up at them both. 'I had scarlet fever and my sister caught it. I lived and she died. She's never forgiven me and she never will.'

January 1942

Dear Peg,

Thank you for your letters. I got a whole batch of them this morning, including Christmas cards from you all and the photographs Marigold took of Flo at the party. Well. If that didn't spur me on to keep fighting, I don't know what will. The lads are all jealous of my beautiful wife, but you'll be amused to know that Albert is now proposing marriage to you. He's a card, but I've never had a truer friend in my life. The party certainly sounded eventful and

I'm glad you persuaded Flo to go. I feel sorry for Marigold, but then I also think she's lucky to have a friend like you. Nancy's Christmas card made us all laugh. She told me she'd asked Father Christmas to send me home on a magic carpet like the one in *Aladdin*. I wish. What I wouldn't give to see you all and be home in wet, cold Blighty after miles and miles of nothing but desert.

Still, we're getting on with things out here. We shot through ███████ like a dose of salts. The Jerries didn't know which way was up. We saw the POWs looking very sorry for themselves as they trudged past their burnt-out tanks and planes. It's hard to feel any sympathy after what they're putting us all through, although I don't shout and jeer at them like some do. None of this feels like anything to crow about. I'm glad Uncle Sam is fighting alongside us now though. I'm going to thank you and Beecher for helping to make that happen, because I know you're working hard, Peg. I know you say that what you do doesn't really make a difference, but it does. Every word, thought and deed towards ending this blasted war is worthwhile, so you keep going and I promise that I will too until we meet again.

Love, Joe

Chapter 16

When she looked back later, Peggy realised she should have noticed the gathering storm. After the party and following months of putting up with Buchan's monstrous ego and unreasonable demands, it was inevitable that the bubble would burst. It's just that Peggy hadn't expected it to burst in such an alarmingly sudden and explosive way.

'Mr Buchan is demanding dinner at the Ritz to celebrate his glittering success in the war effort,' said Marigold wearily as Beecher emerged from his office one day.

'Surely Longforth can entertain him?' he said.

'He seemed adamant that it should be with the people who have worked on his books.' Peggy glanced at her. They both knew it was a ruse on his part to get closer to Marigold.

'Perhaps you could come along, sir?' said Peggy hopefully.

'When is he proposing this government-funded soirée?' he asked.

'A week on Thursday,' said Marigold.

'Sorry, that's Mrs Beecher's birthday,' he said before his face lit up with an idea. 'Why don't we invite Frank

Bauman?' Peggy realised she was holding her breath. 'He's been instrumental in the production of the books after all.'

'Good idea, Mr Beecher,' said Marigold.

'Yes,' said Peggy, the prospect of entertaining Buchan seeming less arduous all of a sudden.

'I'll telephone him now. And thank you again for your efforts. I know how Mr Buchan can be and I'm grateful at how you've handled his demands.'

'Anything for the war effort, sir,' said Peggy. She sank into her chair after he'd gone. 'What on earth do you wear for dinner at the Ritz?'

Marigold smiled. 'You should know by now that your fairy godmother will provide.'

Wilfred Buchan insisted that they book a private dining room. The table was laid with a pressed white linen tablecloth, adorned with a display of creamy roses and set for four. Buchan immediately pulled his chair closer to Marigold so that Peggy felt very much like a spare wheel until Frank Bauman arrived.

'Apologies for my lateness,' he said, offering his hand to Buchan. 'Frank Bauman.'

Buchan raised his eyebrows. 'Bauman? Is that a . . .'

'German name. Yes. I'm a German Jew who has sought refuge in the safety of the Great British harbour.'

'How poetic,' said Buchan frostily.

As the evening progressed, Peggy became increasingly grateful for Frank's company. Buchan ignored the pair of them completely, preferring to shower Marigold with his attentions. Not that he listened to anything she had to say. He was far more interested in sharing his wisdom on everything from the death of English literature ('No one has written anything of merit since Dickens, alas. And don't try to tell me that Orwell is a shining beacon illuminating the way to a bright literary future. A child could write that dross.') to how the war could be won within the week ('Assassinate Hitler. It really is that simple.'). The more Buchan drank, the louder and more animated his opinions became.

'He really does enjoy the sound of his own voice, doesn't he?' murmured Frank to Peggy as the waiter cleared away their dinner plates.

She laughed quietly. 'My grandmother always says to beware of those with the loudest voices. They rarely have the most interesting or important things to say.'

'She sounds like a wise woman.'

'I wish I were more like her.'

'Don't be so hard on yourself, Miss Sparks. I've noticed glimpses of wisdom in you.' His eyes were shining as he said this and she found herself laughing at his teasing.

'Now, now, what do we have here?' said Buchan, slurring his words as he turned towards them. 'Do I detect an air of coquettish behaviour from our fellow diners? That would never do.'

'More wine, sir?' asked the waiter.

Buchan gave a vigorous nod. 'And another bottle if you have one. I'm sure the Ministry will be happy for us to celebrate our success.' He lifted his glass. 'Cheers to us all.' They raised their glasses in reply. Buchan turned his attention to Peggy. 'Come on, Penny, cheer up. You really are a wet weekend in Bognor, aren't you? Don't you ever smile? You should take a leaf out of Marigold's book,' he said leaning towards her. 'She really is the epitome of womanhood, whereas you . . .' He scowled at Peggy. 'Well, you're not much to write home about. I would snap up this chap in an instant if he'll have you. Although marrying a Jew might not be the best idea right now.'

Peggy was aware of two things happening at that moment. Firstly, Frank jumped to his feet, knocking over the plush red and gold chair he'd been sitting on, and secondly, the room resounded with a stinging slap which caused Wilfred Buchan to clutch his face in surprise. It took them all a moment to realise that this had been delivered by Marigold, whose face was crimson with rage. For a split second, the four of them stared at one another before Buchan exploded. 'What in God's name do you think you're doing?' he roared, leaping to his feet, clutching a dinner napkin to his scarlet cheek.

Marigold squared up to him. 'Doing what a good number of women should have done before me, you horrible little man. I loved your books as a child, but I shall burn them all now. A great writer you may be but you're also nothing more than a lascivious bully!'

'How dare you?' he shouted. 'It was you who led me on with your fluttering eyelashes and cooing flattery. I should have you arrested!'

'I wouldn't if I were you,' said Frank, his eyes flashing dangerously.

Buchan turned on him. 'Oh, are you threatening me now? Well, I'm sure the police would have something to say about an enemy alien threatening one of England's foremost writers. I'm sure the press would too.'

Peggy watched Frank's face now. He seemed calm but she could tell there was seething anger simmering beneath his expression. Buchan sensed it too as he took a step back. 'I also believe that the press would be interested in the way that one of England's greatest writers made unsolicited advances towards one of England's most famous aristocrats. I have a friend at the *Herald*, an enemy alien just like me, who would be happy to print a story like that,' he said quietly. 'Or perhaps it would be better if you simply left and we say no more about the matter.'

Buchan stared at Frank for a moment, weighing up his options before throwing down his napkin and making for the door. He paused before he left, jabbing his finger as he spoke. 'I want nothing more to do with any of you, do you hear? And you can tell Longforth that there is no way he's getting another word out of me.' He threw Marigold a final furious look before storming from the room.

Peggy, Marigold and Frank stood in stunned silence before a dawning realisation crept over Marigold. 'What have I done?' she cried.

Peggy stared at her. 'You've just slapped Wilfred Buchan,' she said, as the beginnings of a smile spread across her face. 'You, Lady Marigold Cecily, have just slapped the great Wilfred Buchan across the face.' A bubble of laughter escaped from within.

'Peggy, it's not funny,' said Marigold, putting a hand to her mouth as a giggle burst forth.

'It is funny,' said Peggy, glancing at Frank who was shaking his head in amusement. 'It's very, very funny and also very wonderful because no one deserved a slap across the face more than the great Wilfred Buchan.' They eyed one another for a moment before dissolving into fits of laughter.

The waiter appeared moments later with Buchan's wine. 'Will sir be returning?' he asked.

This prompted further guffaws from Peggy and Marigold. Frank shook his head. 'No. Sir will not be returning,' he said, before joining in their laughter.

'Oh dearie me,' said Marigold, wiping away a tear. 'What are we going to do? Beecher is going to be furious.'

'We'll think of something,' said Peggy. She turned to the waiter who was hovering in the doorway looking bewildered. 'Could you bring us some tea, please?' She glanced at Frank. 'And some coffee for this gentleman.' Frank inclined his head approvingly. 'Thank you for standing up to Buchan,' she said to him.

He shrugged. 'I merely added my voice. I think you both deserve medals for putting up with him.'

'What do you think we should do?' asked Peggy as the waiter brought their drinks.

Frank looked at them both. 'Well. It seems to me that you have three options available to you.'

'Namely?' said Marigold, taking a sip of wine.

'First option. You come clean. Tell Beecher and accept the consequences.'

Marigold and Peggy shared a wincing look. 'What's option two?' asked Peggy.

'Go back to Buchan and beg. Take him a bottle of whisky and apologise for everything.'

'Never,' they chorused.

'In that case, you have only one choice.'

'Which is?' asked Peggy.

'Write the books as Buchan.'

'We can't do that,' cried Marigold.

'Wait.' Peggy stared at Frank. 'Go on.'

'Well,' he said. 'You're familiar with his writing style and I know you're already adept at editing his words.' Peggy looked sheepish. 'And Miss Cecily could still take the photographs with you visiting the women, Miss Sparks.'

'It's risky,' said Peggy. 'What if Buchan phones Lear to complain?'

'He won't,' said Frank.

'Why not?'

'Ego.'

'I beg your pardon?'

Frank shrugged. 'A man like Buchan has an ego which he needs to preserve at all costs. If he telephones the Ministry to report you two giving him a dressing-down, his ego will be deflated.'

'That's brilliant!' cried Marigold.

'Thank you,' said Frank with a grin.

'It is brilliant, and it might just work if you're prepared to help us,' said Peggy.

'I'm surprised you need to ask, Miss Sparks,' said Frank.

Peggy avoided his gaze and turned to her friend. 'Marigold, do we dare?'

Marigold gave her a dazzling look. 'Peggy, we do.'

Peggy was as jittery as a cornered bird as they produced *Flying High with the Wrens* in the weeks that followed.

Despite reassurances from Marigold and Frank, she was certain that their deception would be uncovered at any moment. It was only when the book was published and Mr Beecher had congratulated them yet again on delivering an outstanding piece of work that she began to relax. She knew they would be asked to work on similar titles soon, but for the time being, she could breathe a sigh of relief. Instead, she concentrated on her work with Mrs Pyecroft. Although the US had entered the war, Peggy was still required to write pamphlets which kept up morale, whilst reassuring the women at home that the men, whose return they longed for, were engaged in a war they would win, and soon. Peggy read and reread her brother's letters, making sure that his sentiments about who he was fighting for and how much he valued letters from home were reflected. After years of enjoying his protection, she felt able to offer him some of her own.

So when Beecher called Peggy and Marigold in to his office one day, she had almost forgotten about Wilfred Buchan. However, when she spotted the books fanned out on Beecher's desk and the way he glared at the pair of them like a headmaster dealing with two disobedient pupils, her stomach flipped. Mrs Pyecroft was standing by the window, arms folded as she observed everything with her customary inscrutable gaze.

'I can see from your faces that you both realise what this is about and indeed, how serious it is,' he said by way of introduction.

'Yes, sir,' they murmured.

'Longforth is apoplectic and although we rarely see eye to eye, I'm not far behind him.'

'We were acting with the best intentions, Mr Beecher,' pleaded Marigold.

'Really, Miss Cecily? You would describe slapping one of the most admired writers in the land and then assuming his identity whilst you complete the writing of one of his books as acting with the best intentions?'

'Well, when you put it like that . . .'

'I'm not sure how else to put it. We're lucky that Buchan isn't suing us for impersonation.'

'We're really very sorry, Mr Beecher. I know we should have come to you after what happened with Mr Buchan, but we thought we could handle it,' said Peggy.

Beecher fixed her with a look. 'Oh, you handled it, Miss Sparks. The truth is you handled it a little too well.' He held up a copy of the most recent book. 'Wilfred Buchan's agent said he couldn't believe that the man himself hadn't written it. That's how efficiently you handled this particular affair. And you would have got away with the whole thing if it hadn't been for the fact that the books did so bally well, the agent noticed when he got paid.'

'It's good to know people are enjoying them,' said Peggy, wincing, desperate to offer something positive.

Beecher stared at her in alarm. 'My dear Miss Sparks, it is not good at all because it means that the public want more of them, and in these desperate times we have no choice but to give the public what they want.'

'Oh. I see.'

'And Longforth wants me to sack the pair of you whilst

others feel that this would be unnecessarily drastic, so you can see my conundrum.'

Peggy stole a glance towards Mrs Pyecroft, who seemed intent on studying the carved detail of Beecher's mahogany filing cabinet. 'We do see, sir. And we're both very sorry. Aren't we, Marigold?'

'Dreadfully sorry, although Wilfred Buchan did need to be put in his place.'

Beecher scowled at her. 'You would do well to maintain an air of contrition, Miss Cecily.'

'Yes, sir. Sorry,' said Marigold, staring at the floor.

'Above all, I feel deeply hurt. I placed my trust in you both, and instead of coming to me, you lied and deceived us all. It is bitterly disappointing.' Peggy's cheeks burned. She could take his anger. It was immediate and would dispel in time, but to think that she had disappointed this man who had put so much faith in her, filled her with shame. 'I'm afraid that I have no choice but to suspend the pair of you for the rest of the week.'

'But, Mr Beecher . . .' she began.

He held up his hand. 'I'm sorry, Miss Sparks. My mind is made up. I will review everything with the relevant parties and let you know our decision. That is all.' He fixed his eyes on the document in front of him as Peggy and Marigold rose to their feet. Peggy stole a glance at Mrs Pyecroft who returned it with a blank expression.

Peggy and Marigold retreated to their desks, shoulders hunched. 'Someone's put the cat amongst the pigeons,' said Sheldrake.

'Oh, shut up, Sheldrake,' said Marigold.

'Personally, I think any woman who can impersonate a writer as great as Buchan is to be admired,' said Dalton.

'Oh, shut up, Wallace,' said Peggy. Dalton and Sheldrake shared a wide-eyed look in an unusual moment of comradeship.

Marigold turned to her. 'I'm still proud of us, Peggy. I'm sorry Beecher's getting it in the neck and who knows what he'll decide, but I think we did the right thing, and we did a good job too. Sometimes you have to stand up for the things you believe, don't you?'

Peggy smiled. She admired this new spirit in Marigold. It had become more apparent since the party at Christmas. It was as if she refused to be held back by her past any more. 'You're right, Marigold. You do,' she said, throwing a glance towards Beecher's office and hoping that he'd find a way to forgive their actions and allow them to return to continue their work. The war was still raging and she couldn't rest until it was over.

Chapter 17

Peggy persuaded Marigold to come and stay with her and her family for the rest of the week. She knew Marigold rarely went out in the evenings since Cordy's death and also that Nancy would be over the moon to have her favourite aristocrat to stay.

'You can come and collect me from school,' she told her. 'And we can read books together. I'm reading *Five Children and It* at the moment. It's very good. I think you'd like it.'

'Must be nice to know you won't be bored during your stay,' said Emily wryly.

'Life's never boring with me around, Great-Gran,' said Nancy.

'Don't we all know it.'

'Gosh, I do love being with your family, Peggy,' said Marigold as they walked to the library after dropping Nancy at school. Flo had been grateful for their help as she, Alice and Emily had to travel to a neighbouring town for WVS duties. 'Everyone's so friendly and kind.'

'You wouldn't say that if you saw my gran before

she's had her tea in the morning,' said Peggy. Marigold laughed. 'Here we are.' Peggy led her up the steps, into the hallowed hush of Edenham library. She introduced Marigold to Mr Alderman and Miss Bunce before leading her to her favourite room.

'I can see why you like this place,' Marigold told her. 'It's so tranquil.'

'I'm never happier than when I'm surrounded by books.'

'I'm the same with photographs,' said Marigold, plucking a Cecil Beaton compilation from the shelf. 'So what do you think old Beecher will decide?'

Peggy shrugged. 'I've never seen him so angry. I feel dreadful about letting him down.'

'It was an impossible situation, Peggy. Buchan was a monster. We didn't have a choice.'

'True, but Mr Beecher has been so kind and encouraging to me. I'd hate for him to feel disappointed in us.'

Marigold fixed her with a look. 'We did a good job, Peggy. I'm sure Mr Beecher will see sense, and if he doesn't . . .'

Peggy didn't want to think about this eventuality. She loved her job, and not just because she sensed she was making a difference. It was more than that now. It was as if she'd been asleep for years and had finally woken up to the possibility of what her life could be.

Their conversation was interrupted by the wail of the air raid siren. Mr Alderman appeared at the door. 'If we could make our way to the shelter, ladies,' he said. They followed him to the brick-built bunker in the library garden. It was gloomy until Mr Alderman lit a lamp and

Peggy spotted her gran's friend Dulcie sitting in the corner with a newspaper on her lap.

'Hello, Mrs Twigg,' she said. 'How are you?'

'Oh fine, dear, apart from my rheumatics and a touch of housemaid's knee. And this is Lady Delphinium, isn't it?' she said, twinkling up at them both.

'Marigold,' said Peggy.

'Of course. Now, Peggy, could you tell me, do I need to be worried about German parachutists landing in my back garden?'

Peggy exchanged a look with Marigold. 'I'm not sure Edenham would be their first choice, Mrs Twigg,' she said. 'The gardens aren't really big enough.'

'Good, that's good to hear,' said Dulcie as a fearsome explosion made them all jump.

'That sounded close,' said Marigold, gripping Peggy's arm.

'I'm sure it'll be all right,' she said, as if by uttering these words aloud it would be true. The all-clear sounded a while later and they trooped out into the open.

As soon as their nostrils filled with the cloying stench of sulphur, Peggy knew something was wrong. Then she saw the young ARP warden, Miss Pugh, running towards them, panic etched on her face. 'The school,' she stammered, her expression creasing with horror. 'The school's been hit.'

'Which school?' asked Peggy, knowing full well what she was going to say.

'St Edward's. They're digging for survivors now.'

'St Edward's?' said Marigold. 'But isn't that . . .?'

'Nancy's school,' said Peggy. Marigold grabbed her hand and suddenly they were running. The two of them and then a large crowd all sprinting in the same direction. Peggy knew this school as well as her own reflection. She and her brother and Flo had all been pupils there, and now Nancy was too. Nancy. Her sweet, laughing face was fixed in Peggy's mind as they darted along the street, all sending up the same silent prayer.

Please let it be all right. Please let the children escape with just a few scratches.

Peggy had encountered some horrifying sights during this war. After the bombing of the Café de Paris, she'd seen the wounded and dead as they were rescued from the underground carnage. Every day, she'd passed houses with their sides blown off, rooms exposed so you could see the furniture still in place as if a giant hand had opened it up like a doll's house. She'd smelt the plaster, sulphur, and ash so dense you could almost taste it, but nothing could have prepared her for the sight of St Edward's school after a German plane dropped a monstrous bomb right on top of it.

It was so awful, so horrific that she had to keep telling her brain it was real. She knew she would be changed forever by what she was seeing and hearing. The sobs and screams. The whimpers of children crying for their mothers. The smouldering crater where pupils had lined up for playtime only half an hour before. The blood. The shattered glass. The crumbled brick. The broken bodies. She felt physically sick but knew she had to force herself to keep looking as she walked through the devastation. She couldn't rest until she found Nancy.

Some survivors wandered in a daze, shocked, bewildered. Peggy was struck by how calm everyone seemed, whereas her heart was hammering in her chest as she cast around in desperation. She had lost sight of Marigold in the chaos but she kept walking forwards. A teacher with blood pouring from her head was leading two frightened little girls towards the ambulances, talking to them in a soothing voice, whilst a group of men and women had already formed a chain to lift rubble from a buried shelter in one corner of the playground. Whenever she thought back to this day, Peggy would remind herself of these people, of their bravery and kindness. It was the only glimmer of light in the pitch-black darkness. She saw mothers racing into the playground, calling for the children who would never come home, and one man weeping over a tiny, mangled body.

She spotted a nurse hurrying back to the ambulances. 'Excuse me. Can you help me? I'm looking for a little girl. My niece.' Peggy's voice cracked at these words.

The nurse's expression was heavy with sorrow. 'I'm sorry. You'll have to look yourself. We're trying to help the critically injured. And there are a lot of them. Alert us to anyone who's seriously hurt, comfort the dying. And the living for that matter.' She touched Peggy on the arm. 'I hope you find her.'

'Thank you,' said Peggy, blinking back tears as Emily Marsh jumped into her brain. *No time for weeping and wailing, Peg. Find that girl.* Peggy turned and it was then that she saw her, not crying or, 'making a bleedin' racket', as Emily would say. She was sitting beside a woman who was lying down and clutching a blood-soaked handkerchief to the side of her face while Nancy held her other hand. Peggy flew to her side. 'Nancy,' she cried, wrapping her arms around her small body. 'Oh, Nancy!'

'Auntie Peg, I'm so glad to see you,' said Nancy, brow crumpled with worry. 'My teacher is hurt and I don't know what to do.'

Peggy cupped her head in her hands and kissed her forehead, inhaling the scent of childhood and the hope it offered. 'Shall I take a look and see what I can do?' she asked. Nancy gave a small nod. Peggy moved alongside the woman. 'I'm Nancy's auntie. My name's Peggy,' she said softly. 'Would it be all right if I had a look at your injury?' The woman's breathing was so shallow, Peggy wasn't sure if she could hear her.

'This is Miss Bright,' said Nancy. 'Do you remember, I told you about her?'

'Of course I remember you telling me about your favourite teacher. Well, there's a thing, Miss Bright,' said Peggy, grasping for a moment's reassurance. 'We're Nancy and Peggy Sparks and you're Miss Bright so we can be bright sparks together.' The woman's lips moved upwards with the shadow of a smile, which gave Peggy the courage she needed. 'Now. I'm just going to move your arm a little.'

Miss Bright gave a sharp intake of breath as Peggy touched her hand. 'Elsie,' she whispered. 'Elsie Bright. Don't let Nancy see.'

'I won't.' She turned to her niece. 'Now, Nance. I need you to stay very still by Miss Bright's side, holding her hand. Can you see that big tree outside the playground?'

223

Nancy looked over to where she was pointing. 'The horse chestnut?'

'That's the one. Keep looking at that tree because it's a special one. Every autumn when we were kids, your mum, dad and me would collect the conkers from under that tree and then your granny would soak them in vinegar and bake them in the oven so we could play conkers. Your dad always won,' said Peggy, gently lifting Elsie's head and prying away the handkerchief. She felt a chill run through her body at the sight of the mangled flesh, sinew and bone where the side of Elsie's face had once been. She quickly replaced the handkerchief and fished her own from her pocket. It had been neatly pressed and handed to her by her mother that morning, the elegantly embroidered 'P' with its delicate lavender decoration facing uppermost. Peggy closed her eyes, conjuring up Alice's smiling face as she pressed it gently against the other handkerchief and allowed Elsie's head to rest to one side. She felt her wrist for a pulse and could tell it was weakening with every tiny beat, like a dying star in the night sky. She cupped one hand around Elsie's other cheek. She was a pretty young woman, probably no more than twenty years old with soft caramel curls and a kind face. Peggy could imagine her reading stories to the children whilst they gazed up at her in wonder, or strolling through the park at the weekends with her sweetheart who was probably now goodness-only-knew where. It was all so unjust. These youngsters, robbed of their lives. Elsie gave a shuddering breath as if she agreed and Peggy stroked her cheek. 'Sleep now,' said Peggy as tears pricked her eyes. 'We're here. You're safe. You can sleep.'

'Is she all right?' asked Nancy.

'She's resting,' said Peggy. She knew better than to lie to her niece. Nancy always implored her to 'tell me the truth, Auntie Peg', and her grandmother had always maintained, 'You tell children what's what. They're too clever to believe lies.'

'So Miss Bright is your favourite teacher?' she asked, taking off her coat and laying it gently across Elsie.

Nancy nodded. 'She teaches us songs. You know I like singing.'

'Why don't you sing one now? I bet Miss Bright would like to hear it.'

Nancy looked unsure. 'Will you sing it with me?'

'I can try.'

Nancy thought for a moment. 'There's one I like because it goes on about bloomin' Heather and Miss Bright doesn't mind when we laugh.'

Peggy gave her a look of encouragement and continued to stroke Elsie's cheek as she began to sing.

> 'Oh, the summertime is coming
> And the trees are sweetly blooming
> And the wild mountain thyme
> Grows around the blooming heather.
> Will you go, lassie, will you go?
> And we'll all go together
> To pull wild mountain thyme
> All around the blooming heather
> Will you go, lassie, go?'

Her voice was sweet as a blessing. Peggy noticed others pause to listen and palm away tears when they heard her. She looked over at Elsie and saw that her ragged breaths had stopped. Her face was resting to one side, her mouth raised in a peaceful smile.

'She's dead, isn't she?' said Nancy.

Peggy nodded, blinking back tears and offering her arms. Nancy accepted and Peggy pulled her close. 'You're a brave girl, Nancy Sparks. I'm proud of you.'

'Nancy!' shouted a voice from the school gates.

She looked up. 'Mama?'

Flo dashed towards them, arms outstretched. Nancy ran into them, burying her head in her mother's chest. 'Nancy, oh Nancy. My dear sweet girl,' she cried through her sobs, planting feverish kisses all over her face.

'Peggy looked after me and Miss Bright, but Miss Bright died.'

Flo pulled Peggy into their embrace. 'I'm so glad you were here, Peg. I'm so relieved,' she whispered through her tears. 'Thank you. Thank you.' They stood for a moment, clinging on to one another, allowing love to offer a shield against the dark horror which surrounded them on all sides.

The next day, Peggy was surprised by an unexpected visitor. Alice was working at the greengrocer's, Emily was visiting Dulcie and Marigold had joined Nancy, Flo and Charlie on a trip to the park. Given the gift of a quiet house, Peggy sat down to write to Joe and tell him about the bombing at Nancy's school. They had discussed it as a family and realised that as he was likely to read about it in the newspapers, they needed to tell him the truth.

'You should write the letter,' said Emily to Peg.

Flo nodded. 'Oh, please could you, Peg? You'll be able to tell him what's happened without alarming him.'

Peggy was just trying to do just that when Badger alerted her to the presence of the visitor by pelting down the hall, issuing a rapid succession of machine-gun fire barks. Peggy put down her pen and followed him. 'All right, Badger. I'm on my way.'

'What an excellent intruder deterrent you have there,' said Beecher as Peggy opened the door.

'Mr Beecher, this is a surprise,' she said. 'Won't you come in?'

'If I'm not interrupting. Apologies for the unannounced visit. I heard about the school and put two and two together. I wanted to see how you all are.'

Peggy's eyes stung with the threat of tears. 'That's very kind of you, sir,' she said quietly. 'Thankfully, Nancy was unharmed, but others weren't so lucky.'

Beecher's face was grave. 'So I've heard.' He sent his gaze heavenwards as if searching for some divine inter-vention. 'The evil that men do,' he murmured, seeming to forget that Peggy was there.

'Would you like some tea?' she asked.

'Only if you're having one.'

'Come through to the kitchen.'

She made the tea, placing a cup in front of Beecher and sitting opposite him at the kitchen table. 'This is a cosy room,' he told her, looking around him. 'Reminds me of my mother's house.'

Peggy tried to read his face for signs of what he was thinking. Their last words had been angry ones and she wanted him to know how sorry she was but also knew how futile any apology would sound. What did that matter now? What good did their paltry campaigns, half-baked words and flag-waving prose do if they couldn't prevent a school being bombed? A whole generation who were growing up together, who had barely begun their lives, wiped out or left to go on alone. And why? Because one lunatic decided to inflict horror on the world and no one seemed able to stop him. What an unspeakably senseless waste of human life. She took a sip of tea, welcoming its comforting warmth.

'My son was killed. In the first war,' said Beecher, fiddling with his teacup. 'He was eighteen years old. His name was Harold.' He stared into the middle distance, a tender smile spreading over his face as if he'd just caught sight of his boy. 'He loved cricket. Had hoped to play for Kent. He made his mother and me so very happy.' Beecher looked away, overcome.

Peggy swallowed. 'I'm sorry, sir.'

Beecher regained his composure. 'Thank you. Sir James told me about your father. I'm sorry too.' He lapsed into silence for a moment. 'It makes one wonder why we do what we do, doesn't it?'

'Yes,' said Peggy. 'I was just thinking the same thing myself.'

'And yet, humans continue to make the same mistakes and never really learn from them.'

'I suppose we have to keep trying.'

He glanced at her. 'You're a very wise young woman, Miss Sparks. You don't always make the right decisions, but I get the feeling you're learning from these errors of judgement.'

'I am, sir. Not that it matters now, but I'm sorry for not telling you about Mr Buchan.'

Beecher waved away her concerns. 'Mr Buchan is of no consequence and never has been.'

'I'm sorrier about your son.'

'Thank you,' said Beecher. 'He was our only child. It's hard when you were once a father and can no longer claim that role. It makes you feel rather lost at times. Fortunately, Mrs Beecher is the very best of women. I am blessed.'

Peggy wasn't sure if it was tiredness or sorrow or merely the years of grief and sadness catching up with her which made her leap to her feet and embrace him, planting a kiss on his cheek. 'Sorry, sir. I couldn't help myself.'

Mr Beecher rewarded her with a benevolent look. 'As I said, Miss Sparks, I am blessed.' He drained his cup before standing up. 'Thank you for the tea. I'm so relieved your niece is all right.' He paused in the doorway. 'And I'll see you and Miss Cecily at work on Monday morning.'

'Thank you, sir.'

He nodded. 'Onwards, Miss Sparks.'

She smiled. 'Onwards, Mr Beecher.'

Dear Peg,

Thank you for your letter. I'm sure you can imagine
how I felt when I first got it. I was about to march
straight in to our commanding officer, but the
sergeant met me at the door and asked me where
I thought I was going. I told him I had to get
home, explained what had happened at Nancy's
school. He can be a bit strict, but I noticed his
eyes go soft when I told him about my girl. He
said he understood, told me any father would feel
the same but that I had to understand that it was
impossible. I got angry then, grabbed his collar
and shoved a finger in his face, shouting all sorts.
Luckily, Albert had caught up with me by then. He
put an arm round my shoulder and told me I had
to calm down, that Nancy was all right and that
was the main thing. The sergeant was watching
me but didn't say anything, just told Albert to take
me away and that he'd speak to us later. I was in
a state, Peg, I don't mind telling you. When the
other blokes found out they all crowded round
offering me ciggies, telling me not to worry, that
they would have done the same. I was worried,
mind. Thought they'd court-martial me, but then
the sergeant sent for me. His face was stern and
I was quaking a bit when he took me to see
our commanding officer. He's a nice older bloke,
reminds me of Mum's boss, Mr Miller. Got the
same moustache. I got in first and apologised to

the sergeant. The CO poured us all a nip of scotch. 'We're men,' he said. 'But we're also fathers and if you can't get passionate about your children then what on earth are we fighting this bally war for?' Then he raised his glass and we did the same and he told us to shake hands. 'We'll not speak of this again, but I want you to take leave for a few days, Private Sparks. Private Cobb will go with you.'

So I've got five days' leave and I'm making the most of the time by writing pages and pages to you all. We're staying in a nice hotel with a radiogram and baths, but the best bit is the library, because guess what I found in there – only a copy of *Our Mighty Navy*. I nearly burst with pride when I showed it to Albert. He was impressed. When we arrived he told me that we had to put the war to one side for a few days and make the most of our time. So we have. We visited ███████████████. What a place! You'd love it, Peg. ████████████ ██████████████████████████████████ ████████████████████████ The scents of jasmine, gardenia and spice are heady. I hope you're impressed by how poetic I'm becoming, but I'm taking these moments to look around the world and take it all in before we're sent back to the daily grind. There's a few Americans staying here at the hotel with us. Nice chaps, well-dressed and good company, who work at the embassy. They reckon things are on the up but then the Yanks are always chirpy, especially as these chaps will be heading back home in a few weeks. All right for some! But I can't complain, being here, so I'm as hopeful as I can be.

I miss you all but I have your photos and letters and Nancy's drawings to keep me going and I thank God every night that she came out of that horror unharmed. I'm so grateful that you were with her, but I can't imagine how it must have been to watch her teacher die. Oh Peg, this blasted war. When will it be over? I wish I could talk to you even for just a few minutes. But don't worry, as I'm in good spirits and with Albert, so you know I'm safe. I know it's taking a few weeks for letters to get censored before they're posted so I hope this reaches you soon. Keep writing and we'll meet again.

Love, Joe

Chapter 18

The devastation at Nancy's school sent ripples through the Ministry and particularly Peggy's department. The war was littered with appalling tragedies but none were more harrowing and far-reaching than those where children lost their lives. These were the events which always caused a doubling down of effort as everyone became more determined to end this dreadful war once and for all. People were changed forever. Peggy certainly had been, and she saw it as well amongst her colleagues. Sheldrake was less snappy and Dalton a little less arrogant. She was pleasantly surprised to receive a call from Frank Bauman too.

'Mr Beecher told me about your niece's school. I'm sorry, Miss Sparks.'

'It's kind of you to call. Thankfully, Nancy is all right.'

'I'm glad. And he said you were there? That must have been awful.'

'Yes, but we're the lucky ones.'

'I admire your bravery, Miss Sparks.'

'It's not bravery, Mr Bauman. It's just living.'

'How wise you are.' Peggy hung up the phone after his call and realised she was smiling.

In the weeks following, it was Marigold's behaviour which particularly surprised Peggy. She was quieter, her fizz and sparkle extinguished, replaced with a blank expression and distracted manner. At first, Peggy put it down to the shock. Everyone seemed to be living under a cloud for the first week or so. However, when Marigold's grey mood looked as if it were in danger of cloaking her permanently, she began to worry. 'Fancy a walk around the square this lunchtime?' she suggested one day.

'What?' said Marigold vaguely. 'Oh, a walk. Yes, all right, but not for long. I've got a lot of work to do.' Peggy shared a wide-eyed look with Sheldrake.

'Beautiful day, isn't it?' she observed as they strolled through the gardens. 'My gran always says that a bit of sun on your face reminds you what it is to be alive.' Marigold didn't answer. She had stopped and was staring at a woman walking hand-in-hand with a little girl of about three who had paused to point out a particularly interesting flower. Peggy placed a hand on her arm. 'Are you all right, Marigold? I know what happened at the school must have brought back some dreadful memories for you.'

Marigold's gaze transferred from the little girl to Peggy as her eyes rapidly filled with tears. 'I ran away.'

'I beg your pardon?'

Marigold stared at her in desperation. 'I ran. I helped one man to an ambulance and then turned on my heels and ran away. I couldn't stay. I didn't help. I'm a monster.' She clutched her face in her hands and sobbed.

'Oh Marigold,' said Peggy, putting an arm around her, ignoring a couple of onlookers who stopped to stare as she led her to the nearest bench. 'You're not a monster. You're a human being and it was too painful for you. It's all right. You have to protect yourself sometimes.'

Marigold blinked at her. 'So you don't think I'm a terrible person?'

Peggy shook her head. 'You did your best. And no, I don't think you're terrible. I think you're lovely.'

This brought on a fresh round of tears. 'Oh Peggy. I've been so worried and ashamed.'

Peggy gave her shoulder a squeeze. 'Trust me, there are plenty of people in the world who should be ashamed right now, and you're not one of them.'

Sir James called Beecher, Longforth and their department staff to a meeting towards the end of the summer. Peggy was heartened to see Mrs Pyecroft already in the room. In the public-school-educated, male-dominated atmosphere of the Ministry, she found something both reassuring and hopeful about her constant presence.

'Good morning, Mrs Pyecroft,' said Beecher. She didn't have time to reply before the door flew open and Longforth crashed through it, banging his folders and papers down on the table in front of him. He was accompanied by Mr Lear who acknowledged their presence with a slight tilt of his head before sitting beside his superior. In contrast, Longforth glared down at the papers as if they had greatly offended him and ignored everyone else in the room.

Sir James arrived moments later. 'Good morning, one and all,' he said, smiling at them as he took his place at the head of the table with Mrs Pyecroft to his left.

Peggy noticed her slide a document towards him which he accepted with an appreciative nod before addressing them. 'Thank you for coming today. Firstly, I want to congratulate you all on some first-class publishing. The Official War Books have exceeded all expectations.' Peggy felt her hands ball into fists as she noticed Longforth's self-satisfied grin. 'The excellent work begun by Mr Beecher's department has been continued with similar aplomb by Mr Longforth's department.'

'Some might say superseded,' muttered Longforth to Lear, who smirked.

Sir James glanced at the document before him. 'Sales to date have exceeded twelve million copies worldwide, and reports from our colleagues in Home Intelligence suggest that over half the population have seen these books and responded favourably to their message, so well done.'

'And if I may be so bold as to add,' said Lear. 'Thanks to these sales, we've also contributed a profit which has helped to subsidise other, perhaps less profitable parts of the Ministry's work.' He shot a glance towards Beecher. Peggy realised that she was clenching her fists so tightly, her knuckles were translucent.

'Thank you, Mr Lear,' said Sir James with a slight frown. 'And of course we mustn't forget the Wilfred Buchan titles.'

'Oh, now how could we forget those,' said Longforth, glaring towards Peggy and Marigold. 'Forgive me, Sir James, but was any action ever taken against this trouble-some pair for assuming the identity of one of the greatest writers of our generation?'

Mrs Pyecroft gave a quiet cough as if clearing her throat. Sir James fixed Longforth with a steely look. Peggy had never seen this man display a hint of anger, but now she recognised a different side to him as he spoke. 'Careful, Mr Longforth. You are an excellent publisher, but it would do you a disservice to question my authority.' Longforth continued to scowl but seemed to shrink a little in his seat as Sir James continued. 'As I was saying, the Wilfred Buchan titles have also been a huge success with reports confirming that these have been very well-received, particularly amongst female readers.' Longforth folded his arms and adopted a bored expression. 'And so, to help build on this success, we would like to combine the talents of both your departments to devise a series of titles about Britain with a plan to publish these books worldwide. It will be part of the cultural diplomacy initiative drawn up with the Minister. We've found that it boosts morale both at home and abroad if we produce titles which illustrate the more universal aspects of British life – life in the town, life in the villages and then thematic angles such as life in an air-raid shelter, life in the ration queue and so on.'

'Sounds rather humdrum,' said Longforth.

'Most people's lives *are* humdrum,' said Peggy. The words were out of her mouth before she could stop them.

Longforth glared at her but Sir James offered a look of encouragement. 'Go on, Peggy.'

Peggy felt Marigold give her a gentle nudge. 'Well,' she said. 'I know from my brother fighting abroad that all he really wants to remember is life back home, the ordinary things, the everyday. Going to the park with his children or the pub with his friends, eating one of Mum's home-cooked dinners or my gran's sponge cakes. Doing all those humdrum things we take for granted. That's what he and his fellow soldiers are fighting for. I think a series of books like this would remind them and everyone else what's important. In fact, that's what we should call it – *Britain at Home*'.

'*Britain at Home*?' said Marigold. 'I like that.' There were murmurs of approval around the room with even Lear giving a shrugging nod, whilst Longforth continued to scowl.

'I think it's an excellent idea,' said Sir James. 'Peggy, since you seem to be the most enthusiastic, I would like you and Miss Cecily to write and illustrate the series, as long as that's in order with you, Mr Beecher?'

'I can think of no finer pairing,' he said with a genial look.

'Is there any reason why we can't write these under our own names?' asked Peggy.

Sir James's eyebrows shot up. 'As Peggy Sparks and Marigold Cecily?'

'Why not?' She noticed that Mrs Pyecroft's eyes were fixed on her, alert as a robin's.

Sir James shifted in his seat and Longforth leapt in. 'The reason, young lady, is quite simple. People will simply not buy these kinds of books if they're penned by a woman.'

'He's right,' said Beecher. No one looked more surprised than Longforth at his words. 'I'm sorry, but it's true. Currently the world only listens to Churchill, Priestley and the King.'

'Precisely, Beecher,' said Longforth with satisfaction.

'You may say that the world is peopled by blinkered numbskulls, but I couldn't possibly comment,' he added.

Marigold nudged her. 'They'd still be your words, Peggy.'

'Miss Cecily is right,' said Sir James. 'It's a great opportunity.'

Longforth goggled at Peggy. 'Great Scott, woman, most chaps would give their eye teeth for a chance like this.'

'Thank you, Mr Longforth,' said Sir James firmly.

Most chaps, thought Peggy. *Not women.* They didn't run the show. It was all down to the men, making the decisions, telling women like her what to do, telling them they couldn't use their real names. And yet as she caught sight of Beecher watching her, she knew there were those who valued their work, who encouraged and championed them. She thought of the words Joe had written in his letter before she started this job.

You're clever, Peg. Cleverer than all of us put together and I know you'll show those blokes at the Ministry a thing or two.

She raised her eyebrows at Marigold, who inclined her head in agreement. 'Very well,' said Peggy, noticing the approving look on Mrs Pyecroft's face. 'When do we start?'

'Right away,' said Sir James. 'But the other reason we have called you here today ...' Peggy noted his use of the word 'we' and also noticed the way that Mrs Pyecroft kept her eyes fixed on the document in front of her, '... is because it's come to our attention that there is something of a frosty relationship between our two publishing departments. We feel that in light of the tragic events at St Edward's

239

school, which brought home to each of us the pure evil we're fighting and which affected some of our colleagues personally,' he glanced at Peggy, who felt Marigold squeeze her arm, 'now is the time for more of a spirit of cooperation between you. We are, after all, on the same side, and God knows, desperate to bring an end to this blasted war sooner rather than later. Wouldn't you agree?'

Beecher bowed his head in agreement whereas Longforth ruminated for a moment before answering. 'Hear, hear, Sir James. Bally terrible tragedy. I have grandchildren of that age. Can't imagine anything worse.' Peggy stared in surprise as the most terrifying man in publishing seemed momentarily overcome before fetching a large polka dot handkerchief from his pocket and blowing his nose. 'We'll do our best, won't we, Beecher?'

'We certainly will, Longforth.'

Sir James and Mrs Pyecroft nodded to one another. 'I'm so pleased we're all in agreement,' he said. 'Jolly good. That's all. Good luck, Peggy, Miss Cecily.'

They produced the first book in just six weeks. With Laurie's help, Peggy made good use of the library to ensure that all her facts were correct, whilst Marigold took new pictures and visited her old friends in the Photographs department to source others.

'*Life in the Town* by Basil Eliot and Herbert Bell,' read Beecher as he delivered a finished copy of the slim volume to their desks. 'Based on George Eliot and Currer Bell, I assume,' he added with an approving nod.

'Yes, sir,' said Peggy.

'You should both be very proud. It's a splendid piece of work. Even Longforth was complimentary.' There had been a noticeable change in the working relationship between Beecher and Longforth following Sir James's meeting. They still loathed one another, but there was less of a competitive edge to their dealings.

'Thank you, Mr Beecher,' said Marigold.

'What's next?' he asked.

'I'm taking the photographs for *Life in the Air-Raid Shelter* this week,' said Marigold. 'Peggy's gran and her friend Dulcie have agreed to pose for me.'

'Jolly good.'

Even Sheldrake seemed impressed. 'Not bad,' he said. 'Although it contains a few too many photographs for my liking.'

'Darling Sheldrake,' said Marigold. 'You can never have too many photographs.' Normally this would have received an eye-rolling response, but instead Sheldrake gave a half-hearted laugh. Peggy had noticed a change in him lately. Initially, she had put it down to the tragedy at the school but realised there was more to it when she went to find Laurie one day and discovered the pair of them drinking tea in the librarians' office, deep in conversation. She tapped lightly on the door and was surprised when Sheldrake leapt up as if he'd been bitten.

'I should be getting back to work,' he stammered, darting towards the door.

Peggy touched him on the arm as he went past. 'It's all right,' she said, glancing towards Laurie who smiled. 'You don't need to leave on my account, Mr Sheldrake.'

He paused, eyes down, face scarlet with embarrassment. 'Thank you, Miss Sparks,' he muttered before leaving. Some days she would see the pair of them walking around the square after work. Occasionally, Sheldrake would join her and Laurie for lunch, and Marigold sometimes came along too. Peggy had taken to eating in the canteen on the days when she was working late and the four of them would often dine together. It transpired that the combination of Sheldrake and Marigold as eating companions was invariably highly entertaining.

One day, Sheldrake placed his tray on their table with a shake of his head. 'That dinner lady hates me,' he said.

'Oh, Mr Sheldrake. Surely not,' said Marigold.

'Why do you think that?' asked Laurie.

'Just look at the size of my semolina pudding compared to yours,' he said.

'Well, there is a war on, Mr Sheldrake,' said Peggy, in a mock-scold.

'I know,' said Sheldrake. 'And I'm grateful for my rations. It's just the way she dishes it out and thrusts it towards me in such a bad temper.'

Peggy folded her arms. 'Isn't it awful when people are irritable?'

Sheldrake looked at them all. 'All right. I know I can be a little terse at times.'

'A little?' said Peggy as Laurie and Marigold laughed. 'You nearly bit my head off the day I started.'

Sheldrake turned to her, hand on heart. 'I apologise, Miss Sparks.'

'Apology accepted.'

'Which dinner lady is it?' asked Marigold.

Sheldrake glanced over his shoulder. 'The one who looks like Churchill.'

'You mean Queenie? Oh, but she's an absolute sweetie. At least she is to me. Gave me extra custard last week.'

'Probably because you're landed gentry.'

Marigold considered this. 'She did work as my uncle's cook for years.'

Sheldrake threw up his hands. 'Well, there you are then. There's respect between the aristocracy and the working classes, but where does that leave me?'

'Perhaps you should try to engage her in conversation,' suggested Laurie.

'About what? The consistency of her semolina?' said Sheldrake, dipping his spoon into the pudding and letting the gelatinous gloop fall back into the bowl.

'I always ask about her grandchildren,' said Marigold. 'She's got twelve. Absolutely dotes on them. And she went through a bad patch last year when her husband died. They were childhood sweethearts. William, his name was.'

Sheldrake stared at her in amazement as Laurie leaned over and whispered, 'Perhaps it's less to do with class and more to do with human kindness, eh?'

The visit was a surprise to almost everyone in the department. Only Peggy and Marigold were in the library at the time, busy working together on their next book entitled *Great English Writers*. Peggy had scored a small victory by managing to convince Longforth that they should include four female writers alongside ten male writers. Now she and Marigold were laying out the text alongside the colour plates Marigold had sourced.

They glanced up as Mrs Pyecroft entered the room with three other women. 'Forgive the interruption,' she said. 'But I have some visitors I'd like you to meet.'

The three women greeted them warmly. At first, Peggy assumed they were local dignitaries. Two of the women stood back a little, like planets orbiting the third. It was then that Peggy looked properly at this woman, dressed in a smart but plain wool coat wearing a tilted hat and a fox fur around her shoulders, and realised she was gazing into the face of America's First Lady. Her first thought was to curtsey before she dismissed this as ridiculous. Mrs Roosevelt was obviously used to people behaving in this way around her, offering a reassuringly warm smile as they shook hands.

'It's a great pleasure to meet you both,' she said. 'I told Magdalena that I very much wanted to visit the young woman who wrote the fascinating article on life in south-east London.' Peggy was struck dumb as she continued. 'I remember turning to my husband after I'd read it and saying how impressed I was by the courage of the people of Britain. Of course that was before our nation joined you in the war effort. I want you to know how proud I am that we're fighting alongside you now.'

'Thank you,' whispered Peggy.

'But where are my manners? Allow me to introduce you. This is Mrs Thompson and Colonel Culp Hobby who are accompanying me on this trip.'

Marigold glanced at Peggy, who was still unable to

speak, so she jumped in. 'Marigold Cecily, and this is Peggy Sparks. Do I detect American accents? Where are you from?'

The First Lady pursed her lips in amusement. 'Washington, my dear.'

'Oh, how marvellous. We're so relieved to have you on our side and I know our boys are too. That's what your brother said, isn't it, Peggy?'

Peggy gave a shaky nod as Mrs Roosevelt looked towards her. 'I have sons fighting in the war so I understand a little of how you feel. How old is your brother?'

'Thirty-two.'

'And does he have family?'

'Two children. A girl called Nancy and a boy called Charlie.'

Mrs Roosevelt shared a delighted look with her companions. 'What utterly charming names. And what are you both working on now?'

'A series of books called *Britain at Home*,' said Peggy, finally finding her voice. 'This one is about English novelists.'

'Wonderful,' said Mrs Roosevelt. 'I am deeply impressed by the efforts of young women such as yourselves in this war. I truly believe that we women have a vital role to play in bringing our sons home.'

'I agree,' said Peggy.

Mrs Roosevelt smiled. 'I thought you might. Magdalena, would you be so kind as to send me copies of Peggy and Marigold's books, please. I would love to read them.'

'Of course,' said Mrs Pyecroft.

Mrs Thompson leaned forwards to whisper in Mrs Roosevelt's ear. The First Lady nodded before turning to them. 'Tommy has just reminded me that we have a lunch appointment so I'm afraid we must be away, but I'm so pleased we were able to find time to come and visit you.' She gazed around the room. 'And in such a beautiful setting. I can't imagine anywhere more wonderful to work than a library.'

'It is, and it was a great pleasure to meet you,' said Peggy, wishing that they could talk for longer now that she'd finally found her voice.

'Oh yes. Marvellous,' echoed Marigold.

After the visitors had left, Peggy flopped into the nearest chair. 'I can't believe what just happened. Can you?'

'What?' said Marigold, gazing at her for a second. Peggy stared at her in amazement before the penny seemed to drop. 'Oh, of course. I know. Who'd have thought that Mrs Pyecroft was called Magdalena?'

Later that evening, after spending most of the afternoon reassuring a distressed Marigold that it was perfectly normal not to recognise the wife of the President of the United States, Peggy packed up her things ready to leave. She noticed that Mrs Pyecroft's office door was ajar, the light pooling from her desk lamp on to the document she was studying. Peggy cleared her throat and she glanced up.

'Miss Sparks.'

Peggy ventured forwards. 'May I ask you something?'

'You may. I cannot guarantee that I will be able to answer it.'

'That's funny. Mr Beecher said something similar to me once.'

'Mr Beecher is a wise man.'

'I just wondered how you come to be on first-name terms with the First Lady?'

Mrs Pyecroft's eyes sparkled. 'She addressed me by my first name but I would never presume to call her Eleanor.'

'But she knows you. Quite well, I think.'

'I have had the good fortune to meet her on occasion. I admire her greatly.'

'So do I, but . . .'

'Curiosity is great quality, Miss Sparks, but it's important to understand that you don't need to know everything. Sometimes it's better that way.' She looked at Peggy. 'Do you know what a pyecroft is?'

'It's a place where magpies like to congregate,' said Peggy, remembering her grandmother telling her the word when they saw a gathering of the birds on one of their walks.

'And do you know what magpies like to do?' she asked.

'Steal treasure?'

Mrs Pyecroft pursed her lips. 'I prefer the term "collect",' she said, holding Peggy's gaze. 'I collect treasure and allow it to shine until it becomes dazzling. I recognised your talents as soon as I met you, and rest assured you have been an instrumental part of my endeavours. I have no doubt that you will continue in that vein. Keep dazzling, Miss Sparks. Who knows where it might lead or when you will be called upon again.'

Dear Peg,

Thank you for your letters. They've arrived at different times so it's been strange reading pieces of news out of order, but I don't mind. We're in a hopeful mood out here as things seem to be going our way. It feels as if we're making real progress, so here's hoping we're home in time for Christmas or the summer if we're lucky! We're a tight unit out here now. We look after one another. Poor Albert got hit by shrapnel the other day, but lucky for him, it struck his belt buckle and he got off scot-free. He joked that if it had hit two inches lower, the world would be robbed of any future little Cobbs. He keeps us all laughing. I must say I like ███████. There are a few more trees and it's a little greener than we've been used to, but it's still hot. Not as bad as the desert though. We bumped into an American tank battalion the other day. They were a decent bunch of blokes, sharing their gum and ciggies. It's always good to see the Americans. They're so sure of victory. 'We're on our way to see Rommel,' they told us with big grins on their faces. I told them about you meeting the First Lady but they didn't believe it. I can't blame them. I can hardly believe it myself. It still makes me chuckle that Marigold didn't know who she was.

But here's some other news – I found one of your new books in the camp library! I couldn't believe it, especially when I opened it to find Gran and

Mrs Twigg grinning out at me! It made me want to laugh, cry and hug you all. It gave me such a lift, as if I were talking to you in person. The other lads are all very impressed. Albert said to 'tell Basil that she writes much better than any bloke I've ever read.' I'm proud of you, Peg. And Marigold. It reminded us all of what we're fighting for and why we're going to win this war. For Gran, for you, Mum, Flo and the kids. I've never been surer in my life that we'll meet again.

Love, Joe

Chapter 19

Peggy swept in through the gates of Senate House, pausing to thank the young man who held open the door for her. The ill-mannered receptionist from her first day at the Ministry was long gone and her bright-eyed replacement acknowledged her now with a respectful tilt of the head. Peggy had shrugged off her fear of the creaking lifts and as she pressed the button to summon one, Sheldrake and Laurie appeared beside her.

'Good morning, Miss Sparks,' said the former.

'Good morning, Mr Sheldrake. Laurie,' she said.

'See you both for lunch?' asked Laurie as they parted company at the entrance to the library.

'See you later,' said Sheldrake.

There had been a great deal of change in the department over the past six months. Peggy, Marigold and Sheldrake had all received promotions and been given staff to manage. Peggy and Marigold had moved to an office on the mezzanine level of the library. It was chaotically untidy on Marigold's side and impeccably neat on Peggy's. Sheldrake still sat ever faithful outside Beecher's office but was in charge of two others, including Dalton, who was less than happy about the situation. The other staff member was Mr Fairchild, who had been restored to the department when he finally managed to conquer his war-induced writer's block by producing an instant bestseller for the *Britain at Home* series on his beloved bard. Peggy and Marigold's two staff members also shared this space. Their names were Hilda and Constance Bream. They were two young sisters who had been introduced to them for consideration by Mrs Pyecroft and were as supremely efficient as she promised they would be. They were also immune to the fawning charms of Wallace Dalton, another fact about which he was less than happy.

The *Britain at Home* series turned out to be a huge success, with Herbert Bell and Basil Eliot becoming firm favourites among the reading public. When the first letter arrived from a member of the War Cabinet congratulating 'Messrs Eliot and Bell on a splendid collection of books celebrating the very best of British life', Peggy was pleased but questioned what those outside the government thought. She didn't have to wait long as they began to receive letters from men and women up and down the country praising the titles and asking for more. However, it was Joe's comments in his letter which made her realise the difference they were making. She took it in to work and watched as Marigold blinked back tears and Beecher gave a quiet cough.

'Well, if that doesn't galvanise our efforts, I don't know what will,' he said.

Peggy and Marigold had come to realise that they alone couldn't keep up with demand for the books, and with the cooperation of Beecher and Longforth, began to commission titles from any famous writer who cared to pen one. Longforth and Lear pooled their contacts so that Peggy found herself working with the likes of John Betjeman and her old friend, Graham Greene, whilst Marigold nearly fainted when Cecil Beaton complimented one of her photographs while they were working on a book together. In some ways, it didn't feel real to Peggy, but she firmly believed that their work was making a real difference to the war effort. There was a part of her which would have liked to see their names on the front cover of their books, of course, but she decided that if they needed to assume male identities in order to win this war then so be it. Steadily they increased their print runs and sales began to boom, and then one day Peggy received a call.

'Peggy Sparks. It's Frank Bauman,' barked the voice.

Peggy was thrown by his unfriendly tone. 'Hello, Mr Bauman. How are you?'

'Apart from being worked to death by you and your colleagues, I'm tickety boo, as you English insist on saying.'

'I'm sorry, I don't quite follow.'

'No, I'm sure you don't, because otherwise you might have consulted with your printer before you doubled your order.'

Peggy's hackles rose. 'I'm sorry. Are you complaining yet again because we're giving you more business?'

'Of course not. But I would appreciate a call to warn me that I'm going to have to do battle with Paper Control again. As you know, they're not keen to give extra paper to a company run by German Jews at the best of times.'

'But I thought that had all been ironed out. I didn't realise it was still an issue.'

'No, well, you wouldn't.'

'Now look here. I think it's unfair of you to take that tone with me. How was I to know that this would happen?'

'Oh, of course. How would you know? You just snap your fingers and hey presto, a book appears.'

'Have you spoken to Mr Beecher?'

'No, I have not spoken to Mr Beecher because the name Peggy Sparks is emblazoned on the order, so I'm speaking to you. Or would you prefer it if I deferred to the man in charge?'

Peggy was furious but more because she had done exactly that. 'Well, what would you like me to do about it, Mr Bauman?'

'Well, Miss Sparks, the ever efficient Mr Burbage has demanded a meeting with us on Thursday at ten o'clock. I suggest that if you want your books printed, you leave the cosy confines of the Ministry and come along.'

'Fine. I'll be there,' said Peggy, determined not to give this infuriating man the satisfaction of knowing how annoyed she was.

'Fine. I'll see you then.'

'Goodbye, Mr Bauman.'

'Goodbye, Miss Sparks.'

Peggy glared at the receiver for a moment before slamming it back down on to the cradle. 'That man.'

'What man?' asked Marigold, glancing up from the photographs she was studying.

'Frank Bauman. He just berated me for something I didn't even know I'd done.'

'That sounds a little unfair,' said Marigold.

'Why can't he just be polite? I thought we had an understanding after we worked on the Buchan books.'

'I was beginning to think he was in love with you,' said Marigold casually.

'I beg your pardon?' said Peggy, her cheeks growing hot.

Marigold's eyes narrowed. 'You like him too.'

Peggy huffed, hoping that Marigold didn't spot the bloom of a blush. 'You'll excuse me, I do not. He's the rudest man. Like a Jekyll and Hyde character. Nice as pie one minute and then utterly objectionable the next.'

'Well, make sure you tell him.'

'I will,' said Peggy. 'I'm fed up with these unreasonable men.'

'I think we all are,' said Marigold. 'Boo to Buchan and Bauman.'

Peggy could tell that something was wrong as soon as she turned her key in the front door that evening. It was too quiet. Usually she would be greeted by either Nancy, Charlie, Badger or invariably all three of them hurtling down the corridor towards her. Tonight, both children were absent and Badger merely padded into the hall and stopped, throwing a worried glance back towards the kitchen. As Peggy heard the low murmur of her mother's voice and the occasional hiccupping sob, a chill ran through her body. She was torn between wanting to move towards them and remaining frozen to the spot, unknowing. As she pushed open the door to the kitchen, her eyes were immediately drawn to the telegram on the table.

'Peggy,' said her mother. 'I didn't hear you come in.'

'What's happened?' said Peggy, looking from the telegram to her gran's frowning face, to Charlie nestled on Flo's lap as she cried silent tears.

Nancy, who had been resting her head against Alice's shoulder, rushed forwards. 'Oh, Auntie Peggy,' she cried, throwing her arms around her middle. 'Daddy's been taken prisoner.'

'Prisoner?' said Peggy. Her first thought was one of relief. *He's not dead. Joe's still alive.*

'It doesn't make sense,' said Emily, frowning at the telegram as if this scrap of paper were to blame. 'I thought our boys were on the up in Africa.'

The words swam before Peggy's eyes as she plucked it from the table.

IMPORTANT HAND DELIVERY . . . OFFICIAL INFORMATION RECEIVED . . . PRIVATE J. C. SPARKS IS A PRISONER OF WAR . . . LETTER FOLLOWS SHORTLY

'Oh, Auntie Peggy!' wailed Nancy.

'Hush now, child,' scolded Emily. 'You'll scare your brother.'

Charlie was sitting on his mother's lap, regarding them all through wide eyes, his thumb clamped firmly in his mouth. Peggy noticed Flo pull him closer and stroke his soft brown curls. 'It's all right, Nancy,' said Peggy, sensing she was saying this more for her own benefit. 'Your daddy is safe. They take good care of prisoners of war. It's the law.'

'As if Hitler abides by the law,' muttered Emily.

'Mum,' warned Alice before turning to her grand-daughter. 'Peggy's right, Nancy. Your daddy is safe and we'll get a letter soon.'

'Can I write to him?' asked Nancy.

'Oh yes,' said Peggy. 'He'll be able to get post as usual and he can write to us too.'

'That's good. At least he's all right. Not like poor Alfie Riley's dad.'

Peggy hugged her close. She had seen Mrs Riley in the queue for the butcher's only last week, a child hanging off each arm, her eyes weighted with sorrow, staring into the distance. 'I know. We must be grateful for these things and we must stay cheerful, because that's what your daddy would want.' Nancy nodded.

'Time for bed, young lady,' said Alice, holding out her hand. 'Want me to take Charlie, Flo? You look done in.'

'Come on, give 'im 'ere,' said Emily, holding out her arms.

'I thought you didn't like bedtimes, Great-Gran,' said Nancy, following her up the stairs.

'Well, I'm full of surprises, me,' she told her.

Peggy sat beside Flo after they'd gone. 'You all right?'

Flo shrugged. 'Not really, but it's true what you say. At least he's alive.'

'They have to look after prisoners of war, Flo. It'll be all right.'

Flo stared at Peggy, imploring, eyes brimming with

tears. 'But what if he's not, Peg? What if he doesn't come home?'

Peggy took hold of her hand. 'We'll have none of that. He's alive. He's safe. Everything will be all right.'

'We'll meet again?' asked Flo.

Peggy held her gaze and sent up a silent prayer. 'We'll meet again.'

There was something about the daily drudgery of war that reminded Peggy of a conveyer belt, endlessly moving you forwards. It never stopped and you could never get off. You had no choice but to keep going. There were times when loss or grief, worry or fear would do its best to drag you backwards, but you couldn't allow it. You had to keep moving forwards, to believe that there would be better days ahead. That was why Mrs Cooper was always polishing her front step, why Mr Miller the greengrocer opened his shop the day after his daughter was killed and why, on the morning after they received the telegram, Peggy and her family were up early as usual, getting ready for work and school. Only Nancy seemed reluctant to follow the usual routine.

'But what if a letter from Daddy arrives while I'm at school?'

'Well then, it'll be here when you get back,' said Emily, who was sitting at the kitchen table, plaiting her hair.

'But I don't want anyone else to read it first.'

'Then we'll wait and read it together.'

'But—'

'No buts! That's an end to it, Nancy Sparks. Now stop

wriggling. You're making your plaits all lumpy.' Nancy buttoned her lips together but wore a deep scowl, mirroring Emily's own frown of concentration.

'Look at the pair of you,' said Peggy, watching them from the doorway. 'Like peas in a pod. Right, I'm off.'

'Have a good day, dear,' said Alice, kissing her on the way past.

'You too, Mum. Will you phone me if there's news?'

'Of course. You and Mrs Cooper will be the first to know,' said Alice with a weary smile.

'What's wrong?' said Marigold as soon as Peggy entered the office.

'What do you mean?'

'I can see it in your face. I have a good intuition about these things.'

Peggy cursed the way her expression always betrayed her thoughts. Her mother often joked, 'You're an open book, Peg. It's like reading a story looking at you sometimes.'

'Joe's been taken prisoner.'

Marigold put a hand to her mouth. 'Oh Peggy. I'm so sorry. Why didn't you stay at home today?'

'And done what? Fretted the day away? No, and besides, I've got that meeting with Frank Bauman. Can't say I'm looking forward to it, mind.'

'I'll come with you.'

'You don't need to, Marigold.'

'I want to. We girls must stick together against these objectionable men.'

'All right,' said Peggy, grateful not to be facing the inevitable wrath of Frank Bauman alone. 'Thank you.'

They left the office later than Peggy would have liked due to Marigold telling the department about Joe, which led to visits from every member offering words of encouragement. Beecher told her that his door was always open whilst Sheldrake brought her tea and Mrs Pyecroft assured her, 'If your brother has even half your courage and determination, all will be well.'

They hurried across London and on reaching the correct street, struggled to find the building they were looking for. They had walked past it three times before Marigold spotted a grubby sign and realised they were in the right place. Peggy was thrown into a panic on noticing that they were now ten minutes late. Naturally, Marigold took it all in her stride, which only added to Peggy's vexation. She didn't need another reason for Frank Bauman to find fault with her today.

'Now remember, Peggy, don't let him boss us around. Agreed?'

'Agreed,' said Peggy, turning the door handle and leading them both inside. She was surprised to find that there didn't appear to be a receptionist or indeed a reception. The dimly lit hallway with walls the colour of badly made tea led to narrow corridors on both sides, whose doors remained stubbornly shut. In the distance, they could hear the churn and hiss of a printing press. Peggy's cheeks burned wondering how on earth they were going to make their presence known. Marigold, on the other hand, thought nothing of standing at one end of the corridor and shouting.

'Hello? Anyone home? Hello? Mr Bauman?'

After a pause, a door at the far end opened and Frank's face appeared. 'At last,' he said, looking less than impressed. 'So good of you to join us.'

'Yes, well, perhaps if your sign weren't so dirty, we would have been able to read it properly,' said Marigold.

'I'm dreadfully sorry. I'll get the footman to polish it immediately,' said Frank, folding his arms.

'We apologise for our lateness,' said Peggy.

He regarded her for a moment as if trying to decide if her apology was genuine before ushering them inside. Peggy was immediately relieved to see Rosa sitting at the battered, scratched table as Frank took his place beside her. She glanced up with a reassuring smile. On the opposite side sat Royston Burbage from Paper Control, looking grim. The room was as dim as the hall. Peggy noticed patches of damp in one corner of the ceiling and peeling yellowing paint around the windows.

'Mr Burbage, you were saying?' said Frank impatiently before Peggy and Marigold had even had a chance to sit down.

Rosa held up her hand and turned to them. 'I would like to apologise for Frank's manners. Again,' she said, raising an eyebrow at her brother. Peggy was immediately reminded of how much she liked this woman. 'Miss Sparks and Miss Cecily, welcome. It's good to see you again. I believe you know Mr Burbage?'

'Charmed,' said Marigold, flashing her Hollywood smile first at Mr Burbage before resting it on Rosa.

'We do know Mr Burbage but he perhaps doesn't recall us,' said Peggy, turning to him. 'Good afternoon, sir, and manifold apologies for our lateness. I'm Peggy Sparks and this is Marigold Cecily. We oversee the publication of the *Britain at Home* series at the Ministry. I believe there are issues with paper supplies? I hope we can find a solution which is agreeable to all.' She glanced at Frank, who was regarding her with interest.

'Mr Burbage was just telling us about the *Book Production War Economy Standard*,' said Frank. 'I'm sure you're both familiar with it?'

Peggy knew he was issuing a challenge but before she had a chance to answer, Marigold bowled in. 'Oh, but of course, it's my favourite bedtime read,' she said with a chuckle.

Mr Burbage frowned. 'It is a highly important pamphlet and one with which every individual involved in the production of printed matter should be familiar.'

'Oh, we are, Mr Burbage,' said Peggy. 'Very familiar. Aren't we, Marigold?' she added with meaning.

'Desperately familiar,' said Marigold. 'I feel I know it better than my own family.'

'You no doubt have deep concerns about typographical standards then?' said Frank with one eyebrow raised.

Peggy was used to being underestimated by men and was ready. 'It's a challenge, of course, to decide whether to compromise the number of words on the page or the font size, but we're very strict about adhering to the guidelines. It's vital that paper rationing rules are followed to the letter,' she said, fixing him with a triumphant look. Frank's other eyebrow was now also raised in surprise.

'I'm very glad to hear that, Miss Sparks,' said Mr Burbage. 'And I'm delighted to know that you've taken such great interest in the guidelines. Some on the publishing side of the Ministry dismiss our work as dull.'

'How could they?' said Frank, his eyes glittering with amusement, ignoring the deathly stare coming from Rosa.

'Well, it's our duty, isn't it, Marigold?' said Peggy, determined to maintain the upper hand.

'What?' said Marigold, stifling a yawn. 'Oh yes, our absolute duty.'

'And so to business,' said Mr Burbage. 'These *Britain at Home* titles you're producing . . .'

'Yes,' said Peggy, reaching into her bag and pulling out a copy. 'They're selling very well, hence us needing more paper.'

Mr Burbage picked up a copy of *Life in the English Village* and peered at it in bewilderment. He flicked through the book. 'There are a lot of pages,' he said. 'And illustrations.'

'We could reduce that,' said Peggy. 'And have fewer illustrations.'

'Some of these chapter headings and breaks are rather extravagant,' he said.

'Oh dear me,' said Frank. 'That's one of the watchwords of the *Book Production War Economy Standard*, isn't it, Mr Burbage? We can't have extravagance.'

Peggy narrowed her eyes. Frank Bauman was infuriating. 'We can be far less extravagant,' she told him.

Mr Burbage sighed. 'It's a lot of paper.'

'I know, sir,' said Peggy. 'But these books are part of the Minister's own plans to raise morale both at home and abroad.'

'Because nothing raises morale more than a book about English village life,' muttered Frank. Peggy threw him a dagger glare as Rosa nudged him with her elbow.

'Look, Mr Burbage, we know how busy you are,' said Marigold in a voice as smooth as silk. 'And we are very grateful for your time and the important work you do. So, if Peggy and I personally pledge to make sure that all your standards are adhered to, do you think you could see your way to allowing us a little extra paper? Please?' He gazed at her in the way that Peggy had often seen men gaze at Marigold. He was a planet in her sun's orbit and there was nothing he could do to escape her magnetic charm.

Mr Burbage's stern expression melted. 'Very well,' he said. 'But I shall be keeping an eye on this operation. Mark my words.'

'Oh, Mr Burbage, you are a peach,' cried Marigold, clapping her hands like a little girl who'd just been prom-ised a bowl of ice cream. 'Thank you. A thousand times, thank you!'

Mr Burbage's expression melted further into an indul-gent simper. He held out the copy of *Life in the English Village* to Peggy. 'Oh please, keep it,' she said.

He shook his head. 'Thank you, but no. I'm not much of a reader.'

'Makes sense,' said Rosa, after he'd gone.

'We did it, Peggy,' said Marigold, seizing her by the shoulders.

'We did,' said Peggy.

'Bravo,' said Rosa.

'Congratulations,' said Frank, with an edge of bitterness. 'Interesting to note that your friends at Paper Control capitulate when the cavalry from the Ministry arrives but won't entertain the requests of two Jews.'

'Frank,' warned Rosa.

'What?' said Frank, throwing up his hands. 'Is that not true? We both spoke to them, told them exactly what you just said, almost to the letter, but they wouldn't listen.'

'I'm sorry,' said Peggy. 'I had no idea.'

He held her gaze for a moment. 'That's the problem. Most people don't.' He gathered up his papers and made for the door. 'Thanks for coming along to save the day.' Peggy watched him go with a mixture of indignation and guilt.

'Don't mind Frank,' said Rosa whilst Marigold disappeared to 'powder her nose'. 'He's got a bee in his bonnet.'

'It sounds as if he's entitled to have one,' said Peggy.

Rosa shrugged. 'We are lucky to be safe in England but he worries about our family in Germany. We both do. It's the not knowing which is most difficult. It hangs heavy on us. My brother isn't always able to put these things aside.'

'I'm sorry. It must be hard.'

'I think it is hard for everyone. You have family fighting in the war?'

'My brother is, was, fighting in North Africa. We heard yesterday that he's been taken prisoner.'

'Now it's my turn to be sorry,' said Rosa. 'I hope everything works out.' She stood up and held out her hand. 'It was good to see you and Marigold again, Peggy, and don't mind Frank. Underneath that gruff exterior, he has a kind heart. Now if you'll excuse me, I need to make some telephone calls to source more staff. We're going to be very busy, thanks to you, and we are grateful, despite what Frank might have you believe.'

'I thought that went rather well,' said Marigold as they returned to the Ministry.

Peggy nodded, although Frank's assertions bothered her. She hated the idea that he and Rosa would be treated this way, but she also hated the idea that he might think less of her because of it.

Chapter 20

Peggy and her family had taken to hovering by the front window at different times of day as they waited for word from Joe, hoping to spot the postman or telegram delivery boy. On Saturday morning, a screech went up from the front room, followed by a bellowing cry from Charlie. Peggy came running with Emily on her heels.

'What's all this then?' demanded Emily as she spotted Nancy perched primly by the windowsill while Charlie lay on the floor in a sobbing heap.

'She pushed me off,' said Charlie, pointing an accusing finger towards his sister.

Peggy plucked him into her arms. 'Nancy, did you push your brother?'

'He fell,' said Nancy.

'Liar!' squeaked Charlie as Flo came running downstairs from where she had been changing the beds with Alice.

'Right. That's it,' said Emily. 'We're going to the park. Nancy, you're coming with Auntie Peg, Badger and me.'

'But I want to stay here and wait for the letter,' wailed Nancy.

Peggy handed Charlie to Flo and knelt before Nancy. 'No one will read the letter without you.'

Nancy regarded her with sorrowful eyes. 'Promise?'

'Promise.' Peggy leaned in to whisper. 'And maybe we can visit Mrs Huggins.'

Nancy's eyes brightened. 'For a quarter of barley sugar twists?' Peggy nodded. 'I only really like the orange ones,' said Nancy.

'Orange barley sugar twists it is, then,' said Peggy. 'Come on. Get your coat.'

The weather couldn't make its mind up between clinging on to winter or embracing the promise of spring. The frost-cloaked morning was melting away as the sun began to warm the day and the sky shone icy blue. Peggy pulled up the collar of her coat as she and Emily walked behind Nancy, who was skipping along the street with Badger on his lead, trotting happily beside her.

'What it is to be young and able to shake off your worries with a trip to the park and the promise of a bag of sweets eh, Gran?' said Peggy, linking arms with Emily.

'Mmm,' said Emily with an unusual lack of gumption.

Peggy glanced at her grandmother. She'd noticed a change in her of late. It wasn't a monumental change. She was still as obstinate and direct as she'd always been, but Peggy saw a certain weariness in her demeanour these days. She'd always been the one to chivvy them all along, to keep them laughing or fighting. That spirit was still there but it seemed to Peggy as if she had become worn down by the years and years of being the beating heart of their family. It was hardly surprising. Emily Marsh had survived the death of her husband and her son-in-law, and now her grandson was in danger. Even if you were as strong and resilient as she, these things took their toll.

'You all right, Gran?' Peggy asked as they entered the park and began their stroll around its perimeter.

'What? Me?' said Emily. 'I'm fine, Peg. I'd feel a lot better if we'd heard from Joe, but that's the same for all of us. Especially that one,' she said, gesturing towards Nancy who had just called over her shoulder that she and Badger were 'running up the big hill'. Emily turned her face upwards. 'That's better,' she said. 'A bit of sun on your face always does the trick. So, how's work?'

Peggy's eyes lit up. 'I enjoy it. I feel lucky to be working there.'

'They're lucky to have you, Peg. You've done us all proud.'

'Thanks, Gran.'

'We always knew you would, mind, right from when you were a nipper. You were so full of questions, whereas your brother had all the answers.' Emily chuckled at the memory. 'I remember the day the pair of you turned to your dad and said, "We want to visit the King. Where does he live?" And he told you, "Buckingham Palace." "Where's that?" you said. And I can still see your dad looking over at me with that twinkle in his eye he always got when he was playing along. He took out his pocket watch and said, "You can catch the quarter past ten train from Edenham Station, go all the way to the end of the line at Charing Cross, walk out to the front of the station, turn left and then go through the big arch, you can't miss it, straight down The Mall all the way to Buckingham Palace, past Queen Vic's gold statue, and if the flag's flying on the top of the palace, you'll know the King's at home. Go up to the front door, ring the bell and tell the footman you've arrived to have tea with the King, milk, one sugar, please.'" Emily chuckled again. 'And do you know what you did?'

'Tell me,' said Peggy. She'd heard the story a thousand times before but always loved the way her gran told it.

'You and Joe fetched your coats and shoes and scarpered out the door while our backs were turned. First thing we knew was when the policeman knocked on our door two hours later with the pair of you in tow. You'd got all the way to Charing Cross before someone clocked you.' She chucked Peggy under the chin. 'Your dad sent you to bed without a story and no supper for Joe, but I remember he wasn't really cross. He turned to me later and said, "Well, Ma, they're a pair of bright sparks, aren't they? They're going to do great things one day."' Emily's eyes glistened. 'Turns out he was right, wasn't he? He'd be proud of you and your brother.' She patted Peggy's hand. 'I know I am.'

Nancy skipped towards them now. 'I've thought of some more questions,' she called.

Emily cocked her head towards Peggy. 'And there's another bright spark, right there,' she said with a look of satisfaction before turning back to Nancy. 'Go on then, young lady, what is it now?'

Work at the Ministry offered a blessed escape from all the fretting and waiting. Peggy and Marigold had never been busier, and the Minister himself had even been down to the department to congratulate them both on the *Britain at Home* series which had just published its fiftieth title. After the meeting with Mr Burbage, Peggy made sure to call Rosa once a week to check that everything was running smoothly.

One day, Frank happened to answer the telephone, his voice bristling with impatience. 'Yes?'

Peggy recognised his voice immediately but pressed on. 'I wanted to speak to Rosa if she's available, please?'

'She's in a meeting.'

'Is that Mr Bauman?'

'Is that Miss Sparks?'

She detected a note of amusement in his tone. 'It is. And since Rosa is unavailable, perhaps you could tell me how everything is going.'

He sighed. 'Apart from having too much work and not enough staff, everything is simply top-hole, as you might say.'

Impossible man, she thought, pressing on. 'And you've had no more issues with Paper Control?'

'No. Evidently your Lady Cecily's charms worked wonders on Mr Burbage and his department.'

'I'm glad to hear it.'

'Well, if that's all, I don't really have time for idle chit-chat.'

Something inside Peggy snapped. 'Would it be beyond you to be civil? I know the situation was unpalatable, but I have done my best to sort it out and I don't think I deserve your rudeness.'

'I'm sorry?'

'Apology accepted.'

There was a pause on the other end of the line. 'I am sorry. I shouldn't have spoken to you like that.'

'Again, apology accepted.' There was another pause. 'Well, I best let you get on.'

'Have you heard from your brother?'

The question was as surprising as a proposal of marriage. 'How did you . . .?'

'Rosa told me. Just after she'd berated me for antagonising you the other day.'

Peggy laughed. 'I like your sister even more now. Unfortunately, the answer is no. We've had no news, but no news is good news, as we British like to say.'

It was Frank's turn to laugh. 'You British do love to see the positive side, don't you? Drink tea and keep the home fires burning and so on.'

'What else can you do?'

'True.'

'And what about your family? Any word?'

'Nothing for over a year.'

'I'm sorry.'

'No news is good news, Peggy.'

She heard the change in his tone as he called her by her first name. Friendly. Warm, even. 'Very true, Frank,' she said.

There was a brief pause. 'Well. I best get back to work. I'll tell Rosa you called.'

'Quite right. No time for idle chit-chat. Goodbye,'

said Peggy, placing the receiver in the cradle, wondering why she hoped he would answer the next time she called.

'I'm signing up to be an air-raid warden,' announced Marigold over lunch one day.

'Are you indeed?' said Sheldrake with a sideways glance at Laurie and Peggy. 'I hope you don't chip a nail.'

'Oh, hush now, Cyril,' said Marigold. As their friendship had grown, the four of them had relaxed into first-name terms. 'There are more important things to worry about than broken nails.'

'How profound. I believe Churchill said something similar during one of his recent broadcasts,' he said, gazing towards the ceiling in mock-awe.

Marigold smacked him on the arm as the others laughed. 'Horrible man.'

'Well, I think it's laudable,' said Laurie.

'Thank you, Laurie,' said Marigold. 'You see, Cyril. That's how a true friend behaves.' Sheldrake pulled a face.

'I'd volunteer back home if it weren't so late by the time I got there,' said Peggy.

'Why don't you volunteer round here with me?' suggested Marigold. 'The chief warden, Mr Baggley, said they needed more people, particularly as the Luftwaffe seem to be back with a vengeance. You could stay over at my place after your shifts.'

Peggy considered this. The endless churn of war was exhausting, but the only way to bring it to an end was to do something. She knew that their books were playing their part but there was still a way to go. They needed to pull together and keep pushing forwards. She sensed that if she could help others, she'd be helping Joe too. 'All right,' she said. 'When do we start?'

'Now this is a ceiling pike,' said Ronald Baggley in a slow, deliberate voice. They had gathered for training in the local church hall a few days later with half a dozen other new female recruits, including Hilda and Constance. 'It is over three metres long. The purpose of the ceiling pike is for you to poke the ceilings of damaged buildings to assess their safety. But you must ensure that you are wearing your tin helmet when you do this in case any debris becomes dislodged and strikes you on the cranium. The bill hook on the end of the pike can be used to snag any stray remnants of aforementioned debris.' Peggy's eyes grew heavy at his soporific delivery. She felt Marigold lean against her arm and begin to snore gently. 'Now this is a gas rattle,' he went on, holding it up for them to see. 'The purpose of the gas rattle is to give the public a warning of a potential gas attack. If we give the rattle a spin, thus . . .'

The deafening clatter which followed caused Marigold to leap from her chair in fright. 'Heavens to Betsy,' she cried, clutching her chest.

Mr Baggley continued undeterred, '. . . we are able to alert the general public to the threat of an imminent gas attack or of a gas attack drill. After a gas attack or gas attack drill or indeed an air raid, we sound the all-clear with a bell.' He lifted a brass handbell from the table beside him and gave it a hearty shake. 'Any questions?'

'When do we get our overalls?' asked Marigold, eyeing a pile of navy cotton garments at the back of the room. She had already told Peggy that she was happy as 'blue is very much my colour'.

Mr Baggley smiled. 'I'm glad you're so keen, Miss Cecily. Perhaps you and Miss Sparks could help me with a training demonstration in the back yard?'

'We'd be delighted,' said Peggy.

They all trooped out through the side door and stood in a semicircle around Mr Baggley. 'Now this is a stirrup pump with hose attachment. The purpose of the stirrup pump is to put out small fires. It requires two people to operate it so, Miss Sparks and Miss Cecily, if you would be so kind as to step forward. Who would like to man the pump?'

'I will,' said Peggy, seizing the wooden handle with both hands.

'Jolly good. So, Miss Cecily. You take hold of the hose.'

'Right-ho,' said Marigold, accepting it from him with the guarded suspicion of someone being passed a poisonous snake.

'It's very important that you point the nozzle away from other people,' said Mr Baggley, gesturing towards the other giggling volunteers.

'Away from people. Right,' said Marigold, directing the hose across the yard towards the front gates.

'And then, Miss Sparks, if you would be so good as to pump the handle, please.'

Peggy did as she was told with gusto. A spurt of water leapt from the front of the hose, causing Marigold to drop it in fright. The hose then reared up like an angry cobra, cascading water towards the gate where a couple of men, one of whom was Dalton, were walking past. 'Watch out!' he cried, laughing. 'If that's what happens when you give a girl a hose to operate, it's no wonder they won't give them a gun.'

'Marigold, swap with me,' said Peggy, grabbing the hose from the floor. As soon as Marigold began to pump, Peggy pointed the nozzle towards Dalton and his snickering friend who didn't have time to jump out of the way before they were both soaked. 'Oh sorry,' she called, holding up her hand. 'It's just that I'm a girl so I don't really know how to use this properly. Apologies. Apologies, Mr Baggley,' she said handing the hose back to him whilst the other volunteers fell about.

'This is a very expensive suit,' cried Dalton.

'Oh shush now, Wallace,' said Marigold. 'It's only water.' She peered into the metal bucket and pulled a face. 'Just dirty brown water.' She caught Peggy's eye and they both howled with laughter whilst Mr Baggley looked on helplessly and Dalton and his friend shook their heads in annoyance.

'Well,' said Mr Baggley. 'I think you get the gist of how the stirrup pump works and how it is vital that you avoid pointing it at people.'

'Unless they're patronising dolts like Wallace Dalton,' murmured Marigold.

'Yes, and then the purpose of the stirrup pump is to give them a soaking,' said Peggy before they both burst into helpless laughter again.

They were still chuckling when they reached Marigold's flat an hour or so later.

'Odd,' said Marigold as she opened the door. 'I was sure I double-locked it. Oh.' She stopped in her tracks at the sight of Lady Lavinia Cecily standing in the kitchen doorway. 'Mummy. What are you doing here?'

Lady Lavinia seemed different to the icy individual Peggy had met before. Her frame was hunched, her eyes wrinkled with obvious distress. She frowned when she saw Peggy. 'I didn't know you were entertaining, Marigold.'

'I'm not. Peggy is just staying here after our ARP shifts.'

Lady Lavinia's eyebrows raised. 'ARP, eh? How noble.'

Peggy noticed Marigold's shoulders stiffen, but there was a boldness about the way she responded, a refusal to be cowed. 'Well, we all need to do our bit,' said Marigold. 'And to what do I owe the pleasure? I thought you always stayed at the Savoy.'

Lady Lavinia glanced at Peggy again. 'It's a private matter.'

'I can go home,' said Peggy.

'No,' said Marigold, fixing her mother with a determined look. 'Peggy is my guest.'

'Well then, why don't I make some tea while you talk to your mother?'

Marigold and Lady Lavinia eyed one another reluctantly before Marigold took the initiative, ushering her mother into the living room. Peggy set about preparing tea, doing her best to ignore the increasingly audible exchange which filtered out to the kitchen. After a while she heard the living room door slam and a moment later Marigold appeared in the doorway. 'Well, she hasn't changed one bit.'

'Are you all right?' asked Peggy.

Marigold shrugged. 'She's left my father, not for the first time, I might add. He's known for his affairs and gambling and drinking. I can't blame her, but when I tried to comfort her, she pushed me away like she always does.'

'I'm sorry, Marigold,' said Peggy, putting an arm around her friend's shoulder.

'Thank you,' said Marigold. 'I'm all right. Really. It doesn't upset or surprise me any more.'

Peggy squeezed her hand. 'Would you like some tea?'

Marigold shook her head. 'I'm going to bed. Mother is going to sleep in the other guest room. Will you be all right?'

'Of course. I might see if your mother wants some tea.'

Marigold sighed. 'I wish you luck. Goodnight.'

'Goodnight, Marigold, and thank you for persuading me to come along tonight. I'm glad we're doing this together.'

Marigold smiled. 'Me too.'

Peggy tapped on the living-room door before pushing it open. Lady Lavinia was sitting on the sofa, staring dejectedly at the photograph on the mantelpiece of Marigold and Cordy. 'It's a lovely picture of them, isn't it?' she said.

Lady Lavinia looked up vaguely. 'What? Oh yes, I suppose so.'

'I thought you might like some tea,' Peggy said, placing it before her.

Lady Lavinia's ice-cold demeanour defrosted slightly. 'Thank you – Peggy, isn't it?'

'Yes,' she said, making for the door. 'I'll leave you to it . . .'

'Marigold thinks I'm a monster, doesn't she?'

Peggy froze, momentarily caught off guard. 'I'm not sure I should be speaking on her behalf, but I think monster is a strong word.'

'I wish I could talk to her,' Lady Lavinia said. 'But my mother never talked to me, you see.' Peggy sat down at the other end of the sofa and Lady Lavinia turned to her. 'Do you talk to your mother?'

'All the time,' said Peggy. 'And my grandmother. But everyone is different.'

'I enjoyed visiting your house that time, but I couldn't stay for long. It reminded me of all the things I wish I'd had in my family.'

Peggy was surprised at this shared confidence. 'You know, you could try to talk to Marigold. I think she'd like that.'

'I'm not sure I know how to talk to anyone.'

'You're talking to me now.'

Lady Lavinia blinked rapidly in a moment of realisation. 'Yes. I suppose I am.' She gazed at Peggy. 'Did she tell you about her sister?'

Peggy nodded. 'I'm sorry.'

'Rosamund, her name was.' Peggy noticed how her eyes lit up at the mere mention of her name. 'They were twins. Thick as thieves. Little darlings, the pair of them. She was only six.'

'That must have been very hard.'

Lady Lavinia stared at her in amazement as if it were

the first time anyone had ever acknowledged this. 'My mother told me I had to get on with it, to shut my feelings away. That it was the only way.' Peggy watched her, unsure of what to say. 'So that's what I did. And now I have nothing and no one.'

'You have Marigold.'

'Marigold despises me.'

'She doesn't. If you told her how you felt, she would listen. I know her.'

Lady Lavinia looked unsure. 'She wouldn't understand.'

'She would. She lost her best friend. She's grieving too. And she lost her sister. It's not too late to rekindle things.'

'Perhaps.'

'No perhaps about it. All families have disagreements, but if you love one another, you have all you need and you'll find a way.'

'Those are wise words, Peggy.'

'My gran's, not mine.' She stood up. 'I'm going to bed now. Early start in the morning. Goodnight, Lady Lavinia. I hope you sleep well.'

Marigold's mother nodded, her expression softening. 'Thank you for the tea.'

The letter was delivered one day with the afternoon post while Peggy was at work. Her mother had telephoned, her usual calm voice breathless with relief. 'It's arrived. A letter. In Joe's handwriting. Oh Peg. And I'm here all on my own.'

'Open it, Mum.'

'No. I want us all to be together.'

Peggy glanced at the time. 'But it's only three o'clock.'

'It's all right,' said Alice. 'I'll tell Flo and Mum but hide it from Nancy. Charlie's too young to understand. Oh Peg. He's all right. Joe's all right.'

'Can you read the postmark?'

'It's from Italy.'

'That's good. If things go as planned, the war might be over there soon. He could be sent home.'

'Do you really think so?'

'Nothing's certain, but there's a good chance.' Her mother was silent for a moment and then Peggy heard the sound of quiet sobbing. 'It's all right, Mum. Either way, he's all right. Isn't he?'

Alice sniffed away her tears. 'Yes. And that's all we can ask for.'

Marigold was watching Peggy with wide eyes as she replaced the receiver. 'Sorry to earwig but that sounded like good news.'

'Joe's in Italy. He must be in a POW camp there.'

'Oh, that is good news. What did he say in his letter?'

'Mum won't open it until I'm home.'

'But you must go. This is a family emergency.'

'I don't know. We're very busy. It'll only be a few hours.'

Marigold sighed. 'Suit yourself.' She stood up. 'Back in a tick.'

Peggy stared down at the document she was editing. It was a fascinating book by John Betjeman on English cities and towns in which she'd been thoroughly absorbed until she received the call from her mother. She took a deep breath and did her best to focus, but the words seemed to jump around in time with the beating of her delighted heart. There was a light tap at the door. Peggy glanced up to see Mr Beecher standing there.

'Miss Sparks, might I have a word? In private.'

Peggy was surprised. 'Of course.'

'Thank you.' He stepped into the room and closed the door behind him. 'I need to ask you to do something for me, please,' he said. 'And I need you not to question what I'm about to ask.'

'That sounds serious.'

'It is.'

'Very well.'

'I need to ask you to go home to your family immediately.'

'Marigold told you.'

'Miss Cecily may have mentioned that you've had some significant news. I'm delighted to hear that your brother is safe.'

'Thank you, Mr Beecher.'

'I hope his letter brings you the reassurance you need. Oh, and by the way, I'm having lunch with Frank and Rosa Bauman tomorrow. Would you care to join us? I know you've been working closely on the *Britain at Home* series with them. He said you'd been very helpful.'

'Oh,' said Peggy, hoping her cheeks weren't as pink as they felt. 'Did he?'

Beecher nodded. 'I'm very fond of Frank and Rosa. We're actually related via my wife. She's a cousin of their late mother. We helped them when they first came here.'

'I see. How kind of you.'

'They're good people. So you'll join us? And perhaps Miss Cecily too?'

'I can't speak for Marigold, but I'd love to.'

'Excellent. Well, I've held you up long enough. Godspeed, Miss Sparks.'

April 1943,
Campo 82,
Laterina,
Italy

My dear family,

Where to begin except to say that I am alive and well in a camp in Italy! You can write to me at the sender address given, so please do, and don't worry, I'm fine. I can't tell you what happened, but as you might imagine we're all furious to have been captured by the Italians. It was their luck and our bad luck, but here we are and you have to make the best of it. Anyway, if things go the way we hope in ██████, we'll be all right. I don't want to build up false hope because who knows what might happen in this war, but there's a mood of optimism in here.

What can I tell you about the place? It's huge. There are thousands of blokes from all over. As for the place, it's all right, fairly basic but we're well looked after. The food's adequate, nothing special. What I wouldn't give for Mum's steak and kidney pudding and one of Gran's sponges! I'm happy to report that I'm in a sleeping hut with Albert. I don't know where I'd be without him, to be honest. We keep each other cheerful. We've got straw mattresses and four blankets each, which isn't bad as some of the blokes in the other huts are having to sleep on concrete floors! The good news is that the mail system is working although it can take a month or two for letters to arrive. We're getting Red Cross parcels every week which is helping boost our rations. If you could send some of your socks, Mum, we'd all be grateful. Peg, you'll be glad to know that there's a library in here, but I haven't found one of your books yet. Albert started reading *War and Peace* the other day and we all joked that it'll keep him quiet until the end of the war. I've discovered John Steinbeck and I suppose I don't need to tell you, Peg, how good it is to escape into a book.

We do our best to exercise too, although there isn't enough room to play football, which is what we'd all like to do. Albert and I have volunteered for farm work in return for extra rations. It's pretty hard going and the farmer isn't the friendliest, but it's good to have the distraction of work. So as you can see, I'm all right. I miss you all very much but I'm hopeful about what lies ahead. Nancy and Charlie, I hope you're being good for your mum. I love you, Flo and all of you. Don't worry about me. We'll meet again.

Ever yours, your loving grandson, son, brother, husband and dad, Joe

Chapter 21

Peggy's first thought when she woke the next morning was of her brother, and as she drifted into consciousness, a deep sense of relief filled her bones. Her second thought involved the realisation that she would be having lunch with Frank Bauman later that day which then gave way to a ticklish sense of anticipation. She stepped into her slippers, pulled on her dressing gown and opened the wardrobe, hoping by some miracle that Vivien Leigh had dropped by in the night with a few stylish outfits. She shut the door, annoyed with herself for being concerned about her appearance, and then opened it again with a loud sigh.

'What's up, Auntie Peg?' asked Nancy, peering around the doorway.

'Oh nothing,' said Peggy. 'Just wondering what to wear.'

'But you always wear the same thing,' said Nancy.

'Yes,' said Peggy. 'I know.'

'Oh,' said Nancy. 'Are you going somewhere special?'

'Not really,' said Peggy. 'I'm just going out for lunch and wanted to look nice.'

'Are you going with a boy?'

Peggy laughed. 'I don't think you could call Mr Beecher a boy but there will be another man there. And his sister. And Marigold.'

'I like Marigold. What are the man and his sister called?'

'Frank and Rosa.'

'Oh. I like those names too. Do you want me to help you? I'm good at picking outfits,' she said, holding up the skirt of her pretty floral dress to illustrate her point.

'All right,' said Peggy uncertainly. 'What would you suggest?'

Nancy peered into the wardrobe with a studious frown. 'Hmm, there's not much colour here. Why don't you borrow something from Mum?'

'Nancy! Time to do your hair,' called Flo from her bedroom.

'Come on, Auntie Peg,' said Nancy, seizing her by the hand. 'Let's pretend you're Cinderella and I'm the Fairy Godmother. You shall go to the ball!'

Peggy didn't usually like the faff and fuss of dressing up for work. She was always smart in a simple tweed skirt and demure blouse, and that suited her fine. Stepping out today in Flo's pretty green dress with its nipped-in waist, however, made her feel different. It was as if she grew a little taller and walked with more purpose. She noticed people, men and women alike, glance in her direction. It was as if she were less invisible. It was an odd but not unpleasant feeling.

'Gosh, don't you look lovely,' said Marigold as she entered the office.

'Is it too much?' asked Peggy, smoothing her skirt.

'No, not at all. It suits you. Brings out the colour in your cheeks.'

'Thank you.'

'What was the news from Joe? I've been thinking about you all night.'

Peggy gave her a grateful smile. 'He's in a POW camp in Italy. He sounds in good spirits. Albert's with him so I think that helps.'

'I'm very glad. It must be a relief to you all,' said Marigold. 'And I hear we're going for lunch with Frank and Rosa Bauman?'

'Beecher invited us both yesterday.'

Marigold eyed her mischievously. 'This doesn't have anything to do with your new outfit, does it?'

Peggy busied herself by shuffling through the papers on her desk, avoiding her friend's eye. 'Nothing at all. I just fancied a change.'

'Good for you,' said Marigold.

'It has also occurred to me that I have a birthday coming up, and even at my age, you're regularly written off as an old maid.'

Marigold's eyes lit up. 'Oh, when is your birthday? We must do something to celebrate you not being an old maid.'

Peggy laughed. 'It's next month.'

'Right,' said Marigold. 'Leave it to me. We're going dancing. Invite Flo. You can both stay at mine.'

'I don't know, Marigold . . .'

'No ifs and buts, young lady. We're celebrating. Life is short and we've all been working hard lately. We need to have some fun.'

Peggy looked at Marigold's eager face. 'It doesn't sound as if I have a choice.'

'You don't. I'll organise everything. This is going to be wonderful!'

Beecher, Frank and Rosa were already sitting at the table when Peggy and Marigold arrived five minutes late, thanks to the latter's need to 'reapply her Gala' before they left. The eateries around this part of town were often busy and this one was particularly bustling with local office workers, including some from the Ministry who Peggy recognised. Mr Leach nodded to them from the table he was sharing with a colleague and she spotted Sheldrake and Laurie sitting in the far corner, deep in conversation.

As the waiter led them both to their table, Peggy noticed how Beecher and Frank were laughing over something Rosa had said. If she didn't know better, she could have been watching a father dining with his children. 'Ah, Miss Cecily, Miss Sparks,' said Beecher, standing up. 'I'm glad you were able to join us. You know Frank and Rosa, of course.'

'It's lovely to see you both again,' said Rosa.

'Let's hope it's more fun than our last meeting with that dreadful bore, Mr Burbles,' said Marigold.

'He's called Mr Burbage, Miss Cecily,' scolded Beecher. 'And he has a very important role to play in the war effort.'

'Sorry, sir,' said Marigold. 'But you have to admit, he's jolly dull.'

Beecher pursed his lips and lifted his chin. 'I couldn't possibly comment on that.'

'Case closed,' said Marigold, winking at Rosa as she sat down beside her.

The last remaining chair was next to Frank. He looked up at Peggy with the dark eyes that had flashed with anger in the past but which now lit up in welcome. 'Won't you sit down, Miss Sparks?'

'Peggy. Please,' she said, sliding into the seat as the waiter handed them menus.

'I beg your pardon, Peggy,' he said deliberately, his face creasing with mirth. There was a new laughing kindness to his expression that made it difficult for Peggy to do anything but hold his gaze.

'Now then,' said Beecher, perusing his menu. 'The food here is acceptable if you happen to like spam. They present it in almost every form – as vol au vents, "à la Greque" and indeed in a bold claim as "Steak Diane". The puddings are, however, divine. I highly recommend the spotted dick with custard.'

'You British do love your custard,' remarked Frank.

'Not as much as our tea,' said Peggy.

'Ah yes. Tea. That dreadful drain water you celebrate as your national drink.'

'I suppose you'd rather we drank coffee,' said Peggy.

Frank gave a gracious bow. '*Aber natürlich*. And not that ersatz rubbish made with chicory. Proper coffee made with freshly roasted ground beans.' He closed his eyes and inhaled. 'Ah, pure nectar.'

'I've never had coffee,' said Peggy.

Frank's eyes snapped open. 'You've never had coffee? *Ach du lieber Gott.* Rosa, have you heard this?'

Rosa was deep in conversation with Beecher and Marigold. She glanced up. 'Heard what?'

'Peggy's never tried coffee.' The waiter returned and they broke off their conversation to place their order.

'Forgive my brother,' said Rosa after he'd gone. 'He's fixated on the country he left behind which betrayed him instead of embracing the one which has welcomed him with open arms.'

'We're not always welcome,' said Frank.

'Well, I'd rather take my chances strolling down the Strand than along Unter den Linden,' said Rosa.

'I'm going to march straight back there when this war is over,' he said.

'Do you think you will?' asked Peggy.

He turned to look at her again with an intensity which made her mouth go dry. 'Wouldn't you want to return to your homeland? To the place where you were born?'

'I can't imagine having to leave my home in the first place, so it's difficult to know how I'd feel.'

'You are lucky then.'

'Yes. I know I am.'

Frank's expression softened. 'I'm sorry, Peggy. I know I get a little worked up sometimes.'

'You're entitled to. It must have been hard for you to leave Germany.'

'It was. But tell me about you. Where is your home?'

'South-east London. Not that far from here, but in a town quite different to this part of London. I live with my

mother, grandmother, sister-in-law, niece and nephew –
and my brother, of course, before he was sent abroad.'

'Mr Beecher told me you've heard from him?'

'Yes. We had a letter yesterday.' Peggy was suddenly
aware of Frank's situation with his own family. 'He's well.'

'I'm glad.'

'Peggy's family are absolutely divine,' said Marigold.
'They saved me when I needed saving.'

'They sound like good people,' said Frank, keeping his
eyes fixed on Peggy.

'Like you say,' she said. 'I'm lucky.'

As predicted by Beecher, the best part of the meal was
indeed the pudding. Frank sat back in his chair and held
up his hands with a satisfied grin. 'You win, Mr Beecher.
I am a complete convert to your spotted dick and custard.
That was *ausgezeichnet*!'

Peggy noticed a man sitting alone by the window
look over with a frown at the sound of German being
spoken.

'I'll take it as a small victory,' said Beecher. 'Although
I am of course devastated that you will never enjoy our
national drink.'

'Ah, but I live in hope that I will be able to convert
Miss Peggy Sparks to the joy of *Kaffee und Kuchen*.'

After Beecher had settled the bill, they made their
way outside to say their goodbyes. Marigold and Rosa
seemed to have struck up a friendship and were making
arrangements to meet again when Marigold cried out,
'Oh, but you must both come to help us celebrate Peggy's
birthday next month.'

Peggy felt panic rise up inside her. 'I'm sure Rosa and Frank have better things to do.'

'Actually, I don't,' said Rosa. 'I'd love to. Frank?'

Frank glanced at Peggy. 'Why not? My sister is always telling me I should have more fun.'

'That's what Marigold says to me,' said Peggy.

'Then we must try to have fun together, Miss Sparks.'

Peggy laughed. 'Very well, Mr Bauman.'

'Oh marvellous,' said Marigold, clapping her hands together. She caught sight of Mr Beecher smiling at them all. 'Would you like to join us, sir?'

Beecher stared at her in amazement. 'Touched as I am by the invitation, Miss Cecily, I am usually tucked up with an Ovaltine and an edifying book by nine, but thank you.'

'I look forward to seeing you then, Peggy,' said Frank, offering her his hand.

She accepted with a smile, realising she felt exactly the same.

The man she'd noticed in the restaurant earlier emerged through the door into the street. He seemed irritated that they were in his way and caught Frank's shoulder in passing. '*Verdammte Juden,*' he muttered under his breath.

'Hey,' called Peggy after him, but the man had already disappeared around the corner. She turned back to Frank whose face was clouded with anger. 'Are you all right?'

'Yes, I'm fine,' he said in a way that suggested he was anything but. 'Come on, Rosa. We should go. Goodbye. Thank you for lunch, Mr Beecher.'

Beecher took his hand and grasped it firmly. 'Take care of yourselves,' he told them both, then watched them walk away arm in arm. 'It's a sad truth,' he said, 'that even in this country, the Jews aren't always afforded the compassion they deserve.'

'It makes me very angry,' said Peggy.

Beecher glanced at her. 'Never let go of that anger, Miss Sparks.'

As they entered the Ministry building, Longforth met them in the hallway. 'Ah, good. You're all here. We have a problem.'

'What is it?' asked Beecher.

Longforth inclined his head slightly, lifting his gaze with it. 'That woman sitting over there.' Peggy, Marigold and Beecher all looked to where he was gesturing. 'No! Don't all look at once. Be discreet.'

'Longforth, what is this all about?' said Beecher. 'Why are you so animated about a harmless elderly lady?' Peggy glanced over at her. She was a slight, frail-looking woman, wearing an apricot-coloured beret, wire-framed glasses and a twinkling expression.

'She's asked to see Eliot and Bell,' he whispered.

Beecher frowned. 'But how on earth did she end up here?'

'Because some dolt at the stationery office told her that this is where the writers are based.'

'Can't we just tell her they're out?'

'We've tried that. She says she'll wait as she has an important message for them. What are we to do?'

Marigold and Peggy exchanged glances. 'Maybe you could pretend to be them,' said Peggy.

'Yes, good idea,' said Marigold.

292

It was Longforth and Beecher's turn to exchange looks now. 'I'm not sure that's entirely appropriate,' said Beecher, shifting uncomfortably.

'Why not?' said Peggy. 'We pretend to be them all the time.'

Longforth adopted a wistful look. 'I did tread the boards at Oxford. I'm game if you are, Beecher.'

Beecher shook his head in exasperation. 'Oh, very well. Let's get it over with and keep it short.' Peggy and Marigold grinned at one another. 'I don't know why you two are smiling. You're coming too.'

The woman's name was Miss Dahlia Mackintosh and she had travelled all the way from Edinburgh to voice her appreciation for the work of Mr Eliot and Mr Bell. 'I saved my rations and baked you a Dundee cake,' she told them in a quietly lilting Scottish accent, sliding a paper parcel tied with string across the table.

'Well, we're most grateful to you for making the effort, dear lady,' said Longforth with a gracious bow.

'So which of you is Mr Eliot and which is Mr Bell?' she asked.

Longforth and Beecher shared a brief look of panic. 'I'm Mr Eliot,' said Beecher.

'Yes, and I'm Basil Bell,' said Longforth.

'Herbert,' murmured Peggy.

'Oh, Herbert Eliot,' said Longforth.

'Bell,' urged Marigold.

Longforth gave an embarrassed laugh. 'Beg pardon. I'm Herbert Bell,' he said.

Miss Mackintosh frowned. 'You don't seem very sure.'

'Well, the truth is that these aren't our real names,' said Beecher.

Miss Mackintosh looked horrified. 'Not your real names?'

Beecher threw a panicked look towards Peggy who intervened. 'It's very usual for writers to adopt pseudonyms,' she said. 'Hence the confusion.'

'Oh,' said Dahlia with an edge of disappointment. 'I see.'

'But we're delighted you've enjoyed the books,' said Marigold. 'Peggy and I help to compile them.'

'I think they're wonderful,' said Miss Mackintosh. 'The one on Scottish history is my favourite, of course.'

'Of course,' said Peggy, smiling.

'But if I may be so bold, I have one small criticism.'

'Oh yes?' said Longforth.

'There aren't enough women.'

'Beg pardon?'

'Wo-men,' she said slowly as if addressing a fool. 'The female of the species. You've got Shelley and Byron and Tennyson and Keats, but where is Emily Brontë? Where is Elizabeth Barrett Browning? And where is Mrs Elizabeth Gaskell?'

'We did include some women in the book on English novelists,' said Peggy.

'Quite so. I rubber-stamped that myself,' said Longforth.

Miss Mackintosh fixed him with a beady eye. 'Lip service,' she said.

'Beg pardon?' he asked, cowed by her scrutiny.

'You are merely paying lip service and I believe you can do better, Mr Bell.'

Peggy and Marigold shared an amused look. 'Well,' said Mr Beecher, offering his hand to her. 'We're grateful to you for taking the time to come and tell us, Miss Mackintosh.'

'Not at all,' said the diminutive lady sweetly, shaking each of their hands in turn. 'Enjoy the cake.'

'Pankhurst has a lot to answer for,' said Longforth, as they watched her leave.

'Marigold, how much longer are you going to be?' called Peggy a few days later. It was to be their first ARP shift and she had deliberately told her friend that they needed to be there by six when Mr Baggley had in fact said six thirty.

'Just a tick, Peggy,' replied Marigold from the bathroom. She emerged moments later and struck a pose. 'What do you think?'

Peggy was amazed. Considering the utilitarian nature of her outfit, Marigold was managing to wear it with the flair and glamour of a Hollywood starlet. Her hair was styled into soft curls, framing her beautiful face, and she was wearing bright red lipstick, applied with practised perfection. 'You know we're not going for cocktails at the Savoy, don't you?'

'Darling, just because there's a war on, it doesn't mean that I'm going to stop making an effort. I bought this new lipstick especially. It's called "Victory Red",' she said, smacking her lips together. 'Now come along. We don't want to be late for dear Mr B, do we?'

Peggy shook her head in disbelief. 'God forbid that we should ever be late,' she said, following her out of the door.

'Right then, everybody,' said Mr Baggley as they gathered at the warden's post, which had once been a refreshments kiosk and still displayed signs promising a delectable range of Lyons Maid ice creams. 'As you've learnt from training, we generally remain here unless we hear a siren. Occasionally, we may patrol the streets to ensure that no lights can be seen from the buildings and we address this in a courteous fashion. If we hear a siren, I will remain here and you will patrol the streets to check that people are either in or making their way to their shelters. You will then take shelter yourselves and then when the all-clear sounds, you will leave the shelter and begin your assessment of potential incidents to report or act upon. It is imperative that you alert the authorities either via police boxes, fire alarms or street telephones before treating any casualties. Please do not put yourselves in danger but offer first aid wherever you can. Remember, courage and presence of mind are our watchwords. Good luck.'

Despite Mr Baggley's rousing speech, Peggy and Marigold's first shift was uneventful. After an hour, he sent them both out to patrol the locale which was buzzing with people enjoying a night out. 'Gosh, do you think Mr B would mind if we popped in for a drink?' asked Marigold as they passed by the third blacked-out restaurant from which the tantalising sound of happy diners floated into the still-light early evening air.

'Unfortunately, I do,' said Peggy. 'But we're doing our civic duty and that's far more important.'

'If you say so,' said Marigold, swinging her rattle so that its clattering caused two women to look over in alarm. 'Sorry,' she called. 'False alarm. Please go about your business.'

They passed a group of American soldiers in uniform. 'Good evening, ladies,' one of them drawled. 'Would you care to join us?'

Marigold caught Peggy's eye before bestowing her film-star smile upon them. 'I'm afraid we can't. We're on duty, you see.'

'Aww, sweetie, you're breaking my heart here,' he said, pounding his chest in mock-distress.

Marigold chuckled. 'Maybe later,' she called over her shoulder. 'I could rather get used to this,' she said.

'Have you spoken to your mother since the other night?' asked Peggy as they continued their patrol.

'She was still asleep when we left the next morning. She hasn't called since. Did she say something to you when you took her the tea?'

'She thinks you see her as a monster.'

Marigold laughed bitterly. 'She's more perceptive than I thought.'

'I sense she'd like to talk to you but doesn't know how.'

Marigold turned to face Peggy. 'How difficult can it be if you really want to? You talk to your mother and grandmother all the time. We talk. Heavens, I even talk to Sheldrake these days.'

Peggy shrugged. 'Everyone's different.'

'Don't make excuses for her.'

'I'm not. I just remember what we always say about life being short. Who knows what might happen. You don't want to regret something later you could have done now.'

Marigold gave her a sideways glance. 'Why do you have to be so bally wise all the time?' She threw up her hands. 'All right, Peggy Sparks. I'll try to talk to my monster of a mother.'

Peggy linked an arm through Marigold's and gave a satisfied smile. 'Good girl,' she said.

Chapter 22

'Happy birthday, Auntie Peg!' cried Nancy as Peggy appeared in the doorway of the kitchen, yawning. 'And happy birthday, Daddy,' she added, 'wherever you are.' Peggy pulled her into a tight hug and kissed the top of her head. Birthdays were always harder without her twin, but she was grateful for her niece's fierce love. 'Great-Gran and I baked you a cake each.'

'That was supposed to be a surprise for later,' said Emily. 'Happy birthday, Peg.'

'Two cakes?' said Peggy.

Emily nodded towards Nancy. 'She insisted, so we made two small ones. Lucky Dulcie keeps chickens.'

'Happy birthday, love,' said Alice, leaning over to kiss her daughter. 'Have you got time for breakfast?'

Peggy glanced at her watch. 'I'll just have some tea.'

Emily tutted. 'You young girls, never sitting down for longer than five minutes, existing on tea and thin air. In my day, it was porridge sprinkled with sugar every morning.'

'I don't like porridge,' said Nancy. 'It's too lumpy.'

'Not when I make it,' said Emily.

'Here you go, love,' said Alice, setting down a cup of tea in front of Peggy.

'Thanks, Mum.'

'Happy birthday, Peg,' said Flo, entering the kitchen with Charlie in her arms.

''Appy burfday,' echoed Charlie, holding out his chubby fists to her. Peggy took him on to her lap, laughing as he planted a soggy kiss on her cheek.

'You look worn out, Peg,' said Alice.

'It's been a busy few weeks,' said Peggy, doing her best to suppress another yawn. 'What with the warden shifts on top of work.'

'Why can't you do your ARP bit over here?' grumbled Emily. 'Or join your mum and me for some WVS shifts. We were run off our feet the other night.'

'We've been through this, Mum,' said Alice. 'It'd be too late by the time Peggy got home and it's easy enough for her to stay with Marigold.'

'I'd just feel a bit safer in my bed knowing Peg was patrolling our neck of the woods and then I could make her a nice cuppa from our mobile canteen.'

'Ah, Gran, are you missing me?'

Emily flapped a hand dismissively. 'Oh, get away with you. Here,' she said, sliding a small pile of post towards her. 'Open these. I think you'll like the one on the top.'

Peggy's eyes lit up when she recognised the writing. 'It's from Joe.'

'I kept it secret,' said Nancy, bouncing up and down in her chair as Peggy tore it open. 'Read it, Auntie Peg.'

Peggy smiled. 'Dear Peg, happy birthday. Hope you're impressed as I sent this a month early so it would arrive on time. Glad to receive your letters and hear that you're all fine. All is well with me too. More news soon. We'll meet again. Love, Joe.' She caught Flo's eye as she finished. Peggy knew they were thinking the same thing. What was life really like for Joe? These postcards and letters could only say so much. Part of her longed to step into his world and see for herself, but part of her dreaded what she might find there.

'I wonder what Daddy's doing for his birthday,' said Nancy, voicing their innermost thoughts. 'Do you think he got our parcel? I wonder if Albert baked him a cake.'

Flo stroked her daughter's hair. 'I expect he did.'

Peggy noticed the weary way she said this and longed to make things better. 'Are you sure you won't come out with Marigold and me tomorrow night?' she asked.

Flo sighed. 'I'm too tired, Peg, and I need to be here for the kids.'

'Maybe I shouldn't go,' said Peggy.

'Yes, you should,' said Alice. 'It's your birthday. You need to be out enjoying yourself whenever you get the chance.'

'You wouldn't have caught me missing the chance to kick up my heels when I was a young woman,' said Emily. 'War or no war.'

'You were young once, Great-Gran?' said Nancy with a mischievous grin.

Emily glared at her with indignation. 'I swear these youngsters are getting cheekier every day. If I'd spoken to

301

my great-grandmother like that, she would have walloped my backside.'

Alice plucked a photograph from the dresser. 'This was your great-gran,' she said, placing it in front of Nancy.

'You look just like Auntie Peg,' she said, staring at the photograph of a beautiful young woman, gazing into the distance, eyes full of wonder.

'That was me when I was working as a cook for the Randolph family,' she said. 'Bit younger than Peg. It was taken just before I met Reg.' She patted Peggy's hand. 'Time you met a nice fella.'

'What about Frank?' asked Nancy.

'Who's Frank?' said Emily.

'No one,' said Peggy.

'He didn't sound like no one when you were talking to Mum about him,' said Nancy.

Flo shot a wink at Peggy who drained her tea, avoiding her grandmother's eye. 'Sorry, got to go,' she cried, plonking Charlie on her surprised mum's lap. 'Thanks for the birthday wishes. See you later!' She grabbed her coat and bag from the hallstand and dashed out through the door.

'Don't think that's the end of the conversation, Peggy Sparks,' called her grandmother. 'I'll still be here when you get home.'

The opulent basement bar at the Ritz offered its well-heeled visitors a welcome refuge from the drab existence of wartime life above ground. With its honey-coloured chandeliers, gilded marble floors and plush velvet sofas, it was the last word in decadent luxury.

'César Ritz designed the hotel so that it would bring out the beauty of the female guests,' Marigold told Peggy as the top-hatted doorman held open the door and greeted them with a touch of his brim. 'I thought it was the perfect place to celebrate your birthday. My treat.'

Peggy had become used to the social differences at the Ministry, to the men who'd been schooled at Eton and who asked her to make the tea or assumed she was one of the secretaries from the typing pool. She had learnt to adapt and even relish their surprise when she showed them the books she'd written or edited. Peggy knew she'd been lucky to land in a department with Mr Beecher at the helm and Mrs Pyecroft weaving her quiet magic in the background. However, she had to admit to feeling like a fish out of water as they entered the bar and were confronted by the hedonistic sight of the upper echelons of London society drinking, laughing and dancing the night away. It wasn't even a consolation that Marigold had lent her the elegant, olive-green dress she was wearing or helped to style her hair and apply a little make-up. Peggy felt as uncomfortable as if she were wearing her shoes on the wrong feet.

'Here,' said Marigold, handing her a coupe filled with sparkling amber liquid. 'Drink this. You look like a rabbit caught in the headlights. Cheers.'

'Cheers,' said Peggy, taking a sip and wincing against its sharp fizz.

Marigold laughed. 'You'll be all right. You just need to loosen up a bit. Cordy and I used to have the best nights here,' she said, smiling at the memory.

303

'You must miss her,' said Peggy.

'She was the love of my life,' said Marigold. Peggy stared at her in amazement. She gave a coy look. 'Does that shock you?'

'If you mean am I shocked by the revelation, then no, not really, but I'm surprised as I never suspected.' She thought back to Dalton's comments when they had lunch years ago and the fact that, despite her beauty and charm, she had never actually seen Marigold out with a man.

Marigold glanced around at her surroundings now. 'You have to be careful who overhears these things, but it's pretty safe here.' Peggy followed her gaze, noticing the women sitting in couples who she could see were more than just friends. 'And I know my secret's safe with you, Peggy.'

'Of course.'

'You know our friendship means the world to me, don't you?' she said.

Peggy smiled. 'It does to me too.'

'I feel very lucky to have met you, Peggy Sparks. You've taught me about what's important in life.'

'Dearie me, that makes me sound like a dreadful old school mistress.'

Marigold shook her head. 'No, I mean the way you are with your family, the way you look after one another. It's made me realise who I value and that life is about more than glittering parties.'

'Says the woman drinking cocktails at the Ritz,' teased Peggy.

Marigold laughed. 'You see, that's why I like you. You

never let me get above myself. Happy birthday, my dear friend.' She tapped her glass against Peggy's and glanced towards the doorway. 'Oh look, here's Frank and Rosa now,' she added, waving. Peggy's stomach dipped as she caught sight of Frank. She took another drink to calm her jittery nerves.

'Well, isn't this lovely?' said Rosa, as they reached them.

'I thought we all deserved a treat,' said Marigold. 'Let me get you both a drink.' She turned to the barman. 'Two more champagne cocktails, please, Jim.'

'Champagne?' said Rosa, accepting the glass she was handed. 'You really are treating us, Lady Cecily.'

Marigold looked at her with devilish glee. 'Well, you've got to live for the moment.' She covered her mouth and whispered, 'I don't think they serve real champagne unless you're the Prime Minister, but who cares?'

'Is the Prime Minister here?' asked Frank, glancing over his shoulder. He looked as awkward as Peggy felt.

'No, but I saw our beloved Minister in the foyer on the way in,' said Marigold. 'Darling!' she cried, spotting someone she knew at the far end of the bar. She grabbed Rosa's hand. 'Come with me. There's someone I want you to meet. Back in a tick,' she said over her shoulder to Peggy.

Peggy and Frank stared at one another for a moment. She was wracking her brain for something engaging to say. 'Happy birthday,' he said after a while.

'Thank you.' There was another pause which threatened to inch its way towards discomfort.

'So. How have you been?'

'Quite well. I had a postcard from Joe. He seems fine.'

'Good. That's good.'

'And you?'

'Oh yes. Fine. Busy but fine.' Peggy fiddled with the stem of her glass before taking another large gulp. 'You look very nice,' he ventured.

Peggy looked into his eyes, his soft expression drawing her in. 'Thank you.'

'Beautiful, actually.'

She felt the heat rise to her face and turned away, catching sight of Marigold and Rosa, who were now ensconced at a table talking to a glamorous woman Peggy was sure she'd seen in a photograph in one of Flo's magazines. 'I think we've been abandoned,' she said.

Frank followed her gaze and laughed. 'Look, Peggy. I don't know about you, but this isn't really my kind of place. Would you like to go somewhere else?'

She turned back to him with a smile. 'I would like that very much but I should let Marigold know. She did organise this evening for me after all.'

'Of course. I'll wait for you here.'

Marigold had been unsurprised when Peggy told her she was leaving with Frank. She waved away her apology and kissed her cheek. 'Just call me Cupid,' she said with a wink.

Peggy hoped that Frank didn't notice the scarlet tinge to her cheeks as she rejoined him. 'I know just the place but it's a bit of a walk,' he said. 'Or we could catch a bus?'

'I don't mind walking,' said Peggy.

'Then follow me, Miss Sparks,' he said with a bow.

It was a mild night, the sky alive with stars, the moon a shining beacon above their heads. Despite nearly four years of blackouts, it still always took Peggy a while to adjust to the dark streets, lit only by the occasional passing bus. She moved gingerly before Frank wordlessly offered his arm and she accepted with a secret skip of happiness. They met a few people along their way and whenever someone gave them a smiling nod, Peggy secretly relished the idea that they saw them as just another couple, out for an evening stroll. Part of her had worried that she and Frank would have little to say to one another, but it soon became clear that once they'd escaped the overwhelming atmosphere of the Ritz, all awkward platitudes disappeared. They talked and laughed like old friends. In fact, Peggy was amazed how easy conversation was with Frank. They discussed their families, their upbringings, their work. Peggy told him about Joe, sharing the hopes and fears she rarely shared with anyone else. In turn, Frank confided his deepest concerns for his family in Germany, how he was unsure if they were even still alive, how anger fuelled his work and made him determined to do all he could to help the Allies win the war.

'Some people would say I was betraying my country but they would be wrong. My country betrayed me a long time ago,' he told her bitterly.

'I can't imagine what it must be like to leave your home,' said Peggy.

'It's not my home any more,' he said, shaking his head.

'What about Britain? Does this feel like home?'

He glanced at her, his eyes wrinkling with good humour. 'It's beginning to.'

'So where are we going?' she asked, avoiding his gaze.

Frank pointed towards the grandly ornate building opposite, from where Queen Victoria and her husband looked down at the world with an imperious air. 'I thought we could dine with Victoria and Albert,' he said. 'Or will I get thrown into the Tower for being so informal?'

Peggy laughed. 'Your secret's safe with me.'

As he led her inside the museum, Peggy remembered visiting with her mother as a child and marvelling at the wide, echoing halls and ornate marble staircases, at the huge sculptures, the paintings, the sheer beauty of everything that humans could create if they put their minds to it. Now, large swathes of the Victoria and Albert Museum were shut off with many items having been removed or sandbagged for protection. They made their way to the far side of the museum, along an arcaded corridor into a large room where a canteen had been set up along one wall, the glass display cases she remembered sitting in the centre of the room replaced with tables and benches. A sign at one end announced the 'British Restaurant Menu', promising 'soup, roast beef and 2 veg, treacle tart and custard' for less than a shilling.

'It may not be the Ritz, but I know how much you like your custard,' said Frank.

'It's perfect,' said Peggy. 'And they've even got coffee.'

Frank grimaced. 'It's not the real thing but it'll be better than your tea.' She laughed.

After they'd queued with their trays, they managed to find two seats in the bustling body of the restaurant. Peggy was pleased how easy she found it to be in

Frank's company. There were no awkward gaps or difficult moments in their conversation, and when their talk turned to her job at the library and her love of reading, his eyes lit up. He told her how he had learnt English through reading the short stories of Somerset Maugham and she told him how much she admired the poetry of Rilke. They were still sitting at their table when the stern-looking WVS woman running the canteen asked them if they had homes to go to.

'Where to now?' said Frank as they emerged back on to the street.

Peggy glanced at her watch. 'I need to find my way back to Marigold's apartment. Maybe I should try to catch a bus.'

'I'll walk you home.'

'It's miles,' said Peggy.

'I don't mind if you don't,' he said. 'It's a lovely night and given the lack of sirens, a quiet one too.'

'In which case, I accept your kind offer. And you're right, it is a lovely night,' she said, smiling up at him. He offered his arm again and she took it, leaning in a little more, enjoying the warmth of his touch. They made their way along the dark streets, greeting anyone they met along the way. As they passed a Piccadilly night club, a group of young men in uniform were spilling out on to the pavement, jostling and laughing with one another. As Frank and Peggy passed, one of them caught Frank on the shoulder. 'Excuse me,' said Frank with a touch of irritation.

'What was that, mate?' said the man, turning back with a dangerous glint in his eye.

'Leave it, Jackson,' warned one of his fellow soldiers.

Jackson squared up to Frank. 'Shall we leave it, mate?'

Frank let go of Peggy's arm. 'I'm not your mate, and if you bump into someone I believe it's polite to beg their pardon.'

Jackson stared at Frank for a moment before laughing. 'Oh, you believe, do you? And you're right. You're not my mate. You're foreign. I can hear it in your voice. Where are you from then?' A couple of Jackson's friends pricked up their ears at this, taking their place either side of him, staring at Frank with menace.

'Come on, let's leave it,' called the other man, watching from afar.

'Shut up, Williams,' said Jackson. 'So then. Where are you from?'

'Germany,' said Frank.

Jackson's eyes bulged. 'You're German.'

Frank nodded. 'And Jewish. Poor me, eh?'

Jackson wasn't sure how to react to Frank's sardonic humour. 'Well, shouldn't you be locked up in the Isle of Man or something?'

'We should arrest him,' said the small, wiry man standing next to Jackson.

'Right, that's enough,' said Peggy, pushing her way between them. 'You can all go home. This man is a German Jew working for the government to bring an end to this war. And you are presumably soldiers home on leave from fighting in the war. So no one needs arrest anyone because we're all on the same side. Now leave us alone before I call the police and your commanding officer.'

The men took a step back. 'All right, all right, no need to get excited,' said Jackson. 'Sorry, miss.'

Peggy glared at him. 'Try and read a book every now and then and stop being so ignorant. Everyone in England is a foreigner, given that we're mostly descended from Anglo-Saxons or Romans.'

Jackson stared at her in surprise. 'Right. Sorry.'

'I'm glad you're sorry,' said Peggy, shaking with anger. 'But maybe you should stop apologising to me and apologise to this man instead.'

Jackson looked at Frank, who seemed as astonished as him by Peggy's outburst. 'Sorry, mate,' he said.

Williams clapped him on the shoulder. 'Right, come on, let's go before you get us into any more trouble.' He nodded at Frank and Peggy. 'Pardon my friend. Good night.'

Frank glanced at Peggy as they continued to walk along the street. 'Well,' he said. 'I've never been rescued before. It's quite a heady feeling.'

Peggy shook her head and laughed. 'I'm sorry, Frank. I know you can fight your own battles but ignorant people make my blood boil.'

'I noticed,' he said, his eyes crinkling with amusement. 'Thank you, Peggy Sparks, my protector and friend.'

'I'm just sorry I wasn't quick enough when that man insulted you at the restaurant.'

Frank shrugged. 'Compared to the Nazis, he's a pussy cat, but I'd be lying if I said I don't care about these things. Even in Britain, with your parliamentary democracy and freedom of speech, you still have Oswald Mosley and his Fascists.'

'Thank goodness they've all been interned.'

'Yes, but these views still exist.' They were passing by a Lyons Corner House as he spoke. 'Take this sign, for example.'

Peggy read aloud. 'No enemy alien, whether naturalised or not, is employed by this company.'

'According to the laws of this land, I'm a so-called enemy alien, so you can see why Jackson and his friends think the way they do. It's indoctrination,' said Frank. 'Words have power, as well you know, Peggy. People like me are labelled alien, enemy, Jew. We're all put into groups. Judged. If Britain labels us like this then surely that gives carte blanche for the man we met to label us as "damn Jews". What's the difference?'

Peggy cast her eyes downwards. 'I'm sorry, Frank,' she said.

He reached forwards and lifted her chin. 'You have nothing to be sorry about. You know all this to be true and you stood up for me. No one's ever done that before. You're one of the good ones, Peggy Sparks.'

She held his gaze as he said this, her one thought now that she wanted to kiss him. He smiled as he moved his face towards hers and they met in a moment that felt to Peggy as if a thousand fireworks were exploding in her heart. He stroked her cheek and stared into her eyes as they moved apart. 'Words have power but so do actions,' she said, reaching for him again as he folded her into his arms.

Peggy was at home alone when the visitor came round to call. Flo had taken the children to the park and Emily and Alice were braving the ration queue, so Peggy had offered to stay home and do the chores. She was relishing some time alone away from the bustle of the Ministry and Marigold's endless questions about Frank to enjoy a quiet house without either Nancy or Emily interrogating her on the same subject. Only her mother seemed to understand. 'Enjoy this part, Peggy. The falling. I remember it with your father. I felt as if I'd sprouted wings and was suddenly able to dive and soar in the sky,' she told her, patting her hand. Peggy knew exactly what she meant. Over the past few weeks, Frank had seemed to find numerous reasons to visit the Ministry and before each encounter, Peggy felt a thrill of anticipation which became a dip of longing after he left. So it was a rare treat to be alone in the house with gently soothing band music on the wireless and time to think about him. She was also hoping they might hear from Joe. There had been one letter since the card on her birthday, its tone similarly ambiguous, but still, any word that he was well was enough for Peggy.

Her first thought when she heard the knock at the door was that it was Nancy, having run ahead of Flo and Charlie, demanding to be let in. Peggy was therefore surprised on opening the door to be gazing into the face of a man of around Joe's age with a curly mop of blond hair. She sensed from his expectant expression that she should know who he was but for a moment she struggled to place him.

'Peggy,' he said, realising her confusion. 'It's Arthur. Arthur Morris.'

'Arthur,' said Peggy, her mind immediately transported

back to childhood, to that small boy with the scabby knees and the snotty nose who used to follow her and Joe home from school, asking to join in their games. The man who stood before her now bore none of that youthful innocence or energy. His face had a greyish pallor, his eyes bruised with fatigue. 'Please come in. How are you?'

'Not so bad, thanks,' he said, following her to the kitchen. 'I can't complain really.'

She was already filling the kettle. 'Please. Sit down,' she said. 'I'll make us some tea.'

'Thank you. That's very kind.' There was a slow deliberation to the way Arthur spoke. Peggy remembered him as such an excitable child, eyes always bright and alert, ready to participate in any game into which he was invited. The blue eyes that gazed up at her now had lost that brightness. They were dull and flat, as if someone had extinguished the spark behind them. *That's what war does*, thought Peggy. *It snuffs out the spirit*. She made the tea, placing the pot on the table, and fetched two cups and saucers and the milk jug.

'I'll be mother, shall I?' she said, adding a splash of milk to each cup and turning the pot before she poured.

'Thank you, Peggy. It's nice to see you after all this time.'

'It's nice to see you too, Arthur.'

He took a sip of tea. 'So is Joe out?'

Peggy stared at him in surprise. 'Out?'

Arthur nodded. 'I was hoping to see him.'

Peggy blinked. 'I'm sorry, Arthur. I don't know what you mean.'

314

Panic flickered across Arthur's expression. 'I was in the same camp as Joe and we were all sent home, so I assumed he would be too.'

For Peggy, it felt as if all the joy from earlier had been drained from her. 'Sent home? When?'

Arthur swallowed. 'Last month.'

'Last month?' Peggy's mind raced. If Arthur had made it back, then surely there was a chance that Joe was on his way back to them too. 'When did you last see him?'

'The day before we left. We were all in different huts so I didn't see him when we moved out. I'm sorry, Peggy. I just thought he'd be back by now.'

Arthur looked so forlorn that Peggy reached out a hand to comfort him. 'It's all right, Arthur. You weren't to know, and besides, Joe might be on his way back now but just been held up somewhere. Don't you think?'

Arthur stared at her, desperate for this to be true. 'Yes. I'm sure that's what must have happened.'

Peggy squeezed his hand. 'I bet your mum's glad to have you home. Joe told me you've got a young lady. She must be pleased to see you.'

'We're getting married next month.'

'That's wonderful. Congratulations.'

Arthur looked uncertain. 'I just wanted to talk to Joe, you see. Not many people understand what it's like, you know?'

Peggy could see how tortured he was, how the horrors of war lived on inside his brain, how they probably never disappeared even when he closed his eyes at night. It was all very well being freed from the toil of fighting a war, but she got the feeling you could never escape the things you'd seen. She squeezed his hand. 'I'm sure Joe will be home soon,' she said, hoping that by uttering this aloud it would turn out to be true.

> Kriegsgefangenenlager,
> August 1943

I'm safe. I'm a prisoner of war in a German camp. Don't worry about me. More news and address to follow. We'll meet again.

Love to you all, Joe

Chapter 23

Peggy was determined to uncover even the smallest nugget of information about her brother after watching her family's reaction to Joe's message. Flo had stared at the telegram for the longest time as if willing the words to transform into something more hopeful before turning to Peggy with tears in her eyes.

'I don't understand,' she whispered. 'How is Arthur home but not Joe?'

Emily folded her arms. 'We need answers. Why on earth is he in Germany? He should be at home with us.'

Alice sat at the table with her head bowed. She looked defeated. Peggy placed a hand on her shoulder. 'It'll be all right, Mum. Joe has said he'll send more news soon. He told us not to worry. I'll go and see Sir James tomorrow. Ask if he can help.' As her mother gazed up at her with a weary nod, Peggy's heart fractured a little. It was hard to keep going, to tell yourself that everything would be all right when there seemed to be no respite from the relentless churn of worsening news.

Sir James's secretary gave her little cause for hope. 'I'm afraid Sir James is out of the office today and his first available appointment is . . .' she traced a manicured finger down the pages of his diary, '. . . a week on Thursday.' She glanced back up at Peggy with a brisk smile which didn't reach her eyes.

'Oh, but I was hoping to see him sooner. It's rather important, you see.'

'May I ask what it relates to? Is it Ministry business?' asked the woman, peering at her over the top of a pair of horn-rimmed spectacles.

It would have been so easy to lie, to claim that it was about some vital aspect of their publishing strategy, but Peggy believed in telling the truth. Perhaps this woman would understand. 'No. It's about my brother, you see. He's been taken prisoner in Germany and . . .'

'Well, I'm very sorry for your brother, obviously, but I hardly think this is a matter for Sir James. I'm sure you understand. Good day.' The woman gave a tilt of her head and returned to her work, leaving Peggy no alternative but to return to the library, her cheeks burning with frustration.

'Goodness,' said Marigold, who was talking to Sheldrake. 'You look angrier than Mama when Father's been on one of his gambling sprees.'

'I went to ask Sir James if he could help find out where Joe is, but his secretary was less than helpful,' Peggy told them, just as Mrs Pyecroft emerged from her office.

She fixed Peggy with a steady gaze. 'I am sorry to hear about your brother,' she said.

'Thank you,' said Peggy. 'Apologies if I disturbed you.'

'I'm glad you did,' she said.

A few days later, Peggy received an unexpected visit from Sir James's secretary. She was no more friendly than before, delivering her news with a strained air. 'Sir James has had a cancellation in his diary and is free to see you now if you would like to come with me.'

'Oh. Thank you,' said Peggy, following her.

'Ah, Peggy. It's good to see you,' said Sir James, ushering her into his office. 'Thank you, Daphne.'

'Sir,' said Daphne, throwing Peggy a final cold look.

'Thank you for seeing me,' said Peggy, taking a seat on the other side of the solid oak desk, glancing around the room at the book-filled shelves, the picture of the King gazing down benevolently at them.

'Of course. Always happy to help if I can. I understand this is about Joe,' Sir James said solemnly. 'I was very sorry to hear about him ending up in a POW camp in Germany.'

'I was wondering if you might know what happened? We're all desperate for news, and as you can imagine, Gran was particularly keen that I speak to you.'

'Of course. Dear Mrs Marsh.' There was a pause before he answered as if he were choosing his words carefully. 'All I know is that Joe was unlucky to be picked up by the Germans. They are rather reluctant to accept the fact that the Italians will soon be out of the war.'

'Unlucky,' said Peggy quietly. 'That's one word for it.'

Sir James regarded her with concern. 'I'm sorry, Peggy. You know if I could offer more information, I would. However, I do at least have an address for you so that you can write to him.'

Peggy accepted the government-headed notepaper with

319

a heavy heart. 'Thank you. So what do we do now? Watch and pray like the rest of the nation?'

'It's all we can do, I'm afraid. I remain optimistic that the tide will turn as soon as the Italians capitulate. Take heart, Peggy.'

She knew Sir James was right, but this cycle of hoping for good news and then being knocked back by bad seemed never-ending. It was impossible for it not to take its toll. She could see the weariness in Flo's eyes, the despair in her mother's face and the endless disappointment for Nancy as she returned home from school day after day, longing for a letter from her daddy. Only Emily remained stoic and determined, and Peggy did her best to emulate her.

'That boy will win the war for us all and be back before you know it,' she'd say whenever one of them voiced even a grain of doubt. 'He'll never give up and it's our job never to give up either.'

That evening, she took the address from Peggy before turning to them all. 'Right. We're going to write letters to Joe this evening and I'll post them tomorrow. It's like you always say, Peg, words can keep the spirits alive, so we've got to do that for our boy.'

'I'm going to do my best handwriting,' said Nancy.

'Good girl,' said Emily.

They sat around the kitchen table and wrote by lamp-light. Peggy watched their faces: Flo's soft gaze as she thought of her darling husband, Nancy's brow screwed up in concentration, determined to perfect every word, Alice smiling gently and Emily nodding with satisfaction as she signed off her letter with a kiss. She could imagine families all over the country sharing these moments that had nothing to do with the struggle of war and everything to do with the love of a family. She turned back to her own letter now, wondering what Joe would like to hear, eager to make him understand how much she loved and missed him and longed for his return. Theirs had always been a jovial, easy relationship, and life these days was anything but. Still, she knew she needed to try to keep him cheerful, to lift him up. Life in the camp must be a cold, hard slog. She raised her pen and poured out her heart, telling him of her ARP adventures with Marigold, of joyful moments spent with Nancy and Charlie, and of Frank, of how happy he made her and how she couldn't wait for Joe to meet him.

We miss you very much. You've always been my fiercest protector and now I will do all I can to protect you and bring you home. I love you dearly. I can't wait for you to return and meet Frank and be with us all again. We'll meet again. I promise. Ever, your loving sister, Peg.

By Christmas, the Italians had indeed capitulated, but this had only served to make the Germans more doggedly determined. On Christmas Eve, Mr Beecher stood before them and in the absence of anything more intoxicating, raised his teacup. 'I want to take a moment to wish you all a happy Christmas. I know I've said this every year, but I truly hope it will be the last one of the war.'

'Hear, hear,' said Dalton. 'No more murkey for Christmas dinner.'

'Or tinned pears for afters,' said Hilda.

Peggy smiled, but all she could think of was Joe's return, of what life might be like with him sitting at the table with them, pulling crackers, laughing and singing. It felt like an age since they'd sent their letters, but there had been no word; nothing since Joe's first postcard. Everyone said that the post from prisoners of war was erratic at the best of times, that they shouldn't worry, that there would be a letter soon, but Peggy could see that even Emily was starting to struggle with the daily reality of no news. 'Penny for them?' asked Marigold, appearing at her elbow.

'Just thinking about Joe, wondering how he is. He's never far from my mind,' said Peggy.

'One of my mother's friends has a son who's a POW and he's in good spirits, all things considered. They've even set up a university in the camp and he's carrying on his studies. They have concerts and play sport, too. Hopefully it's the same for Joe.'

'Thank you, Marigold,' said Peggy. 'So what are your plans for Christmas? You know there's always room at our table.'

'You're a peach, but actually, I'm entertaining.'

'Oh yes?'

She gave an enigmatic smile. 'Rosa Bauman is joining me, given that her brother has other plans.'

Peggy laughed. 'Gran was insistent. I didn't think Frank would want to come, but he assured me that it was entirely appropriate as he hasn't practised his faith for some time.'

'Are Nancy and Charlie excited about Christmas?'

'They're more excited about meeting Frank. I think Flo sees it as a blessing, as toys are a bit scarce this year.'

'I'm happy for you, Peggy,' said Marigold. 'I think Frank's a splendid chap.'

'Me too,' said Peggy.

They were interrupted by the arrival of Lady Lavinia, looking immaculate as usual but different somehow, her expression milder and more relaxed. 'Hello, Mama,' said Marigold, moving forwards to greet her mother with a kiss from which she did not recoil. 'I've booked us a table at the Russell if that's all right with you.'

Lady Lavinia nodded. 'Thank you, dear.' She turned to Peggy before they left. 'Happy Christmas, Peggy. Please give my best regards to your family.'

'Happy Christmas, Lady Lavinia.'

'So do you think my daddy is eating Christmas dinner like we are?' asked Nancy, eyes fixed on Frank as they had been ever since he'd arrived two hours earlier. Peggy shot him an encouraging look. Since he'd stepped through the door, he had been questioned on every subject from Winston Churchill's health to when he thought sweet rationing might end to whether he preferred Winnie the Pooh or Piglet.

'Yes,' said Frank without hesitation.

'Hmm,' said Nancy, picking over her dinner with her knife and fork. 'I hope he likes mutton more than I do.'

'Can I have yours?' squeaked Charlie.

Nancy frowned at him. 'I'm not finished, you little piggy.'

'Nancy!' scolded Flo. 'You shouldn't call your brother names.'

Charlie shrugged. 'I like little piggies.'

Frank turned to him. 'In German we call them *Ferkel*.'

'*Ferkel*,' repeated Charlie with glee.

'*Ferkel*,' replied Nancy, giggling.

'What have you done?' said Peggy as they all laughed.

'Don't go saying it at school,' warned Frank. 'You'll get into trouble.'

'Why?' asked Nancy.

'People don't like anything German at the moment,' said Alice.

'But I like you and you're German,' Nancy told Frank.

'Well, I don't feel very German any more,' he said. 'I think I would prefer to be British like you.'

Nancy clapped her hands together. 'Good, because then you could marry Auntie Peggy and we could have every Christmas together.'

Frank caught Peggy's eye. 'We'll see,' she said. 'Now, are you going to finish your Christmas dinner or give it to that little *ferkel* of a brother of yours?'

Charlie chuckled again. '*Ferkel*.'

Peggy noticed Emily watching the scene unfold from the head of the table, a look of contentment on her face. After they'd finished dinner, Nancy persuaded Frank to play a game of Snap with Charlie and her in the front room, whilst Alice kept order. Peggy and Flo cleared up the dinner things whilst Emily and Dulcie looked on.

'You're unusually quiet today, Gran,' said Peggy, winking at Flo who laughed.

'Cheeky girl,' said Emily. 'I'm just taking a moment to

be grateful for those around me, but thinking about the ones who aren't with us.'

'Like dear Joe,' sighed Dulcie.

Emily nodded. 'Precisely.'

'Where is he again?'

Emily rolled her eyes. 'Germany.'

Dulcie pulled a face. 'I 'ate the Germans.'

'Don't let Peggy hear you say that,' said Emily. 'Her young man's a German.'

Dulcie looked horrified. 'Is 'e? Peggy, did you know this?'

Peggy shared a look of amusement with Flo. 'Yes, Mrs Twigg. He's Jewish. He had to flee Germany because of the Nazis.'

'Oh yes,' said Dulcie. 'I remember you saying now. Poor man. What's his name again?'

'Frank,' said Emily.

'Oh yes, Frank. Very handsome,' said Dulcie. 'Lovely eyes. Like that nice Gary Grant.'

Flo giggled into the washing-up. 'I think he's lovely, Peg,' she said. 'Don't you, Gran?'

Emily glanced up and gave a brief nod. 'He'll do,' she said.

Alice wouldn't hear of Frank not staying the night and Frank wouldn't hear of Peggy giving up her bed for him. 'I'll be very snug down here,' he said, gesturing at the camp bed set up in the corner of the front room beside the small sparkling Christmas tree.

Peggy glanced over her shoulder. Dulcie had gone

home and she could already hear her grandmother's steady snoring from upstairs whilst Alice and Flo read bedtime stories to the children. 'I'm glad you decided to spend Christmas with us,' she said, wrapping her arms around his neck and kissing him.

'Me too,' he said, pulling her closer as the kiss intensified. Eventually, they pulled apart and he cupped her face in his hands. 'I love you, Peggy Sparks.'

It was the first time he'd said this and as she gazed into his sweet, kind face, she realised she felt the same. 'I love you too.'

'Then shall we grant Nancy her wish and get married?'

Peggy had never been the kind of woman to hanker after a knight on a charger. She'd always thought that fairy-tale endings were exactly that. There were no happy ever afters in real life, especially when there was a war to contend with. But standing there in front of Frank, gazing into his eyes, seeing nothing but love and kindness, she realised that falling in love could be easy, that moments of happiness were there to be seized. 'Are you asking me to marry you?'

He took hold of her hand and kissed it. 'I am.'

She grinned up at him as she replied. 'Then I accept.'

Kriegsgefangenenlager,
December 1943

Had a good Xmas, meat pie, cake, beer and your letters! Your happy news cheered me no end. Cold and frosty here but in good spirits. Sang carols with the lads and thought of you all. Albert is organising

326

concerts and revues to keep us busy. We're all well so don't worry. More news soon. Please write and send socks if you can. We'll meet again.

Love as ever, Joe

Chapter 24

Peggy and Frank were married in the spring. It had been Emily who dismissed her misgivings that they should wait until Joe's return.

'Who knows how long this bleedin' war's going to last?' she said. 'You have to make the most of these moments, Peg. Mark my words, Joe wouldn't want it any other way.'

'Mum's right,' said Alice. 'And we can celebrate again when he's home.'

'I'll be dancing in the street at that party,' said Emily.

Peggy smiled. They often talked about what they'd do once Joe was home, about the celebrations they'd have. They never gave voice to the thought that this might not happen. No one ever did if their loved ones were still alive. You had to keep hoping. It was the only way to get through a war.

Frank wore the one suit he'd brought over with him from Germany with a carrot-top buttonhole and a joyful grin. Peggy's outfit was the product of much deliberation between her three bridesmaids after they reviewed first Peggy's, then Flo's and finally Marigold's wardrobes in search of something they could adapt for the occasion.

'Do I have any say in the matter?' asked Peggy as they roundly rejected the contents of her wardrobe and seized upon a combination of Flo's dresses and the selection of outfits which Marigold had brought with her.

'Not really, darling,' said Marigold, pecking her on the cheek. 'Please don't take it to heart, but your wardrobe somewhat lacks the colour palette required for a wedding.'

'It's a bit drab, Auntie Peg,' said Nancy.

'Nancy,' scolded Flo. She offered Peggy a consoling look. 'We'll make sure you look lovely, won't we, girls?'

'Oh yes,' chorused Nancy and Marigold with glee.

In the end, Peggy wore a cherry-blossom-patterned dress courtesy of Flo and an orchid-pink fitted jacket borrowed from Marigold. 'You look beautiful, Auntie Peg,' said Nancy as she handed her the matching cherry blossom bouquet she'd made with help from Emily. In the absence of Joe and given his role in Frank's life, Peggy had asked Mr Beecher to escort her into the registry office. As they stood in the entrance hall, he turned to her.

'If Mrs Beecher and I had been blessed with a daughter, I'd have hoped she'd be as remarkable as you, Peggy. Frank is a lucky young man.' She kissed his cheek and he patted her hand in reply.

Peggy could hear the sniffles of joy as she and Frank made their vows, culminating in a loud nose blow from Dulcie Twigg, which made Nancy and Charlie giggle. She gazed up at her new husband as they shared a look of pure joy.

'Hello, Mrs Bauman,' he said.

'Hello.'

Alice and Emily excelled themselves with the reception, celebrated in the room above the pub where Alice worked. Rations had been saved, arms had been twisted and the array of meat and fish paste sandwiches, vegetable salads and the madeira wedding cake were made thanks to the kindness of neighbours and friends. Peggy gazed around the room at Mr Beecher and his wife laughing with Rosa and Marigold, at a bemused Sheldrake trying to hold a conversation with Dulcie, at Laurie looking amused as Nancy tested his knowledge of books whilst Alice and Frank chatted like old friends.

'Happy, Peg?' asked Emily, appearing at her shoulder.

'Very,' she replied. 'You?'

'You know me. If my family are happy then I'm happy.'

'I wish Joe were here.'

'He'll be back,' she said, patting her arm. 'Right, I better go and rescue your friend from Dulce. She gets a bit giddy at weddings.'

'Gran?' said Peggy.

Emily turned back towards her. 'What?'

Peggy wrapped her arms around her neck and hugged her. 'Thank you.'

Emily's eyes sparkled as they pulled apart. 'Daft apeth,' she said, chucking her under the chin.

A few weeks later, Peggy was sitting at her desk, reviewing the layout for a new book about women's organisations which, following the visit of Miss Dahlia Mackintosh, had been agreed with Longforth's department as part of their Official War Books series. Peggy was particularly pleased with it as the author, a Mrs Grace Halfpenny, had adopted a familiar, chatty tone which reminded Peggy of the reports she used to write herself. She had also interviewed several women and managed to reflect their quietly significant deeds, whether they were running a WVS canteen or offering support to those in need or, as in the case of eighty-seven-year-old Winnie Bagshawe, knitting over two thousand pairs of socks since the beginning of the war. Peggy was still smiling at Winnie, who beamed back at her from the photograph Marigold had taken, as she answered her telephone.

'Publishing?'

'Peggy Sparks?'

'It's actually Peggy Bauman,' she said, admiring her wedding ring. It had belonged to Emily who asserted that it was 'more use on your finger as I'm resigned to the fact that Clark Gable will never propose, and besides, it won't fit over my gippy knuckles any more.'

'Actually, that's what I need to discuss with you. This is Mrs Gower from the Women's Staffing department. Do you have a moment to come and see me now?'

Peggy stomped back into the office half an hour later, slammed the door shut and flung herself into her chair.

'Gosh,' said Marigold, glancing up from her desk. 'Who's rattled your cage?'

'The powers that be won't allow me to use my married name at work.'

'Oh.'

'German-sounding names on the staff list are not desirable, apparently.'

'Oh. I see.'

Peggy was irritated by Marigold's blithe acceptance. 'It's wrong though, isn't it?'

Marigold shrugged. 'Perhaps, but I can also see the Ministry's point of view. Anyway, if I'm honest, you'll always be Peggy Sparks to me.'

'But that's not the point, Marigold. Why should I be told which name to use?' Peggy was brimming with fury now.

'I don't know. I'm sorry.'

Peggy's phone began to ring again. She snatched it to her ear. 'Publishing?'

'Miss Sparks? It's Lear.'

'Oh, hello, Mr Lear,' she said, not bothering to correct him following her deflating conversation with Mrs Gower.

'Mr Longforth has asked me to call you. We need to bin the Women's Organisations book.'

'I beg your pardon?'

'The book. About the women's organisations? It's no longer required.'

'Why?'

Lear seemed stumped. 'I'm sorry?'

'Why is the book no longer required?'

Lear hesitated, sensing an ominous edge to Peggy's voice. 'I think Mr Longforth isn't quite sure if there'll be the readership,' he said, choosing his words as carefully as if he were picking through broken glass.

'For a book about women and their part in the war?'

'Erm, I don't think he put it quite like that.'

'Well, how did he put it then?' Peggy didn't give him a chance to answer before she continued. 'Because it seems strange that Mr Longforth doesn't deem there to be a readership for a book like this given that half the people in the country are women, and there are a good number of men who would be interested too.' Marigold stared at Peggy, who was now riding the wave of disgruntled anger which had begun following her conversation with Mrs Gower. 'I also find it strange that Mr Longforth doesn't have the gumption or courtesy to deliver this message to me in person, given the amount of time and effort Miss Cecily and I have put into it, not to say the time Mrs Halfpenny has invested. So please, do tell Mr Longforth that I await his apology in person at his earliest convenience. Good day, Mr Lear,' she said, replacing the receiver before he had an opportunity to respond. In the days preceding life at the Ministry, Peggy had shied away from conflict, but she welcomed the indignant fury she felt today like a new friend.

'Golly,' said Marigold. 'That told him.'

'Well, really,' said Peggy, gesturing towards the pages in front of her. 'Do they think we have nothing more to do with our time than create books for them to cancel on a whim? What do I tell Mrs Halfpenny?'

'I'm sure she'll understand.'

'But why should she, and why aren't you getting as cross as me about all this?'

Marigold shrugged. 'What's the point? Longforth won't change his mind so you'll get all worked up for nothing.'

'But shouldn't we be getting worked up about things that matter to us? Taking a stand? Isn't that what this blasted war is all about in the first place?'

Marigold sighed. 'I suppose. Perhaps I just don't have your fighting spirit.'

'Maybe that's because you've never had to fight for anything in your life.' Peggy might have regretted the words escaping from her mouth if it weren't for the fact that she was stoked with fury.

'Now hang on a minute,' said Marigold. 'That's not fair. You know I've had more than my share of struggles. You don't really know the truth of what it's like for me.'

'Don't I?' said Peggy. 'I know that you've never wanted for anything in your life, that it's all been handed to you on a plate, that people fall over themselves to help you because of who you are and how you look. I know that much.'

Marigold's face grew scarlet. 'That's not true.'

'Oh, isn't it? What about during that meeting with Mr Burbage? He wouldn't entertain the thought of helping Frank and Rosa until you swanned in and batted your eyelashes at him.'

Marigold's eyes blazed with anger. 'Well, we can't all be getting on our high horses every second of the day, can we? Sitting up there, assuming that anyone who has a title or an education is a villain.'

'I don't do that.'

'Yes, you do. You do it all the time. You did it to me the first time we met, in fact. The truth, which you can't bear, by the way, is that you and I really aren't that different. In fact, you're luckier than me, Peggy. Far luckier.'

Peggy snorted her derision. 'Oh really? The girl with three houses has less luck than me. How can that be, Marigold? What could I possibly have that you don't?'

Marigold's eyes filled with tears as she answered. 'Love.'

Kriegsgefangenenlager,
April 1944

Dear Peg,

The first thing I have to say is congratulations! I was tickled pink to get your news about your wedding to Frank. Gran is right, I'm glad you went ahead. I hope it was a wonderful day. I'm sorry I missed it, but as you say, we'll have all the more to celebrate when I'm home. Just writing that word – 'home' – brings me joy. I feel as if you're a long way from me, but picturing you celebrating in the room above the pub makes me smile. I can't wait to meet Frank. He sounds like a good bloke. I'm glad you've found someone who makes you happy, Peg. No one deserves it more.

As for me, I'm all right. I do my best to keep my spirits up but I can't lie to you, it's hard to keep going. Sometimes it feels as if this war will never end, and every time I think we're winning or there's a chance I might get home, it's all dashed away from us. Albert won't let me dwell on this. He says we have to keep on hoping and praying. In some ways, he reminds me of you. I know you wouldn't let me dwell on it either. I hear that in your letters. I read and reread them, Peg, because they remind me of everything and everyone I miss and love, and that spurs me on. At least the winter's past and it's spring again. Mind you, as soon as the weather warms up, the flies put in an appearance and stay like unwanted house guests until winter comes again. We've managed to get hold of some fly papers, though, so it's not too bad. The food is improving a bit too and the Red Cross Parcels are getting through, which helps. It's a good job I like potatoes, bread and turnip as we eat these nearly every day! I also got your parcel. Thank you. I enjoyed the book, even though the story was a bit strange, but I like the title – *Brave New World* – it makes me think of life after the war. The other chaps are reading it now so it's getting quite tatty, but it's a good distraction. You always said that books make everything better and I see what you mean now.

Albert and I are working in a rubber factory near to the camp. It's another distraction, although they work us hard. Mum would do her nut if she knew that I only have one shower every ten days. Albert jokes that it's a good job there are no women around. They wouldn't come near us if they caught a whiff! All in all, I'm all right. Our RAF lads often pass over because we're near to the factories. We hold up sheets spelling out 'POW' during the raids so they know to avoid us. It gives me fresh hope every time they fly over. Sorry if this letter isn't as cheery as some. It's been a long war but we'll meet again.

Love, Joe

Chapter 25

The two-bedroom flat which Peggy now shared with Frank and Rosa was cosy. It belonged to a friend of the Beechers who had retired to the Kent coast but wanted to keep the property to let. It was ideal for Peggy as it was situated within walking distance of the Ministry. However, she couldn't help but experience a pang of longing every time she thought of her mother's house. She missed her early morning chats with Nancy about everything from whether Badger was getting fat to Field Marshal Montgomery's favourite food (Nancy was certain it was suet pudding). She missed her grandmother telling her to eat breakfast and her mother kissing her goodbye. She missed her evenings gossiping with Flo and her reading Peggy's horoscope, and she missed Charlie's warm body as he wrapped his sweet little arms around her neck and held tight. She loved being married to Frank, of course, kissing him goodnight and waking up beside him in the morning. She enjoyed evening suppers with him and Rosa, sharing tales of their day, laughing and chatting. If Rosa was out, she would light some candles and they'd enjoy dinner together, then she'd take his hand and they would dance to music on the wireless or gramophone before going to bed to make love. Peggy was happy. She knew she was and she knew it was natural to miss her family. It was all different and new and that would take a while to get used to, but being with Frank made her feel as if she'd found a piece of herself she hadn't even realised was missing.

Life at the Ministry was less joyful. She hadn't spoken to Marigold since their disagreement, and when she came to work the next day and Marigold's desk remained empty until gone nine thirty, Peggy assumed she had reverted to her old tardy ways. However, as the hours ticked on, she became more concerned.

'Hilda, do you know where Miss Cecily is today?'

'Mr Beecher said she was on leave.'

'Oh. I see,' said Peggy.

A short while later Mr Beecher appeared in her office. 'Might I have a word, please, Mrs Bauman?' Despite the Ministry's refusal to accept her new name, Mr Beecher had respectfully adopted it and Peggy was quietly grateful. The advantage of her marrying 'an enemy alien' was that she wasn't forced to give up work as a married woman. 'I am the silver lining to your cloud,' Frank had told her with a wry smile.

Peggy noticed that Beecher's face was grave as she followed him to his office. He closed the door and took a seat, indicating for her to do the same. 'As you know, I'm not a man who minces his words so I'll come straight out with it. Miss Cecily has requested a transfer.'

'Oh,' said Peggy, unsure of how to respond. 'Did she say why?'

'No. She said she felt that her time here had come to an end.' He studied her face as if searching for the truth.

'I see,' said Peggy, avoiding his eye.

Beecher sighed. 'Look, Mrs Bauman. Peggy. This isn't a school playground and I'm not your headmaster. However, I feel that it's my duty to ask if the pair of you have had a falling-out?'

Peggy hesitated. She had come into work with the intention of smoothing things over with Marigold. It had been a silly spat, after all, but hurtful too. Now, she felt a fresh wave of indignation that Marigold had taken matters into her own hands. 'We may have had words,' she said quietly.

'Was it anything to do with the cancelled publication on the subject of women's organisations?'

'Partly. I was very annoyed.'

'So Mr Lear said.'

'I think I was right to be annoyed, sir.'

Beecher held his palms open. 'I'm not disagreeing with you. All I would say is that it's probably not worth losing a valued colleague and friend because Mr Longforth has perhaps made an error of judgement.'

Peggy was silent for a moment. She knew he was right but was still peeved. 'So you think it was an error of judgement?'

'I do.'

'Will you speak to him about it?'

'I will not.'

Peggy did her best to hide the impatience in her voice. 'May I ask why, sir?'

Beecher considered the question. 'Do you know how I spent the first ten years of my career?' Peggy shook her head. 'I spent it challenging authority. And do you know how I fared?'

'I'm guessing badly, from your expression.'

'Very, very badly. I infuriated my superiors, stayed exactly where I was in my pay grade and made myself thoroughly miserable.'

'So you're saying I should comply without question?'

Beecher shook his head. 'Oh, good heavens, no. You merely need to learn to pick your battles.'

'I thought I was.'

'No, Peggy, you're not. You're taking issue with every injustice you see, which is admirable, but there are bigger, more important battles to fight.' He picked up the front cover of *Women's Organisations*. 'If you go to war with Longforth over this, he'll make every other book you work on as difficult as it can be, but if you accept it and allow time to move on, you may even be able to persuade him to publish it at a later date.'

'Are you telling me to let this go?'

'Oh no. You're far too intelligent for me to dictate to you. I am merely offering the benefit of my experience. It's up to you whether you choose to listen.'

Peggy sighed. 'What about Marigold?'

'She's taking some overdue leave, but I believe she's still in London. I don't want to sign her request. I think you're a stellar team. I hope you can find a way to patch things up.' Peggy nodded. 'And by the way, you don't need to lose that fighting spirit. You merely need to learn the art of diplomacy. They complement one another rather well, particularly in times of war. As do you and Miss Cecily.'

Peggy left Beecher's office with a sense of defeat. She'd achieved so much since taking the job here, and yet she hadn't been able to help Joe and she'd lost the one true friend she'd made since the war started. Peggy glanced in through Mrs Pyecroft's door on her way past. She looked up from her desk. 'Ah, Mrs Bauman. Might I have a word?'

'Of course,' said Peggy, stepping inside.

'Shut the door behind you and come and sit down, please.' Peggy did as she was told. Mrs Pyecroft eyed her for a moment before she spoke. 'Your brother is a prisoner of war in Germany, I understand?'

Peggy nodded. 'He was in Italy first but instead of being sent home was captured and transferred by the Germans.'

'A dreadful business, when loved ones are taken prisoner. And how is Mr Bauman?'

'Very well, thank you.'

Mrs Pyecroft spoke slowly, picking over her words with care. 'What I'm about to tell you is top secret.'

'I understand,' said Peggy.

Mrs Pyecroft continued. 'I have recently become involved with the work of a secret organisation helping prisoners of war to escape.' Peggy stared at her. 'We have had some notable successes and are looking at new ways to generate more. One idea is to plant our so-called escape kits in the stitching and spine of the books we send via the Red Cross to prisoner of war camps.'

'I see,' said Peggy.

'My proposal is to ask you to produce a book which would offer the suitable bulk whilst your husband helps us with the printing and securing of these items.'

'But how will the prisoners know what's inside?'

'We have agents on the ground, some of them working at the camps. Very brave men and women. It's highly dangerous work.'

'We'll do it,' said Peggy without hesitation.

'Don't you need to consult with your husband first?'

'I know him. I know what he'll say.'

'Very good,' said Mrs Pyecroft. 'We start work tomorrow.'

Peggy called on her publishing contacts to reprint *The Grapes of Wrath*, which at 464 pages delivered a wide enough spine for the button-sized compass and miniature map which would be stitched inside. Each map needed to be tailored to the particular prisoner of war camp. Mrs Pyecroft agreed that Rosa and the Baumans' trusted associates should be drafted in to help with the painstaking work.

'I'm amazed they're letting Germans take on this task,' joked Frank one day.

Peggy wrapped her arms around his neck and kissed his cheek. 'You're more trustworthy than half the British people I know,' she told him. She didn't ask Mrs Pyecroft if these books might end up in Joe's camp. It was never discussed, but then one day she came to Peggy. 'Your brother is in Stalag 344, correct?'

'Yes, Mrs Pyecroft.'

'You know I can't promise. These things are decided at a higher level.'

'I know.'

Mrs Pyecroft nodded. 'Onwards, as Mr Beecher likes to say.'

'Onwards, Mrs Pyecroft.'

Peggy hoped she would see Marigold at an ARP shift. She valued Mr Beecher's opinion and knew he was right about the foolishness of losing a friend over something so trivial. Sadly, she was to be disappointed.

'Called in to say she'd had to go away, unfortunately,' said Mr Baggley as he handed out their warden's torches and whistles.

'That's a shame,' said Peggy.

'Indeed it is. If it's anything like the last few weeks, we're in for a busy night.'

Mr Baggley's prediction turned out to be right. Since the middle of June, the Wehrmacht had begun to scatter their deadly new rockets on towns and cities across the land, with London bearing the brunt. After the bombing of Nancy's school, Peggy couldn't claim immunity to the horrors she'd seen, but there was a sense in which war and the tragedy it dragged with it had become part of the everyday. That's not to say that she didn't weep at the lives cut short or feel her stomach writhe at the sight of the broken, bloodied limbs and bodies, but you had to develop a certain amount of grit – 'a spine of steel' – was what her grandmother called it. If you didn't, it would surely drive you insane.

When this fresh round of bombings first began, Frank had begged Peggy to give up her ARP role. 'It's too dangerous,' he told her. 'I'm going to spend the nights pacing and worrying.'

'Join up with me and we can pace together,' she joked.

'It's not funny, Peggy,' said Frank. 'Besides, I'm an enemy alien, aren't I? They wouldn't have me for fear that I'll find a way to brighten the moon so that the Luftwaffe can see their targets more easily.'

'Now who's joking?' said Peggy, wrapping her arms around his neck and kissing him.

He raised one eyebrow. 'Would it help if I, as your husband, ordered you to give up?'

She pursed her lips. 'I think you know the answer to that, having met my grandmother.'

'Please be careful, Peggy. It's dangerous out there.'

She gazed into his eyes. 'It's dangerous everywhere, Frank, but we have to keep fighting.'

The first siren sounded ten minutes into Peggy's shift. 'Right,' said Mr Baggley. 'Let's move in an orderly fashion and make sure people get to the shelters safely. I know everyone's weary after these blessed bombs falling day and night, but we must continue to do our duty. Courage and presence of mind will get us through as it's always done. Good luck.'

In the absence of Marigold, Peggy had been paired with a new recruit called Phyllis Bickerstaff, who looked considerably younger than her eighteen years, eyes skittering left and right as they made their way outside. When the first bomb fell in the distance, she grabbed hold of Peggy's arm, causing her to jump in alarm too. 'It's all right, Phyllis,' said Peggy. 'Remember what Mr Baggley said and take courage.'

'Courage. Right. Yes. I'll do that,' said Phyllis, even though she looked as terrified as a rabbit in a corner. 'I'm sorry. It's just it's my first time, you see, and I'm worried. My nan keeps going on about these new bombs. Says they're even more terrifying than the doodlebugs. She reckons they'll end up gassing us all in our beds.'

'Well, it's probably best not to worry about something until it's happened,' said Peggy. Another bomb exploded, a few streets away this time, causing Phyllis to scream. Peggy turned and seized her by the shoulders. 'Look, Phyllis. You need to try to stay calm, all right? It's not going to help you, me or anyone who needs us if you're yelling your head off. Do you understand?' Phyllis nodded at her, wide-eyed. 'Good girl. Now. You need to breathe and stay calm because we have to go towards where that bomb landed and see if anyone needs help. Can you do that for me?'

'I think so. Thank you, Peggy.'

Peggy patted her hand. 'It's all right. Everything will be all right. Now, shine your torch downwards so that we don't break our necks. We're going this way.'

At the sound of another bomb, Phyllis grabbed Peggy's arm again. 'I don't think I can do this.'

Peggy stopped. 'Do you know what my gran always did when I was scared?' Phyllis shook her head. 'She used to sing to me. Shall we try it, as we walk along?'

Peggy wracked her brain for which song to sing and smiled as she remembered Joe. 'We'll meet again,' she began, wondering at the unusual sight of two women walking arm in arm in the middle of a raid with one of them doing her best Vera Lynn impression. It was then that she heard Phyllis's sweet, clear voice join in. Peggy nodded encouragement as they walked and sang, noticing Phyllis's grip loosen on her arm as her voice grew stronger and more confident.

The scene which greeted them was one of familiar devastation. Two buildings had crumpled like sandcastles overcome by the sea. Other wardens had already arrived and a stretcher team were lifting bodies from the wreckage, the lucky survivors gazing heavenwards with bloodied, frightened faces, the unlucky ones covered by blankets.

'Come on. We have to help,' said Peggy.

To her credit, Phyllis didn't hesitate. They dashed over to where a chain of people were lifting rubble, wood, brick, furniture – anything that needed to be cleared in a desperate hunt for survivors. The smoke and dust was suffocating but they kept going. Peggy had never felt more determined in her life. She thought of everyone she loved. Other people's loved ones were buried under there and she had a duty to them and to her own family to help. Deep down she felt that if she could save one person, the universe might save Joe too. After an hour, a shout went up. 'Mother and baby here!' Peggy raced to the spot, her heart thumping as she saw a woman emerge with her baby in her arms, bruised, bloodied but alive. Peggy raised her eyes heavenwards. *Thank you*, she mouthed.

'Come on, Peggy,' urged Phyllis. 'No time to rest. There's more needs clearing over here.'

'Your grandmother will be proud of you, Phyllis,' she told her as they formed part of the next chain of rescuers.

Phyllis smiled. 'Yours too.'

Peggy arrived home a little after midnight, exhausted, her brain still buzzing after that evening's events. She wasn't surprised to find Frank waiting for her as he usually did but didn't expect him to meet her at the front door as soon as she turned her key in the lock. It was his expression that alerted her that something was wrong. Even though he worried about her during a shift, he always rewarded her with a relieved, loving look. Tonight, however, his face was etched with distress, pale and fretful.

'Is something wrong?' she asked, as he grasped her hands.

'I think you should come and sit down.'

'What is it? Is it Rosa?' she asked, as he led her to the kitchen and sat beside her at the table.

He shook his head. 'Rosa's fine. She's out with a friend.'

She searched his expression for the truth. 'Then what? What is it, Frank? You're scaring me.'

He cast his eyes downwards and swallowed before gazing at her with sorrowful eyes as the words tumbled from him. 'It's your grandmother. Your mother found her in the garden. She'd been picking tomatoes. Said she didn't suffer. They think it was a heart attack. I'm so sorry, Peggy.'

Peggy stared at him. Surely this was a dream? She had only seen her grandmother at the weekend. They'd climbed up Edenham Hill with Nancy and Badger and sat on a bench at the top laughing while Nancy told a story about Alfie Riley terrifying their poor class teacher, Miss Winslow, when he brought his pet mouse to school and it escaped from his desk. How could she only have been sitting next to her gran in the park on Saturday, weeping tears of laughter and clutching Emily's arm as Nancy re-enacted the chaotic scene? How could that ferocious love from the woman who'd been a second mother to her, be gone forever? Snuffed out in an instant. How could that be the last time she would ever sit beside her, watching her wryly amused face, catching a note of her rose-scented perfume, hearing her infectious laugh wrap itself around them like an embrace?

Chapter 26

The world seemed to blur and muffle around Peggy after Frank delivered the news. It was as if she was listening to everything with her head underwater, struggling to comprehend what he was telling her. Peggy listened in silence as Frank repeated that it would have been quick and instant, that she wouldn't have been in pain. One minute Emily Marsh was alive, the next she ceased to exist. He held Peggy's hands and stroked her face, telling her how sorry he was, how he understood what a shock this was, what a wonderful woman Emily had been. She gazed at him unblinking, unable to believe that any of this was real. Then she let go of his hand, rose from her chair, her coat still on, and made for the front door.

'Where are you going?'

It was a reasonable question, but Peggy didn't have the first clue. She just knew she needed to keep moving. 'Out,' was all she could think of to say.

'Let me come with you.'

'No,' she said abruptly before softening her tone. 'Thank you. I need to be alone.'

Frank approached and pulled her into his arms. Peggy

remained rigid, stock still. She knew he was being kind but there was no comforting her today. She was numb and needed to escape. He kissed the top of her head before letting her go with tears in his eyes. 'I love you.'

Peggy nodded and hoped he understood that she loved him too but couldn't find the strength for the words today. She left the flat and walked out into the street. The world was ink-black, the sky cloaked with cloud with not even a glimmer of stars or glow of moonlight. Peggy hurried along the pavement, eyes fixed down following her torch's steady beam. She knew now where she needed to go; it would be a long walk. Her limbs were weary, her bones aching, but dogged determination forced her to keep putting one foot in front of the other, a single thought powering her on. *Emily is dead. My beloved grandmother is dead.* The one who kept everyone going, who never allowed them to entertain the thought of giving up for even one moment, had given up. She was gone. How could this have happened? How could this be? Peggy glared at the sky, willing the Luftwaffe to appear so she could shout, scream, wave her fist as she searched for someone to blame. The stress and strain of the war had finally taken its toll on her grandmother and Hitler was to blame. Angrily, she palmed away hot, salty tears and pressed on. There would be time for crying, but for now, she had to keep going. She marched through London's bruised and battered streets, past the wreckages of places where children once played, the bombsites that people used to call home, the gaping holes where others had worked, feeling angrier and angrier with every step. She glimpsed the Ministry's towering form, rising above it all, a menacing presence in the darkness, and it provoked a fresh fury and indignation. What had she been thinking, taking a job here, thinking she could make a difference to the war effort? What astonishing arrogance had she shown as she produced those useless pamphlets and books? What good did they do? Did they protect the ones you loved? What had been the point of it all given that Emily was now dead and Joe was a prisoner enduring goodness knows what? What a fool she'd been to think that any of it mattered, to believe that she could change anything. She quickened her step, desperate to get away from this place. She should never have come here in the first place. She should have stayed at the library, stayed at her mother's house, taken care of her family properly, praying her way through the war like everyone else.

Within an hour, Peggy had reached the river. She stared into its silty depths and urged herself to keep going. She imagined Emily at her shoulder willing her on, although she knew she'd call her a 'daft apeth' for undertaking such a journey. As she made her way over the bridge and began to trudge along the road, a vegetable truck pulled up alongside her.

'Peggy?' said a voice. 'What on earth are you doing here?'

She turned in surprise, recognising the man immediately. 'Mr Miller,' she began. 'I'm . . .' Fresh tears sprang to her eyes at the sight of the kindly greengrocer for whom her mother worked, who was gazing at her now with a look of deep concern.

Mr Miller seemed alarmed at the outburst. 'Ah now, don't cry, Peggy. Come on. Hop in. I'll take you home.'

The mere mention of home brought a new round of tears from Peggy but she managed to climb inside the truck. 'Thank you,' she said weakly.

He reached into his pocket and fished out a clean handkerchief. 'Here. Have this. What on earth has happened, my dear?'

She gazed at him through tear-stained eyes. 'My grandmother's dead,' she stammered.

Mr Miller's face fell. 'Oh, my dear. I'm so sorry. She was a wonderful, wonderful woman.' Peggy nodded. He turned the key in the ignition. 'Right, hold tight. We'll get you home as quickly as we can.'

Peggy rested her head against the cab window as Mr Miller sped through the streets of south London, the weight of sadness pulling her down as if she were plunging to the bottom of an ocean. She slipped into a fretful sleep and woke with a start a while later as he pulled up outside her mother's house. 'Here we are,' he said.

Peggy noticed his sorrowful expression, remembering how he'd lost his own daughter, how he must miss her every day, how the pain and sadness never really go away. Their eyes locked in a moment of understanding. She reached for his hand and squeezed it. 'Tell your mother I'm deeply sorry,' he said.

'Thank you.' She walked up the path feeling as if her body were cast from marble. The house was dark but as she approached the front door, Peggy glimpsed a sliver of light from the kitchen. She fished her key from her pocket and turned it in the lock. As she pushed open the door, her mother appeared. Alice's eyes were red-rimmed, her face blanched with grief. She looked surprised to see her daughter for a moment and then overcome with tearful relief as they flew into one another's arms.

'Oh Peg,' cried her mother, burying her head into her daughter's shoulder. 'She's gone. She's gone, Peg. Whatever will we do now?'

Peggy clung to Alice, not wanting to ever let go. 'I don't know, Mum,' she sobbed, giving in to the avalanche of sorrow which engulfed her. 'I just don't know.'

Peggy ran her hand along the soft spines of the books in Edenham library's fiction section and selected one at random. She carried it through to the reading room and slid into one of the chairs set around the walnut table, placing it in front of her. Opening the book, she smoothed down the first page and began to read. It didn't matter to Peggy what the story was, she barely noticed the words. It was the routine and rhythm of sitting in this hallowed space and methodically turning the pages which seemed to be the only thing which could calm her grief-stricken mind at the moment. She had telephoned two people the day after she arrived back in Edenham. The first was Frank. He begged her to come home, to let him take care of her.

'I am home, Frank, and this is where I need to be for now. I hope you can understand that.'

'I love you, Peggy, so of course I understand. I'll call again soon and visit at the weekend.'

'I can't wait to see you.'

The other person she called was Mr Beecher, who was stunned into silence when she told him what had happened. When he finally regained his voice, it was cracked with despair. 'Oh, my dear Peggy. I am most dreadfully sorry. Please accept my deepest condolences and take all the time you need.'

'I won't be returning to work, Mr Beecher.'

'You've had a great shock, Peggy. Please don't make any rash decisions yet.'

'I'm not. My mind is made up. I'll send you my formal letter of resignation in the morning.'

He paused before answering. 'This saddens me greatly, but I respect your decision if it's final.'

'It is.'

Peggy was amazed how grief brought everything into sharp focus. It was as if she were seeing the world for what it really was for the first time in her life. She had never been surer that she was in the right place, taking care of her family, comforting them, offering support. Ever the stoic, Alice had of course gone straight back to work. 'What good does it do sitting at home?' she asked Peggy. Mr Miller, who had opened the shop the day after his daughter died, didn't question the decision.

In the evenings, of course, when they were alone, they wept for Emily but they also shared stories about her, of the impossible things she'd said, of her fire, determination and wicked sense of humour.

While her mother was at work, Peggy would often go to the library. She could tell that Mr Alderman was in two minds as to whether he should comfort her when she first set foot back inside the building. He looked visibly relieved when she told him, 'I'm all right, Mr Alderman. I just want to sit and read.'

'Of course, my dear. Miss Bunce or I will be happy to help if you need anything. Anything at all.'

'Thank you.'

Miss Bunce was as kindly as Peggy remembered. She would offer suggestions or set aside titles she thought Peggy might like. Really, Peggy just wanted to sit quietly amongst the books because she felt safe there. She feared that if she had too much time to think about Emily or the fact that she would never see her again, she would be driven into a dark pit of despair from which she would never return. She preferred to sit, to turn the pages of the books and imagine that Emily were still with her.

So you've given up your job, have you?

It's for the best.

Seems a shame, given how hard you worked.

Some things aren't meant to be.

That's true. Best to accept them. Else you'll go potty. What about Joe? Have you told him about me yet?

No, we've decided he's got enough to deal with.

Poor lad. You can pretend my letters went astray.

Something like that.

What about Alice?

I'm looking after her.

She's strong. She's put up with more than most. She'll be all right. So will you.

'Are you having one of your imaginary chats with Great-Gran?'

Peggy didn't realise Nancy had entered the library until she noticed her standing right beside her. 'Where did you spring from?'

'I wanted to come and find you. Besides, I like the library too.'

Peggy kissed the top of her head, inhaling the comforting scent of Sunlight soap. 'I'm glad you're here, and to answer your question, yes, I was chatting to Gran in my head. It makes me feel better.'

'I knew you were. You get that far-off look when you do. And I understand. I think it's nice.' She sat down beside Peggy at the table. 'I miss her.'

Peggy squeezed her hand. 'So do I.'

'Even though she used to tell me that I chattered on too much.'

'She was a fine one to talk.'

Nancy chuckled. 'Do you think she's in heaven with Grandad Charlie?'

Peggy regarded her for a moment. Her family had never been religious, but she liked to believe that Emily Marsh was still somewhere, offering her no-nonsense opinion to whoever needed it, watching over them with her father. 'What do you believe?'

'I think she definitely is.'

'Then that's what I think too.'

Nancy gave a satisfied nod before taking out the copy of *Little Women* she was reading. 'Shall we just sit here quietly then, Auntie Peg?'

'I'd like that,' said Peggy, turning back to her book and beginning to leaf through with Nancy beside her, tracing each line with her finger, mouthing the words as she read.

It was standing room only in the church for the funeral of Emily Marsh. Peggy gazed around from her position between Frank and Nancy in the front pew and wondered what her grandmother would make of all the fuss.

Why's Edna Cope sitting at the back weeping and wailing like that? She couldn't stand me.

She's just paying her respects.

Respects, my foot. She never forgave me after I criticised her dusting at the library. It was inch-thick, Peg.

Well, I think it's lovely that so many people have turned out for you. There's a whole row of WVS women. Even Mrs Pike is here. Said there was no one quite like you.

That's a back-handed compliment if ever I heard one. Now you keep an eye on Elsie Cooper at my wake. She'll be emptying plates of sandwiches into her handbag if you don't watch her.

I miss you, Gran.

I'm always here, you daft apeth.

Peggy reached into her pocket for the handkerchief her gran had embroidered with a looping lavender 'P' and wiped her eyes. She smiled as Frank took hold of her hand and squeezed it, noticing Sir James appear at the back of the church with Beecher, Sheldrake, Laurie and Marigold in tow. She turned to face forwards, concentrating her gaze on the catafalque at the front. She'd wondered if Sir James would attend but hadn't reckoned on a whole Ministry delegation. She hadn't spoken to Marigold since their argument and wasn't sure she had the strength to face it today.

'Is that where Great-Gran's coffin will go?' whispered Nancy from her other side. Peggy nodded, catching her mother's eye from the end of the row where she sat beside Flo and Charlie. She and her mother had planned the funeral together, imagining what Emily would have to say about everything from the flowers ('pink roses fresh from the garden – nothing better') to the hymns she'd prefer ('anything but that bleedin' awful "All Things Bright and Beautiful"').

'All rise,' came the vicar's voice from the back of the church.

Everyone agreed that it was a beautiful service, that Emily would have loved it, that she was in a better place now with 'her dear Reggie'. Peggy appreciated their sentiments and thought that the Reverend Edward Blythe summed up her grandmother perfectly when he told the congregation that 'Mrs Marsh touched so many lives and left no one in any doubt as to what she thought.' For Peggy, though, the truth was that Emily wasn't in a better place. She should still be here, and she knew her mother believed this too. As they joined the mourners at the wake held above the pub in the same room they had celebrated Frank and Peggy's wedding months earlier, Peggy felt like an onlooker. The mood was muted, hushed even. She noticed Alice talking to Sir James, the way he inclined his head towards her with genuine sorrow. She saw Mr Alderman, nursing his tea in sad reflection. She spotted Dulcie, sitting beside Nancy and Flo, looking utterly lost.

Emily Marsh had indeed touched many lives and it would seem that no one really knew how to go on without her.

'I'm going to get some air,' she told Frank. 'You stay here.' He kissed her cheek before she left. She smiled, appreciating his quiet, consoling presence. Peggy knew she was distant at the moment but took heart from the fact that Frank seemed to understand. She made her way down the stairs and out through the bar.

'Peggy,' said a voice as she reached the door.

She turned to see Marigold gazing at her, her expression one of sorrow and regret. 'Hello, Marigold. It was kind of you to come.'

Marigold's eyes misted with tears. 'Of course. I thought your grandmother was a queen amongst women. I'm so deeply sorry, Peggy.'

'Thank you.'

'Do you have five minutes to talk?'

'All right,' she said.

'Will you have a drink?' Peggy shook her head. They sat in a corner of the pub. 'I want to apologise, Peggy, for what was said.'

'I think I'm the one who needs to apologise, Marigold. I'm sorry.'

'Well, it all got a bit out of hand, but I did wonder if you really thought those things of me. I must confess I was a little hurt.'

Peggy studied the beer-stained table. 'I'm sorry. I was angry. I lashed out. It was unkind. And you're right. I do get on my high horse, but I know full well where I get that from.'

'Your grandmother.' Peggy nodded. 'I must confess to feeling jealous of you with your mother and grandmother in your corner. You know how it is in my family.'

'How is your mother?'

'Things are definitely improving between us. I telephoned her last week and she sounded genuinely upset when I told her about your grandmother. She asked me to pass on her condolences to you and your family.'

'That's kind.'

'She and my father are planning to divorce, and that seems to have lifted a weight from her shoulders. She even said she'd seen some of my photographs in one of our books and thought they were rather good.'

'Heavens, Marigold. That's praise indeed.'

She laughed. 'Rather. We'll never be close as you and your family, but it's something. And I feel as if I have the gumption to deal with it all better these days.' She stole a glance at Peggy. 'Mr Beecher said you'd handed in your resignation. I'm sorry to hear that.'

'Don't be. It's the right decision.'

'Are you sure?'

'I should never have been there in the first place.'

'Why on earth not?'

'The Ministry isn't a place for people like me. I should have stayed here in Edenham, caring for my family, my community. If I'd done that, my gran would still be alive today.'

Marigold looked astonished. 'You don't honestly believe that, do you?'

'What else is there to believe? If I'd been here, I would

360

have noticed something was wrong. Got her to a hospital before it was too late. It's as simple as that.'

Marigold gave her a sorrowful look. 'You can't save everyone, Peggy. I was with Cordelia the night the bomb went off. She died, I lived. It's not fate or destiny or anything within our control. It's an awful tragedy and there's nothing anyone can do to stop that.'

Peggy gazed at her for a moment. She could see the truth in what Marigold was telling her but still felt the burden of responsibility like a boulder in her stomach. 'Did you feel guilty after Cordelia died?'

'Every waking hour,' said Marigold. 'I kept replaying it in my mind. What I could have done differently. What would have happened if she'd been dancing with my chap. If I could have saved her life in the immediate aftermath. It nearly drove me potty.' She took hold of Peggy's hands. 'You're grief-stricken. You've lost one of the most important people in your life. Trust me, I understand how that feels. It breaks you apart.' Peggy stared at her as a creeping truth began to take hold. 'But do you know what saved me?' Peggy shook her head. 'You did. You and Beecher, Laurie and heavens, even Sheldrake, but particularly you, Peggy.'

'I don't know what to say.'

Marigold rested a hand on her shoulder. 'My dear friend, you don't need to say anything, but you could let me help you. You're still needed, you know.'

'At the Ministry?' Peggy shook her head. 'I don't think so. Like I said, it's not a place for someone like me.'

'Someone like you? What does that mean exactly?'

'Someone from a place like this,' she said, gesturing around the room. 'Someone who never had elocution lessons or a nanny or a maid.'

'You mean as opposed to someone like me who had all those things.'

'You have to admit that there are far more people like you than me at the Ministry.'

Marigold shrugged. 'So what? So you get the odd ignorant comment and stupid remark, but most people respect you for your intelligence and work. People like Beecher and Mrs P and Sir James. Forgive me, Peggy, but I really think you have a chip on your shoulder. I don't think your grandmother would approve of that, particularly if it stops you doing something worthwhile.'

'Is it worthwhile?'

'I think so and I know you used to. And for what it's worth, I think you'd be a fool to give it all up after you've worked so bally hard. You were a shrinking wallflower when I first met you and now you're a towering oak. And that's me getting up on my high horse.'

'I thought you'd asked for a transfer,' said Peggy, amused.

Marigold adopted a prim look. 'It's a lady's prerogative to change her mind. You could too if you wanted to.'

Peggy hesitated. She could see the sense of what Marigold was saying. There was still a war raging with Joe in the middle of it. It was just that she had tried so hard to bring him home but it had made no difference. Even Mrs Pyecroft's books hadn't seemed to work. It was difficult to see what else could be done except hope and pray. 'I feel as if I'm needed here at the moment,' she said quietly. 'I'm not sure I can go back.'

The door to the staircase swung open and Dulcie appeared. As soon as she caught sight of Peggy, she made a beeline for her. 'Ah, Peggy, the very girl. I need to speak to you. It's of national importance.'

'Oh really,' said Peggy, raising one eyebrow.

'Would you like me to leave?' asked Marigold.

'Oh no, Your Ladyship,' said Dulcie with a curtsey. 'This concerns the both of you. I've had an idea. About your books.'

Peggy glanced at Marigold. 'Oh yes?'

'Yes,' said Dulcie. 'You need to write stories about women like your gran, about real women who do their bit without asking for anything in return. They look after their families but look out for everyone else at the same time. Your gran was always helping others, moaning about them as she went, but she'd do anything for anyone.'

'That is true,' said Peggy.

Marigold's eyes lit up. 'I think it's a terrific idea. We could find different groups of women to interview, I'll take some photographs. Use some material from that book Longforth cancelled. Dedicate it to your grandmother's memory.'

'It does sound wonderful,' Peggy admitted.

'I won't ask you for a penny for the idea,' said Dulcie. 'Just doing it for the memory of my oldest friend will be reward enough for me.'

'That's very generous of you, Mrs Twigg,' said Peggy.

'There is just one small detail,' said Marigold.

'What?'

'You'll have to come back to work.' Marigold fixed her with a look as Dulcie nodded enthusiastically. 'The Ministry needs you, Peggy Bauman.'

Kriegsgefangenenlager,
September 1944

Dearest Peg,

Thank you for your letters. They come in dribs and drabs with no rhyme or reason. I've had two from you, three from Flo, one from Mum but nothing from Gran for a while. I'm glad to hear your news. I must tell you that this is the hardest letter I've ever had to write. You'll remember I told you that we would hold up sheets to spell out 'POW' during air raids. Unfortunately, the raids have been coming thick and fast lately and it's been too dangerous to do anything but take cover. One day last week, Albert and I were playing cards when the siren sounded so we were a bit slow getting out. By that time, one of the shelters was nearly full and Albert shoved me inside and told me he'd go to the other one and then meet me back in our quarters so he could take the rest of my money. Had such a grin on his face. 'In your dreams,' I shouted back. That was the last I ever saw of him, Peg. A direct hit, right on top of their concrete shelter. Killed half the men inside and the rest are so badly injured, most of them wish they were dead too. I'm sorry to be blunt but I have to get it down on paper. I know you of all people would understand this.

After the raid we spent the next three days and nights helping survivors and burying the dead. I won't go into details but I'm not ashamed to admit that I wept like a child through the whole thing. I would never have got through this war without Albert Cobb. A truer friend you'd never hope to find. I wish you could have met him. I'm not sure where we go from here. I'm sorry to bring such sad news. Rest assured, I'm all right, so please don't worry, but please pray for me.

Ever your loving brother, Joe

Chapter 27

'I've got a surprise for you,' said Frank one weekend as they strolled around Edenham Park with Badger and Nancy in tow. Spurred on by the combined will of Marigold, Dulcie and Emily's spirit, Peggy had recently returned to the Ministry. She had resolved to continue to stay at her mother's house, however. Alice assured her that she was absolutely fine, that Peggy should return to her marital home, but something held her back. She hadn't said anything to her mother or Frank about her niggling worry that Joe hadn't signed off his last letter with the usual promise of 'we'll meet again'. Peggy told herself it was foolish superstition, but she knew it meant that Joe had reached rock bottom and this ate away at her. So whether it was the loss of her grandmother or fresh nagging concerns for Joe, she couldn't tear herself away from the place where she felt closest to both of them. Peggy knew people would find it questionable for a wife to live apart from her husband but also knew that Frank wasn't one of these people. He bore it all with kind patience and she loved him all the more for it.

'I love surprises,' said Nancy, skipping alongside them. 'Is it chocolate?'

'Better,' said Frank with a wry grin.

'What on earth could be better than chocolate?'

'Over there.' He pointed towards a row of houses.

'A barrage balloon?' asked Nancy with a frown.

Frank laughed. 'No. Come with me. I'll show you.'

Moments later, they found themselves standing outside a dilapidated Victorian red-brick house with missing roof tiles and pigeons roosting in the porch.

'Sorry, Frank, but it doesn't look better than chocolate,' said Nancy solemnly.

'Well, the man who lived here didn't really look after the place so it needs some attention, but that also means it's not as expensive as other houses,' he said, opening the front door.

Peggy stared at him in astonishment. 'But, do you mean . . .?'

He nodded. 'It's ours if you like it, but only if you like it. I've been talking to a few estate agents on my recent visits.' He gazed at her with a look of pure tenderness. 'I just want you to be happy, Peggy, and I know you'd be happy living near to your family.' He stood to one side to let them in. Peggy walked from room to room, taking in the damp walls, peeling wallpaper, broken floorboards and more pigeons, who scattered out through the broken windows as soon as Badger bounced through the door and barked his greeting. 'It's got three bedrooms and indoor plumbing, but that might need a bit of updating. And there's a garden, more a patch of scrubland at the moment, but it could be wonderful.' Peggy remained silent as they climbed the stairs to the first floor and walked into a large room looking out across the park.

'I like it,' declared Nancy, drawing a smiling face on the grime-encrusted window. 'I could wave at you from the duck pond.'

'And I didn't bribe Nancy to say that, did I?' said Frank.

'You did say we could go to see Mrs Huggins for some lemon sours on the way home.'

Frank laughed before turning to his wife. 'Well, my love. What do you think?'

Peggy looked around at the grubby fireplace, towards the large, filthy windows, out across the wide open landscape of London. Battered and mangled but still standing.

He's a good man, Peg.

I know.

Fancy him finding this place for you. It's a tip, but with a bit of elbow grease you'll have it right as rain in no time. Be a nice place to bring up kiddies, too.

Oh, Gran.

You got to keep moving forwards, Peg. You know that, don't you?

'Peggy?'

She turned back from the window and caught Frank's eye. So kind and loving and desperate to offer some spark of hope. She moved towards him, sliding her arms around his neck and kissing his cheek. 'Thank you, Frank,' she whispered through her tears. 'Thank you.'

Peggy and Marigold spent the next few months interviewing the women who would feature in the book which was now entitled *A Woman's Place is in the War.* They were also determined to write it under their own names.

'You know you don't need to convince me on that point,' said Mr Beecher. 'But Mr Longforth might have other ideas. Press on, though, and we'll address these bumps in the road as we drive over them, wouldn't you agree, Mrs Pyecroft?'

'Most certainly,' she said with a gentle nod of her head.

As they travelled from place to place, Peggy couldn't imagine stories more inspiring and moving than those of the women they met. There was Rosemary Draper, who was a radar operator for the ATS. She had joined up after her fiancé was killed in action in France.

'I wanted to do something, anything, to help, to stop others dying and other women like me losing their futures. At first, the chaps were a bit condescending, but once I stepped up and showed them I was just as capable as them, they soon shut up. As a woman, I'm not allowed to fire a gun, of course, but I'm right in the thick of it. I've heard some pretty awful stuff over the radio transmitter, but I've saved lives too. I'm proud of what I do. I know it's made a difference. I can't imagine going back to normal life once this war's over. I used to work in a bank but I'm not sure I fancy being stuck behind a desk after this. It's opened my eyes. I'll never be the same again and I'm grateful for that.'

Peggy and Marigold then travelled to Cornwall to meet Maggie Burrows and her fellow Land Girls. They were a joyous bunch who cheerfully admitted that they'd 'never been to the country before, let alone milked a blinkin' cow'.

'So what would you say you've learnt most from coming here?' asked Peggy.

Maggie glanced at the others before answering. 'That a woman can do what any man can.'

'Even if they get paid less for it,' said her friend.

'True,' agreed Maggie. 'But I would never have had the chance to learn to drive a truck back home in Leytonstone.'

'Or deal with rats,' said another woman.

'Yeah,' said Maggie, chuckling. 'Turns out I'm a champion rat catcher. But you know what the best thing is?'

'The overalls,' cried someone.

Everyone laughed. 'This lot,' she said. 'We're a family. Ain't that right, girls?'

Peggy and Marigold grinned at one another as the cheers rang out.

Next they interviewed a woman from a munitions factory, who left home at five a.m. every day for her job fitting and finishing shells. She confided her heartfelt hope that one of them would 'land on the head of the Hun who killed my brother'. They met Wrens, members of the WAAF and a Fire Watcher, who reminded Peggy of Emily when she told her that she'd once carried on baking a cake whilst an ARP warden defused an unexploded bomb which had landed in her front garden. Apparently, she gave him tea and a slice after he'd successfully completed the task.

'I think we've done a whizzo job, Peggy, if I do say so myself,' said Marigold as they married the photographs with the text one day. 'I'm particularly proud of this photograph of Maggie and her compatriots.'

'So you should be. You've really captured their spirit, Marigold. It's wonderful.' She picked up her note-book. 'Right. Let's go and conduct this last interview. Unfortunately, Mr Longforth has decided that he wants to sit in on this one. Apparently, he wants to make sure our book doesn't reflect badly on his department.'

'Couldn't Mr Beecher send him off with a flea in his ear?'

'He told me that I was more than capable of dealing with Mr Longforth.'

Marigold grinned. 'And so you are, my friend. Who are we meeting today?'

Peggy glanced in her notebook. 'Actually, the introduction came via Mrs Pyecroft. She's head of the Beechwood Women's Voluntary Service. A Mrs Margery Travers.'

Marigold gave a shiver. 'WVS women are notoriously terrifying.'

Peggy shrugged. 'Perhaps that's just a myth.'

It proved to be far from a myth as they emerged from the lift to be greeted by the scowling glare of Margery Travers. She glanced at the clock above their heads. 'You are three minutes late,' she said by way of introduction.

'I do beg your pardon,' said Peggy.

'Mmm,' replied Mrs Travers.

'We thought we could conduct the interview over tea in the cafeteria if that's acceptable to you?' said Marigold with one of her most dazzling smiles.

Mrs Travers regarded her with a look which suggested she was immune to such attempts at charm. 'I have served more cups of tea than you have had hot dinners, young lady. I hope it is both strong and piping hot.'

371

'I'm sure it will be,' said Peggy. 'It's this way.'

'Miss Sparks?' barked a voice.

She turned. 'Mr Longforth. We were just about to escort Mrs Travers to the cafeteria to conduct the interview, if you'd care to join us.'

'Very well.'

Mrs Travers turned her icy gaze towards him. 'And who might you be?'

He looked at her in surprise before offering his hand. 'I beg your pardon, dear lady. I am Henry Longforth, Head of Publishing,' he said.

'And so you should beg my pardon. You are seven minutes late,' she said, tapping her watch before turning away and following Peggy.

As the interview progressed it became rapidly clear that Henry Longforth had met his match. 'You see, while you sit here, telling the country what to think and do, we at the Women's Voluntary Service are hard at work, making sure we win this war,' Mrs Travers told them.

'Oh really?' said Longforth with wry amusement. 'You don't think it has anything to do with our boys fighting overseas?'

Margery rolled her eyes at Peggy and Marigold as if they were in the presence of a blithering fool. 'Well, of course it does, but who supports them in their endeavours? Who sends them the socks to keep their feet dry, or parcels to keep them fed, and who keeps Britain going while the war rages around us? Who provides tea and sympathy for our wardens, police and fire service operatives? Who offers comfort and support to those bombed out of their homes? Who will make sure there's a Britain to come home to?'

'Oh bravo,' cried Marigold, clapping her hands in spontaneous applause.

Margery pursed her lips into something resembling a smile before she turned to Longforth. 'Who is it who does all those things?' she said. 'Because I don't think it's you, is it?'

'Crikey,' said Marigold as they made their way back to their office afterwards. 'I've never seen a human being turn the colour Longforth did when Margery Travers put him in his place. What would you call it? Crimson? Violet?'

Peggy chuckled. 'Beetroot. He looked like a prize pickled beetroot.'

'Ah, Mrs Bauman, Miss Cecily,' said Mrs Pyecroft, meeting them by the door to their office. 'How did it go with Mrs Travers?'

Peggy and Marigold shared a look. 'Let's just say I don't think we'll have any more issues with Mr Longforth about the book,' said Peggy.

Mrs Pyecroft gave a satisfied nod. 'Excellent. Jolly well done, as Miss Cecily likes to say.'

Mr Beecher insisted that the entire department go to the printers to see the first book roll off the press. With the tide of the war surging very much towards victory in Europe, it felt as if it wouldn't be long before their work at the Ministry was done.

As Frank handed the first copy of *A Women's Place is in*

the War by Marigold Cecily and Peggy Sparks to the two authors, Mr Beecher applauded whilst Rosa, Sheldrake, Hilda and Constance whistled and cheered.

'It's as if we're taking delivery of a new baby,' said Marigold, smoothing the front cover of the book from which a montage of all the women they'd interviewed gazed out at them with similar pride. She opened the front cover and squeezed Peggy's arm as they caught sight of the dedication.

In memory of Emily Marsh, 1870–1944

'If I may have your attention for the briefest moment,' said Mr Beecher. He turned to Peggy and Marigold. 'Congratulations to you both, not merely on the publication of this book, which is a fine, fine piece of work, but for all your hard work over the last few years. I am immensely proud of this department, of everything we've achieved.' He nodded to them all as he said this. 'Some might dismiss the work of the Ministry, to label us as a government mouthpiece peddling propaganda, but I truly believe that we have done our best to work with integrity, to seek to boost the morale of our nation and to offer hope which will see us through to brighter days. It's an honour to work with you all. If we lived in different times, I would toast you with the finest French champagne, but today all I can offer is praise and pride. Thank you.' He caught Peggy's eye and they shared a smile.

'Am I allowed to tell my wife how immensely proud I am of her too?' asked Frank, pulling her to one side.

'Of course,' said Peggy. 'Actually, it's funny what

Marigold said about the book reminding her of a baby.' She looked up at him with eyebrows raised.

'Really?' said Frank, his face lighting up.

Peggy nodded. 'Really. I'm hoping we'll be celebrating a new life and an end to the war next year.'

Frank held her close, kissing the top of her head. 'We better look sharp about it with the new house then.'

Much to the satisfaction of Henry Longforth, the book didn't sell in great quantities. 'I warned Beecher it was sentimental hogwash,' Sheldrake overheard him saying. 'Readers aren't really interested in what women are up to. They want tales of bravery and adventure.'

'Sorry,' said Sheldrake as he told them what he'd heard over lunch one day.

Peggy shrugged. 'I couldn't give two hoots what Henry Longforth thinks, and besides, I didn't expect it to sell thousands. I just wanted to tell these women's stories.'

'What's wrong with being sentimental anyway?' said Marigold. 'That man has no soul.'

'Well, I thought it was wonderful,' said Laurie. 'And so did my mother. And all her friends.'

'That's reward enough for me then,' said Peggy. She stood up and stretched her arms. 'I'm going for a turn around the square,' she added. 'Baby's orders. I'll see you in a while.'

The sky was billowing with pale grey and white clouds as Peggy made her way outside. On crossing the road, she spotted Mrs Pyecroft at the entrance to the square. She turned and raised her eyebrows in greeting. 'Mrs Bauman. Do you have time for a lunchtime stroll?'

Peggy was pleasantly surprised. Over the years, their interactions had been functional, merely part of the work they were doing, but she had always been intrigued by this woman, always secretly longed to share a proper conversation with her. 'I do.'

They walked in silence beneath skeletal trees to which the last remaining leaves clung defiantly. 'Are you disappointed by the reception to the book?' asked Mrs Pyecroft after a while.

'Not at all,' said Peggy. 'I'm proud of it.'

'As you should be.' She reached into her pocket. 'By the way, I received this message today. I thought you might be interested to read it.'

Peggy unfolded the note she passed and was amazed to see the White House insignia at the top.

My dear Magdalena,

I trust you are well. Just a short note to thank you for sending me Peggy and Marigold's book. I thought it was wonderful. Please extend my congratulations to them both. I feel confident that with women like those represented in the book at the forefront of our efforts, we will be able to bring home our boys soon and bring an end to this terrible war.

With all good wishes.

Yours, Eleanor

Peggy stared at Mrs Pyecroft who was at that moment gazing at a robin, observing them from the ground a few feet away as it plucked a stubborn worm from the earth. 'Such a clever bird, the robin, wouldn't you say? Determined. Resilient. I've always admired them.'

'Yes, they're certainly plucky little birds, but can I ask you about this letter?' Peggy stumbled over her words. 'How did you . . .? When did you . . .? Why did you . . .?'

Mrs Pyecroft looked at her. 'Life is full of questions, Mrs Bauman. Some need to be answered and others don't. Take me, for example. People ask all sorts of questions about me. They want to know where I come from, who I am, what I do. If they had this information, they would make assumptions and judge. If they knew that I am a German, for instance, they would judge. They would class me as an alien. An outsider. A spy, even. So I have found that if I keep quiet and do what needs to be done, I am able to achieve much. I can see that you and thousands of young women have done this too. The war has offered a great opportunity to us and we would have been fools not to take it.' She fixed her gaze on Peggy as she spoke. 'You may not see the direct consequences of your good works, and a man like Henry Longforth would want you to believe that they don't exist. For instance, he would not believe that one of your most recent works has led to the escape of over five hundred prisoners.'

Peggy stared at her. 'Five hundred?'

Mrs Pyecroft nodded. 'Who in turn were able to offer key information about the enemy, so you see, your work has become far-reaching and vital.'

'Thank you, Mrs Pyecroft.' Peggy held out the note.

'Keep it,' she said. 'Show it to Miss Cecily. And make sure it's framed on your wall for when Mr Longforth next visits. Small endeavours cause great ripples, Mrs Bauman.'

Post Office Telegram

Regret to inform you that your husband Joseph Charles Sparks is reported missing as the result of an escape on the night of 30th Jan '45. Any further information received will be immediately communicated to you pending receipt of written notification from the Red Cross.

Chapter 28

The victory bells rang across the world in May, but for Peggy the word 'victory' felt hollow. What could possibly be victorious about a war which had claimed the life of her grandmother and into which her brother had disappeared? There had been no word of Joe's whereabouts, and as the weeks became months, the Sparks family began to face the prospect that he would never return.

VE Day arrived in a flurry of bunting with street parties held on every road and avenue in Edenham. When Peggy, Frank and Nancy looked out of the upstairs window of Alice's house, there was a line of trestle tables as far as the eye could see with mothers rolling out tablecloths and setting down plates, chatting and laughing, carefree after years of hiding away. Nearly every house in the street had a Union Jack flag at the window and children skipped back and forth wearing home-made paper crowns and mile-wide grins.

'I don't want to go to the party, Auntie Peg,' said Nancy. 'It doesn't feel right to be having fun with Daddy missing.'

Peggy glanced at Frank and put an arm around her shoulder. 'I know where we can go. Let's ask your mum and gran too.'

Although it was a public holiday, Peggy knew Mr Alderman would be at the library. There were those for whom an end to the war in Europe was cause for great celebration, whose husbands and loved ones would return and who felt pure relief that these dark days were now over. But there were others for whom the war – whether it be this one or the previous one – would never be over. While some could sing about a 'Land of hope and glory', cheer and dance the night away, for others, VE Day was one of sad reflection. Peggy knew Mr Alderman was one of these people. During her more recent trips to the library, she had taken to visiting him in his office. His benevolent presence reminded her of Mr Beecher's, and she found their discussions reassuring. One day she had appeared in his doorway to find him gazing at a photograph, a gentle smile on his face. Peggy cleared her throat to announce her presence. He glanced up and ushered her in.

'I hope I'm not intruding,' she said.

He looked down at the photograph again and hesitated, unsure of whether to share a confidence. Something persuaded him that he should as he slid the photograph towards her. 'My wife and son,' he said.

Peggy gazed down at the pair. Mrs Alderman was beautifully attired in white frills, a pearl choker at her throat, with her son perched on her lap. They stared out at Peggy with such mirth and joy that she found herself smiling in reply. 'It's a beautiful picture,' she said.

'Today would have been my wife's seventy-second birthday,' he said. 'She died shortly after the end of the first war. The doctors said it was her heart and I agree. It broke when Monty was killed in 1916.'

'I'm sorry, Mr Alderman.'

He gave a gentle smile. 'I was lucky to have known them,' he said. 'Lucky to have those memories.'

'Is it all right if we come in, please, Mr Alderman?' said Nancy. 'We don't feel much like celebrating today.'

His face lit up as he stood back to let them through the door. 'Of course. I'm very glad to see you. And I wouldn't usually permit this in the library, but I think we could make an exception and have some tea.'

'I was hoping you might say that,' said Alice, holding up her basket. 'I've baked some of Mum's queen cakes.'

'Sublime,' said Mr Alderman.

'I'll make some tea,' said Peggy.

'I'll help you,' said Flo.

'And I'll eat Emily's buns,' said Dulcie.

'I'll help you,' said Nancy and everyone laughed.

For Peggy, there was no better place to be today. They could hear enough of the hum and cheer of the celebrations outside to remind themselves that they were living in peaceful times, but there was something reassuring about being cocooned together, drinking tea in this book-lined haven. Mr Alderman joined them for one cup before disappearing into his office with a book of Robert Graves poems tucked under his arm.

'I can see why you like it here, Peg,' said Flo, as she and Charlie turned the pages of a book of *Aesop's Fables*. 'I feel calmer than I have done in weeks.' Peggy smiled.

The war had taken its toll on all of them, but it pained her deeply to see her oldest friend suffer. Alice did her best to support Flo but she had similarly lost her husband, her mother and now, in all likelihood, her son. It made Peggy long for a magic wand to make everything all right, impossible as that was. She looked over at Frank as he read *Emil and the Detectives* to an enthralled Nancy and felt the baby kick, reminding her that there were tiny seeds of hope germinating, reasons to move forwards and keep going.

Dulcie snapped shut the Agatha Christie novel she'd been reading and shoved it to one side. 'I knew it!' she declared. 'I knew he did it. I could tell he was a wrong 'un from the off.'

Emily Alice Bauman was born on a July day that was as bright and hopeful as her arrival. The midwife declared that she had 'never come across a baby with a louder pair of lungs', which made Alice and Peggy cry tears of joy for the fact that Emily Marsh's spirit lived on. When she handed Frank his new daughter and saw how he gazed down at her with such tenderness, Peggy felt her heart swell with a joy that was only tinged by the absence of Joe. With every day that passed, the lack of news moved them closer to a world without him. It was only bearable because there'd been no official word to quash that final germ of hope.

Baby Emily brought with her a fresh sense of purpose. Frank worked tirelessly during evenings and weekends to finish the house whilst Peggy stayed with her mother, savouring precious moments with her new daughter.

Marigold had called for a visit one day, reporting that they were packing up operations at the Ministry.

'It's a bit sad, but then I suppose all good things must come to an end,' she told her.

'True,' said Peggy. 'What will you do now it's all over?'

'Rosa and I are going to Europe.'

Peggy was amazed. 'Really?'

Marigold's smile was uncharacteristically coy. 'We've become very close.'

Peggy saw the secret happiness in her expression, the unspoken truth and a new joy which had been absent ever since the death of Cordelia. 'I'm so happy for you, Marigold.'

'I'm happy for us both, Peggy. Oh, and by the way, I thought you might like one of these. I've given one to everyone in our department.' She reached into her pocket and fished out a photograph. 'Do you remember, I set the timer and got everyone to pose that Christmas?'

Peggy gazed at the photograph of Mr Beecher standing beside Mrs Pyecroft, their eyes sparkling with amusement, of Sheldrake with a slight frown, of Dalton grinning like a dolt beside a benignly smiling Fairchild, and Peggy and Marigold, sharing a joke as the camera captured the moment. 'We look like a strange little family,' she said.

Marigold laughed. 'That's precisely what we were. A strange little family.' She grinned at Peggy. 'Don't tell the others, but you were always my favourite sister.'

Peggy pulled her friend into a tight embrace. 'Be happy, Marigold. You deserve it.'

Marigold kissed her cheek. 'I'm not a religious woman, as you know, but I pray for Joe every night.'

A few days later, Peggy found herself alone at her mother's house. She and Frank were planning to move to their new home at the weekend and she was sorting through books and photographs, ready to pack them into the grocery boxes Mr Miller had lent them. Peggy picked up a photograph of herself and Joe and wiped the frame. They couldn't have been more than five years old. Peggy could remember him being cross because the photographer had told him to face forwards instead of looking at his sister. Consequently, he was wearing a petulant scowl which always made her and Alice chuckle when they caught sight of it. Peggy was about to place it carefully in the box when she heard the telephone. She hurried from the living room and picked up the receiver.

'Edenham 3175?'

'Peggy.' The voice reached through the telephone like a child asking for a hug. It was so familiar but so unexpected, as if she'd found a treasure she'd thought she'd never see again. She yelped and clutched a hand to her mouth as tears sprang to her eyes. She had longed for this moment, dreamt of it every night, but had started to fear it would never happen.

Somehow, she managed to find her voice. 'Joe?' she whispered through her tears. 'Joe? Is it really you?'

He chuckled, a soft sound that was love and relief and joy all rolled into one. 'I told you we'd meet again, Peg.

You didn't think I'd let you down, did you? Thank you for the compass, by the way. Came in very handy.'

Edenham,
12th March 1946

My dear Marigold,

Thank you for your letter and the photographs. I'm so pleased you and Rosa are settled in Paris. Your work documenting the aftermath of the war sounds extremely interesting. It makes me very happy to see the joy in your faces. You deserve to be end-lessly happy. I'm glad to hear that your mother is planning to visit you. I hope it's the start of a better understanding for you both.

Life is good with us. Emily is a wonderful baby, growing fast, crawling now and keen to get moving. She reminds me so much of my grandmother, which is a great comfort although tinged with sadness that they never got to meet. I get the feeling they would have been the greatest of friends. We're settling in well to the new house. Frank has nearly finished decorating and it's everything I've ever dreamed of. Nancy is a frequent visitor and adores her new cousin. She's also very excited as Flo is expecting another baby! Joe is hoping for a boy as he wants to call him Albert after the friend he lost. He's returned to work at the garage, but in truth, he's a different man. Sometimes he tells me about the things he saw and I think that helps, but other times, I can see how he struggles. I know he's happy to be home, to see Flo and the kids again, but as we all know, war changes a person. I think it's changed us all and the world has been changed forever by it. I know it's changed me, for good and for bad.

We've all suffered, but I know I was lucky to work at the Ministry. Mr Beecher came to visit with his wife recently. He and Frank have become very close and they are both wonderful with Emily. I get the feeling that they will be part of our lives forever which makes me very happy. Laurie and Sheldrake are also in touch and I hear they're planning to visit you in Paris. I can only imagine the fun you'll have! I was intrigued to hear that Mrs Pyecroft disappeared after the war. I daresay she's been sent to dispense her quiet magic somewhere that needs her. Weren't we lucky to work with these people? I have your photograph on the mantelpiece and smile at it every day. Of course, yours is the friendship I value the most, not that I believed that when we first met! We had some wonderful adventures, and the memories of these raise my spirits and spur me on. I'm proud of us, Marigold, proud of everything we achieved. We gave the world hope when it needed it most. I can't think of anything better than that.

Ever yours, your loving friend, Peggy

Historical Note

The Ministry of Information was established on 4th September 1939 with the principal aim of managing the flow of information to the public during the war. It was divided into over twenty departments with categories including Press Censorship, Empire, Film and Official Artists. Its existence was fairly chequered, with it being criticised for a patronising approach towards the public in terms of campaigns (the 'Keep Calm and Carry On' slogan was never used because of this) and accusations that they were spying on the British public. It was also dismissed as a laughing stock for being too big to be able to keep secrets properly. It was, however, a fascinating place where the likes of Laurie Lee and George Orwell worked and it served as an inspiration for the Ministry of Truth in the latter's novel, *1984*. The Ministry of Information also became a highly successful publishing business with its bestselling range of Official War Books which by 1943 had sold over twenty million copies.

The Mass Observation Project, set up by three former Cambridge University students in 1937, was designed to record the everyday thoughts and lives of members of the public through their diaries. During the Second World War it was often commissioned for research by the Ministry of Information and proved a valuable resource as the MOI sought to manage the flow of information to the public.

Acknowledgements

Thank you to my editors, Sherise Hobbs and Priyal Agrawal for their brilliant guidance and to the fantastic team at Headline – Rebecca Bader, Ollie Martin, Hannah Sawyer, Kashmini Shah and Isobel Smith. Special thanks to Caroline Young for the stunning cover. Thank you also to the wonderful Ellie Wood and to the equally wonderful Hachette Australia for connecting me with some of the loveliest readers on the planet. Thank you as always to my agent, the one and only Laura Macdougall, to Olivia Davies and the whole team at United Agents.

Love and thanks to Celia Anderson, Jenna Bahen, Kerry Barrett, Carol Baylis, Kay Fox, Ruth Hogan, Helen Holden, Melissa Khan, The Littles, Sarah Livingston, Pam and Rip Pugh, Lisa Timoney and Sally Wells for your support and friendship.

Huge thanks to Kelly and her Beckenham Bookshop team, to Cat and everyone at Waterstones, Bromley, to Jaynie and all at Waterstones, Orpington and to the librarians of Bromley and beyond, for spreading the love.

Special thanks to the readers who send me messages nearly every day and to the book community who do so much to share a love of stories and reading.

My final biggest thanks to Rich, Lil and Alfie for their love, support and nights spent bingeing *The Wire*, and of course to Nelson for the head-clearing dog walks.

Historical resources

The following proved particularly useful while I was writing this book:

Books

Mrs Miles's Diary by Constance Miles, edited by S. V. Partington, Simon and Schuster, 2013

Ministry of Morale by Ian McLaine, George Allen & Unwin, 1979

Britain by Mass-Observation, 1939

Eve in Overalls by Arthur Wauters, 1942

The Battle of Britain issued by The Ministry of Information, 1941

Wartime Britain 1939–1945 by Juliet Gardiner, Headline, 2004

Life Among the English by Rose Macaulay, Collins, 1942

Blitz Spirit 1939–1945 by Becky Brown, Hodder & Stoughton, 2020

Websites

MOI Digital

The Imperial War Museum

WW2 People's War – BBC